"CARR

He swept
bedroom an
bed. A single lamp cast long shadows. ...
watched with a certain disbelief as he went to the
door and latched it, then came back to look down
at her, his face grave and intent.

He pulled back the wrapper and fumbled with
the ribbons at her bodice and still she did not
move. But when the shirred material fell away
to leave her breasts bared, she realized the enormity of what was happening. She mustn't . . .
she couldn't do this . . .

"No . . ." she said. But her voice was soft
and trembling and strange.

He laughed deep in his chest. "Don't pretend
to be shy," he said. "I've wanted to do this since
the first moment I laid eyes on you . . . and
you've wanted it, too."

And all the time he was talking, he was stripping her out of her gown and robe and she was
thinking frantically. If she stopped him . . . if
she could stop him . . . would he take out his
anger on the others at Kingston Landing?

Also by Betty Layman Receveur
Published by Ballantine Books:

MOLLY GALLAGHER

CARRIE KINGSTON

BETTY LAYMAN RECEVEUR

BALLANTINE BOOKS • NEW YORK

Library of Congress Catalog Card Number: 83-91129

ISBN 0-345-30401-2

Manufactured in the United States of America

First Edition: February 1984

To my sons—
Don, Rick, and Brett.
Rebels all, in their way.

And—I can't resist adding—
to my own special Yankee. Always.

1

U PRIVER FROM NEW ORLEANS, RICH DELTA LAND SHIMMERED and steamed in the mid-morning sun. A chestnut gelding with a white blaze picked his way along the vine-tangled path beside the Mississippi, the dark-haired girl who rode him sitting easily in the sidesaddle, her back very straight, her head high. The breeze, always stronger near the river, ruffled the surface of the muddy water, made sweeping lines of pale cream foam, and tugged at the strands of gray-green moss that trailed from the gnarled oaks along the bank.

Carrie Kingston pulled Majestic to a stop and sat motionless, those big amber eyes turned inland toward that sweep of acreage that lay untended and overgrown south of the sugar house and the mill. Dry and blackened cane stalks stood in mute testimony to the early freeze that had put an end to the cutting and sugarmaking that past October—though in truth there hadn't been enough hands left on the place to do it properly anyway—and now, where the stubble cane pushed valiantly upward out of the earth, it was choked and matted with wild morning-glory vines and thick coco grass. The once meticulously kept drainage ditches were clogged and useless against heavy summer rains.

This was only a small part of the vast acreage of Kingston's Landing, but the other fields were in no better condition. As Carrie surveyed the ruin, quick tears glistened, but it was hardly a moment before she raised an impatient hand to brush them away. Though the dark green skirt of her riding habit revealed a hint of the long, slender legs beneath it, and the matching jacket curved softly over breasts that were already well developed for a girl barely eighteen, there was about her a certain strength, a determination that was echoed in the firm curve of her mouth and in the dark eyebrows that slanted sharply upward to peaks and then down like wings.

She had inherited them from her father, the brows and the mouth, and there were those who found them unseemly features in a girl. God, they said, she reminded you of the old man. It was as if Adam Kingston himself had come back from the grave and stood there in a slip of a girl. And wasn't it too bad, they said, that it hadn't been her brother George Pierre who had inherited the grit of old Adam.

Carrie thought of her father now, felt a painful gratitude that he could not see what had become of the plantation. It would have broken his heart. No, she corrected herself instantly. It would not have broken his heart! He would have done something about it! And so should she . . . somehow. But the war. . . .

"Damn the war!" she said out loud, mildly surprised at herself for using that word. "Damn the war! And the Yankees!" she added defiantly.

There was a sudden dry rustling in the nearby thicket, and Carrie whirled, her body poised to put the horse beneath her into instant flight. She waited, breath stilled, her heart pounding, and then to her immense relief a large gray rabbit darted out of the underbrush and away.

She let her breath out and laughed, feeling slightly ridiculous. Still, there was no telling who was about these days. There had been reports of jayhawkers riding in Louisiana since shortly after the war had started—bands of unscrupulous men, marauders, who took advantage of the unsettled times. And since New Orleans had fallen to Federal gunboats this last spring and Union troops had pressed northward nearly to Baton Rouge, it was not uncommon to see Yankee soldiers in the area.

So far, they had let Kingston's Landing alone, but other plantations along the river had reported visits from the troops, and by their accounts the Yankees had certainly not behaved in a gentlemanly fashion. But that was hardly surprising since General Butler himself, who headed the new military government, had insulted every decent woman in New Orleans with his so-called "Woman Order."

She sighed, pulled her horse around, and leaned to pat the smooth, warm neck when she caught a movement out of the corner of her eye, back among the trees, the way the rabbit had come. Her hand froze as she waited, watched, her heart once again beginning a slow steady pounding, and then she saw the clear outline of a man's shoulder behind a slender maple, edging back as if the trunk were not quite big enough to hide him.

"You there!" she heard herself saying, "you there among the trees! Step out so I can see you!" Despite the hammering of her heart and the sudden dampness of her palms, she was determined to find out who the person was and what he was doing on Kingston's Landing. Probably a runaway slave, she told herself. Lord knew there were plenty of those about. All heading toward New Orleans and the Yankees.

For a minute there was no movement, and then Carrie saw the figure shift slightly, twigs and branches obscuring him still.

"Who are you?" she called, her voice steady. "Step out and show yourself at once!"

"Carrie? Carrie Kingston? Is that you?" the man's voice carried back to her, and as he stepped out and she saw the gray Confederate uniform, she caught her breath.

"Paul! Paul Gayerre!" His name escaped her before she could stop it, but she quickly motioned him back, knowing at once what danger he was in being here. She took a careful look around to be sure that she was not being watched by anyone, and then she slid down from her horse. Leading the gelding, she made her way into the thicket where it was cool and shady, the ground slightly spongy underfoot.

The Gayerre plantation lay across the river from Kingston's Landing; the house three miles upriver. And as Carrie came up to Paul Gayerre now, noting the fine dark Creole features, for an instant she was reminded of her brother, who was himself off fighting with the Confederate Army somewhere. George Pierre's mother, Papa's first wife, who had died when George Pierre was only four years old, had been Creole.

"Paul," she said. Her eyes took in the exhausted look of the man and the dirty gray uniform streaked with mud, his jacket torn in one place, the trousers wet to the knees. "Paul . . ." she

3

whispered. "Good Lord, what are you doing here? Come, we must get you to someplace safer."

He had swept the battered hat from his head as she approached, those elegant Creole manners not forgotten even now, and he bowed rather formally, though the dark eyes betrayed his anxiety. "I know . . . but first, please tell me, Carrie, do you know anything of my wife and my mother? I went to the house and it is closed, the windows shuttered and locked—"

"They're safe," Carrie interrupted. "When it seemed certain that New Orleans would fall to the Yankees, Aurore and your mother decided it would be best if they went up to Natchez."

"Natchez? I have an aunt there. They must have gone to *Tante* Collette."

Carrie nodded. "They took their personal servants and were able to get aboard one of the last of the steamboats to go upriver before the Yankees closed it to commercial traffic. They left your overseer in charge of things at the plantation."

"But it is deserted. No one is there."

"I know. I'm afraid the man packed up and went off to New Orleans the first chance he got."

"And the slaves?"

Carrie shook her head. "They ran off."

Paul swore under his breath and ran a long-fingered hand over the days-old stubble of beard.

"They would have anyway. Most of ours have," Carrie said gently.

He was silent for a moment, looking off through the trees toward the river. Everything might change, wars might come and go, but the river stayed the same, impersonal and constant, and wildly beautiful.

"I went to Maisonfleur," he said finally, referring to the fine old manor house about a mile downriver. "It, too, seemed deserted. What of Monsieur Moreau?"

"Uncle Etienne is with my sister Susannah and me at Kingston's Landing. He doesn't want us to be there alone while my brother is away."

Paul nodded, and Carrie saw him sway slightly. "Are you hurt? Wounded?" she asked quickly.

4

"No, no. Only tired. I have not slept for more than two days."

Carrie saw the lines of fatigue cutting into his face from nose to mouth. Paul Gayerre seemed to have aged ten years since she had last seen him a year ago. "Come," she said, "you'll be safe at Kingston's Landing. Can you swing up behind me on Majestic?"

He hesitated. "I shall only be putting you in danger. There is a Union patrol about. I saw them. That is why I left home and crossed the river to hide. Perhaps I should—"

"Nonsense," Carrie cut him off. "You'll be safe with us. We've had no trouble with the Yankees so far. Besides, there are plenty of places to hide you at Kingston's Landing. Come on now before we're seen."

He agreed finally and helped her mount the horse, then stood there looking up at her for a moment. "Was Aurore all right?" he asked anxiously. "She was expecting our child, you know."

"She was fine." Carrie smiled down at him. "She was very happy about the baby. I saw her often before she left. The only thing she worried about was you."

Though he looked half-embarrassed at that, he smiled and a little of the anxiety left his eyes. He swung up behind her and settled himself behind the sidesaddle.

"Aurore wrote to you every week," Carrie said as she deftly put the horse into motion.

"But I got no letters after I was transferred from Richmond. I was half out of my mind not knowing what had happened to her. And then when New Orleans fell . . . Poor Aurore," he said, "she must be as worried as I have been."

Carrie knew every inch of the plantation. She headed the horse back through the wooded areas and stayed away from the road along the river where they might conceivably run into someone. She did not even take the main drive up to Kingston's Landing, but emerged from the magnolia trees and tall sweet olive bushes, which framed the big house.

Square white columns supported the second-story galleries, which extended across the f. nt and around either side of the house, shading the lower porches. A giant, old bougainvillea vine, heavy with purple blossoms, climbed up one corner of the structure, clinging along the gallery railings and reaching up still

5

farther, almost to the roofline with its captain's walk—the small room at the highest point of the building from which steamboats on that great highway of a river could be signaled when a passenger wanted to come aboard.

Carrie guided the horse around toward the back where Benjamin, a Negro slave who had been with her family since before she was born, was chopping wood near the summer kitchen. As they came into view, he swung toward them and squinted against the sunlight, his blue cotton shirt damp with sweat, shoulders still powerful though they were beginning to show a slight rounding with age. Perspiration glistened on the dark face as he peered at the two of them on the horse, and then recognizing who was with his mistress, he dropped his axe and hurried toward them.

"Mist' Gayerre," he said, his hushed voice revealing his understanding of the danger. He helped Carrie down, and Paul Gayerre swung to the ground himself though it was clear that he was almost too exhausted to stand.

"Benjamin," Carrie said, "assist Lieutenant Gayerre into the house, and you and Lafitte get him settled in one of the guest bedrooms. See that he has whatever he needs."

"Yes, Miss Carrie."

"I'll send up some food," she said to Paul, turning away toward the summer kitchen.

"Carrie, wait . . ." Paul stopped her. He struggled with the pocket of his uniform blouse—a loose field coat. "Here . . ." He pulled out a packet of crumpled and dirty envelopes and pressed it into her hands. "From your brother."

"You've seen him? George Pierre is safe?" Her throat was almost too full to speak as she looked down at her brother's careful and deliberate handwriting.

"Yes. And your betrothed. Lieutenant Morrison. There are letters from him also."

"Oh . . ." She breathed a sigh of gratitude. There had been no word from either George Pierre or J. D. since before New Orleans had fallen and the Yankees cut off communication with the rest of the Confederacy. "Where are they?" she asked anxiously. "Still at Montgomery?" She put up a restraining hand at once. "Don't answer. We can talk later. Go and rest now."

She watched as the weary soldier allowed himself to be helped into the house. Then she put the letters into her skirt pocket and went the short distance to the summer kitchen. All the heating of water and most of the cooking was done away from the main house to keep it cooler during the hottest months.

The pleasant room smelled of vanilla and cloves. Copper-bottomed pots hung along the brick wall, and sturdy shelves bore jars of spices and rice and dried beans. Chloe, a stout, broad-faced Negress, her graying hair tied up in a white kerchief, stood at the scrupulously clean wooden counter and beat a huge bowlful of glistening egg whites, her ample hips bouncing with each stroke. She turned and looked back over her shoulder.

"There you are, Miss Carrie, honey. Thought I heard your voice out there."

"Chloe, Lieutenant Gayerre is here," Carrie said.

"Mist' Gayerre? Mist' Paul Gayerre from . . ." Her head cocked in the general direction of the river and the Gayerre lands.

"Yes. Apparently he's gone through a very bad time to get here. He didn't know that Aurore and old Madame Gayerre had left and gone upriver. Benjamin is taking him up to one of the guest rooms. Could you fix him a plate? I don't know how long it's been since the poor man has eaten."

"Indeed I can." Chloe put the bowl of egg whites aside and took a sugar- and pepper-encrusted ham from a large covered crock. She cut several thick slices, which she put into a black iron skillet.

"And, Chloe," Carrie said, "he's seen George Pierre and J. D. and they're safe! Paul brought letters!"

"Praise the good Lord!" Chloe swung round, the butcher knife poised in midair, her face beaming with joy.

At that moment, Carrie's sister, Susannah, came bursting through the door, her honey-brown curls dancing, cheeks pink with excitement. Just turned sixteen, Susannah had put on her first grown-up long skirts only two months ago, and she still hadn't quite learned how to manage the unwieldy hoops.

"Carrie! I've just seen Paul Gayerre!" she said. "Benjamin was seeing him upstairs. And do you know what he said to me? He said, 'Why, Mademoiselle Susannah, I hardly recognized

you, you have grown up so since the last time I saw you.' "
Susannah struck a pose with her head high and waved her hand
with a flourish, then giggled. Carrie grinned at her pretty little
sister.

"Well, it seems like to me that a certain Miss Somebody so
grown up would stop tearin' the ruffle most off her petticoat,"
Chloe grumbled, but the fond look she turned on the girl belied
her scolding tone.

"I tripped, Chloe," Susannah explained. "I got my hoop
caught coming out the back door and . . ." She gave a discouraged sigh and, carefully maneuvering her skirt, sat down in one
of the chairs by the long oak table. "See, I think I'm getting
better at it," she said.

"Suzy," Carrie burst out, unable to contain herself any longer,
"Paul brought letters from George Pierre!"

"Letters?" Susannah's ladylike posture was forgotten as she
sprang eagerly from the chair. "Oh, Carrie, is there one for
me?"

"Now, let me see," Carrie teased, knowing full well that there
was. She quickly retrieved the packet from her pocket and gave
Susannah hers. "Here's one for Uncle Etienne, too."

"George Pierre's at Vicksburg!" Susannah exclaimed as she
got her letter open and began to read.

"Vicksburg?" Carrie came to the old oak table and sat down,
her head bent over her own letter. "Yes, I see," she said,
reading eagerly. "He was transferred from Montgomery nearly
three months ago. And he's well," she added for the benefit of
Chloe who, though she couldn't read a word, was hovering
anxiously over Carrie's shoulder, meanwhile keeping a sharp eye
on the ham slices sizzling in the skillet.

" 'The Confederate defeat at Shiloh,' " Carrie read aloud,
" 'was bitter news indeed, but the bitterest news for me was
when word reached us that our own New Orleans had fallen to
the enemy. I have been desperately worried about you and
Susannah, and everyone at Kingston's Landing. I pray daily for
your safety . . .' "

Chloe's eyes were suddenly damp as she went to turn the ham
slices. "Lord, Lord," she said, "but I hate to think of that child
all that way from home. Seems like just yesterday he was the

littlest boy playin' out under the apple trees.'' Shaking her head sadly, she started to cut a thick wedge of cornbread from the pone left from breakfast.

"He says they turned back an attack by Yankee gunboats,'' Susannah said.

"Yes, in mine, too,'' Carrie said. " 'We must hold Vicksburg at all costs,' '' she read. " 'We are all in good spirits here, and I believe this time next summer, the war will be ended and I shall be back at Kingston's Landing.' ''

"He says,'' Susannah put in, " 'Tell Chloe I am hungry for some of her peach cobbler.' '' And the Negress grinned delightedly.

A pretty girl in her middle twenties, skin the color of rich chocolate, came in the doorway balancing a small wicker basket on one hip. She moved across the kitchen floor, swaying with each step as if she were dancing, her starched petticoat rustling pleasantly.

"Lafitte says to tend to Mist' Paul Gayerre's clothes,'' she said, wrinkling her nose at the muddy and torn uniform in the basket. Lafitte had been the head houseman for many years.

Chloe favored her daughter Mattie with a patient look, her eyes slightly squinted; Chloe had grown nearsighted with age. "I'll take a look and see what needs to be done,'' she said. "Fetch me that tray from the shelf there.''

"Yes, Mama.'' Mattie put down the basket and brought the tray to her mother. She was the only surviving child of Chloe and Benjamin. There'd been a son, young Benjamin, who'd drowned in the river, and two other girls who had died in infancy.

Chloe piled the hot ham on the plate by the corn bread and cold sliced sweet potatoes. She added a dish of fresh peaches and a pot of strong hot coffee and put it all on the tray. "Here,'' she said, "take this up to Mist' Gayerre. And then you come back here,'' she added as the girl started toward the door, "and I'll tell you what to do about these here clothes.''

"Yes'm,'' Mattie said.

"Mattie,'' Carrie put in quickly, "no one must know that Lieutenant Gayerre is here. Only us. Do you understand?''

9

Susannah looked up from her letter. "Who is there to tell anyway?" she asked.

"Well," Carrie answered as offhandedly as she could, "someone could ride by. Unexpectedly. You never know."

"You mean Yankee soldiers, don't you?" There was sudden concern in Susannah's green eyes. "Carrie, what would they do if they knew Paul Gayerre was here?"

Carrie picked her words carefully. There was no use frightening her sister. "The Yankees haven't come here to Kingston's Landing so far, Suzy. There's no reason that they should now. I just meant—since we are in captured territory, and since Paul is a Confederate soldier—it might be best if we just said nothing to anyone about his being here. Okay?"

Susannah shrugged. "Okay," she said. "Is it all right if I take this letter to Uncle Etienne? I think he was sitting in the garden earlier. I bet he doesn't even know that Paul Gayerre is here."

"Of course," Carrie said, and handed her sister the letter. But once the girl was gone, Carrie and Chloe exchanged level looks. "Tell Benjamin to keep a sharp eye. Lieutenant Gayerre told me that he'd seen a Yankee patrol about. If they should come this way, we must be ready to hide him quickly."

And Chloe nodded solemnly.

Carrie passed through the back part of the house and entered the coolness of the front hall, her footsteps barely audible on the fine old Oriental carpet. The sunlight filtered softly through the fanlight above the big front door.

Rooms opened along either side of the foyer, rooms furnished with lovingly aged furniture, redolent of supple leathers and wax and lemon oil, but Carrie headed straight up the big staircase toward her bedroom where she could read J. D.'s letter in private.

As she reached the top of the stairs, she saw Lafitte come quietly out of one of the guest bedrooms at the end of the hallway. The tall black man was carrying the food tray that Chloe had sent up, and as Carrie drew closer she could see that at least some of it had been eaten.

"Is Lieutenant Gayerre comfortable, Lafitte?" she asked in a low tone.

"Yes, Missy," Lafitte said. "He is asleep." He spoke in that carefully precise, French-sounding accent that was typical of slaves in Creole households. Usually they were of West Indian origin. Carrie's father had acquired Lafitte along with the plantation years before and had promptly made him his personal manservant. Touches of gray were now creeping about the Negro's ears.

"You know we must be careful, Lafitte," Carrie said, "careful that no one find out that Lieutenant Gayerre is here." She glanced to the door behind which Paul Gayerre slept.

"I know, Missy," he reassured her. "Benjamin and I will keep watch."

"Thank you, Lafitte," she said, and felt a rush of gratitude for her house people as she watched him go along the length of the hallway and down the stairs, his thin body garbed as always in a dignified black.

Inside her room, she closed the door firmly behind her then took out the two letters still left in her pocket. She looked at the strong, rather brash slant of the handwriting on the envelopes and smiled. Putting the one addressed to J. D.'s parents on her nightstand, she settled herself into the chair by the open window and eagerly broke the seal. She pulled out the two sheets of paper.

> Dear Carrie,
> Oh, Lord, how I miss you, honey! But what a stroke of luck that Paul Gayerre is going to slip through the lines to see about his wife and baby, and I can get this letter to you. It is the first chance I've had to send any word since the Union troops took New Orleans and moved north. I hope to God you are all right, honey. I think about you all the time. Especially at night when I am rolled up in my blanket.

Carrie felt her face grow warm.

> How I wish, Carrie, that we had gotten married before I left so that I could have the memory of you as my wife. But we'll take care of that the minute I get home.

Carrie felt the stirring of an old unease. She turned away from the letter, looking out the window over the garden, which was not as beautifully kept as it once had been but was still lovely in the noonday sun.

J. D. was so impatient. He wanted everything *now*. He probably would insist that they get married as soon as he arrived home.

John Danfield Morrison. Her betrothed—that's what Paul Gayerre had called him. Lord, that seemed strange, even to think of J. D. that way. Her betrothed. Though it shouldn't. Hadn't everyone always assumed that she and J. D. would get married someday?

As far back as she could remember, the Morrisons had visited Kingston's Landing often, coming up from New Orleans to stay overnight or a weekend. And the Kingstons had gone down to the city just as frequently in those years before the accident that had taken her parents' lives. And though she had been only thirteen when that happened, the families had already come to speak of a wedding between Carrie and J. D. not as a possibility, but as if it were a fact that time would effect, like summer following the spring.

And somehow, to make a formal commitment *had* seemed the thing to do once the war started . . . with J. D. looking so splendid in his gray uniform with its shiny brass buttons, and Carrie knowing that he might be going off to die in defense of Louisiana and the South. J. D.—who had put a tadpole down the top of her shirtwaist when she was eight years old, and who, when she was nine, fished her out of the river after her attempt to walk a mud-anchored log behind him and her brother George Pierre. That time he had even engaged her mother's attention long enough so that she might slip up the stairs unnoticed, thereby escaping a lecture on what was ladylike and what was not.

Somehow it was all those things that had been in her mind when, two days before he and George Pierre were to leave with their outfit, J. D. had slipped a gold ring with three small emeralds onto her finger.

"There now," he'd said. "Guess that makes it official." And he'd swept her into a hug that had all but broken her ribs.

12

"J. D. . . ." she'd protested, but he'd lowered his head with that thatch of blond hair bleached nearly white in the sun, looked at her with eyes that were blue as the sky on a clear morning, and kissed her, his mouth open and wet and hot.

He had kissed Carrie before, perhaps a half-dozen times in all, but they had always been proper kisses with his lips together, and he had certainly never done that with his tongue before. She'd thought she was going to suffocate!

She squirmed and pushed her hands against his chest until finally he let go.

"All right, all right . . ." He grinned down at her, that devilish hint of mischief playing about his face, the fair eyebrows raised in amusement. "But I'm a man, honey. All grown-up. And I kiss the way a man does. Don't get mad at that."

"I'm not mad, J. D. It's just that . . . that . . ." She stammered and felt her face flush, all the time angry at herself that she wasn't handling it better and wondering if what she'd heard about J. D. and her brother George Pierre were true—that they frequented those houses in New Orleans where women actually let men do things . . . for money!

Old Miss Esther Beauchamp had whispered that, not too softly, to Geraldine Brighton on the steps of the First Presbyterian Church in New Orleans. Leaning heavily on her walking stick, Miss Esther had added that she was not so old that she wasn't on to the likes of those rascals, and she had fastened George Pierre and J. D. with a disapproving eye as the young men brought the carriage around in front of the church. And then, upon seeing Carrie standing nearby, Miss Esther had favored her with a look only slightly less fierce . . . as if Carrie had overheard on purpose.

J. D. broke into her wondering to tip her still blushing face upward, a gentle hand beneath her chin, his features as sober as she had ever seen them. "Let's have the wedding now, hon. Right now. Before I leave."

"J. D., that's impossible!" Carrie's voice held a touch of panic. "You're leaving tomorrow afternoon and . . . and I don't have a wedding dress . . . and your mother would be all upset . . . She'll want to plan the reception. And there wouldn't be time enough for our friends . . ."

J. D. sighed. "All right," he said finally, "but you get together with Mama and decide on everything. We'll do it on my first leave for sure."

But J. D. hadn't been home on leave. Just when it seemed that he might get permission from his commanding officer, New Orleans had fallen and the Union lines had moved northward almost to Baton Rouge. And though Carrie was desperately worried about him, as well as George Pierre, there were painfully honest moments when she admitted to a certain guilty relief that she wouldn't have to tell J. D. that she thought they should wait until after the war to get married.

And even then, she told herself now, J. D. needed some time to get settled . . . and they needed time to get used to each other again. After all, it had been over a year since they'd seen one another.

Carrie drew a long breath and went back to the letter, the rest of which was mostly J. D.'s brash assurances that now that Louisiana men had arrived at Vicksburg, the safety of that strategic point was assured. "Better for the Yankees," he said, "if they just packed up and headed back up North again."

He ended with rather extravagant protests of his love and the request that she send the letter for his mother and father on to them in New Orleans if she could. There was a postscript:

> Carrie, honey, I hope you haven't had any trouble with the Yankees. Knowing how you love Kingston's Landing, I don't suppose it will do me any good to suggest this, but maybe it would be better if you took Susannah and went to stay with my parents in New Orleans until I get back.

Carrie sat looking down at the letter. J. D. was right. She did love Kingston's Landing, so much sometimes that it made a fierce ache inside her. She might go down to New Orleans later in the year. She would have to if she were to accomplish what she had in mind to do. But she would not stay away from the plantation any longer than needful. And unless the Yankee patrol had caught sight of Paul Gayerre and started to comb the area to find him, there was no reason to suppose that their luck wouldn't

14

hold so far as the Yankees were concerned. Perhaps General Butler and his "brave" men would content themselves with insulting and harassing the people of New Orleans, she thought scornfully, helpless women and men too old to be in the army.

Her gaze moved to the top of the walnut chest where stood the daguerreotypes of J. D. and George Pierre. They had been taken three days before the men left and both looked stiffly ill at ease in the new gray uniforms. How ironic, she thought, that all the area boys had joined the Confederate Army with such haste and then had been away fighting to the north and east when New Orleans had fallen to the enemy. Farragut had been able to bring his gunboats up the Mississippi from the Gulf and take the all-but-helpless city with ease.

Shaking her head and rising from the chair, she put the letter on her dresser and then slipped out of her riding habit. In camisole and pantalettes, she splashed her face with water from the ironstone pitcher and bowl, then patted it dry with the linen towel that hung alongside the washstand.

Nearly five feet six inches tall, she was very slender in the waist, her figure rounding beautifully to hips that were just full enough and thighs that were well-shaped and tapering. Her young, full breasts pushed at the ruffled top of her camisole.

She was aware that she did not meet the accepted standards of beauty for the day. She was too tall. Her face wasn't delicate enough, her eyebrows too strong. The full, coral-colored lips were too definite, not at all the small rosebud mouth so generally admired. And yet from the time she was sixteen, she had been aware of a smoldering, only half-hidden heat in more than one masculine eye. J. D. was not the only boy around who had wanted to court her.

Sometimes she thought about the apparent contradiction of it, but not today. Today her thoughts still lingered on J. D.'s letter, and it was with a certain impatience that she pulled the ribbon from her dark hair and let the long tresses, which curled slightly and held a strong glint of chestnut highlights, swirl down about her shoulders.

She applied the tortoise-shell brush vigorously, catching back the tendrils that wanted to curl about her ears, and then she tied the thick mass firmly back again. With one last look at J. D.'s broad, fair face looking so intently into the camera, so unlike him because he wasn't smiling, she pulled back the white woven coverlet on the tall-posted bed and lay down.

Whatever was the matter with her? She loved J. D. She was going to be his wife. And to worry about the exact timing of their wedding was foolish.

She turned her face into the coolness of the sheets and thought about how it would be when the war was finally over and George Pierre was back home . . . and she tried to imagine what it would be like to be married to J. D.

Paul Gayerre slept through that first day and most of the next, and fortunately life at Kingston's Landing went on as usual. Only old Toby, one of a handful of ancient slaves left in the quarters, had ambled up to the house to get some sweet oil for his wife Nadine who had an earache. And he had gone back none the wiser that a certain Confederate lieutenant slept in one of the guest bedrooms upstairs.

Toward evening of the second day, Lafitte informed Carrie that Lieutenant Gayerre was awake and would be down shortly, and thirty minutes later Paul Gayerre presented himself to Carrie and Susannah in the parlor, his uniform clean and mended, the dark stubble of beard gone from his face.

He greeted them with Creole charm, and then as the girls' uncle joined them, he bowed rather formally as a mark of respect to the older man. "Monsieur Moreau, how are you, sir?"

"Well, thank you, Paul." Etienne Moreau stood tall in his well-cut, always perfectly pressed even if old black suit, his light gray waistcoat buttoned over the spotless white ruffles of his shirtfront. He inclined his head graciously, a pronounced streak of silver through the black hair gleaming in the candlelight.

He was thinner than ever, Carrie noted suddenly, aware of the delicacy of those aristocratic features. Dear Uncle Etienne. He had been the brother of Papa's first wife, Dominique, and owned Maisonfleur, that lovely old house about a mile downriver. Carrie could never remember a time when he was not a constant visitor. Adam Kingston had always treated him like a brother.

"I regret," he was saying now to Paul Gayerre, "that I was unaware of your arrival yesterday until you were already settled in your room. I am afraid I have started to make a habit of sitting in the morning sun and enjoying the garden. One grows lazy as one grows old.''

Paul smiled. "No matter. I am delighted to see you now, sir. And I think I should like nothing better than to sit a while in a sunny garden myself.''

"You look quite rested, Paul," Carrie said.

"Indeed I am, thanks to your kindness." His gesture took in the three of them.

"Then come . . ." Carrie had just seen Lafitte nod at her from the hallway. "I believe dinner is ready. Let's go in.''

They entered the dining room with its crystal wall sconces and needlepoint-covered chairs. Three white candles were arranged in the center of the snowy white linen cloth, blue ageratum clustered about them.

Despite the circumstances, the occasion was taking on a festive air. It was so seldom, Carrie thought, that they had a dinner guest since the Yankees had captured New Orleans.

Susannah's cheeks were rosy as Paul Gayerre held her chair for her, and she looked up at him, dimples showing. "Chloe made a burnt-sugar cake," she offered brightly.

"Well, Mademoiselle Susannah, I shall certainly look forward to that." He grinned.

"To have news of George Pierre has been so welcome," Etienne said once they were all seated, and Lafitte and Mattie had begun to serve.

Paul nodded. "He will be just as anxious to hear that all of you are well. I shall have to describe every minute of this dinner to him and Lieutenant Morrison. It is not often that we get to sit down to such a meal in the army. Though, the good ladies of Vicksburg do occasionally invite us to join them and their families for dinner.''

"Is the food in the army not adequate? Not good?" Carrie asked anxiously.

"It is fine," Paul reassured her at once. "It is just that the army has no time for the niceties of dining. And, I must confess, no cooks that can equal your Chloe." He watched approvingly as Lafitte served him from the large platter of fish and river shrimp, which had been freshly caught that morning. Bowls held

17

potatoes, fried okra and eggplant, and thick slices of tomatoes from the garden. Mattie passed the basket of hot rolls.

"Tell us, then," Etienne said when all the plates were full, "how is the war really going? We are never quite sure."

"The newspapers in New Orleans can only print what General Butler wants them to," Carrie said. "He has closed down at least one whose editor defied him."

"Butler!" Paul Gayerre said scornfully. "We hear only bad things of him. Let us hope that soon we shall drive him and his men from Louisiana."

"Let us drink to that." Etienne raised his wineglass, and they all followed suit.

"To the Confederacy," Paul said. "May she be triumphant soon." And as Carrie raised the glass to her lips, she saw those dark eyes glitter with a bright resolve.

The toast ended, and Paul answered Etienne Moreau's question. "Stonewall Jackson and Jeb Stewart are fighting brilliantly in the east. I shouldn't be surprised if before too long we are able to take Washington and end this war once and for all. Meanwhile, it's certain that Grant will eventually try to take Vicksburg. He has to if the Union is to have complete control of the Mississippi. But I am confident that we shall hold him off. Vicksburg occupies high ground on the east bank of the Mississippi, and the Yazoo River enters just a short distance north of the city with steep bluffs along its left bank. It is like a natural fortress and General Pemberton has manned it fully. I think the mighty Grant will have met his match."

There were smiles around the table, and Susannah tossed her head pertly, curls dancing. "Well, I'll be glad when it's over," she said, her smile turning to a pretty pout. "Carrie wouldn't even let me go down to New Orleans to visit for my birthday. Not with the Yankees there."

"Oh, that's too bad, Mademoiselle Susannah," Paul said. "To be deprived of such a lovely young lady is New Orleans's loss."

Susannah blushed and dimpled prettily, and Carrie was struck by how much she looked like their mother.

It was clear that Paul was hungry after his long sleep. He

finished his plate and made no protest when Lafitte refilled it for him.

The conversation turned to happier times, to trips to the city, and to plantation parties. Susannah listened with rapt attention, her cheeks still pink.

"I remember well," Paul said, "one of the parties that your father gave here at Kingston's Landing. Let me see, what year was it? I was only a boy . . ." He was relaxed and reminiscing when suddenly there was a great clatter outside in the hallway, and Carrie stiffened, feeling her heart leap almost into her throat.

Paul Gayerre started from his chair in a half-crouch, dark eyes wary, his hand moving to his side where his gun would have been if he had not left it in the bedroom upstairs.

They were frozen there for an instant, all eyes turned toward the door, when Lafitte's tall form appeared holding a silver coffee pot before him.

"Mattie accidentally dropped the tray, Missy," he said quietly to Carrie. "She is cleaning up now."

Carrie felt her breath come out in a rush. She had not realized that she was holding it. "It's all right, Lafitte," she said. "Tell Mattie it's all right."

The black man nodded and put the pot on the sideboard.

Paul gave a nervous laugh and sank back into his seat while Etienne Moreau looked relieved. They resumed eating, trying to act as if nothing had happened, but the earlier mood of gaiety had been broken. The weight of the war hung heavy in the room.

"I have not tasted such shrimp since I left home." Paul's attempt at heartiness rang slightly false.

"I must remember to tell Chloe how much you enjoyed it," Carrie said lightly, trying to match his effort. Only Susannah seemed unaffected and chattered on as usual.

They had finished their cake and coffee when Etienne asked Paul if he would care to retire to the study for cigars and brandy.

"I regret that I must say no," the young Creole answered. "I think it best that I go now."

"So soon?" Etienne protested. "I had hoped that you could stay until tomorrow. That we might have a game of chess or—"

"I thank you," Paul broke in gravely. "I thank all of you for your hospitality. But I have put you in danger for too long as it is.''

''That's not true,'' Carrie said.

Paul smiled and stood up. ''Aurore and I will remember,'' he said, his voice very quiet. There was a moment's silence in the room, and then he went on matter-of-factly. ''Besides, it is much safer for me to travel at night. And I must get back as soon as possible.''

''Of course,'' Carrie said. ''I'll have Chloe pack some food to take with you.''

And a short time later, Carrie waited with Paul Gayerre in the shadows of the front gallery. A pale sliver of a moon disappeared from time to time behind patches of dark clouds, and Benjamin stood patiently at a distance from the porch, holding a horse that was saddled and ready. Etienne and Susannah had gone to fetch their letters to George Pierre. Carrie had already given Paul hers for J. D. and her brother.

''I should apologize for my appearance yesterday when you first saw me,'' Paul chuckled. He seemed more relaxed now that he was ready to leave. ''I am not accustomed to calling on a neighbor in such a disreputable state of dress, but I needed to put some distance between myself and that Yankee patrol. And the only boat I could find was Pompey's old fishing boat. It was half-rotted out, but luckily I made it almost across the river before it started to sink.''

Carrie grinned. ''I'm glad I came by at the right time. Do you think they saw you? Before you crossed the river?''

''I do not think so. I had reached home and found it deserted and decided to sleep a while when I heard them. Right outside the window.'' A deep frown suddenly appeared between his eyebrows. ''It was the strangest thing, Carrie,'' he said. ''The first voice I heard was a man giving orders in a Southern accent. I thought they were Confederates until I looked through a crack in the shutters and saw their blue uniforms. I got out through the back.''

''That is strange,'' she said.

He shrugged, his forehead smoothed. ''Perhaps I was mistaken. I may have dreamed it. That the man spoke like a Southerner, I mean. The patrol was certainly there.''

The waiting horse stamped at the soft earth and blew through his nose. Benjamin quieted him.

"And what of you?" Paul changed the subject. "George Pierre worries about you, you know."

"Yes, I know. He said so in his letter. But there's no need."

"He is afraid too much will fall to your shoulders. After all, you are but a girl. He has spoken to me about it. He is afraid . . ." Paul's kind concern was suddenly mixed with embarrassment. "Forgive me if I presume too much. He is afraid that there is not enough money."

"Money? Oh, of course there is," Carrie lied, hoping that her face didn't betray her. "You tell George Pierre that everything is fine here at home. Tell him he's not to worry."

The truth was she'd sat up many nights going over the books, trying to find a way to stretch what little money they had left and wondering how George Pierre could have let so much of Papa's money dribble away in such a few years. But it wasn't his fault, she reminded herself. He couldn't help it if he didn't have Papa's business sense. And after all, he'd only been nineteen when Papa had died and he'd had to take over Kingston's Landing.

"You have no slaves left?" Paul asked now.

"Only three or four in the quarters, too old to run off."

"Three or four in the quarters, and your house people."

Carrie hadn't even counted her house people. They were like her family. It had never occurred to her, or for that matter to them, that they might run off.

Paul shook his head. "Then there's no way you can get a crop in next spring."

"Yes, there is," she said quickly.

"How?" He looked puzzled.

"They say there are plenty of runaways in New Orleans who'll hire out to whomever will pay them."

"Pay them?" Paul said angrily. "They should be returned to their owners by the authorities! But the Yankees probably delight in seeing plantation owners losing everything!"

"We'll not lose," she said sharply. In her mind's eye she could see the untended fields and the all but empty quarters, the stables that needed painting and the broken-down levees. She would put it right somehow, she vowed to herself once again. If

21

she were a man, she would go off to New Orleans tomorrow, round up her runaways, and bring every last one of them back. And she would work in the fields alongside them, if necessary. That's what Papa would have done. "You don't ever ask your people to do anything that you wouldn't do yourself." She'd heard him say that a hundred times.

Her thoughts were broken by Susannah coming out onto the gallery with her letter for George Pierre. She was followed almost immediately by Etienne.

The letters safely inside Paul's blouse pocket, the four of them looked at each other, almost awkwardly. A night bird called, shrill and plaintive in the still air.

"Will you try to go to Natchez?" Carrie asked.

Paul nodded. "And as soon as I've seen Aurore and the baby, I shall be on my way back to Vicksburg where I'll deliver these." He patted his pocket. "Once I get through the Yankee lines there will be no trouble at all."

The waiting horse nickered, and Etienne Moreau embraced Paul after the Creole custom. "God go with you," he said.

"Be careful," Carrie added.

"Do not worry." Paul's white teeth flashed. "I know the country better than they do."

2

CARRIE FINISHED THE LAST OF HER CINNAMON BUN AND SHOVED the empty oatmeal bowl aside. "I don't know how I could have slept so late," she said to Chloe, who had a pan of fresh green beans from the garden in her lap. "You should have sent Mattie up to wake me."

It was two days after Paul Gayerre's visit to Kingston's Landing, and they were in the summer kitchen, sitting at the long oak table, its well-worn top mellowed to the color of honey. Carrie had chosen to eat there because she'd missed breakfast with Uncle Etienne and Susannah, who'd had theirs as usual in the dining room.

"I figured you be needin' your rest," Chloe said, snapping off the ends of a long, plump bean and whisking away the strings. "You was up mighty late last night. I thought I heard a noise, and when I got up to see about it, I saw that the lamp was still lit in the study."

Carrie nodded, suppressed a sigh. Her session with the accounts, poring over the ledgers at Papa's old desk, had proven fruitless. There was so little money left, she dared not use it for planting or repairs. She must take care of Suzy and the others still here at Kingston's Landing who depended on her. Heaven knew how long she'd have to make the money last. And though Uncle Etienne was a partner of a sort—the two plantations had been managed together by her father—she suspected that he had little money left for himself. She couldn't ask him.

"Don't hurt a thing to sleep in once in a while," Chloe was saying.

Carrie put her napkin on the table and stood up. "All the same," she said, "I should have gotten up earlier. I promised Uncle Etienne that I'd go over to Maisonfleur with him this morning. Where's Susannah? I thought she might like to ride over with us."

"That child . . ." Chloe leaned from her chair to retrieve a green bean that had fallen to the brick floor, "that child went out to the garden to cut some flowers 'most an hour ago, and she ain't come back yet. Promised she'd bring me some sage, too," she added.

"I'll go see if I can find her," Carrie said.

She went the few short steps to the main house, passing under the latticed arbor of blooming bougainvillea. She went in through the back, moving quickly through the rear halls where the workrooms were, the warming kitchen and pantry and the room off to the side that held a copper shower and tub. In the front part of the house, still cool and dim, the draperies drawn against the sun, she crossed through the sitting room where the muted colors of a Persian rug blended with the soft sheen of waxed walnut woods and well-cushioned leather.

When Carrie walked out onto the south gallery with its heavy cypress chairs and old green swing hanging from the ceiling, she saw her sister at once, out in the garden, which was a charming tangle of blooms.

"Suzy," she called, and the girl straightened and waved. Catching up her basket and skirt, Susannah ran toward the gallery, skipping gracefully over the stepping stones, her petticoats showing to a disgraceful degree.

Carrie shook her head and laughed. "Keep your skirts down. Your legs are showing," she admonished.

Susannah slowed at once, smoothed her dress, and came the rest of the way at a prim and proper pace, which was belied by the saucy toss of her head and the sparkle of her green eyes.

"Look, Carrie," she said, holding out the basket of pink, red, and yellow roses, "aren't they lovely!"

"They are." Carrie leaned down to catch the fragrance. "I like this one." She gently touched a huge, dark red bloom. "Did you get Chloe's sage?"

Susannah poked a finger into one corner of the basket. "Right here."

"All right. Come on, we'll put the roses in water." She slipped an arm about her sister's waist, and they walked around the house together, past the sweet olive bushes and the clumps of wild ginger.

"What took you so long?" Carrie asked. "Chloe said you've been gone nearly an hour."

Susannah shrugged. "It was a pretty day. I walked down to the river."

"Really," Carrie chided, "you mustn't go far from the house alone. With the way things are these days . . . it's best to be cautious."

"You ride about by yourself all the time," Susannah reminded her tartly.

"That's different. I can look out for myself."

"Well, I just guess I can, too!"

"Will you *please* do as I say!"

24

Susannah drew a long sigh, and Carrie softened, giving her sister a quick hug. "And next time you're out in the sun, wear a hat. You're going to get freckles," she teased as they came into the kitchen.

"Did you get my sage?" Chloe asked.

"Right here, Chloe."

"Thank you, honey lamb."

Carrie reached up to the top shelf of a cupboard and brought down a thin bristol vase, which she filled with water and carried to the table along with a sharp knife to trim the rose stems. "Uncle Etienne and I are going to ride over to Maisonfleur," she said to Susannah. "Do you want to come along?"

"That dusty old place?" Susannah said. "Why would anybody want to go there?"

"Why, Suzy, Maisonfleur is one of the loveliest houses in Louisiana. If it's dusty, it's because it's closed up. There's no one seeing to it." She held up one of the pink roses, looked at it thoughtfully. "You know," she said, "maybe we should do that. Maybe we should go over one day and clean it. I think Uncle Etienne would like that."

"Oh, pooh!" Susannah said, her pink underlip pushing out in a pout. "We never do anything that's fun anymore. Not since George Pierre left. Why can't we go down to New Orleans?"

"Because," Carrie said, clipping off the stem end of the pink rose, "New Orleans is not a good place for ladies to be since General Butler and his Yankees took over."

A sudden mischievous sparkle lit Susannah's green eyes. "And why not?" she asked innocently.

"Well . . ." Carrie and Chloe exchanged quick looks, and then Carrie took her time in positioning the flower in the vase. "Well," she went on finally, "it just isn't. Not with the war and everything."

"I do wish," Susannah drew her petite figure up as tall as she could make it, "that you would stop treating me like a child, Carrie Kingston. I know about General Butler's old 'Woman Order' as well as you do. *'When any female shall, by word, gesture, or movement, insult or show contempt for any officer or soldier of the United States, she shall be held liable to be treated as a woman of the town plying her vocation'*," Susannah parroted the infamous order, which had been posted all over New Orleans. "And," she added saucily, "I know what *woman of the town* means, too!"

"Suzy!"

"I bet if your Mama was alive, she'd wash your mouth right out with soap," Chloe said, but it was obvious that she was trying to keep from grinning.

Carrie sighed. "Well, if you know all that," she said, "you know why we haven't gone down to the city."

"I still don't see why not," Susannah persisted. "The Morrisons sent word that they were all right, Yankees or no. And Paul Gayerre didn't seem to think it would be so terrible if I got to go."

"Paul was just being nice to you." Carrie put the last rose in the vase and handed it to her sister. "Come on, we'll put these in the house. They'll look nice in the front hall."

Susannah followed along, still grumbling. Once they had reached the front hall, they put the roses on the walnut table.

"I still don't see why we couldn't go. Just for a short visit. We could stay with J. D.'s folks."

"Not right now, Suzy. Maybe, just maybe, we'll go a little later this year."

Susannah saw a sign of weakening and pressed it. "If a Yankee soldier would dare to say anything to me on the street, I'd just say to him, 'Good day, sir,' and pass right on by."

"What is this about a soldier? A Yankee?"

The two girls turned to find Etienne Moreau coming down the stairway, his fine, dark Creole eyes ablaze.

"A soldier has had the effrontery to speak to you?" he demanded, his head high, that streak of silver through the black hair accentuated by the sun through the fanlight.

Susannah giggled and ran to him. "No, Uncle Etienne." She gave him a big hug and dimpled prettily. "That's what I'd say to one if he *did*."

"Well," he said, looking only slightly mollified, "if one did, there would be no need to say anything to him because he would answer to me!"

Carrie looked at the two of them and smiled. "That's *just* the reason we're not going down to the city," she said firmly. "Are you ready, Uncle 'Tienne? Let's get started to Maisonfleur. Shall I call Lafitte to get the buggy, or would you rather ride?"

Carrie had worn her straw bonnet with the bright yellow ribbons that tied beneath her chin and set off her big amber eyes, which could turn golden in an instant if the light was right. She was grateful now for the ample brim that shaded her face from the sunlight, though they stayed to the cool shelter of the trees as much as possible.

Majestic blew softly through his nose and danced sideways, feeling good. The gelding that Etienne Moreau rode shied, but the Creole brought him quickly under control, his long thin fingers intertwined with the leather reins. Carrie smiled; he was a fine horseman.

"I have been thinking of Paul Gayerre," he said. "I do hope he has moved safely through the enemy lines."

"So do I," Carrie said. "At least it's been quiet around here. No sign of the Yankee patrol he saw across the river."

"May it continue to be so." Etienne smiled wryly.

They were silent for a few minutes, the horses' hooves a rhythmic thumping against the soft earth. Carrie caught a whiff of honeysuckle. "We should do this more often," she said.

"Yes. I had forgotten how pleasant it is to ride along here . . . near the river." The dark eyes seemed less somber than usual.

When Carrie was twelve years old, she had imagined that Uncle Etienne, who had never married, must have had an early and tragic love affair to put such a sad look in his eyes. But she had long since decided that that rather melancholy look must go with the Creole blood. Sometimes she could catch a glimpse of it in her brother George Pierre.

The horses were coming up over the rise now, and Carrie could see the whole stretch of river on one side and the fallow fields on the other, overgrown and matted, palmettoes springing up here and there. In the distance were the bayous; egrets and ospreys rose against the blue sky.

"Did you know," Uncle Etienne was saying, "that all of this

land was once a separate plantation with Maisonfleur as the manor house?''

"Yes, I did, Uncle 'Tienne," Carrie said. But he went on as if she hadn't answered.

"That house once made a king welcome . . . future king," he corrected himself. "King Louis Philippe of France when he was still the Duke of Orleans. As a matter of fact, the chess set I wish to bring back with us today was given to my uncle, Pierre Dubonnet, by the duke. Your brother George Pierre was named after Uncle Pierre, you know."

"Yes. He was your uncle on your mother's side, wasn't he?"

"That is correct," he said. "My mother was a Dubonnet, my father a Moreau."

Though Carrie had heard it all many times, she never failed to encourage her uncle. She loved hearing about the Dubonnets and the Moreaus, old line Creole aristocracy. Even the names rolled off Etienne Moreau's tongue like music, rich and exotic.

But today, he seemed disinclined to pursue family history except to say, "The Maisonfleur lands became a part of Kingston's Landing when your father married my sister Dominique. Adam took charge of everything," he added, "and he did a splendid job. I am afraid that I was never much help to him . . . as I have not been a help to you, Carrie, in this past year."

"Uncle 'Tienne . . . please don't say that."

"No, no, it is true." There was a certain weariness about him. "Your father always said that Creoles had no head for business. And he was right. Ah, Carrie, sometimes I think that I have come to live too much in the past."

"Dear Uncle 'Tienne . . . I don't know what Suzy and I would do without you. Truly I don't." Carrie's sincerity was evident in her voice, and Etienne Moreau smiled. For a moment there was something quite boyish about his face.

"Even when you were a little girl, *ma chère*, you always seemed to find the right words to say."

Though it was not yet in view, they were not far from Maisonfleur now, and up ahead was the place that Adam Kingston had long ago set aside for the family plot. "I'll just be damned if I want to bake in one of those ovens down in New Orleans after I'm dead!" Adam had often proclaimed, referring to the practice of laying the dead to rest in above-ground tombs. The old city was like a huge catchbasin—lower than the river and dry only because of the levees around it. Any attempt to dig a regular grave resulted in a hole full of water.

But along this wooded stretch of road that led to Maisonfleur, the land sloped enough so that it drained properly, and the plot itself was flanked by two huge and twisted live oak trees.

"I thought I might stop for a few minutes, Uncle 'Tienne. I'll be along shortly," Carrie said.

"Take all the time you need, *ma chère*." Etienne turned slightly in his saddle as the horse plodded on. "Call out to me when you enter the house. I shall probably be upstairs in Uncle Pierre's old room. I believe the chess set is in a chest he kept at the foot of his bed."

"All right," Carrie said.

Across the road and down a short distance from the family plot were graves with small stone markers that bore names like Plato and Zsamelda, Cinta and Julene and Young Benjamin, trusted family servants, near but always apart, in death as in life. But it was to the four graves beneath the oaks that Carrie turned.

Old Monsieur Dubonnet had been buried there. And Armand Moreau, Uncle Etienne's father—Carrie could just barely remember him, an old man in a tall-backed wheelchair. And there were the graves of Adam and Molly Kingston, side by side and a little apart from the others, with fine white Italian marble tombstones rising above.

Wild vines crept around and clung tenaciously to the carved marble flowers and grape clusters, and Carrie worked for the next few minutes pulling them away, grateful for the leather riding gloves that protected her hands against the tough and prickly plants. The other graves were in need of attention, too. She'd send Benjamin or Lafitte over one day to see to them.

She could feel the perspiration on her throat and the nape of her neck as she tugged at the stubborn vines. Finally finished, she retrieved the lace-edged handkerchief from her small reticule and patted her face and neck after removing her bonnet and lifting up the heavy mass of dark hair. Contrary to fashion, she liked wearing her hair loose, or at most tied back with a ribbon.

Cooler now, she took the two roses she'd brought with her

over to the graves and sat down in the sweet-smelling grass
beside the spot where Molly Gallagher Kingston lay. She put the
pink rose there for her mother and tried to remember her with
that same sharp and bittersweet keenness that she could remember her father.

Mama had been so pretty . . . and smelled of lemon. Carrie
remembered her eyes best, green with gold speckles. It was as if
she'd divided the coloring between her daughters; Susannah had
gotten that clear green, Carrie the amber gold, really the only
thing about her that was her mother's.

There was never any doubt that Molly Kingston loved her
children—not only her own daughters, but her stepson just as
much. But even as a child, Carrie had always had some deep-
down knowledge that Mama loved Papa even more. And that
seemed right somehow . . . to love Papa more than all the other
people in the world.

After five years, Carrie could see them yet as they'd stood that
day at the steamship railing waving goodbye . . . Papa so tall
and handsome, Mama turning her face up to him for a moment
with all that love in her eyes. Then she turned to wave again and
smiled at Carrie and the others on shore.

It was to be a summer holiday in Philadelphia, where Papa
would see to a business matter or two and Mama would shop for
the latest fashions. But just above Baton Rouge a faulty boiler
exploded and more than two-thirds of the people aboard had
never seen Philadelphia or anyplace else again.

Mama had been killed instantly, Papa thrown into the muddy
water, his legs crushed. Lafitte, unhurt himself, had pulled his
injured master from the river.

At home, the tall-backed wheelchair that old Monsieur Armand Moreau had once used was brought from the storage room,
and when Adam Kingston was well enough, he sat in it, that
once lusty body wasted, gaunt.

"There are some sins that take a lot of paying for. Remember
that, Carrie honey." He'd said that to her on a hot September
afternoon when the smell of roses was heavy in the air and bees
buzzed in the garden. "But I've had your mother for a while
. . . and you children. And I've had the land. I've had Kingston's
Landing. God has let me have that ... ."

He had died soon after that.

Now Carrie moved over to her father's grave and put the blood-red rose, the one that was her favorite, there by the tombstone. She closed her eyes. "I'll make Kingston's Landing the way it used to be . . . for you, Papa," she said aloud. "I don't know how, but I will."

She stayed still for a moment, eyes closed, and then some small, nagging thing that she had refused to notice for several minutes tugged at her senses, demanded attention. Faint sounds carried on the breeze—almost like men shouting and once a higher pitched sound like a horse whinnying.

She swung round quickly and saw smoke rolling high into the sky above the trees, perilously close to Maisonfleur, billowing blackly, blotting up the blue of the sky, and she was aware of the sudden, faint odor, the slight stinging in her nostrils.

Dear Lord . . . maybe it was one of the barns. Or the sugar house even . . . Let it be one of those.

She caught up her skirts, threw herself into the saddle of the startled Majestic, and brought her crop down to send him bolting along the road.

When Etienne Moreau had left Carrie at the family cemetery, he had continued along toward Maisonfleur, lost in the memories that seemed to dominate him of late, memories of the past and of the great house up ahead. Of the parties, the dancing, the elegantly dressed gentlemen, and their lovely, dark-eyed ladies.

He chuckled softly as he recalled the first time he had brought Adam Kingston to a plantation party there. The Creoles had been outraged, shocked, that an *American* would be a guest in the magnificent old manor house where three generations of Dubonnets had lived.

The Dubonnets and the Moreaus had been in Louisiana from the beginning. Gaspard Dubonnet and Achille Moreau had been officers under the command of Bienville himself when he first laid out the city of New Orleans in the name of France. And for a hundred years after, those two families had been the backbone of the Creole aristocracy that had turned a frontier settlement into the most civilized and cosmopolitan city of the continent, a city that had entertained royalty more than once and had grown in grace and culture.

But then, with the Louisiana Purchase, the Americans had taken over, and slowly everything had changed. The elegant and genteel Creoles who had once been the lords of the city finally, inch by inch, had to give way to the aggressive Americans, but through it all they had maintained a stiff-necked aloofness.

His own father, Armand Moreau, Etienne thought now, had been wiser than the others. He had said many times that the Creole and American cultures must meet, must accommodate one another. He had given his consent for Dominique to marry the American, Adam Kingston, and not entirely because Adam was a rich and powerful man. Though there was that, too, since they needed money to avoid losing Maisonfleur. But he had sincerely believed that the Creoles could not survive unless they learned to live with the Americans.

When the predictable storm of disapproval swept through both the Creole and the American sections, Armand Moreau stood firm. And Dominique, gentle Dominique had been above it all, steadfast in her love for the big American.

Etienne closed his eyes for a moment, remembered how Dominique had looked in her wedding dress on the day of her marriage, remembered the big dark eyes and raven hair. He felt a dull ache, as he always did when he thought of her. She had died too soon. Too tragically soon.

He brought himself up stiffly in the saddle, impatient with himself. Those days were long ago, and he was the last of the Moreaus, as Uncle Pierre had been the last of the Dubonnets. Even Adam Kingston, the man Etienne had come to admire more than any other in the world, except perhaps his own father, even Adam was gone . . . and dear, sweet Molly. He had to think of the children now, Adam's children. He had to see them safely through the war. And he would do it gladly. Were they not the nearest to his own that he would ever have?

There were times when he longed for the quiet serenity of Maisonfleur with its high, molded ceilings and graceful fan windows, longed for the proud assurance on the faces of his ancestors who looked down from their gilded frames on rooms of fine old French furniture and mantelpieces of veined marble.

Ah, well, he drew a sigh, once the children were safely back together again he could go home. And meanwhile he would find Uncle Pierre's old chess set today, and he would check all the shutters and make sure that they were securely bolted, and—

He was startled as he heard a shout, a deep male voice calling out a name that he couldn't quite make out, followed almost immediately by an answering call.

He spurred his horse and emerged from the trees at an angle to the big house that allowed him to see the circular drive and the shaded front galleries. Eight or ten men milled about, some down from their saddles, others still atop horses that whinnied nervously and chopped at the soft earth with their hooves.

Etienne reined his own horse up sharply, too stunned for a moment to believe the scene in front of him.

One of the big windows in the front exploded suddenly in a shower of glass, as if something had been thrown through it from the inside, and in the next instant a big black horse carrying a heavy-browed man in a slouch hat and a red neckerchief came out of the open front door, the horse's hooves clopping loudly against the wooden floor of the gallery, stumbling slightly on the three wide steps that went down to the white gravel drive.

The man hefted a silver candelabrum in one hand and grinned. "Don't forget this here!" he shouted. "Ought to weigh six, eight pounds if'n it weighs a ounce!" He tossed it to a bull of a man who was on the ground bending over a sheet spread out and piled high with silver pieces.

"I ain't got no more room," the big man bellowed.

A red-cheeked boy in the blue uniform of the Union Army, his shirt now streaked and tattered, sprinted out the door. "Put it in here," he yelled and waved the white linen pillowcase, which he had pressed into service.

Etienne stared, frozen in place, but his brain was racing. Jayhawkers, that was what these men were, that strange name that Americans had given to such bands of thieves. That boy there in blue was a deserter, from the army. . . .

He seemed unable to move as the rage mounted in him. And men were shouting and passing out dusty bottles of wine from his wine racks. Another deserter, wearing the blue cap and dirty jacket of a Union uniform with a pair of baggy dark green trousers, came through the front door triumphantly waving a small clock. Even at this distance, Etienne recognized the timepiece. It was silver inlaid with Russian enamel, and it had once belonged to his mother.

That was perhaps what freed him, the sight of that clock profaned by the man's touch. He brought his heels smartly against the horse's side and put the animal into a brisk and determined trot toward the house. His back was as straight as it had been when he was a young man, his head stiffly erect.

Etienne was almost there before they saw him. The man in the slouch hat had his head thrown back drinking from a wine bottle, his huge Adam's apple pumping up and down, when he caught a glimpse out of the corner of his eye. He swung round, red Bordeaux dribbling over his chin, and gurgled a warning to the others.

Etienne saw a big-jawed man swinging a bottle above his head, bearing down fast on a spotted pony, but he kept his measured trot. For an instant he wished that he had his old sword. He had been an excellent fencer in his youth, as skilled with the saber as the foil. He was aware of the blood that surged through his veins, that pounded at his temples . . . the Moreau blood . . . the Dubonnet blood.

As the two horses almost collided, the big-jawed man let out a resounding whoop and brought the bottle around in a vicious arc against the side of Etienne's face. The blow knocked him from the saddle. There was a flash of pain, and the white gravel of the drive and dust in his mouth . . . and blackness enveloped him, left him only vaguely aware of a far-off throbbing in his head, a sick heaving in his stomach.

After a time, the pain grew worse, nagged him back to full consciousness. He stirred, spat gravel, and caught his breath in a great rush of air. He realized that someone, or something, was tugging at his hand, and he opened his eyes to see one of the young deserters, the one who had had his mother's clock, hunkered down beside him. There was a pleased grin on the ferrety face as the boy stripped the heavy gold signet ring from Etienne's finger, and the Creole had just opened his mouth to protest when he saw the awful sight, saw flames licking out the lower windows of Maisonfleur, smoke belching from up above. A great cry tore from his throat, lost in the shouting of the others.

"Let's get outta here . . . Come on, boys!"

"Wait up! Not without this! They's some good French brandy here!"

"Shit! Don't be leavin' no good drinkin' liquor behind!"

Etienne could hear them, and the horses stomping, snorting, as he slowly, painfully pulled himself to his feet, swaying slightly.

"Look there. The Frenchie's gettin' up!" one of them called out.

"Messieurs," Etienne said in a strangely level voice, "you will leave behind everything that you have stolen . . ." The man nearest him, the one in the slouch hat, wheeled his horse almost into Etienne, who went on as if nothing had happened except that he couldn't quite get his breath anymore. "And you will," he gasped, "ride . . . from my property . . . at once!"

"Is that a fact, Frenchie?" The big man roared with laughter, the roof of his mouth gaping pink and wet. And then he swung the butt end of his rifle around and down in a crushing blow to Etienne's skull that sent him reeling backwards to fall heavily to the gravel.

Eyes open, staring up at the sky, Etienne was only vaguely aware when the men pulled their horses into line, two abreast, and with raucous shouts and curses spurred them away, pillow-cases and sheets with tied corners bobbing. Nor did he see Carrie emerge from the trees at a point somewhat farther toward the front than he had.

All he was really aware of was the pain in his head, and even that seemed far removed, apart from him. He thought for a moment that he could see his father, dressed all in black as always, except for the white ruffled shirt, tall and slender and regal as a king. And Adam . . . *Mon Dieu*, but they were so alike. He had never really noticed that before. Perhaps that was why he had loved them both so. . . .

He was still staring at the smoke-blackened sky when Carrie reached him, and with an agonized cry she threw herself down from the saddle and dropped to her knees beside him.

"Uncle 'Tienne . . . Oh, dear Lord, Uncle 'Tienne!" She

slipped her arm beneath his shoulder and pulled his head onto her lap.

The side of his face was swollen and discolored, but it was the wound atop his head that caused her to catch her breath in a fearful gasp. Bright red blood oozed and gathered in darker pools, staining that handsome silver streak of hair. His eyes were clouded, unfocused, but his lips moved.

"Dominique . . ." he whispered to Carrie, "is that . . . you . . . Dominique?" And a deep shudder passed through his body. He trembled violently for a moment and then relaxed as a long hissing sound escaped through his lips.

"Uncle 'Tienne!" she cried, the horror thick in her throat. "Uncle 'Tienne!" she screamed again as she looked down on that terrible stillness. "Oh, please . . . Uncle 'Tienne . . ."

She sat there in the gravel and rocked, his head still in her lap, unmindful of the blood on her dress, or the smoke that seared her nose, or the heat from the roaring flames on her tear-streaked face. She was seeing again that quick image she'd gotten as she'd come out of the trees, as the marauders had disappeared behind the burning house. She had only seen one of them clearly, the last one in line, but she had seen that flash of blue, that Yankee cap.

There could be no doubt about who had done this thing. *Soldiers of the Union Army had killed Uncle Etienne . . . had destroyed Maisonfleur.*

3

EITHER CHLOE OR MATTIE HAD TURNED BACK THE BED, AND Carrie slipped out of her clothes and into the soft white muslin gown and wrapper. She tied the pink ribbons at her throat, then walked slowly to the chest, picked up the daguerreotype of George Pierre, and looked into those dark, sensitive eyes. If only she could tell him about Uncle Etienne. Though maybe it was kinder that he not know until he came home. It would hurt him terribly, Carrie was sure of that.

She sighed, put the daguerreotype back on the chest beside the one of J. D., and then went to the dressing table to give her long dark hair a few half-hearted strokes with the brush. She studied the faint smudges beneath her eyes, which were proof of how little she'd slept these past three nights.

It had been two days now since Uncle Etienne had been laid to rest beside his father and his uncle, near to Mama and Papa. Carrie had pulled herself together enough to do what had to be done. Since Uncle Etienne had been a Catholic, she had sent Lafitte upriver a few miles to a small church that served the scattered Cajuns who hunted and fished the bayous. The lone priest had come, a big, raw-boned man with hands as rough as a farmer's and a half-stubble of beard on his chin, but he had chanted the Latin that Uncle Etienne would have wanted.

Old Monsieur Cirrillo, a neighboring planter who in recent years had been Etienne Moreau's closest friend, was there. Benjamin had taken the word to the Cirrillo plantation, and the old man had come, limping badly with an attack of the gout,

37

tears running down his wrinkled cheeks as he was helped from his carriage to the graveside.

Justice had come over in a wagon from his small farm north of Kingston's Landing. Justice, thick-set and solemn, had always been there in time of trouble for the Kingston family. He had once been a slave on the place and then had risen to be its overseer and Adam Kingston's strong right arm. In fact, for many years Justice's word had been second only to Adam Kingston's on the plantation.

"I'm surely sorry about Mist' Etienne, Miss Carrie," he had said, and Carrie had reached out to press the dark hand. Then he had stood a little aside with his wife Tana until it was time to lower the coffin into the dark earth, when he stepped forward to help Benjamin and Lafitte.

It was then that Susannah had begun to sob so piteously that Carrie had finally delivered her into the comforting arms of Mattie who took her back to the house. But Carrie herself had stood staunchly through the burial of that dear and gentle man. She had kept her face carefully set, trying her best to say the right things to the priest and old Monsieur Cirrillo while she fought to hold the flood of images from her memory . . . agonizingly sharp pictures of Uncle Etienne lying in the dusty gravel before the burning Maisonfleur.

It was not until the night, when she could finally climb into bed, that she turned her face into the pillow and let the tears come until she could cry no longer. Then she lay wondering what she should do now that Uncle Etienne was gone, shivering as if she had a chill, though the night was warm.

And now, as she looked at her reflection in the mirror, she saw the full-lipped mouth begin to tremble, the big amber eyes fill with tears. None of them must know how frightened she felt, she told herself sternly. She was responsible for them and she must be strong—as strong as Papa had been. Somehow she had to keep things together.

She heard footsteps coming along the hall, and she hurriedly wiped away the tears and turned toward the door as the light knock sounded. "Come in," she called, and made a great show of busying herself with the hairbrush.

"It's just me, honey." Chloe entered the room, carrying a tray. "Brought you some good hot tea."

"Thank you, Chloe."

The big woman, her snowy white kerchief as spotless and crisp as when she had tied it on that morning, cleared a space on the bedside table for the tray and then poured the dark brew into a delicate china cup. "Should've brought up some warm milk instead," she said, almost as if talking to herself.

"I hate warm milk, Chloe," Carrie said firmly.

The wide face broke into a grin, making crinkly lines around warm brown eyes. "I know you do. That's why I brought you this here tea."

Carrie laughed in spite of herself and put the brush aside.

"Just the same," Chloe went on as she stirred in a spoonful of sugar, "a little warm milk would do you good. Maybe fatten you up some. I don't believe you eatin' enough these days."

"Oh, Chloe, of course I am. I'm fine."

Chloe passed her the cup. Carrie inhaled the fragrance and sipped. "Oh, it's good," she said gratefully. "You put orange peel and cinnamon in it."

Chloe nodded. "There's some more in the pot if you want another cup. I'll just leave it," she said and started toward the door.

"Chloe, wait . . ." Carrie called her back. "Don't go yet. Sit down. I need to talk to you. Here, we can both sit on the bed." Carrie put her cup down on the tray and climbed up on the big tall-posted bed, gesturing for Chloe to take the place next to her.

Chloe's eyes were troubled. She put a gentle hand to Carrie's cheek. "What's the matter, honey?" Carrie hesitated. "Come on, now. You can tell Chloe. Ain't you been my baby since the day you was birthed? My baby much as you was your Mama's and your Daddy's?"

Carrie nodded and suddenly found herself in Chloe's strong and comforting arms. They hugged each other for a long moment, Chloe's hand patting steadily at Carrie's back, and Carrie sniffed back the tears that were ready to start again. With a grateful smile, she sat upright.

"Let's talk, honey," Chloe said. "What you got on your mind?"

"I think I'd better go down to New Orleans for a while," Carrie said. "I need to see Leroy Tate at the bank about Uncle Etienne's will. Though I don't think he left anything much. The house . . . ." She sighed, remembering how the ruins of Maisonfleur reached jagged and black toward the sky, the windows gaping squares. It was as if the magnificent old house were a living thing that had been tortured and blinded and left to stand, helpless against the sun and rain.

"I know," Chloe said, shaking her head. "I know . . ."

"And," Carrie drew a long breath, then went on, "despite General Butler and his men, I think now that it might be safer to have Suzy in New Orleans. I'm sure J. D.'s parents would take her in."

"Safer for you, too."

Carrie shook her head. "I'll only stay long enough to get my business finished. I'm afraid to leave Kingston's Landing even for a short time. And there are the people left down in the quarters, old Nadine and Toby. They depend on us."

"I'll stay here, honey. Me and Benjamin . . ."

Carrie was quiet for a moment. "I don't like to leave you here," she said. "The same thing that happened at Maisonfleur could happen here, too."

"Hmmph!" Chloe's lower lip stuck out, her eyebrows knitted. "Ain't no Yankees better come sneakin' round here and messin' with this here place! I'll send 'em packin'!"

Carrie smiled, squeezed Chloe's hand. "All right. You could send for Justice if anything happened. He'd do whatever he could."

Chloe nodded.

"I have to get some money to put in a crop the first of the year," Carrie said. "I'm going to ask Leroy Tate to make me a loan."

Chloe looked at her, the dark eyes shrewd and knowing. "Your Papa's money?"

"Not a lot left," Carrie said quietly. "But I don't want Suzy to know how bad it is."

"Mmmm mmmm," Chloe hummed. "Time was when it seemed like Mist' Adam had all the money in the world. But that sweet boy George Pierre—"

"It wasn't all his fault," Carrie protested.

"Course it wasn't. He did the best he could."

Chloe stood up and pulled the light cover on the bed back farther, then plumped up the pillow. "Here now," she said, "if you goin' to be doin' all this, you goin' to need your rest."

Carrie slipped out of her wrapper and climbed into bed, resting her back against the soft pillow, while Chloe poured the cooled tea into the waste bowl and refilled the thin china cup with more of the hot brew from the silver pot.

"You drink this 'fore you go to sleep," she directed.

"I will, Chloe," Carrie promised.

"When you think you be leavin'?"

"In a few days, I guess."

Chloe nodded. She turned down the wick of the big brass lamp on the table, cupped her hand over the top of the chimney, and blew the flame out. "I'll leave the other one on," she said, gesturing to the lamp on the bedside table. She started toward the door, then turned back for a moment. "Don't you worry none, honey. I'll be takin' care of Kingston's Landing while you gone."

Carrie smiled at the woman who had been like a second mother to her. "I know that, Chloe. I think you're the only one left now whom I could trust Kingston's Landing to."

After she had finished the tea and put out the lamp, she settled down in the depths of the goose-feather mattress. Chloe was right, she thought. She did have to sleep. Somehow she knew that she had to be at her best in the days to come.

"Are we, Carrie? Are we *really* going down to New Orleans!" Susannah said, her eyes shining, a healthy glow of color coming back into the pretty face that had been so woebegone since Uncle Etienne's death. And when Carrie assured her that they were, Susannah rushed upstairs and began to drag out trunks and hatboxes, even though the planned departure was still three days away.

It had been decided that Mattie and Lafitte would go along, and the shapely black girl's reaction was no less enthusiastic than Susannah's. She muffled a shriek of pleasure and danced through the halls. Lafitte was somewhat more dignified. He merely drew his painfully thin, tall frame up as far as it would go and nodded his head.

"I remember the first time I accompanied your Papa into New Orleans, Missy," he said.

"New Orleans ain't New Orleans no more," Chloe scolded him, "not with them Yankees there. And you just make sure that you take care of these here girls, you hear me, Lafitte?"

Lafitte threw her an outraged look. "I shall attend them," he said. "Have I not always seen to my duties?"

"All right," Carrie intervened, "it's all settled. And we have a lot to do if we're going to be ready to leave on time. Chloe, would you make a list of the supplies we're short on? We'll take advantage of this trip to do some shopping. And, Lafitte, I think we'd better take the big carriage because of the luggage. We haven't used it for so long . . . maybe you'd better ask Benjamin to see that it's ready."

"Yes, Missy."

They both hurried off. Carrie went into the study, closed the door, and spent the afternoon going over the books, putting together the bills that were outstanding and must be taken care of as soon as she reached New Orleans. She would have to go to the bank to draw some money from the account. And she would speak immediately to Leroy Tate about a loan for the cane crop. She was positive he'd advance it. Hadn't Papa done business with the Tate Bank of New Orleans ever since he had first come to Louisiana?

Carrie leaned back in the big swivel chair and put her head back for a moment. The sun was slanting in the window, throwing a golden shaft of light across the patterned carpet, touching the oak desk and the ink bottle and the open ledger with its rows of small, neat figures. It was getting late.

She heard the sound of hooves. Benjamin must be taking the horses from the pasture over to the barn lots, she thought. And then suddenly the door burst open and Lafitte stood there.

"Miss Carrie," he said, "there are soldiers outside!" In the next instant, Carrie heard a loud shriek that she recognized as Mattie's, not the joyous sound the girl had made a few hours ago, but a cry laced through with fear.

The sound had come from out in front. Carrie jumped to her

feet and pushed past Lafitte into the big front hall. She caught a glimpse of Susannah, petticoats flying, coming down the stairs. "Stay inside, Suzy!" she yelled back over her shoulder and then pushed open the big oak door and stepped out onto the front gallery.

She stopped short as she saw four men in dusty blue uniforms, horses stamping as they leaned down from their saddles, grinning and poking at one another. A soldier on the ground had one arm around Mattie's waist, holding her up in front of him easily despite her struggling. Mattie emitted periodic little shrieks, her feet kicking uselessly well off the ground, her big breasts bouncing beneath the thin cotton of her dress.

"You're sure enough a pretty thing," the big soldier said. "Hold still now . . . I ain't gonna hurt ya." And his begrimed and scraggly partners snorted and howled.

"He jist wants a little squeeze, sugar baby!" one of them yelled out, and the others let out new whoops of laughter.

Carrie could feel her heart pounding against her ribs so hard she was afraid she might faint, but she took a deep breath and walked determinedly down the wide front steps and toward the men, who pulled their horses back a pace or two when they saw her.

The soldier who held Mattie stood his ground, and the young black girl stopped struggling and looked at her mistress with big, frightened eyes. "Miss Carrie . . ."

Carrie's mouth was dry, but she bit the side of her tongue and tried to remember how Papa had sounded when he gave a command that he expected to be obeyed.

"You there," she said in a loud and surprisingly firm voice, "you put her down at once!"

The soldier stared at her for a moment, surprise in his eyes, and then he threw back his head and laughed, tobacco-stained teeth showing. "Looks like this place is full of spitfires!" he chortled.

"Damned if it ain't!" another one joined in.

"Did you hear me, sir!" Carrie demanded, taking a step toward him, though her legs were trembling so she was afraid for a moment that she would fall. "I said put that girl down!"

There was a long moment of silence as the soldier eyed her

43

insolently. Then suddenly from behind her there came a deep
masculine voice with a decidedly Southern drawl.

"I do believe, Corporal, that you'd better do as the lady tells
you."

"Yes, sir," the soldier said reluctantly as Carrie whirled
around to look up into a pair of the grayest, most direct eyes
she'd ever seen.

There stood before her a man of impressive stature. Though he
was slender and well made, he was even taller than J. D., she
would remember thinking later. Almost as big as Papa had been.

He grinned. "Allow me to apologize for my men, Miss." The
soft Southern accent was startling since he was garbed in the
unmistakable, if dusty, uniform of an officer in the Union Army.
"I'm afraid the corporal forgot himself," he said quietly.

Carrie stared at him, unable to find her tongue yet, but aware
of a fine straight nose above a dark, well-trimmed mustache and
a decided cleft right at the middle of a rather firm chin.

"If you'll permit me to introduce myself," he said, sweeping
off his hat. "Captain Rance Stewart, aide to General Benjamin
Butler, military commander of New Orleans. My men and I have
been on a special assignment for the general and—"

"Captain Stewart," Carrie interrupted frostily, "do your men
make a habit of going onto private property and forcing their
attentions upon innocent females?"

"Certainly not, Miss, uh . . . ?" The gray eyes probed.

"Kingston," she said grudgingly.

"Most certainly not, Miss Kingston," he said with a certain
amusement in his eyes. "Again, my apologies."

Carrie caught a movement out of the corner of her eye and
glanced quickly toward the front gallery. Susannah, who had
been standing beside Lafitte, edged down to the lower step. And
in that instant, Carrie realized what a tempting picture her little
sister made, not a little girl any longer but a very fetching young
lady with that mass of tawny curls, pink cheeks, and a swelling
young figure.

Carrie could have slapped her. Didn't she know this was the
patrol that Paul Gayerre had seen? Very likely these same men
had killed Uncle Etienne and burned Maisonfleur. Why hadn't
she done as she was told and stayed safely out of sight?

"We're on our way back to New Orleans," Captain Stewart was saying, "but I'm afraid we met with a minor mishap earlier today. One of our packhorses stumbled down an embankment and into the river. He swam to shore, but most of our supplies were ruined."

Carrie watched him warily, said nothing.

"My men are tired and hungry, Miss Kingston," he went on in that smooth, deep voice. "Too tired and hungry to continue on to New Orleans before morning. And while I very much regret the intrusion upon your privacy, I find that I must beg the hospitality of your plantation for the night."

Carrie took a deep breath. "And do we have a choice, Captain?"

Rance Stewart looked down at her, gray eyes level, unperturbed. "Miss Kingston," he drawled, "while there *are* regulations governing the occupied territories, I'm sure it won't be necessary to invoke them. I've never known a Southern lady to refuse the hospitality of her house to a weary traveler."

They stared each other down for a moment, and then Carrie dropped her eyes, inclined her head. "Very well, Captain," she said. "But I would ask you to see that your men behave as gentlemen while they are here at Kingston's Landing."

"You have my word," he said.

Suddenly there was a loud howl, and a scrawny soldier burst from the far side of the house, his skinny arms flailing. Chloe, right behind him, was vigorously applying a broom to his head and shoulders.

"Chloe!" Carrie said. The black woman lowered her formidable weapon and scowled at the group of men, while the unfortunate fellow who'd been the recipient of her attention grinned sheepishly and scuttled toward his compatriots, greeted by derisive hoots of laughter. "Chloe, it's all right," Carrie said. "These . . ." she paused deliberately, "gentlemen will be staying the night."

"Yes, Miss Carrie," Chloe said, her eyes still darting suspiciously, her lower lip well out.

"Have Benjamin set up tables out in back for the men. Captain Stewart will dine with us."

"My thanks, Miss Kingston." Rance Stewart inclined his head slightly. "If it wouldn't be too much of an imposition, I wonder if I might clean up a bit?'' He ran a long-fingered, well-shaped hand over his chin, which showed a shadowy trace of whiskers.

"Lafitte will see to you, Captain," Carrie said, and Lafitte, standing on the steps, nodded his head. "And, Lafitte, once you get the captain settled, put some soap and towels and buckets of water out back for the others."

"Yes, Miss Carrie," Lafitte said.

"I'll just have a word with my men and then be right along," Captain Stewart said.

"You do that, Captain," Carrie said pointedly.

Mattie, who had gotten over her initial fright, was beginning to look on the whole thing as a lark and was now swaggering about, moving her shoulders in a way that caused the soldier who had grabbed her to nudge the man next to him.

Carrie and Chloe exchanged looks, and Chloe gave her daughter a yank that almost pulled the girl off her feet. "I be needin' you in the kitchen!" she said. And once all the women were safely inside, she gave the girl another yank. "Git yourself to your room, girl, and put on your camisole underneath there. And put on your checked dress, the one with the collar right up to your chin! And when you ready, git out in the kitchen and start fryin' up some side meat!"

"Yes, Mama," Mattie said meekly and sped away.

"And you go find an apron and put it on," Carrie said to Susannah. "Start peeling potatoes. We'll need lots of them."

"I just never knew," Susannah bubbled, "how downright *charming* a Union officer could be!" And she made off for the kitchen, grinning, her face flushed with excitement.

Carrie started to call her back, but Chloe touched her arm. "Let her go, honey. She ain't no more'n a baby yet. She don't know."

Carrie sighed. "I guess you're right, Chloe."

The older woman's eyes were somber. "What we goin' to do?"

Carrie put her hand up to her forehead, looked away for a moment. "I don't know," she said, her mind racing. There wasn't even a gun on the place except for Papa's collection of old dueling pistols. And Carrie wasn't sure if she could fire one of them.

"I 'spect the first time Lafitte has a chance, I better send him out to warn Benjamin before he comes in and sees all those Yankees about. It might scare him most to death."

"Yes," Carrie said, but she hardly heard Chloe. She was too busy thinking. She turned suddenly. "You know, Chloe . . ."

"Yes, honey?" Chloe waited expectantly.

"Those men out there do seem to do just what the captain tells them to."

The two women looked at each other for a long moment.

"Now what you got in your head, honey?" Chloe asked, an uneasy tone in her voice.

"Chloe," Carrie grabbed her hand, "I don't know if it'll do any good . . . but you go in the kitchen and make the best dinner you can. Make your smothered chicken, and the peas with mushrooms, and some of those little brown-sugar tarts. I'll help you. And we'll get out the best china. And I'll cut flowers for the table. Chloe—" Carrie stopped short and took a deep, frightened breath, "we have got to entertain Captain Rance Stewart, entertain him well enough so that . . . ." She left the rest unsaid.

The dinner was ready in the kitchen. In the dining room, the finest damask tablecloth had been laid out, a lovely arrangement of roses and baby's breath was in place, and the best wax candles graced silver candlesticks.

Upstairs in her room, Carrie had just finished sponging herself clean with lavender soap and cool water. She patted her long white legs dry, brought the towel up over the smooth-skinned stretch of belly and waist to gently dry the high and firm young breasts with their well-formed pink nipples, then twisted to get any last drops of water still on her back.

She picked up the bottle of lavender water on her dressing table and touched the glass stopper to wrists, earlobes, and the bend of her elbows. Then she hurriedly pulled on stockings, soft white cotton drawers with lace edges, and a camisole. She seldom wore stays, in fact hated them; they always made her feel as if she were suffocating, and she certainly needed all her breath and wits tonight, she told herself, as she shoved them aside in the drawer.

An inspection of the dresses in the big double-doored armoire proved disappointing. She hadn't had any new clothes made for a long time. She hadn't wanted to spend the money. But tonight she needed something special. She had to catch Captain Rance Stewart's eye, had to hold his attention and keep any thought of harming Kingston's Landing from his mind.

At the far back of the wardrobe, she caught a glimpse of pale cream silk. Of course! She had forgotten that dress! J. D.'s mother had insisted that Carrie have it made last fall. "Something special," she had said, "in case J. D. can get home on leave for the holidays. Because of course you'll want to go to the Christmas ball at the St. Charles." But J. D. hadn't come home, and the dress had gone unworn.

Carrie pulled it out now and looked at it. As she recalled, it had made her feel slightly self-conscious when she'd tried it on for the final fitting . . . something about the way the bodice fit so snugly. It *was* cut a bit low right there in front.

Though her mouth was dry, her hands shaking with nervousness, she eyed it shrewdly. It was perfect for tonight, she decided, and drew her mouth to its most determined line.

She put on hoops and petticoats, tying the tapes in place about her waist, and then slipped the dress over her head and down. She struggled to reach the hooks in back, all but stamping her foot in vexation as the trembling fingers refused to work properly. Finally she managed to get the dress fastened and went to stand in front of the full-length mirror.

The pale cream color was most becoming with her dark hair, she thought objectively . . . but the fit of the dress was even more provocative than she remembered. Though the sleeves were quite demure, covering her entire arm and ending in a graceful swirl of lace at the wrist, and though the skirt hung sedately in soft, full flounces, the bodice fit like a second skin, not only outlining each breast clearly, but pushing them up so that there was more than a hint of cleavage showing at the neckline.

For a moment she panicked. Oh, Lord, I can't . . . *I can't*, she thought, and her fingers flew to the hooks, feverishly trying to get them undone.

But then she stopped herself, took a deep breath. What choice did she have? She had to try to charm or entertain or sweet-talk that man who, despite the gentlemanly Southern accent, was very likely responsible for burning Maisonfleur. She shuddered at the memory of that blackened shell, of those last awful moments when she'd held Uncle Etienne.

She'd do anything to keep that from happening at Kingston's Landing. There was Suzy to consider, and the others. And this house . . . dear Lord, she had been born in this house.

She grabbed the comb and quickly ran it through the long dark hair, which glinted in the lamplight with chestnut highlights. She pinned it high on either side to cascade in soft curls at the nape of her neck, and then tucked a small yellow velvet bow just over her left ear. She stood back to view the results with a certain satisfaction.

On a sudden and daring impulse, she touched a drop of lavender water to the hollow between her breasts, then turned away from the dressing table and walked to the door. And as she grasped the knob, as she prepared to go downstairs and put on the biggest act of her life, there was a small inner voice, questioning, demanding. Just how far was she prepared to go to save Kingston's Landing?

4

CARRIE PAUSED OUTSIDE THE SITTING ROOM FOR ONLY THE barest instant, and then she swept through the door in a rustle of silk and a delicious scent of lavender, smiling her most charming smile.

"Captain Stewart," she said, "do forgive me for being late. I hope I haven't kept you waiting too long." She extended her hand, and Rance Stewart bowed over it, his eyes boldly appraising her, his lips brushing her fingers.

"Not at all, Miss Kingston," he said. "As a matter of fact your most charming sister has been keeping me well entertained."

"I'm happy to hear that, Captain." Carrie smiled at Susannah. Her sister was staring in amazement at the low-cut silk gown and was just opening her mouth to say something when Chloe, who was taking the captain's empty wineglass from the table, gave her an unobtrusive little nudge. The girl closed her mouth and kept quiet for the moment.

"As a matter of fact," Captain Stewart was saying, "whatever the delay, it was certainly well worth the wait. You look lovely, Miss Kingston."

"Why, thank you, Captain . . . how gallant. But come, you must be starving. Is everything ready, Chloe?"

"Yes, Miss Carrie," Chloe said.

"Then if you will serve, please. Captain . . ." She turned toward him, and some part of her had to admit that he was a very handsome man now that he had availed himself of the hot tub that Lafitte had prepared for him, now that his uniform was brushed and pressed, the dark thick hair neatly combed.

She felt a pang of guilt for even thinking such things. General Butler himself might be a handsome man for all she knew, but he had earned himself the name "Beast" Butler in the months since he had assumed control of New Orleans and the surrounding captured territory.

She was careful that her face didn't reveal her thoughts as Rance Stewart smiled down at her and Susannah in turn and crooked an elbow on either side. "I don't know when," he drawled, "I've had the pleasure of escorting two such lovely ladies into dinner."

The candles on the table and in the crystal wall sconces about the room cast a pleasant glow, and there was the faint smell of roses in the air as Rance held the chair first for Susannah, who barely suppressed a giggle, and then for Carrie before he seated himself.

"I told Captain Stewart," Susannah said, "that we are *finally* going down to New Orleans. And that you didn't want to before because of General Butler's old 'Woman Order.' "

Carrie felt her cheeks grow warm. "Suzy," she said, "I don't think we should discuss that with Captain Stewart."

The captain regarded her with the same look of cool amusement that she had seen in his eyes before. "The order was an unfortunate one," he said.

"Oh? Does that mean you don't approve of your general's harsh treatment of the people in the occupied territory, Captain?"

The dark brows raised slightly. "It means that it is the general who is in command, Miss Kingston. Not I. However, to give General Butler his due, some of the ladies of New Orleans did go out of their way to express their displeasure at having Union troops in the city. Some of the soldiers were actually spat upon."

Susannah gasped. "You mean they walked right up and spat on them?"

"That," Carrie said crisply, "would hardly seem to be a proper subject for the dinner table."

"Forgive me." Rance lowered his head slightly and gave her a mocking look, and Carrie was relieved when Chloe and Lafitte entered the room and began to serve the dinner.

"Ah, here we are. I believe Chloe has outdone herself this evening, Captain Stewart. You'll find she's an excellent cook."

"I'm looking forward to it," Rance said.

And as Chloe and Lafitte brought the big platter piled high with chicken and the bowls of green peas and mushrooms, candied sweet potatoes, fried okra, and cold sliced tomatoes sprinkled with pepper and sage, Carrie forced a warm smile to her lips.

"We haven't had much opportunity to entertain the way we used to, Captain. Not since the war. It's a real treat to have a dinner guest this evening." Under the guise of straightening her wineglass, she threw a warning glance at her sister to say nothing of their most recent guest.

"Oh?" One of Rance Stewart's dark eyebrows slanted sharply upward. "I'm glad to hear that. I confess there were times earlier today when I wasn't at all sure that I was entirely welcome."

"Well," Carrie parried, "your arrival was somewhat unexpected and," she added, "the behavior of your men was not exactly what we are accustomed to here at Kingston's Landing."

He chuckled softly. "I'm sure that's true. And I do apologize again. I'm afraid soldiers in the field are not always as civilized as they might be, Miss Kingston."

"And their officers?" Carrie pressed.

"Even they." He regarded her steadily with a smile on his lips and helped himself to a hot roll as Chloe passed the platter.

"Well, I'm glad you came," Susannah interjected. "Nothing much nice happens around here since George Pierre left."

Carrie sent another look Susannah's way. She was certainly not anxious to discuss their brother with a Yankee captain.

"Miss Susannah tells me that your brother is with the Confederate Army," he said.

Carrie's reply was cautious. "That's right, Captain." And all the while she was hoping that Susannah hadn't foolishly said anything about hearing from George Pierre. Rance Stewart just might want to know how they had gotten the letter, and that could prove compromising.

"She tells me," he went on, "that you have heard nothing of his whereabouts since before New Orleans fell." There was a certain smug look in Susannah's green eyes as she regarded her sister from across the table.

"Just one of the hardships that your army has brought to our people, Captain," Carrie said coldly.

Captain Stewart chose to ignore that barb. "When you do hear," he said, "I hope the news will be that he's safe and well. Too many good men have been lost on both sides, Miss Kingston."

For a moment, Carrie was touched by the sincerity in his voice, but she quickly recovered her guard and reminded herself who he was. After a moment of silence, she passed the condiment tray nearer to his plate. "Do try some of Chloe's cucumber pickles," she said. "She's famous for them."

"If this chicken is any indication, she should be famous for all her cooking," he said, and set about eating with obvious relish, completely at ease with Susannah's chattering, answering questions about the latest theater offerings in New Orleans.

The conversation between the two of them allowed Carrie a short respite, and she reminded herself that her plan required that she be nice to Rance Stewart. She would certainly not be able to charm her enemy if she kept allowing her true feelings to show through. She would, she vowed silently, be nicer to him. Even if it killed her!

"Why, Captain, that sounds most amusing," she said after hearing a brief resume of a play he had attended recently in New Orleans. And after that, she smiled often and leaned toward him from time to time, both pleased and frightened to see how his eyes strayed toward the exposed tops of her breasts.

"Did you know, Carrie," Susannah was saying as Chloe brought in the brown-sugar tarts, "that Captain Stewart is not from the North at all? He's from South Carolina."

"Is that so?" Carrie said, still smiling, but barely able to hold back the anger that flashed within her. That a Southerner should sit before her in that uniform! "I must confess I noticed the accent," she said lightly.

"And you were too polite to comment on it," he drawled.

"Perhaps I was simply puzzled, Captain," she said, and as Chloe placed the dessert plate before her, the black woman gave an almost imperceptible nod of her head toward the doorway. Carrie saw Benjamin standing out in the hallway, and even at this distance she could see the hint of trouble in the way he stood, in the way his hat was crumpled in his big hands.

"Would you excuse me please, Captain?" she said. "I'll only be a moment. Please don't get up." And she was up and out of the room before he could stand.

Benjamin was a man who was more at home with the horses than in the polished front halls of the house, but Carrie knew that the worried frown on his face had nothing to do with where he was.

"What is it, Benjamin?" she whispered.

He leaned his big head down, spoke close to her ear. "I ain't likin' what's goin' on out there in the barn where them soldiers are, Miss Carrie."

"What are they doing?" she asked quickly.

"I seen 'em passin' a bottle around. And they beginnin' to talk loud and stir around. I don't like it."

Carrie drew a deep breath. "All right" she said. "You did the right thing to come and tell me. Go back and keep an eye on them. Report back to me if anything else happens. But, Benjamin" —she put a hand to his arm—"don't let them see you. Stay out of their way."

"Yes, Miss Carrie," he said, and she watched him go, jamming the crumpled straw hat down on his head.

Carrie turned back to the dining room, hesitating at the door while she made up her mind whether or not to speak to the captain about his men. She would, she decided, and stepped into the room.

"Captain Stewart—" she began, but at that instant the loud report of a gunshot echoed from the direction of the barns, followed by a second and then a third.

Rance Stewart was on his feet at once and striding toward the door. "You will stay in the house until I come back," he rapped out without a backward glance. And then he was gone, and they could hear the sound of his boots across the front hall, the slamming of the big front door.

Carrie sank into her chair, annoyed that he should be giving her orders in her own house, and even more annoyed that she was following them.

"Carrie," Susannah said, her eyes wide with excitement, "that was a gun!"

"Yes, I know."

"Well, come on! Let's go see what's happening out there!"

Carrie took a quick sip of her wine in an effort to compose herself. "No," she said. "We'll stay right here as the captain has requested. At least for now," she added. "Let's continue with our dinner." She steadfastly took a bite of the brown-sugar tart even though she found it difficult to swallow. Susannah stabbed at hers with her fork.

"I don't see why you have to be so bossy, Carrie! I am not a child, even though you treat me like one!"

"I'm sorry, Suzy," Carrie said absently, but her sister was not to be put off.

"For instance," she said, her voice breaking with indignation, "I'm sure you thought I'd be silly enough to say something about"—she stopped and looked around to make sure the captain wasn't coming back just yet, and then lowered her voice to a whisper—"about Paul Gayerre being here. Honestly, Carrie, you don't give me credit for a lick of sense." Some of the anger had gone out of the girl's voice, and that beautiful little lower lip began to tremble noticeably.

"Oh, Suzy, honey," Carrie reached a quick hand across to her sister, "of course I do. And I *am* sorry. It's just that we have to be careful with Union soldiers on the place."

Mollified, Susannah began to eat her tart. The minutes passed, the ticking of the big clock in the hall audible as Carrie waited for something to happen. If there was another gunshot, she was going out there no matter what Captain Rance Stewart had said. But the silence continued, the rhythmic sounds of the big brass pendulum a jarring reminder.

Carrie's apprehension must have been contagious because, while Susannah still tried to eat, she began to look at her sister with uneasy eyes.

"Miss Carrie . . . ." Carrie jumped so at the sound of Benjamin's voice she knocked over her glass of wine.

"I'll get it," Susannah said and started to mop at the spreading stain with her napkin while Carrie hurried to the door.

"What's happened, Benjamin?"

The big man was breathing heavily as if he'd run all the way from the barn. "Them men . . . 'cause they likkered up, they put up bottles on the fenceposts, Miss Carrie, and they was shootin' at 'em. I don't think they hit nothin' in the dark." He paused to catch his breath.

"Suzy, bring some water for Benjamin," Carrie said, and her sister quickly poured a glass from the pitcher and brought it to the winded man.

He nodded his thanks and drank deeply. "After I heard them shots, I run around back of the barn and I hid in the bushes," he said, "and I seen the captain come runnin'. He lined them soldiers up and told 'em plain, 'You ain't doin' nothin' less you hear me tell you to.' That's what he said. '*Nothin'* less I tell you.' " Benjamin took a long breath. "And I run off here 'cause I thought you'd want to know what's happenin', Miss Carrie."

"Yes, thank you, Benjamin. I suppose there's nothing to be done, for now. Let me know if anything else happens." And as he turned to go, "Benjamin, have you had anything to eat?" she asked, concern for him cutting through her fears.

"No," he said.

"Then go to the kitchen now and have Chloe or Mattie fix you something."

"Yes, Miss Carrie," he said. "I'll be watchin', though."

"All right." She turned back to find Susannah smiling and rosy again.

"You see," her sister said with a relieved shrug, "Captain Stewart took care of it. He really is nice, don't you think, Carrie?"

"Suzy!" Carrie said sharply. "He's a Yankee!"

"Not really," Susannah said innocently. "He's really from South Carolina."

Carrie wanted to shake her sister. "Don't you know that he's probably the one—" Her hand flew to her mouth. She had almost said, *He's probably the one who killed Uncle Etienne and burned Maisonfleur!*

She turned away for a moment, angry with herself. What was the use of frightening poor little Suzy half to death.

"The one? The one who what, Carrie?" Susannah pressed, a small note of fear creeping into her voice.

56

"The one who . . . is probably closest to General Butler. He said he was his aide," Carrie recovered quickly, "so we can hardly regard him as a Southern gentleman, but . . . he does seem to be taking steps to see that his men behave properly."

The tight little lines around Susannah's mouth eased away. "And he *is* nice," she persisted. "Isn't he?"

"I suppose he's nice. For a Yankee," Carrie said grudgingly. She could only think that the captain had not ordered the men to respect the people and property of Kingston's Landing, but only to follow his orders.

It was another five minutes before he returned, but when he did, Rance Stewart stepped into the dining room, calm and unruffled and smiling. "Do forgive me for being away so long. I hope Chloe didn't take away my dessert. Ah, good!" he said as he sat down at the table. "I see it's still here." And he set about eating it with obvious appreciation.

The moon was the color of thick cream and high in the sky, casting a mellow half-light on the gallery nearest the garden where Carrie and Captain Stewart took their coffee. The gardenia bushes nearby filled the night air with their sweetness.

They had moved out onto the gallery at her suggestion once she'd sent Susannah up to bed, and Carrie had flirted with Captain Rance Stewart outrageously, carrying on a light and, she hoped, witty conversation, smiling and leaning toward him from time to time, once even touching his arm lightly as she made a point. Yet all the while, she took whatever small opportunities that came her way to remind him that she was the mistress of the manor and, as such, not to be trifled with.

Now, as a silence fell in the conversation, Rance's eyes went boldly to the exposed tops of Carrie's breasts, lingered for a moment, then swept upward to her throat and lips and hair, finally met her gaze directly with an intensity that made her throat close. And Carrie realized once more what a dangerous game she was playing.

He regarded her with a look, half-speculative, half-puzzled, leaned forward in his chair, and put his coffeecup on the cypress table beside them. "I must confess that you have been something of a surprise to me, Miss Kingston. When I rode in here this afternoon, I had no idea that the evening would be so interesting. Despite the fact that we find ourselves on opposite sides of the war, you have proven to be a most charming and fascinating hostess.''

"Why, thank you, Captain," Carrie said. "I'm so glad you're enjoying yourself."

"I am." He lowered his head slightly, and Carrie found herself blushing under his gaze for the longest moment. Then he seemed to make up his mind about something and stood up abruptly. "However," he said lightly, "it's been a long day, and I think, with your permission, that I'll retire to my room now."

"Oh, but, Captain Stewart," she protested quickly, certain that if she could just keep him with her and entertained, Kingston's Landing would be safe, "it's early. Besides, you haven't yet told me how a Southern gentleman happens to be in a Yankee uniform."

He smiled. "Under the circumstances, I didn't think it would be entirely appropriate."

"On the contrary. I can't think of anything I'd rather hear about. Come"—she slipped her arm through his and hoped he didn't notice how her hand was trembling—"let's walk in the garden. It's lovely tonight."

He allowed himself to be led down the stone steps and along the path that wound among rose beds that had been encroached upon by creeping phlox and blooming impatiens and baby's breath, and she realized that she was aware of his physical presence as she never had been with any man before. She was conscious of the way he moved, with that assurance of command, aware of the subtle and clean smells of bay rum and a very mellow hint of tobacco, though she hadn't seen him smoke.

Her awareness of him irritated her. Though, she told herself briskly, it was certainly understandable. It wasn't every day that one had the opportunity to study a Yankee captain at close range.

"Tell me of your family," she said, and at once felt a certain drawing away in him.

"There isn't a lot to tell. My mother died very early. I hardly remember her. My father and brother and myself spent some part of each year in Charleston at our house there. But most of the time we were at our family plantation a few miles up the coast. It's not altogether different from this place, though we raise rice in that part of the country, not sugar.''

"And do they, your father and your brother, share your Union sympathies, Captain Stewart?''

"No,'' he said shortly. And after a pause, ''My father is as ardent a Rebel as you are, Miss Kingston.''

They had reached the pair of stone benches and stopped, though they did not sit. Carrie turned toward him. ''Then he must have been very disappointed in you.'' She had said the words before she looked up into his face to see it set in hard, ungiving lines.

"He couldn't understand,'' he said, and there was some deep current in the very timbre of his voice, whether of anger or hate or pain Carrie couldn't tell.

"Nor can I,'' she said, thinking of Maisonfleur, and could not prevent the cold edge in her voice.

He looked at her steadily. ''I did not expect that you would,'' he said. ''After all, you . . .'' He stopped as if searching for the right words.

"Are the vanquished, Captain? Is that what you were going to say?'' The strain of the evening got the better of her, and words tumbled out. ''I am the vanquished and you the victor! And each of us Southerners! There is the puzzle!''

"I believed, and still believe, that the preservation of the Union, Miss Kingston, *has* to be more important than who comes from the North or the South!'' His eyes flashed with a dangerous kind of fire. ''My decision was not an easy one, though God knows I owe you no explanation!''

"And that justifies your allying yourself with a man who insults Southern women, who steals Southern land from its rightful owners, and worse, Captain, even worse!''

"General Butler does not consult me when he makes command decisions!'' he snapped. ''I am a soldier, and I follow my orders the same way that your brother follows the commands of his officers!''

"And what of *your* brother, Captain Stewart? You mentioned a brother! What does *he* think of your Yankee general!''

There was a sudden silence, and Carrie saw Rance pull himself up to his fullest height, his eyes suddenly dark as slate. He stood absolutely still for a moment, the moonlight etching the strong lines of his face, the dark, thick mustache, the deep cleft mark in his chin.

"My brother was killed at Bull Run," he said. "Six months to the day after he enlisted in the Confederate Army." He bowed slightly, his arms straight down, hands at his sides. "And now if you will excuse me, Miss Kingston, I'll bid you good night."

Stricken, Carrie watched him go, watched that tall, stiffly erect figure with the surprisingly wide shoulders walk toward the gallery. Her instinctive regret at causing him pain gave way to a growing panic. What had she done? Was he even now on his way to turn his men loose on Kingston's Landing? To pillage and burn . . . perhaps kill?

"Captain Stewart . . ." she called out, and as she saw that steady stride falter, she caught up her skirt and ran along the stepping stones to him.

As he turned, two deep lines were evident between his brows, the line of his jaw was hard and set. Carrie's fears mounted. She had no idea what a pretty picture she presented with the quick rising and falling of her bosom, the rich touch of color in her cheeks, the dark tendrils of hair that had slipped loose and curled softly about her face. She only knew that she had to make amends, and quickly.

"Captain Stewart," she said, and her voice sounded a little breathless, "please accept my deepest apologies. I had no idea . . . I would never have presumed."

"Don't trouble yourself about it," he said crisply.

"But I must." She put a hand out to his arm. "I had no right to pry into your personal life . . . no right at all. And if I have caused you any discomfort, I hope that you will forgive me. Please," she said softly, and she could feel the tremor in his arm.

His face softened. "Of course," he said finally. "There is nothing to forgive. After all, I didn't have to tell you. Sometimes we inflict our own pain, Miss Kingston."

They looked at each other for a long, slow moment, and then she realized that her hand was still on his arm and she took it quickly away.

"I'll say good night again," he said.

Carrie nodded. "I'll show you to your room."

Inside the house they made their way up the wide, curving staircase. Crystal wall sconces cast their pleasant, flickering light, and Carrie could see Rance Stewart's shadow on the far wall, hear the soft tread of his boots on the carpeted steps behind her.

"Here we are," she said, stopping at the second door to the left at the top of the stairs. "I do hope you'll be comfortable. If there's anything you need, just pull the bellcord and Lafitte will come."

"Thank you." He smiled down at her, and she did not detect any of the amused mockery that had been there earlier in the evening. "We'll be leaving early," he said, "so in case I don't see you again—"

"Oh, I'll be up," she said.

"Very well. Good night then." And his eyes held hers for that last long moment before he turned and went into his room and left her standing in the hallway with a strange weakness in her legs, with tremulous and unexplainable feelings that swelled within her. She was unable to decide if she wanted to laugh or cry.

In her own bedroom directly across from where Rance Stewart was, Carrie sat fully dressed, her hands gripping the curved arms of the cherry rocking chair as she listened for any sound from the room across the hall. For a moment she had let her guard down, she chided herself. It didn't matter how charming the captain was, or how well-bred he seemed, he was a Yankee, by choice if not by birth. And Yankees had killed Uncle Etienne, had burned Maisonfleur . . . She must not be foolish enough to trust those clear gray eyes.

She had been sitting for more than an hour, straining for any sound, any sign that his going into his room had been only a ruse and that his real intentions were to rouse his men and work his will upon Kingston's Landing. But so far she had heard nothing, and after so long in the same position, one leg had gone to sleep and her fingers, curled so tightly about the arm rests of the chair, were beginning to cramp.

She stood up and stretched, aware how tired she was and how tight was the bodice of her dress. Did she dare get out of it and into something more comfortable? Surely he was asleep by now.

After listening for a long moment, she slipped out of her clothes and, as if to cover herself, put one hand to her naked breasts, the other over the thick patch of dark hair between her thighs while she ran to the tall chest of drawers for her nightgown. Hurriedly she chose one of printed lawn, delicate blue flowers on a white background, and felt a definite sense of relief as she drew it over her head, felt the cool material slide down around her. It was almost, she thought uncomfortably, as if he could see right through the walls.

As she tied the blue ribbons at the front, she heard the soft sound of Chloe's old felt slippers coming along the hallway and hurried to the door to let her in.

The slippers were the only concession Chloe had made to the lateness of the hour, otherwise she was dressed as always. "You all right, honey?" she whispered, pressing back against the closed door.

"I'm fine," Carrie said in an equally low tone. "Is Benjamin keeping an eye on the barn?"

"Everything's quiet." Chloe rolled her eyes in the direction of the hall. "He over there?"

"Yes."

Chloe gave her a worried look. "You want me to stay up here with you, honey?"

"No." Carrie squeezed her hand. "I'm really fine."

"All right. But if anything's goin' on up here you don't like, Miss Carrie, you just yell loud and I'll hear you in my room downstairs and come runnin'."

"I will," Carrie said, and let her out the door, watching as she went along the hall and down the stairs. After a look at the closed door across the way, Carrie went back into her own room and stood there helplessly, not knowing if she could dare to lie down.

She was tired. Surely now that Captain Stewart had been quiet this long, he would sleep through until morning.

She debated with herself for several minutes before she finally decided to risk it. But she had barely reached her bed when she heard something . . . a small metallic click that might have been a doorknob turning. She caught her breath and stood poised, listening intently, straining to catch the smallest sound. And then, in all that silence, she heard the door across the hall close, followed closely by the creak of a floor board.

Her heart pounding, Carrie grabbed her wrapper and only had it halfway on as she burst out into the hall to see Rance Stewart, fully dressed and starting down the stairs.

"Captain Stewart," she called, forcing a smile to her lips as the most awful possibilities formed in her head.

He turned back, his eyes taking in her state of dishabille, a half-smile coming to his face. "Miss Kingston," he said, "I'm sorry. I thought I was being very quiet."

"Is anything wrong, Captain? Is there anything I can get for you?" She went to him, suddenly aware how thin the nightgown was and struggling to get her arm into the other sleeve of her wrapper.

"Allow me," he said, holding the sleeve while she quickly slipped her arm through and drew the material protectively about her, her cheeks flaming.

"Thank you," she said, and tried her best to act as if there were nothing at all unusual about standing in the hall half-dressed and with a man.

"I was just on my way out to the barn. I thought I should make one last check on my men," he said.

Dread gripped her as it had all evening and put aside her feelings of embarrassment. "Oh, Captain," she said, giving him a coquettish look, "I know you military men take your responsibilities seriously, but isn't there a time to put duty aside? I'm sure your men are quite comfortable. Probably asleep. Benjamin has seen to all their needs."

He looked at her, his eyes narrowing, that gleam of amusement back, and something else, a kind of heat that made her feel suddenly breathless.

"And what," he drawled, "would you suggest that we do instead, Miss Kingston?"

She stood there, fastened by that direct gaze, and she felt the trembling begin in her legs, move upward. "Why, I . . . I . . .

suppose we could go downstairs and . . . I could fix you some brandy. Some of our brandy is very . . .''

Her voice trailed off as he moved closer to her, so close that she had to tilt her head back to look up at him and she could smell the tobacco smell again, could see the hard line of his jaw, could hear the sound of his breathing. Afterwards, she would ask herself why she hadn't stepped away from him. But now she stood there as if unable to move, helpless with an unlikely mixture of fear and fascination that left her weak and trembling.

"Or we could do this," he said, his voice low and almost gruff, his hands grasping her arms. He brought his mouth down over hers, ignoring the small whimper that escaped her, his lips warm and definite, moving, the thick hair of his mustache scratching her face.

She felt an incredible surge of warmth between her thighs and up into her belly that left her trembling even more, and once he took his mouth away she found, to her chagrin, that she was clinging to him, her face against his chest.

"Carrie," he said, "Carrie . . . that is your name, isn't it?'' He tilted her face back up and brought his mouth down again, this time open, his tongue demanding entrance. And his arms closed about her body, too strong to escape even if she'd tried, and he pulled her against the length of him, against that hard maleness of him, and for a moment she thought she might faint with the rush of feelings that left her light-headed with their intensity.

"Carrie . . .'' he said again, and swept her up, carried her into his bedroom, and laid her down on the high walnut bed with its tall, square posts.

There was a single lamp burning by the bedside, and it cast long shadows against the ceiling and wall. Carrie watched with a certain disbelief as he went to the door and latched it, then came back to look down at her, his face grave and intent. He pulled back the wrapper and fumbled with the ribbons at her bodice, and still she did not move.

But when the shirred material fell away to leave her breasts bared, the nipples dark pink and swollen and thrusting up at him, she realized the enormity of what was happening. She mustn't, she *couldn't* do this. . . .

"No . . ." she said, "no . . ." But her voice was soft and trembling and strange sounding.

He laughed, deep in his chest. "Don't pretend to be shy," he said. "I've wanted to do this since the first moment I laid eyes on you . . . and you've wanted it, too."

And all the time he was talking, he was stripping her out of her gown and robe, and she was thinking frantically. If she stopped him, if she *could* stop him, would he take out his anger on the others, on Kingston's Landing?

She was naked now and terribly aware of it as he drew back and looked at her. "Good God, you're magnificent!" he whispered, his eyes burning, searching out every rise and hollow of her.

She closed her own eyes tightly as he began to shed his clothes, but finally she couldn't stand not *knowing* and she opened them at that last second, that moment when he stood there beside her, tall and lean and muscular, his chest and legs covered with fine dark hairs that curled damply, the skin below his waist paler, as if he'd taken off his shirt in the sun. And that most obvious part of him, the part that she could bring herself to look at only fleetingly, was in such condition as to leave no doubt about what was going to happen.

It was not too late, an inner voice clamored. She could run from the room. She could scream, and Chloe would hear her . . . Benjamin would come running . . . and Suzy. No! She didn't want that. He might turn his men loose on them. No, better this. . . .

It was impossible to grow up on a plantation and be ignorant of sex. She had seen the animals copulating, though she'd always pretended not to, seen the stallions and their mares. She knew what to expect. It would be over quickly, she told herself in an effort to calm her racing heart, and then surely he would be content, surely he would sleep.

She braced herself as he slid onto the bed beside her, but the feel of his naked body against hers sent shock waves coursing along her thighs and belly, made her nipples feel taut and hard. To her surprise, he did not go about it at once, but slipped his arms about her and began to kiss her again, his mustache hard against her face, his mouth open and moving very slowly, his tongue touching hers. . . .

She wished he wouldn't do that. She'd rather he'd just do the other and get it over with. Because this made all those sensations of warmth flood through her again, made it hard for her to think clearly.

He moved his mouth along her throat, and she gave an involuntary little moan. "Captain . . ."

"My name is Rance," he whispered, still nuzzling at her neck and moving slowly downward. "Say it, Carrie . . . say it."

"Rance . . ." She gasped as she felt his hands caressing her breasts, and then his mouth was there, warm and wet and sucking. She heard herself moan, though she felt far removed from the sound, plunging ever faster into the waves that washed her, carried her against her will.

"I couldn't sleep for thinking of you," Rance was murmuring. "I kept wondering what it would be like to touch you all over . . . to feel your bare skin." And as he talked, he was doing just that, his hands moving, exploring her slowly so that a fierce kind of pleasure rippled through her, his mouth lifting to hers and then coming back to nip gently at her nipples. "I kept wondering what it would be like to have you naked under me . . . and do this." His voice sounded hoarse now as he slid his hand down between her legs and moved them apart, and then he was thrusting into her. She drew in her breath and cried out with the unexpected pain that brought her crashing back to reality.

Above her his head jerked up, his eyes wide with the sudden knowledge. "Goddamn!" he swore softly, staring down at her, incredulity plain on his face, deep frown lines marking his forehead. "Goddamn!" he breathed again, but then he groaned and thrust again as if he couldn't stop, and again, each time deeper, the stinging, hot pain between her legs sharper.

She set her teeth, determined not to cry out anymore, until finally she knew she had taken the whole length of him and it didn't hurt so much after that.

He moved against her with hard quick strokes, his face strangely intent, as if now he were the one who wanted it over quickly, and a moment later she felt the long shuddering release, and then the full weight of his body came down on her, lay limp while the air exploded from his lungs in a long breath.

They lay that way for what seemed a long time but was really only a minute or two. She could feel his heart beating. And then he pulled away from her, rolled onto his side and sat up on the edge of the bed.

"Why?" he demanded. "*Why* . . . ?"

He reached for his trousers and started to pull them on as Carrie, suddenly stricken with the full realization of what had happened and still throbbing with that dull pain between her legs, scrambled to retrieve her gown and wrapper, which had fallen to the floor beside the bed. She quickly slipped the gown over her head and down around her.

His fly buttoned now, he brought his full attention to her, his face like a thundercloud. "Just what kind of game have you been playing?" he demanded, his voice low, ominous.

"Why, Captain," she said, still trying to cling to the deception, desperately afraid that it was the only chance that she or Kingston's Landing had, "if love is a game, it is certainly an interesting one." Despite her effort, her trembling voice betrayed her.

"Stop that," he barked, "or I'll take you across my knee and paddle that beautiful bottom of yours!"

She was choking back the tears, and she turned quickly and started toward the door but felt his strong fingers close about her wrist.

He swung her around, and there was no way to avoid those eyes that pinned her mercilessly. "Why, goddammit? All evening you've been damned near asking me for it. You led me to believe that you were"—he stopped, shook his head in exasperation—"a . . . a woman of experience!" The lamplight caught and glistened in the black hair on his chest, gleamed along the clearly defined muscles in his shoulders, along his arms. He looked at her narrowly. "How old are you?"

"Eighteen," she mumbled, looking away.

"What did you say?"

"Eighteen," she said again, this time louder and with a flash of her usual spirit. She brought her eyes up to meet his squarely. "How old are *you*?"

He snorted. "Old enough to have known better than this!" He

shoved his arms into the sleeves of his shirt, pulled it over his head. "All right, tell me," he ordered. "Why did you flirt outrageously with me all evening? Why did you let me think that you wanted me to make love to you?"

"Because I didn't want you to harm Kingston's Landing!" she said defiantly. "Or the people here!"

"Harm Kingston's Landing? Whatever gave you the idea that I—" He stopped, and Carrie glared at him.

"Was it you and your men who killed my Uncle Etienne? Who burned Maisonfleur?" she demanded. "Were you the ones?"

"Killed? Burned? What on earth are you talking about?"

The amazement on his face was so evident that Carrie was taken aback for an instant, but she pressed on, her hands clenched at her sides, her head high. "Four days ago," she said, her voice only partly controlled, "my Uncle Etienne was clubbed down and killed by Yankees! I know! I saw them! They burned Maisonfleur . . . and they left him lying there in the drive!" She was still trying to hold the tears at bay. She would not give him the satisfaction of seeing her cry.

"Union troops?" he said, his voice fallen to a bare whisper. "You're saying Union troops did that?" There was a puzzled frown on his face. He took a step or two away, turned back. "Where was this?" he said. "Where is this Maisonfleur?"

"It *was* about a mile downriver. And he was just an old man trying to protect his home."

"Four days ago . . ." He paced back and forth, his hand to his forehead. "That's impossible!" he turned back to confront her. "I know about troop movements in this area, and there were no Union troops there then."

"You're mistaken, Captain Stewart." Carrie's voice was cold and clipped. "They didn't get away fast enough. I saw one of them, saw his cap, his blue coat."

Rance shook his head. "I don't know what you saw, but there were no Union troops scheduled to patrol this area four days ago except us. And I assure you that my men had nothing to do with it." He shook his head again. "Outlaws, maybe . . . jayhawkers. And there is no shortage of deserters." He looked at her, something close to sympathy in his eyes. "Deserters from *both* sides, Carrie."

She just stared at him silently, trying to keep her mouth from trembling, and then she turned away, started for the door.

He caught her hand. "Carrie . . . wait," he said, but she wouldn't turn to face him. "Carrie, I'm sorry," his voice came to her, "I'm sorry for what happened at Maisonfleur . . . and for what happened here tonight. Please believe me when I say that I never had any intention of harming Kingston's Landing . . . or you."

Carrie could feel his strong fingers grasping hers, and then she jerked away and ran from the room all but blinded by her tears.

𝒥 5 ℚ

RANCE STEWART AWAKENED TO THE SOUND OF A DOOR SLAMming down below and Chloe's voice calling out to Mattie to hurry up with the fried potatoes. For an instant, he wondered where he was, and then Carrie Kingston's face was there behind his eyelids, at once proud and vulnerable, the effort to keep her mouth from trembling requiring all her strength, those incredible golden eyes of hers accusing. . . .

"Jesus!" He opened his eyes, rubbed his hand over a chin in need of a shave. And in spite of himself, he remembered that instant when he suspected—no, was certain—that she was a virgin, and he groaned aloud, felt the hard muscles of his thighs tighten, the hot rise of desire.

What did she expect? he thought angrily. She had thrown herself at him the whole evening. He was a man, after all, and would make no apologies for that!

He threw off the linen sheet that covered him and eased out of bed. Across the room on the washstand, his razor and soap and brush were neatly laid out beside a bowl and pitcher that steamed faintly from the hot water within. Clean white towels were draped over the towel rod that pulled out from the side of the stand. The man Lafitte must have been in already.

Rance lost no time in working up a rich lather in the shaving mug and applying it to his face. The sooner out of here and back to New Orleans, the better. He would, of course, express his regrets to Carrie Kingston for any—inconvenience—he and his men might have caused her. His mouth drew down wryly, and he swore under his breath as he applied the razor carefully around the edges of his mustache.

The girl had spunk, there was no getting around that. She had stood right up to him. "How old are *you*?" she had flung back at him. His chuckle was dry and without mirth. He could have told her that he was ten years older than her and still too much of a jackass to see that a proud and lovely girl, who had apparently been through hell just days before, was not only frightened half to death but willing to give herself to him so that her sister and the others would be safe . . . so that her plantation would be left untouched.

Goddamn the war! Would it ever be over? And how many lives would be ruined before it was?

The door opened, and Lafitte came into the room carrying one of Rance's shirts over his arm. "Good morning, Captain," he said.

"Morning, Lafitte."

"I took the liberty of looking in your clothing pack, Captain. I found this, clean but wrinkled, so I had Mattie press it for you."

"That was very thoughtful of you."

"Is there anything else I can do for you, sir?" Lafitte stood tall and dignified, waiting, in his thin dark face a certain resignation to the years and the changes they brought.

"No, thank you." Rance smiled at him.

"Breakfast will be served in the dining room whenever you are ready."

Rance nodded, wiped the last vestiges of soap from his face. "I'll be down shortly."

Ten minutes later when he walked down the stairs to the front hall, there was no one in sight. He went out through the front way and walked over toward the stables and the barn. Huge maple trees bordered the drive on either side. In the distance, toward the river, he could see the sugar house, red bricks rising solid and substantial. It must have been a hell of a plantation before the war, he thought.

His men were out beside the barn, lounging under the cool shade of the trees. They struggled up half-heartedly at his approach.

"At ease." He waved them back. His eye fell on Hagerty, the big, overgrown kid who had started the trouble with the Negro wench yesterday. Damn him anyway, Rance thought. If he hadn't done that, maybe Carrie wouldn't have been so quick to believe that he and his men meant to do them all harm.

"Hagerty," he barked, "you hardly look like a corporal in the Union Army! Button your blouse!"

"Yes, sir," Hagerty said, throwing him a puzzled look. The captain was not usually such a stickler for regulations.

"Is everything in order? You've all eaten?"

"Yes, sir."

"Horses ready?"

"Logan is seein' to 'em, Cap'n."

"Very well. I have some business yet to attend to in the house. One of you go around to the kitchen and fill the canteens with water."

"I'll do it, sir," Hagerty piped up.

"Not you. Clater, you go." Rance turned his sternest gaze toward the corporal. "You're not to touch that girl, Hagerty. Don't let me catch you even near her. That goes for the rest of you, too. While we are on this plantation, we will conduct ourselves as proper guests and in a manner befitting soldiers of the Union Army. Do you understand me?"

"Yes, sir," they said, sliding questioning looks toward one another. What had happened to get the captain's back up?

None of it was lost on Rance, and he felt a quick surge of anger, knew it was more at himself than at them. "Be ready to leave when I come out," he snapped, turned on his heel, and strode back toward the house.

Chloe was ready with breakfast, and Rance sat at the big dining-room table alone.

"Will Miss Kingston be joining me?" he asked.

"Which Miss Kingston? Miss Susannah done eat and out in the garden . . . and Miss Carrie's in her room. She ain't comin' down 'til later." The woman looked at him with speculative eyes, and Rance wondered how much she knew about last night. It was hard to keep anything from the servants of a household. He knew that from home.

He felt vaguely uncomfortable under her scrutiny, but she served him hotcakes, sausage, eggs, and fried potatoes, and he ate with a good appetite despite his mood.

Susannah came bouncing into the room, light brown curls charmingly disheveled, dimples showing. She was carrying a basket of freshly cut flowers. "Rance . . ." she called breathlessly, "good morning." And then she caught Chloe's disapproving look. "Oh . . . forgive me," she said. "I meant to say Captain Stewart."

Rance grinned at her. It was impossible not to grin at Susannah, she was so young and bubbly. "I tell you what," he said. "I would take it as a downright favor if you would call me by my given name. That is, if I may call you Suzy."

"Oh, indeed you may," Susannah threw Chloe a triumphant look and plopped herself down in the chair across from Rance. "Would you bring some water and a container for these, Chloe? I want to fix them for the table here."

Chloe left the room, her starched petticoats rustling.

"I thought soldiers got up early," Susannah said, helping herself to an orange from the silver epergne in the center of the table.

"I guess they're supposed to," Rance said wryly. "It was a hard day yesterday."

"I waited to have breakfast with you, but when it got so late and Carrie wasn't down either, I just went ahead."

"Good," he said.

"I thought maybe you'd like these flowers on the table when you ate."

"That was very nice of you, Suzy, but I'm afraid I'll have to miss them." He drank the last of his coffee and put his napkin before him. "I want to say goodbye to your sister, and then my men and I had better get started back to New Orleans." He pushed his chair back and stood up.

"Oh . . ." Susannah made her mouth into a charming pout. "Couldn't you stay another day, Rance? It's really nice to have company. Nothing *ever* happens out here since the war . . . except"—that pretty face sobered—"except for bad things. Our Uncle Etienne got killed. Carrie was there."

"I heard about that. I'm sorry, Suzy," he said gently.

"Carrie said that Yankees did it. Could that be true, Rance?" Susannah looked up at him with eyes that were trusting.

"I believe it was jayhawkers who killed your uncle, Suzy," he answered. "There are men willing to take advantage of the war to steal and murder. But I intend to make a report of it to General Butler when I get back to New Orleans. If those men are found, you can bet that justice will be done. There are some who call the general a hard man . . . perhaps he has to be in the line of duty. But I don't believe that he'd condone such acts as that." Even as he said it, Rance had to acknowledge to himself that the chances of finding the band of outlaws, much less identifying and bringing them to trial, were remote indeed. Jayhawkers struck and got out, never staying in one place long. They were probably in Texas by now.

Susannah sighed. "I bet it would be fine with Carrie if you wanted to stay another day."

"Thanks, but I think not," he said. He grinned at her. "But I will stick my head back in the door and say goodbye before I go."

"Okay," she said, smiling again.

Out in the hall, Rance met Chloe coming back with the water for the flowers. "I wish to speak with your mistress before I leave," he said.

Chloe eyed him darkly. "Miss Carrie say she ain't comin' down this mornin'."

Rance drew his head back slightly, narrowed his eyes, and fastened her with a look that left no doubt that he meant exactly what he said. "You tell her that if she doesn't come down here . . . I'm going up there."

Chloe weighed the look for a moment and then reluctantly

nodded, but before she could move, Carrie Kingston's voice came from the top of the stairs.

"That won't be necessary, Captain," she said. Rance looked up, startled, saw her standing tall and regal in a gown of green flowered muslin, that mass of dark hair caught back with a ribbon of the same green, her head held very high above that slim neck.

She swept down the stairs, managing the hoop skirt gracefully, and Rance felt an inexplicable excitement race through him. He inclined his head. "Good morning, Carrie," he said. She did not return the greeting.

"You wished to see me about something, Captain?" she said icily.

"Yes." Rance waited, and she just stood looking at him with scorn in those big amber eyes, stood as if she expected him to speak in front of Chloe who was looking suspiciously from one to the other. "Privately, if you please," he said pointedly.

"You may go ahead with whatever you were about, Chloe," Carrie said, and then to Rance, "In here." She led him across the hall and into the study with its deep leather chairs and glass-fronted bookshelves and storage cabinets. In front of the windows was a huge old oak desk, its top mellowed by countless scratches and an ink stain or two. He closed the door behind them.

"I really don't see that we have anything to say to one another, Captain," she said, refusing to meet his eyes.

"I have something to say to you, Carrie," he said firmly.

"Very well. Say it if you must."

"I want to thank you on behalf of my men and myself . . . for allowing us the hospitality of Kingston's Landing . . . and . . . I want to tell you . . ." He stopped. Jesus, he was stammering like a schoolboy! And all because of this girl!

He cleared his throat, began again. "I'm sorry, Carrie, for what happened last night. Sorry that you . . . that I misunderstood. But you are," he said almost angrily, "a very beautiful and desirable woman. I doubt that many men could have resisted."

She had thrown him a startled look at the word "beautiful,"

74

but her lower lip still drew in scornfully. "You took advantage," she accused.

"But, Carrie, you practically . . ." He broke off as he saw the glint of tears.

"No Southern gentleman would have behaved so basely!" Her voice was low with shame and fury. "No wonder you wear that uniform!" she said. "You're not fit to wear a Confederate one!" She turned abruptly and walked from the room.

Rance just stood there for a moment, and then he brought his fist crashing down against the desktop to set the ink bottle dancing.

On his way out he slammed the big front door behind him, and out in the barn lot he snapped the men to attention, ordered them to mount, and gave the signal to move out quickly.

And all the way back to New Orleans he could see nothing but Carrie Kingston's face . . . those enormous amber eyes, angry and accusing.

Carrie busied herself with preparations to leave for New Orleans, the knowledge that her sacrifice might possibly have been useless a torment of humiliation. She could not think of Rance Stewart without a sharp upsurge of resentment and anger so strong it made her feel light-headed. And it certainly didn't help to have Susannah chatter away about Rance and her hope that they might see him again when they reached New Orleans.

"I hardly think it would be proper, or *loyal*, for the sisters of a lieutenant in the Confederate Army to socialize with a Yankee!" Carrie had replied tartly.

"But, Carrie, he's so nice," Susannah pleaded.

"Yankees are Yankees . . . and they're not nice!"

Chloe made Carrie even more nervous by hovering over her constantly, her eyes worried, questioning. "You all right, honey?" she asked several times during that day and the next.

"Of course I am, Chloe," she answered each time, and each time she gave the same forced smile and wondered if Chloe knew, if she had seen her that night after she left Rance's bedroom, running blindly down the stairs to the back of the house.

She had locked herself into the room where the tall round cisterns outside fed water to the copper shower, stripped naked and, bare feet against the cool brick floor, had scoured herself with strong soap. She had rubbed until her skin was red and burning, and then she'd gone to stand under the shower and pulled the lever that let the water flow down cold around her. And she'd wished that it were hot, wished that it were scalding so that she might burn away some of her shame.

Time would help, she knew that. And she had plenty to keep her mind occupied. Getting Suzy to New Orleans where she'd be safe was the first thing. Whether it had been jayhawkers or Yankees—and she wasn't at all sure that she believed Rance Stewart's declarations—Uncle Etienne was just as dead, and Maisonfleur, except for a few blackened columns, was gone.

Once Suzy was safe, she would see about getting the loan for the crop. And what had happened with Rance Stewart was her secret. No one need ever know. Not J. D., not anyone.

By Thursday afternoon everything was packed and ready, the trunks and hatboxes and leather valises waiting in the front hall for their departure the following morning when yet another unexpected, but this time very welcome, guest rode up the drive to Kingston's Landing.

Despite the fact that he was a man of color, Prosper Durant had been her father's closest friend. To the disapproval of New Orleans society, the well-known fencing master, who was something of a dandy in dress and manner, had been a frequent caller at Kingston's Landing over the years, and Adam Kingston had simply ignored the mutterings of friend and foe alike. Liaisons between well-to-do Creole men and women of color were common, their offspring numerous in New Orleans, but neither Creoles nor Americans socialized with such "free people of color." Under the circumstances, one might have a private drink or two with the fellow, but to bring him *home* . . . it simply wasn't done!

But Carrie could never remember a time when Molly Kingston hadn't welcomed her husband's friend as warmly as Adam did himself. She had always greeted him with a hug and a kiss. And as children, Carrie and George Pierre and Susannah had always rushed to Prosper, who invariably had small tins of sweetmeats or wrapped chocolates or pralines for them.

Now, at an age that must be approaching sixty, he drew his horse abreast of the front gallery, dismounted with a grace and ease many a young man would have envied, and gave an ebullient shout as Susannah, followed closely by Carrie, ran out to greet him.

The huge cameo he always wore was pinned to the snowy white ruffles of his shirtfront, and the plum-colored velvet waistcoat contrasted perfectly with the light gray, well-fitted broadcloth suit. He grinned broadly, skin the color of *café au lait*, teeth very white in a face that, while it bore the marks of time, was still handsome.

"*Mes chères!*" he shouted and swept them up in a great hug, Susannah on one side, Carrie on the other, his arms incredibly strong from those years of foil and épée and saber. Carrie felt her feet leave the ground for a moment, and then he set them both in front of him. "Let me look at you, *mes chères!*"

"Prosper!" Susannah danced about happily and then darted in to hug him once more. Carrie stood quietly and smiled, feeling an enormous relief that he had come.

"I know about Etienne," he said, his grin fading. "I came as soon as I heard."

"But how? Who told you?" Carrie asked.

"In New Orleans, the servants know everything," he said. "Father Perez's housekeeper, Matilda, told the Anderson's girl, Agnes, that a priest from upriver had sent word that he officiated at the burial. Agnes told Caspar who is butler in the Dubois household, who told Emile at the French Market, who told my Delphine who comes in to clean for me every other day."

"I should have sent word to you, Prosper," Carrie said. "I'm sorry . . . I suppose I haven't been thinking very clearly since it happened."

"No matter. I am here now, and I want to know everything."

"Come," Carrie took his hand, "let's go inside. You must be tired."

"Not a bit. I rode in very good time. Less than three hours." He gestured toward the sorrel mare that Benjamin was leading away. "Juno is like me. Though no longer young, she has several good years left."

Carrie drew him along, noting that after so long a ride his clothes were impeccable, the still dark hair, which formed deep, even waves back from a rather high forehead, was neatly in place, the long mustache waxed to stiff, curled points. Even his shoes did not bear a trace of dust. She couldn't recall ever having seen him perspire, though the Louisiana heat could sometimes be sweltering.

Hearing all the commotion, Chloe came from the back part of the house and broke into a broad grin as she entered the front hall and saw Prosper. "Mist' Prosper," she said, "it's sure fine to have you come visitin'!"

"It is fine to be here, Chloe."

"Would you bring Prosper something to eat?" Carrie asked Chloe. "You must be starving," she said to Prosper.

"I got some cold chicken and some peach shortcake in the kitchen."

"Just the thing, Chloe." Prosper's eyes twinkled. "Especially if you have a little sherry to go with it."

"I'll get the sherry," Susannah said.

Later, when Carrie got a chance alone with Prosper, she told him everything—almost. She told him about the men who had killed Etienne Moreau and burned Maisonfleur. About her certainty that they had been Yankee troops. And about a small group of Union soldiers arriving at Kingston's Landing and claiming the hospitality of the place for the night.

"They did no harm," she said carefully. "In fact, when I spoke to their captain about what had happened at Maisonfleur, he insisted that it must have been jayhawkers."

"Well," Prosper said, his face unnaturally grave, "I am glad you are all packed because you are coming home with me. I shall take you to my house on Dumaine Street."

"Oh, Prosper, we couldn't . . . I wouldn't impose—"

"Nonsense," he said. "It once belonged to your own Papa, you know. I bought it from him years ago."

"Yes, I know that. But I'm sure we can stay with J. D.'s parents. Abby Morrison will probably insist."

Prosper's dark eyes suddenly probed. He had caught the underlying reluctance in Carrie's voice. "But," he leaned forward with an understanding grin, "you would not really wish to stay there?"

"Well, I . . . they're wonderful people, you understand . . ." Carrie stammered. The truth was Abby Morrison constantly tried to tell her what to do, and she hated it. "I'm sure they would make us quite welcome," she finished lamely.

"But you do not wish to stay there," Prosper pressed.

"No," Carrie admitted.

"Then it is all settled. You and Susannah will stay at the house on Dumaine Street for as long as you wish, and I shall move into the apartment over the fencing salon. No protests!" he headed her off. "Delphine has been scolding me unmercifully about having so much work to do in that house when there is only me . . . now that my sweet Jeanette is gone." There was a flash of pain in the dark eyes, there and gone as quickly. "At the apartment, Delphine will be finished in half the time and off to see her lover Emile who sells crabs in the French Market."

"But, Prosper—" she began.

"No buts. We shall leave in the morning."

And for the first time since Adam Kingston died, Carrie, numb from the events of the past week, was content to let someone else make decisions for her.

They left early to escape at least a part of the day's heat. Nearly four hours later—it took longer to make the trip in an unwieldy carriage than on horseback—they were approaching New Orleans, following the curve of the river, when Carrie, who was sitting next to the window, caught a flash of a blue uniform up ahead. She leaned her head out to see a detail of Union soldiers.

"Yankees!" she said.

"Do not be alarmed." Prosper's voice was calm. "It is a routine checkpoint." He directed Lafitte to slow the horses and pull over to the side of the road.

A sergeant with a pimply face and scraggly yellow hair peered into the carriage, and Carrie drew back at his oniony breath.

"I am Prosper Durant," the jaunty little fencing master said grandly as he whipped out his identification, "and these ladies

79

are the daughters of the late Adam Kingston. They are coming down from their plantation upriver for a visit to our fair city.''

Susannah's eyes were wide, and Carrie reached out and took her sister's hand.

"That right, Miss?" the sergeant demanded of Carrie.

She nodded.

'' 'Fraid we'll have to look at your trunks,'' he said matter-of-factly, and jerked his head to the men behind him.

"Sergeant," Prosper protested, "is that absolutely necessary? We have driven a long way. The ladies are tired . . .''

The Yankee shrugged. "For all I know you could have them trunks filled with gunpowder and be aimin' to blow up General Butler's headquarters.'' He shifted a wad of tobacco from one cheek to the other and turned his head to spit into the dusty road.

Prosper got out of the carriage, but Carrie and Susannah stayed inside and listened as the trunks were taken down and opened. They could hear the creak of a hinged top and the rough stamping of booted feet. There was a muffled guffaw.

"Really, Sergeant," Carrie heard Prosper's voice, heard the decided edge to his voice, "I do believe you can see we are carrying no gunpowder. Or anything else of interest to the Union Army.''

"They're poking around in our things!" Susannah hissed, that perfect little mouth set angrily.

Carrie kept control of herself with an effort. "It's all right," she said to soothe her sister, but she was near to bursting through the carriage door herself and demanding that they be allowed to proceed when she heard the sergeant's voice.

"All right, boys. Close 'em up. Hoist them trunks back up there and tie 'em down tight.''

And moments later they were again underway and soon rocking gently along the St. Charles Road, past the huge old mansions of the American Section, with their tall hedges and masses of crepe myrtle and oleander bushes.

The house on Dumaine Street in the old city, or the French Quarter as it was called, was a lovely house of typical Creole design, really more Spanish than French. A stuccoed wall along the street presented an unbroken front except for a small iron gate and a pair of green doors with great iron hinges that when opened admitted horses and carriage to an inner courtyard of privacy and flowered coolness. The carriage house and stables were in back. Inside the house the furniture was French and old enough to be mellowed and comfortable.

"Oh, Carrie, I love it here!" Susannah sang out exuberantly once she had, with Mattie's help, unpacked her things and gotten them neatly put away in deep drawers and tall armoires.

"Yes, it's very nice," Carrie said half-heartedly. She was still depressed over seeing the line of Yankee gunboats anchored midstream, menacing in their very ugliness. Closer in, the moored frigates and schooners and steamboats had seemed so fragile, so helpless by comparison. Even the big merchantmen had taken on an air of clumsy impotence under the threat of the guns.

In the heart of the city the streets had been just as busy as ever with carts and carriages, buggies and drays. People shopped in the French Market and strolled along the banquettes as they always had. But the blue-clad soldiers with their harsh Northern accents seemed everywhere, and Carrie had detected on the faces of the citizens a certain tightness about the mouth, a distant and guarded look in the eye.

"Can I go to the dressmaker's tomorrow?" Susannah pleaded now. "I need everything new. Really, I do, Carrie."

Carrie thought of their dwindling money supply. "Not tomorrow. Perhaps next week," she said firmly. She would have to see Leroy Tate at the bank.

"Oh . . ." Susannah pouted, but brightened at once. "Why don't we go over to the Morrisons' and let them know we're here. Perhaps they'll want us to go to the theater with them or something."

"Well . . ." Carrie considered it for only a moment. "We wouldn't want to intrude on their plans. Tell you what. Let's send Lafitte over with a message that we're here, and we'll call on them at their convenience."

But J. D.'s mother didn't wait for them to come to her. Abby Morrison was at the house on Dumaine Street within the hour.

"Carrie . . . Susannah!" She put aside her parasol and embraced them in turn. "It's wonderful to see you, but what are

81

you doing here?'' She was still an attractive woman, with hair just a shade darker than J. D.'s pulled back into a large chignon. Her skin was clear and fair, her eyelids rather pronounced and shaped like half-ovals, which gave her blue eyes a very round and wide look. And now she turned that questioning gaze first to Carrie then to Susannah.

"Well, with Uncle Etienne dead," Susannah burst out, "Carrie thought—"

Abby Morrison gasped. "Etienne Moreau *dead*?" she said. "Merciful heaven . . . When? How?"

They went into the parlor and sat down, and Carrie told the story once again, leaving out the worst details to spare Susannah. Abby shook her head sadly.

"Oh, you poor dears . . . and poor Etienne," she said, and sat silently for a moment. "Will this terrible war ever be over?" she burst out, a thin, shrill note of desperation in her voice. "Soldiers on the streets of New Orleans! They're rude and loutish . . . no manners at all! There's no money to speak of . . . no supplies! Why, Seth may have to close down the distillery altogether if he can't get more corn and sugar."

Carrie leaned forward in her chair. "I didn't know it was so bad."

"It's awful . . . and General Butler is probably making a fortune out of it!"

"I don't understand."

"Well," Abby clasped her hands together in her lap, "Butler has allowed his brother to come in and practically steal from us! The man goes about openly, buying up goods that we need, buying them for a song! Then he ships them north to sell for twenty times the purchase price. He boasts that he's made a fortune already. Why should we believe that the general himself is not in on it, too? It's common knowledge."

"I wonder if Rance knows about that?" Susannah said innocently.

"Rance?" Abby questioned, and Carrie felt that quick tightening in her throat.

"Just some Yankee captain who insisted upon quartering his men at Kingston's Landing overnight," she answered offhandedly.

"Yankees at Kingston's Landing! Merciful heavens! I never

thought you two should stay out there after George Pierre left anyway,'' she said with her positive air. And then her face grew wistful. "I don't suppose that you've heard anything . . . from J. D.'' Her mouth trembled, and she passed a blue-veined hand quickly over her eyes.

"Oh, my goodness!'' Carrie jumped to her feet. "I don't know how I could have forgotten!'' She sped to the small case she had left on the writing desk in the sitting room and quickly drew out the letter from J. D. "Forgive me. There's just been so much,'' she said as she handed the envelope to Abby Morrison.

"How on earth . . . ?'' Abby's voice quivered.

"Paul Gayerre slipped through the lines and brought it.''

Abby eagerly broke the seal, and it was fully thirty minutes later before she had finished reading and re-reading it aloud, wiping away tears ever so daintily with a small lace handkerchief, and exclaiming several times how brave her son was, all of the boys were, to stay cheerful in the face of such adversity.

But finally she slipped it into her reticule and smoothed the tucks at the front of her dress. "Well,'' she said, her blue eyes still red-rimmed, "I wish we'd known about poor Etienne. Seth would have come right after you.''

Carrie nodded.

"No matter. Now that you're here, we must get you moved over to us at once. Before, when I asked what you were doing here, I didn't mean here in New Orleans, I meant *here*. Here in that Durant man's house.''

"Prosper asked us to stay,'' Susannah said.

"He has very kindly let us use his home while we are in New Orleans,'' Carrie said.

"But, Carrie, my dear,'' Abby's voice dropped to a confidential tone, "he's . . . he's part darky.''

"He was Papa's friend.''

"Oh, I know that. You don't have to tell me anything about Adam Kingston. We all loved him, but he was a stubborn man. Nobody could give him any advice. Heaven knows Seth tried, and so did I.''

"Prosper has been a friend to Susannah and me, too,'' Carrie said stiffly. "He's inconvenienced himself so that we could stay here. He's moved into the apartment above his salon.''

"Well, that's very nice, I'm sure," Abby said, "but I still think it best that you come to Seth and me. After all, we're relations . . . practically."

"Thank you," Carrie said, "but I think we'll stay here for now." Her tone was apologetic, and she felt vaguely annoyed with herself for that. After all, she was not married to J. D. yet.

Abby's lips thinned ever so slightly. "I'm sure," she said sweetly, "that after you think about this, you'll change your mind."

Carrie ignored that. "Would you like some tea . . . perhaps some coffee?" she said. "I'll have Mattie bring some."

"Oh, no, thank you. It's really too late for tea. It would simply ruin my appetite." Abby gathered up her reticule and parasol, and pulled her gloves on. Carrie noticed a small mended place on one of the fingers. "I know you must be exhausted today after your trip, and Seth isn't coming home until late. Business, you know. But do plan to come to dinner tomorrow evening. There'll be a gentleman there you must meet . . . a Mr. Beau Canfield. He's been so helpful to Seth and me. Oh," her hand fluttered to her ample bosom, "that reminds me! I haven't told you the good news yet! Melissa is in a family way!"

"How nice," Carrie said automatically. Melissa was J. D.'s sister, older by several years. She had married and moved away from New Orleans when Carrie was still young.

"I just wish I could be with her now," Abby was saying. "A girl in that condition needs her mother right at her side . . . especially when she's a little older. Not that twenty-six is old, but for a first baby . . ."

Somehow Carrie was not hearing anything except "in that condition" and "baby," and there was a sudden hollow feeling in her stomach. She felt a fine perspiration spring out around her mouth.

"We would never have known," Abby was rambling on, "not with her being in Philadelphia, if Beau hadn't brought a letter from her. He's such a *dear* man. But then you'll see tomorrow night."

"Yes," Carrie said, "we'll see you tomorrow."

Abby peered at her. "Carrie, my dear, you don't look at all well. You're quite pale."

"I'm fine," Carrie said. "It's just . . . it has been a long day."

"Of course. A light supper and early to bed will be just the thing. And if you change your mind about moving over to the house . . ." Abby lingered, and Carrie wanted to scream.

"Yes, thank you . . . We'll let you know."

Finally J. D.'s mother was gone, and Susannah looked anxiously into her sister's face. "Are you sure you're all right, Carrie? You do look funny."

"Just tired," Carrie said. "I think I'll go lie down for a few minutes before dinner."

And upstairs in her room, Carrie lay on the bed and stared at the ceiling. Dear God, could it be possible?

6

"OH, I DO WISH THAT BEAU CANFIELD HADN'T HAD TO send last minute regrets. I wanted you girls to meet him." Abby Morrison took the tray from the young Negro housemaid and poured the coffee herself, passing the wafer-thin demitasse cups to Carrie, Susannah, and then to her husband, Seth. They sat in the Morrisons' well-furnished parlor, with its velvet love seats and marble-topped tables.

"I'm sure it was unavoidable, Abby. Beau's a busy man." Seth Morrison eyed the fragile piece of china that seemed so out of place in his stubby fingers. "Good Lord," he said, "don't we have anything big enough to hold a decent drink of coffee? There's not even room in this thing for a touch of brandy!"

"I'm sorry, dear. Penelope . . ." Abby gestured, and the house girl sped away to bring a bigger cup. "All the same,"

Abby stirred cream into her own coffee, "I'm disappointed that Captain Canfield couldn't be with us for dinner. However, he did say that he might be able to come by later."

"*Captain* Canfield?" Carrie said.

"Beau has his own ship," Abby replied brightly.

Seth settled himself deeper into his big overstuffed chair, waistcoat buttons straining. "He's master of a small merchant ship. And a clever young man."

"He runs the blockade into Charleston whenever he's a mind to," Abby said.

"Abby!" Seth Morrison leaned forward to take a quick look toward the door as if to make sure that none of the servants was about.

"Well, it's all right to tell Carrie and Susannah, Seth. After all, they're practically family. They're not going to say anything where it might get back to the wrong people."

"All the same," Seth gave his wife an exasperated look, "Beau is playing a dangerous game, and we can't be too careful."

"This Beau Canfield runs the blockade into Charleston, and yet the Yankees let him make port in New Orleans?" Carrie said.

"I said he was clever." Seth lowered one eyelid in a half-wink, the furrows above his heavy dark brows pulling deeper. "Now that Abby has let the cat out of the bag, you may as well know the rest. But it's in the strictest confidence, you understand."

Carrie and Susannah nodded.

"Beau comes in bold as brass and lets the Yankees think he's a Union sympathizer. He's got them convinced. They don't know that he's really helping the Confederacy. He goes in and out of Northern ports as he pleases."

"Yes," Abby said. "That's how we were able to get the letter from Melissa. Oh, he's been so helpful to us, and he's a most charming man. You'll see."

Susannah's eyes were shining. "How exciting! And how brave of him! I've always thought it must be wonderful to go to sea," she said.

Carrie smiled at her sister, and all conversation ceased as Penelope brought a more suitable cup, filled to the brim with coffee and laced generously with her master's favorite brandy.

Seth sniffed at it approvingly and gave the leggy girl an appreciative nod, then waited until she padded back down the hall toward the back of the house.

"I declare," Abby said, "I would hate to think that either Penelope or old Thomas would repeat anything they heard said in the privacy of our home."

Seth shrugged. "Things have changed, Abby. I know for a fact that a few of those people down on Ship Island are doing hard labor because of something their house Nigras reported. And we certainly don't want to risk getting Beau found out. He's pulled my potatoes out of the fire for me. At least so far. I wouldn't have been able to keep the distillery open this long without the sugar he's brought me from the Indies." He shook his head. "Of course, I don't know how much longer we'll be able to keep on . . . even with a limited production."

Abby sat very straight in her chair, her hands folded in her lap. "The Yankees think," she said, "that because we have so little now, they're going to break us . . . But, they'll not."

Carrie saw the tightly laced fingers. That things were considerably changed since the fall of New Orleans was readily apparent. The dinner they had just had, though certainly adequate, was by no means the lavish table that the Morrisons were accustomed to setting. And Carrie remembered the small mended place she'd seen in Abby's glove. In the old days, Abby would have just gotten a new pair, and the old ones would have gone to Penelope.

"Was it very difficult in those first days?" Carrie asked. "When the city fell?"

"It was dreadful!" Abby said. "We had thought we were perfectly safe with not one, but two forts downriver. And then the word came that Farragut had gotten past both Fort Jackson and Fort St. Philip, and there was nothing to stop him from taking New Orleans."

"There was a relatively small Confederate contingent here. They left just ahead of the invasion," Seth said.

"I never understood why they didn't stay and protect us." Abby's voice was bitter.

"There weren't enough of them, Abby. They had no choice."

"No choice. I bet J. D. wouldn't have left. Nor George Pierre."

"Perhaps not." Seth gave his wife an understanding smile. "But," he went on to Carrie and Susannah, "though the Yankees managed to take New Orleans, they didn't get as much as they thought they would. When we knew it was inevitable, we burned everything that we thought would be a help to them. Burned all the cotton stored along the wharves. Burned the sugar, the molasses, salt meat, everything we could lay a torch to. I touched off one of my own warehouses. Filled to the rafters."

"The fires burned all through the night," Abby said. "Lit up the sky so it was almost like daylight. And the smoke hung everywhere."

They were quiet for a moment.

"Did the soldiers do any harm when they first came into the city?" Susannah asked finally.

"Not at first," Abby said. "But then Butler decided to make an example of one poor boy who had climbed up and hauled down a Union flag. He ordered a public hanging for the lad. And, as Seth told you, some people have been sent down to Ship Island to the prison camp there. Most of the time for nearly nothing!" Abby's voice crackled with resentment. "Oh, he's high-handed, the general is, with his special taxes and his general orders and his loyalty oaths!"

"Loyalty oaths?" Carrie said.

"One of his general orders was that we must all take an oath of loyalty to the United States government," Seth explained.

"Of course we'll not do it," Abby interjected. "I don't know a single person in New Orleans—that is, anyone who belongs here—who would swear allegiance to the Union. I just hope that when New Orleans is finally rescued by our soldiers that General Butler gets what he so richly deserves! I hope that—"

"Now, Abby," her husband interrupted, "it could be worse. And it does no good to work yourself up to a sick spell."

"You haven't heard the latest, Seth," she said. "Do you remember that handsome pair of bays that Miss Esther Beauchamp keeps for her carriage?"

Seth nodded.

"Well, today Geraldine Brighton told me that last week they were confiscated for 'military purposes,' and two days later they were seen hitched to General Butler's carriage when Mrs. Butler attended the theater.''

"Well, my dear, I can understand poor Esther's outrage, but if confiscated horses were the worst thing we had to contend with . . . Besides, the girls here have had their own troubles. I was sorry to hear about Etienne Moreau," he said. "I always liked him.''

Carrie nodded. "It was a terrible loss for Suzy and me. Uncle Etienne was . . . always so good to us.''

"I know he was," Abby said. "God rest the poor man's soul." She gave a long sigh, then squared her shoulders and stood. "Enough of this distressing talk. Come, I want to show you the gloves and scarf I've been knitting for J. D.," she said to Carrie. "If I ever get a way to send them, they'll be ready.''

Carrie followed along to the sitting room where Abby had left her knitting basket and admired the well-made gloves and scarf.

"I don't know how cold it gets in Vicksburg in the winter," Abby said. "Perhaps I can find a way to get them to him before then." She looked down at the basket. "I'm going to make several pairs. For J. D. and his friends . . . for George Pierre." Her voice was forced and bright.

Carrie felt a sudden quick sympathy for the woman. "That's very good of you, Mrs. Morrison.''

Abby turned those round blue eyes to her. "Oh, please . . . won't you call me mother. You're going to be a Morrison yourself just as soon as J. D. comes home. It would be a great comfort to me, Carrie. I'm so glad to have you here in New Orleans.''

The two of them regarded one another for a long moment, and then Carrie impulsively put out a hand to the older woman. "Of course," she said. "Thank you, Mother Morrison.''

Abby smiled, a sudden wry set to her mouth, the barest twinkle in her eye. "I don't suppose I'm going to be able to persuade you to come over here to stay.''

Carrie shook her head. "Not just now.''

Abby grinned. "I do believe you're as stubborn as your father was. But if you change your mind, you're welcome anytime. You and Susannah.''

"I know. And I'm truly grateful for that.''

The doorbell echoed softly through the house, and Abby turned. "Now who do you suppose that is? Perhaps Beau was able to come after all."

They came into the foyer just in time to see Penelope admit a handsome man in his early thirties. He swept off his tall-crowned hat to reveal a good head of curly blond hair.

"Beau," Abby said, and the young man quickly passed his hat and gloves to the house girl. He came forward to take Abby's outstretched hand and swept it to his lips.

"My dear lady," he said, his voice velvety, his teeth very white and even, "I hope you have forgiven me for missing your lovely dinner. My business was pressing. However, once it was finished, I decided that it was not too late, and so here I am. Don't tell me—" His gaze shifted to Carrie. "I'll wager this enchanting young woman is Miss Carrie Kingston."

As Carrie's mouth flew open in surprise, Abby's laughter filled the hallway. "This enchanting young woman is indeed Carrie Kingston, and my son's fiancée. Don't forget that, Beau Canfield," she teased. And to Carrie: "When Beau sent his regrets for dinner, I sent a note back by his man telling him that you and Susannah would be here this evening."

"It's a great pleasure, Miss Kingston," Beau Canfield said, and as he lifted his head after bowing over her hand, Carrie was struck by his eyes, which were deep-set and dark, and held an admiration that he made no effort to conceal.

"Captain Canfield . . ." She nodded, an unsettling warmth stealing into her cheeks. He was the handsomest man she had ever seen, with a broad forehead, perfectly shaped nose, and sensual lips. His manners were excellent, warm and polished; the Morrisons' friend was certainly every inch a gentleman.

Abby beamed. "Come, you must meet Susannah." She took his arm and drew him along. "Seth will be so glad you could make it."

In the parlor, Carrie watched her little sister fall completely under the charm of Beau Canfield as he swept her hand up to his lips and declared that it was indeed his good fortune that he had been able to conclude his business in time to stop by.

"I do think it's a terrible shame," he added, "that two such lovely young ladies have kept themselves hidden away on a plantation upriver. But now that you have decided to allow us the privilege of your company, we must do our best to keep you here." He smiled at Susannah, looking fully into her eyes, and her already pink cheeks deepened to a charming rosy glow.

"I don't believe that would take too much persuasion, Captain Canfield." She dimpled prettily and shot Carrie a pleased little look.

Seth had stood up to greet his guest warmly, and now the two of them stood side by side, Seth's short and stocky body making Beau Canfield's average height seem quite tall by comparison.

It was unusual to see a young man out of uniform these days, and Carrie admired Canfield's elegant attire. He was suited in gray broadcloth of the best quality and fit, his waistcoat of a blue flowered brocade. The white ruffles at his shirtfront were edged with a tiny blue piping, and he wore small pearl cuff-buttons with a matching stickpin. Not at all, she thought, what one would expect the captain of a merchant vessel to look like. In truth, Seth Morrison looked more the seafaring man with his thick body and slightly bowed legs.

"Earlier this evening, Captain," Susannah was saying, "I was telling everyone how exciting I think it must be to go to sea."

"Well now, it's not always quite as glamorous as it sounds, Miss Kingston," Canfield said as he sat down. "In fact, most of the time it's downright uneventful."

"You're being too modest, Captain."

Carrie could see how earnest Susannah's face was, and she tried to send a warning look her sister's way, but it was too late. Susannah rushed ahead.

"You see," she said, her gaze direct and filled with admiration, "we *know*, Captain Canfield. We know . . . about your work for the Confederacy . . . and how you fool the Yankees."

There was a sudden and awkward silence. One of Canfield's perfectly shaped eyebrows lifted slightly.

"I . . . I'm afraid it's my fault, Beau." Abby was the first to speak. "I told them. Rather impulsively, I suppose. But they're family. They're the daughters of the Kingstons who were our closest friends. Carrie's going to marry our son. They wouldn't betray you any more than we would."

"I see," Canfield said slowly.

"I do hope you're not angry with me."

The handsome captain favored her with his best smile. "My dear lady, I could not be angry with you no matter what you did."

Seth grinned. "Your secret's safe with them, Beau. They're a pair of Rebels, and that's the truth."

"Oh, your secret *is* safe with us," Susannah said, her voice ringing passionately. "And I want you to know," she went on, her green eyes burning with admiration, "that I think it's just about the bravest thing I've ever heard!"

"Suzy," Carrie interjected quickly, "perhaps Captain Canfield would rather not discuss—"

"That's not it at all." Beau held up a strong, well-manicured hand and then turned back to Susannah. "It's just that I fear you give me too much credit, Miss Kingston. It is our brave soldiers at the front who should have our praise. And what small contributions I've been able to make to that cause are negligible in comparison."

"I believe my sister is right. You are too modest, Captain." Carrie was impressed by his sincerity. "You've run the blockade?"

"Several times. I was in Charleston last month. Spirits are high there."

"And what news of the war in that part of the country?"

"McClellan's army was within nine miles of Richmond, but that was as close as he could get," Canfield said. "Unfortunately, the commanding general, Joe Johnston, was seriously wounded in the fighting. President Davis has named Robert E. Lee as his replacement, and that appointment was being hailed in Charleston. It is said that Lee is the most brilliant officer in the Confederate Army."

"Well, at least," Abby said, "we have been able to learn the truth about some of our victories from Beau. General Butler will hardly allow the New Orleans papers to print anything."

"Now don't start, Abby," Seth scolded her gently. "Let's not allow Butler, or the war, to ruin the evening." He changed the subject. "I do hope, Beau, that your business this evening was successful. You missed a good supper."

"Oh, indeed it was. In fact, I think that I may have some

good news for you, but perhaps we should save that for later. We wouldn't want to bore the ladies, would we?''

"Certainly not," Abby said firmly. "Besides, you've only just arrived." She rang for Penelope to bring more coffee and brought out a tin of sweetmeats that she had been saving for a special occasion. But before long it was clear that Seth was anxious to speak with Canfield privately, and the two men retired to the study for brandy and cigars.

"Well," Abby said resignedly, "since we've been abandoned by the gentlemen, you two girls can help me hide the silver."

"Hide the silver?" Carrie was mystified.

Abby gave a helpless shrug. "Any silver found in a Confederate household is confiscated. General Butler's orders," she said. "I only brought it out tonight because I wanted your visit to be special."

"You mean the—the Yankees," Susannah sputtered, "would take the silver off your table?"

"I'm afraid they would. And have. We know of several instances."

"I don't believe Rance would do that! Do you, Carrie?"

"I don't know," Carrie said shortly. She felt a surge of emotions at the mention of his name. Shame. Anger that she could have been so easily used. Fury that Rance Stewart had been so willing to take advantage of her. And, of course, there was still that nagging fear. . . .

"Well," Susannah prodded her, "we had our silver right there in front of him, and he didn't bother it."

"No, I suppose he didn't."

"You're lucky," Abby said.

They went into the Morrisons' dining room with its heavy mahogany table and ornately carved sideboard. The silver had been washed and dried and left in orderly rows by the polished chest.

"Honestly, what has the world come to," Abby was saying. "I've had Penelope for twelve years, and I cannot believe that she would ever tell a Yankee anything. But Seth insists that I must never let her know where I hide it."

Carrie tried to sympathize, but it was difficult because she was preoccupied once again with the mental arithmetic that told her how long she would have to wait until she *knew* . . . five days. Dear Lord, it seemed an eternity.

Absently she helped Abby Morrison and Susannah count the pieces of silver, and then with all of it safely locked away in the large flat chest, they took it upstairs to Abby and Seth's bedroom and placed it in a trunk with a false bottom that stood at the foot of the bed. Once there, the chest fit snugly in place, and no one would be the wiser when the bottom was replaced and the quilts put back in.

"I had all but forgotten that space was there," Abby whispered. "The trunk belonged to my mother. I used to hide things there when I was a girl."

She tucked the last quilt in and closed the trunk lid. "The silver teapot, sugar and wastebowls, all my bigger pieces are buried out in the stable under the feed bins."

Their task finished, they went back to the sitting room where Susannah declared her intention to help with Abby's knitting project for their soldiers at the front and, despite her deficiencies in that area, began at once under Abby's careful supervision.

After nearly an hour of clicking needles and idle chatter, Carrie, still restless, excused herself and walked out onto the gallery at the far end of the house to catch a breath of air.

The verandah, floored with large, flat ballast stones, was long and wide, the pale crescent moon casting deep shadows along its length. Atop a low railing at the gallery's edge, large urns spilled out a variety of vines and foliage, and the air was sweet with the scent of gardenias.

Glad to be alone for a little while, Carrie walked to the railing, maneuvering her wide skirts past the low stone benches and around small potted plants, her crinolines rustling softly. She looked out across the expanse of lawn. Unlike the houses in the heart of the city, the homes here in the American section were located on spacious grounds, some the size of a city block. Magnolia trees and live oaks made lacy dark patterns against the night sky.

She breathed deeply. Oh, she did miss Kingston's Landing already. Not that it wasn't exciting to be in the city. But despite the sweetness of the gardenias, the very air seemed different here . . . as if it could never quite rid itself of that taint of discarded vegetables at the French Market, crayfish left in the sun too long, slops thrown carelessly into an alleyway.

She sighed. She would have to go see Leroy Tate at the bank soon. She must remember what she had come here to do. And she must forget Rance Stewart and what had happened, put that night completely out of her mind. It was over. It was finished. Unless. Oh, Lord, what would she do if. . . .

As if to answer her own question, she lifted her head high. "I'll do *something*!" she said aloud, her voice laced with a flinty determination.

A low, masculine chuckle came from somewhere behind her, and she started, whirled about. "Now I just bet you will." Canfield, all but hidden by the shadows, leaned back comfortably in a big cypress chair, cigar in hand.

"Forgive me, Miss Kingston." He rose leisurely and came over to stand beside her. "I should have made my presence known to you at once. I confess I found you so lovely there in the moonlight I simply wanted to enjoy the sight for a few quiet moments."

"Why, Captain . . . Captain Canfield," Carrie stammered, flustered, her hand still at her throat where it had gone at first sight of him, "I . . . I had no idea you were there."

"I know." He grinned at her, very self-possessed, watching almost coolly. "I expect we're both here for the same reason. A breath of air."

She nodded.

"Do you mind the cigar?"

"No. Not at all," she said. "As a matter of fact, my father used to enjoy a good cigar."

"I don't know that I should take that as a compliment. A man of my age compared to your *father*. And by such an attractive young woman."

"Oh, Captain Canfield . . . I didn't mean . . . I wasn't suggesting . . ."

He gave that throaty chuckle again, and Carrie realized that he'd been teasing her. "Shouldn't we dispense with the 'Captain Canfield' and 'Miss Kingston,' Carrie?" he said smoothly. "After all, I am a close friend of the Morrisons."

"If you wish. Of course."

She moved a pace away, turning once more toward the dark stretch of lawn that swept out to the hedges and the road beyond. Her hand moved nervously to the lace that edged the small round collar of her dress, a blue challis print that buttoned primly to her chin.

"Let me see now," Canfield said. "You were talking to yourself a moment ago. What was it you said?"

"Oh, it was nothing," she said quickly. "I was just thinking out loud."

" 'I'll do *something!*' That was it, wasn't it? Let me guess . . ." His teeth gleamed in the moonlight, the perfect bones of his face highlighted, framed by the thick, curling hair. "I'll wager there's a man behind that statement."

"Certainly not, Captain Can—" she caught herself at the chiding slant of his eyebrow, "I mean . . . Beau. I was just thinking about . . . about Kingston's Landing."

"Your plantation?"

"Yes."

"I hear it's one of the finest upriver," he said.

"It *was*. And will be again if I have anything to say about it."

"Ah!" he said. "So that's where your passions lie."

It was a strange word to use—passions—but she smiled. "I suppose."

"It must have been very difficult for you to keep things going after your brother left for the army."

"Yes. Particularly after most of our slaves ran off. But if things go as I hope they will here, I'll be able to get a crop in next spring."

"You need money for that," he said, his voice knowing, quick.

"Yes," she admitted reluctantly, wondering how she had been drawn into such a personal conversation with a man who was virtually a stranger.

He puffed on his long, thin cigar and turned his head to blow the smoke away from her. "Abby has told me that Kingston's Landing is a beautiful place," he said.

"It is. The most beautiful place in the world," Carrie said softly.

"She's also told me that you're a most interesting young

96

woman, and I certainly agree.'' Those deep-set dark eyes regarded her for a long moment, and then he flicked the ash off the end of the cigar and tossed it away.

"I understand," he said, "that while you're in the city, you'll be staying at a friend's house on Dumaine Street."

"Yes."

He inclined his head slightly. "I'd like your permission to call."

Carrie stared at him in surprise. "I'm afraid not, sir," she brought herself up stiffly. "Under the circumstances I don't believe it would be at all proper. I . . . I thought you understood that I am engaged to marry J. D. Morrison."

"Oh, I do beg your pardon, Carrie," he said. "I fear I did not make myself clear." He seemed hesitant to say more, but then with the air of a man caught, plunged ahead. "It is . . . your sister Susannah whom I wish to call on."

"Oh . . ." Carrie said, and felt her cheeks flame in an agony of embarrassment. How could she have made such a fool of herself? She half-turned away in an effort to regain her composure.

She took a deep breath and steeled herself to face him again. "I must apologize for making such a silly mistake," she said.

He was the picture of solicitude. "I'm sure the fault was mine."

"It's just that . . . Susannah is very young yet. I had not thought—"

"Oh? I understood that she is only a couple of years younger than yourself."

"Well," Carrie stammered, "that's true, but—"

"And she is a most charming young lady."

Carrie nodded. "Yes, she is."

"I felt," Canfield said, "that in your brother's absence, you were the one to give your permission for me to call on her. And"—those sensual lips curved in an engaging smile as he inclined his head slightly toward her—"let me assure you that I would have every intention of conducting myself in an entirely proper manner so far as your sister is concerned."

Carrie was quiet for a moment, feeling thoroughly flustered. "Well," she said finally, "I don't suppose there's any harm in your coming to call on Suzy. So long as she doesn't have any objections.''

And even as she said it, Carrie was certain that her little sister would not only have no ojections to Beau Canfield coming to call, she would be ecstatic.

"Why, Beau Canfield,'' Susannah bubbled as Mattie showed their visitor to the sitting room, "what a pleasant surprise!''

Carrie suppressed a giggle. Her little sister had done nothing but fuss and fidgit in the three days since she'd met the handsome captain at the Morrisons' and he had announced his intention of calling. Now she was greeting him as if he were the last person she'd expected to see.

His smile was engaging. "I consider myself fortunate indeed to find such a charming young lady unoccupied.''

Susannah dimpled.

"It's nice to see you again, Carrie,'' he said.

"And you, Beau.''

His arms were filled with a large, beribboned box of confections and a bouquet of yellow roses. Any other man, Carrie thought, might have looked uncomfortable, but Beau seemed quite at ease.

"For you . . .'' He handed the pink box of candies to Susannah who cooed with pleasure.

"Oooh, how lovely of you, Beau! Shall I open it now?''

"Of course.'' He smiled as Susannah attacked the satin ribbons, then turned to Carrie, the bouquet extended. "A small remembrance for my charming hostess.''

"That wasn't necessary,'' Carrie protested, though she felt a rush of pleasure as she looked down at the exquisite roses. "Thank you. They're beautiful!'' She gave them to Mattie to take back to the kitchen and arrange in a vase. "Do come and sit down, Beau.''

She waved him into the comfortable room with its mint green silk love seats and white damask chairs. He chose one of the chairs nearest to the French doors.

"What a charming courtyard,'' he said, looking out over the pink bricks and neat flower borders.

"Yes, it is,'' Carrie said. "The whole house is lovely. It

belongs to our friend, Prosper Durant. Suzy and I are fortunate that we're able to use it during our stay in New Orleans."

"Oh, Carrie," Susannah trilled as she removed the lid from the huge box of confections, "just look!" She popped a small coconut bonbon into her mouth and ate it daintily. "Won't you have some?"

They both declined, Beau grinning. She put the box aside and came to join them.

"Tell me," she settled gracefully into the chair opposite Beau and gave him a coquettish smile, "have you been involved in some terribly exciting and dangerous intrigue since we saw you last?"

He laughed. "Hardly. I confess I've been enjoying myself shamelessly, because—" He paused slightly. "If certain things work out, I shall be back at sea shortly."

Susannah's face clouded. "You'll be leaving soon?"

He nodded. "But only for a short time. I come into New Orleans often."

She brightened. "These *certain things* . . . Do they have anything to do with—" Her voice dropped—"with your brave work that we discussed at the Morrisons'?"

"Suzy!" Carrie chided, taking a quick look out into the hall to make sure that Mattie had gone back to the kitchen. "I'm sure Beau would prefer not to discuss his activities with us."

He held up a hand. "It's quite all right. I know you're aware of how much is at stake. And after Seth's and Abby's assurances, I trust the two of you as I trust them. But the truth is my work involves other people of whom I have no right to speak. Besides, I have nothing to talk about at the moment. I just know that our Confederate wounded are in need of medicines and if I am successful in some rather delicate negotiations here . . ." He left the rest unsaid but Susannah's eyes blazed with admiration.

"You . . . you will be careful, won't you?" Her voice quivered.

"My dear Susannah," he said lightly, "I am always careful."

Her sister's expression was terribly earnest and Carrie thought it best to change the subject. "I think some tea would be nice," she said. "I'll just go have Mattie make us some."

"Oh, we don't want any tea, do we, Beau," Susannah said

willfully. "Perhaps . . ." She blushed as she looked at her gentleman caller. "Perhaps you'd like to walk in the courtyard?"

"Why, I can't think of anything I'd rather do," he rejoined. "That is," he turned toward Carrie, "if we have your sister's permission."

Carrie hesitated only a second. "Of course," she said.

But moments later, she felt a vague unease as she watched them stroll along the brick path, headed toward an inviting scrolled iron bench in the shade of two huge old magnolia trees. Beau made her feel uncomfortable. He was too handsome, his features too perfect, along with all his other charms. It was impossible not to respond to him. How on earth could Suzy, who was still such a baby, be expected to keep her head in the face of attentions from such a man? He was older. Obviously worldly. A blockade runner to boot.

She settled herself into the chair nearest the door so that she could keep an eye on them. Too bad, she thought wryly, that he didn't have at least a slight crook in his nose or a heaviness about the jawline. It might make him less overwhelming.

7

CARRIE STOOD ON THE BANQUETTE IN FRONT OF THE TATE Bank of New Orleans and took a deep breath. There was no reason at all to be nervous, she assured herself. This was usually a man's business, but since the war women had done many things that they hadn't been called upon to do before. And she could handle this. Especially now that she was sure the night with Rance Stewart would have no lasting effect on her life. Thank heaven it was really over. And she must try to forget that it had ever happened. She must get on with the most important thing—getting Kingston's Landing back on its feet again.

She had to make a good impression on Leroy Tate. She smoothed at her skirt with hands clad in her best silk gloves, straightened her straw bonnet, checked the fetching bow tied beneath her chin. A gentleman on his way out swept off his hat and smilingly held the door for her.

Trying to show more confidence than she felt, she swept into the bank with its twin rows of teller's cages and wide green window shades pulled halfway down against the afternoon sun. There was a desk behind an oak railing where a clerk worked, and Carrie made her way to the man who sat, round-shouldered and squinting, scratching numbers onto the ledger pages before him.

"Excuse me, sir. I would like to see Mr. Tate, please. Tell him that Miss Kingston is waiting."

"Certainly, Miss. Won't you have a seat." He bobbed his head and disappeared through a door in back of him.

In barely a moment, Leroy Tate was there, bespectacled and balding. "Miss Kingston," he said. "Miss Carrie Kingston, isn't it?" And at Carrie's nod: "Do come in."

He swept the railing gate open and showed her into his office, seating her in the big leather chair across from his desk.

"This is an unexpected pleasure," he said. And once he had settled into his own chair, he leaned forward, his heavy-jowled face solicitous. "And what can I do for you, Miss Kingston?"

In a clear and straightforward manner, Carrie informed him of Etienne Moreau's death, to which he gravely offered his sympathy.

"Then you've come about the settling of the estate?" he said.

"That's right."

"Your brother is . . . away?"

"George Pierre is with the Confederate Army," she said.

"Of course. I had heard that. No problem. I can see to everything for you."

He got up, went to a long row of cabinets in the back of the room, pulled out a heavy, deep drawer, and began to search through it. Carrie waited nervously. The room smelled musty, like old books.

At last he found what he was looking for and came back with a thick envelope, the contents of which he looked through quickly.

"As I thought, Miss Kingston, Mister Moreau's will leaves everything to you and your brother and sister. The house known as Maisonfleur and everything in it, as well as the land immediately surrounding."

Carrie quickly informed the banker that Maisonfleur had been burned to the ground.

"Oh, that's too bad. Such a lovely old house. I was there once. With my uncle. Well"—he ran a hand over the sparse hair atop his head—"he had a third interest in the lands that originally made up the Maisonfleur plantation. Of course, your father owned the other two-thirds, which came to your brother at the time of his death. There is a little money . . ."

He scanned the records, calculated quickly, and then wrote the amount on a piece of paper and shoved it across the desk to Carrie.

She looked at the figure with a certain resignation. She had already guessed that Uncle Etienne had very little left. What there was would help them to get by a while longer, but it certainly wouldn't finance a crop at Kingston's Landing.

"There are some formalities to be seen to," Tate was saying. "Give me a week or two to clear it up."

"Mr. Tate," she plunged in, "there is something else."

Calmly and in detail she told him of her plans for Kingston's Landing. He listened, at first with a look of astonishment, and later with a small gleam of admiration in his eye.

"I've made inquiries," she said finally, "and I'm told that there are blacks here in New Orleans willing to do plantation work for four or five dollars a month. I don't see how I could get by with fewer than twenty or thirty men at the very least. That, with the other expenses I've spoken of, means that I need to borrow several thousand dollars from your bank."

Finished, she looked unflinchingly into Leroy Tate's eyes, and he leaned back in his chair and surveyed her for a long moment, elbows propped on the arm rests, fingertips touching. He drew a deep breath. "I must say, you are your father's daughter, Miss Kingston."

She smiled.

"Frankly, if any other woman had come to me with such a proposition, I would have had a hard time not laughing, but . . . You've got me darned near convinced that you could do it!"

"I can. I know I can," Carrie said eagerly. "My father taught me everything there is to know about running a sugar plantation."

Tate looked at her again, played along his upper lip with a bony finger. "My Uncle Rhymer, who as you know founded this bank, thought an awful lot of your daddy. He always said Adam Kingston was not only the best businessman he ever saw but also one of his close personal friends."

"I know," Carrie said. "That's why I came here."

"Lord, Lord . . ." Tate got up and paced the length of the floor and back. "I wish I could help you."

"Mr. Tate . . . I don't understand," Carrie said, a small, cold knot of nervousness growing bigger in her throat.

"The fact is," the banker sat back down, "there's no money for loans. Not at this bank or any of the others. You see"—he lowered his voice slightly as if fearful of being overheard—"when it was obvious that New Orleans would be captured by the Union Army, we sent all the gold and silver out of the city by rail to keep it from falling into the hands of the enemy. Then with the arrival of General Butler, Confederate money was declared worthless, which left us with only greenbacks in reserve. I'm afraid the banks of New Orleans are in no better shape than other businesses here. I'm sorry, Miss Kingston."

"Oh . . ." For a moment, Carrie had to fight to keep the tears back, but then she lifted her head high. "I understand, Mr. Tate," she said. "That means I'll have to find it elsewhere." She rose, managing a half-smile. "I do thank you for your help in the matter of my uncle's estate. Good day, sir."

She was almost to the door when he stopped her.

"Miss Kingston . . . wait a moment."

She turned back to find him standing, hands braced against the smooth oak desk. "There might be a way. Private sources, perhaps. I . . . I could at least make inquiries."

"Oh, would you, Mr. Tate?" she said earnestly.

He smiled. "Of course. It may take a while. And I'm not promising anything . . ."

"I understand," she assured him.

"Can you stay on in New Orleans for a while?"

"Of course. For as long as necessary. And I do thank you so much, Mr. Tate." She felt her lips tremble, for a moment revealing the fierce hope that this small offer had awakened in her. Clearly touched, he straightened his spectacles and self-consciously came forward to offer his arm.

"I'll do my very best, Miss Kingston," he said, as he escorted her out onto the banquette and handed her up into the buggy that Prosper Durant had made available to her and Susannah. And it was only after Lafitte had touched the reins lightly to the sorrel mare's back to put the vehicle in motion that Leroy Tate turned and went back into the bank.

Lafitte, in his usual dignified black suit, skillfully guided the horse through the narrow streets. The sun shone on the fine old stuccoed buildings with their intricate iron-lace balconies. Vegetable carts moved toward the French Market as in the old days. Carriages and buggies maneuvered past each other. A fat Negro woman strolled along the banquette, offering her pralines for sale in singsong gombo, that lovely sounding patois that the slaves of the early Creoles had originated. It was almost like the New Orleans Carrie remembered and loved, except for the Yankees. They were everywhere.

One tall and lank-haired soldier stepped off the banquette to cross the street, swept off his cap, and winked at her. She jerked her chin up, gave him a frosty look, and turned away, then held her breath and trembled inwardly as she remembered General Butler's "Woman Order." Abby Morrison had told her that some women had actually been accosted on the streets.

She stole a quick look and was relieved to see that the Yankee was merely grinning and continuing on his way.

Once on Royal Street, Lafitte pulled up in front of the dressmaker's shop where they had left Susannah earlier and climbed down to assist her to the banquette. The sun was high overhead.

"Why don't you wait down there in the shade, Lafitte. If I know my sister, this is going to take a while." And as the black man grinned and did as she said, Carrie turned to the dressmaker's shop that had once belonged to Prosper's wife, Jeanette.

Carrie remembered her as a beautiful, tall woman with caramel skin and white teeth, her head always bound in a brilliant-colored tignon. She had wasted away from a terrible malignancy in her breast, and when the news of her death came, Mama had cried. Carrie could remember that so well. Mama's beautiful green eyes with their golden speckles had filled with tears, and she had turned away to weep softly into her handkerchief until Papa had taken her into his arms to comfort her. They had left immediately to come down to the city and be with Prosper.

Now the shop was owned by Madame Louisa Costeau, who had once been an apprentice to Jeanette Durant. She was small and quick with a heart-shaped face and skin the color of milk chocolate, though it was clear from her features that she had almost as many white ancestors as black.

"Mademoiselle Kingston," she greeted Carrie at the door as the entrance bell jingled merrily, "how fortunate that you have arrived! You can help your sister decide whether she wants tucks or ruffles on the bodice here." She gestured toward the table where Susannah was bent over an open book of fashion prints. Other tables and shelves along the wall were stacked high with multicolored bolts of materials, cards of laces, bindings, and buttons.

"Carrie, I love this one! Look!" Susannah pointed to a dress with a yoke that formed a deep V in the front and revealed a good bit of neck and bosom.

"Oh, Suzy . . . I don't know."

Madame Louisa smiled. "A lovely narrow ruffle right there at the neckline would make the dress eminently suitable for Mademoiselle."

"Oh . . ." Susannah pouted.

"Just a little one," Madame coaxed, her forefinger and thumb showing the exact amount intended.

"That'll be perfect," Carrie said. They looked at the materials Susannah was considering and finally decided on a yellow checked silk taffeta and a soft blue challis.

Susannah tilted her head, her pretty face flushed with happiness. She loved being in town and at the dressmaker's. "Are you *sure* I can't have three new dresses instead of two? I really need them."

Carrie remembered how little money they had left and shook her head reluctantly. "I'm sorry, Suzy."

"Well then," her sister persisted, "why don't you get something for yourself, Carrie? I don't know when you've had anything new."

"No, I'm fine," Carrie said. But she couldn't help sneaking a long look at herself in the full-length, gilt ormolu mirror that was mounted on a stand and could be tilted back or forth as needed.

She'd had the green silk dress she was wearing for over two years now, but it was still quite stylish. It hugged her waist to show off its smallness, and though the bodice was cut quite modestly, it did outline her breasts beautifully. The neckline curved just low enough to reveal a stretch of smooth white throat. The cuffs were beginning to wear a tiny bit. But not badly.

"You know"—Madame Louisa stood back to survey her— "that dress is really lovely. It shows off your figure to advantage. But . . ." She went to one of the worktables against the wall and came back with a length of soft ecru lace. "Look." She gathered a bit of it around Carrie's wrist, and they both studied the effect in the mirror. "Do you see what I mean?" The cuffs were like new. "A touch here . . . and here . . ." She caught up the material of the skirt to make two small flounces on either side and arranged the lace so that it peeked through. "And *voilà!*"

Carrie smiled in spite of herself. "It's very nice. But really—"

"It would cost very little, Mademoiselle. The truth is, there are many ladies in New Orleans who are refurbishing their old wardrobes these days instead of buying new things. A new lace collar here, a touch of ruching there." She picked up Carrie's straw bonnet, which was lying on the table, held a wide strip of white ruching to the underside of the brim, and put it on Carrie's head.

Carrie looked at herself in the mirror. Her hair spilled out from the close-fitting bonnet, curled in small tendrils about her cheeks, and the white ruching framed her face, brought out that hint of red in the dark tresses.

She laughed, suddenly self-conscious. Susannah, who had wandered over to look at the cards of buttons, wasn't the only one with cheeks pink from excitement. Her own cheeks were rosy as could be, her eyes shining gold. It would be lovely to have something new.

"Are you sure," she said, feeling guilty already, "that it wouldn't cost too much?"

"Positive," Madame Louisa said. "I tell you what to do. Bring over several of your dresses, and we'll see what can be done with them. All of it together will be less than half the cost of one new garment."

Carrie took a deep breath. "All right," she said. "I'll do it."

When Susannah had chosen the buttons she wanted, they gathered up their things, made their goodbyes, and went outside to signal to Lafitte, who was waiting patiently down the street in the shade.

"Oh, I do wish," Susannah said plaintively once they were headed back toward the house on Dumaine Street, "that I could have had one of my new dresses for tomorrow afternoon. Beau is taking me to LeGallienne's Sweet Shop, and I want to look my absolute *best.*"

"You'll look fine in your pink taffeta," Carrie said.

Beau Canfield had called twice now, and Susannah was beside herself with happiness even at the mention of his name. Carrie's unease was deepening.

"Suzy," she said carefully, "I know that you're enjoying the attentions of Captain Canfield, but . . . Do remember, honey, sometimes it's better to go slowly until you really get to know a person."

"You're talking about Beau?" Her sister bridled.

"Well . . ."

"I *do* know him!" Susannah set her small mouth stubbornly. "He's the bravest man I ever knew! A man who risks his life to aid the Confederacy!"

Carrie sighed. "Yes, I know. But, Suzy, you're still very young. A man like Beau might—"

"Take advantage of me?" Susannah demanded, her delicate eyebrows knitting. "He would never think of such a thing! He's too much of a gentleman!" She gave her head a toss that set the tawny curls dancing. "I do believe you're jealous, Carrie Kingston! Jealous because Beau prefers me to you!"

The sting of the words caused Carrie to catch her breath. "That's not true," she said softly, but her sister stared straight ahead, bright spots of color at each cheekbone.

They did not speak for a moment. The hoofbeats of the mare sounded hollow against the cobblestones, and always the good servant, Lafitte pretended not to have heard and whistled an old gombo tune.

Suddenly Carrie felt a small tug at her elbow and turned to find Susannah, green eyes filled with tears.

"Oh, Carrie, I'm sorry. I didn't mean that."

Carrie hugged her sister quickly. "I know you didn't."

"It's just that you always try to treat me like a baby . . . and I'm much more grown-up than you think. I'm quite able to conduct myself properly with Beau Canfield or any other man."

She had moved nearer to Carrie on the buggy seat, as near as their hoops would allow. And Carrie was reminded of how they used to sit close together and talk when they were little girls. She squeezed her sister's hand.

She had to admit that Susannah did seem more grown-up since Beau Canfield had announced his intention to come calling. She even sounded more grown-up when she talked. And Carrie hadn't seen her little sister mismanage her crinoline even once in the last two weeks. Still, she would insist on the proprieties.

The next morning, she took Mattie aside. "You know that this afternoon Captain Canfield is taking Miss Suzy to the Sweet Shop?"

Mattie nodded.

"Well, I want you to chaperone. You can keep a suitable distance, but you are always to have Miss Suzy and Captain Canfield in sight. Do you understand?"

"Indeed I do, Miss Carrie," Mattie said. "You can depend on me."

Carrie nodded. "We have to take care of her whether she wants us to or not."

Mattie had been running the feather duster over the mantel, but now she stayed her arm, narrowed her eyes. "You know, Mama always told me you got to be careful of a sportin' man. And I got it in my head that that's just what Cap'n Canfield is . . . a sportin' man. Do you think so, Miss Carrie?"

Carrie observed the serious expression on Mattie's pretty face and didn't know whether to laugh or be annoyed. "Wherever do you get such ideas, Mattie? Captain Canfield is a close friend of the Morrisons' and he's been perfectly charming to Miss Suzy and to me. I just feel that, war or no war, we must do things properly.''

"Yes, Miss Carrie," Mattie said and went back to her dusting.

8

PROSPER DURANT, RESPLENDENT IN A DEEP BLUE VELVET WAIST-coat beneath a superbly fitted white jacket, huge cameo breastpin in place, leaned forward in his chair to accept the cup of steaming coffee lightened with milk and dusted with cinnamon.

"I think you'll like it," Carrie said. "It's even better with pure cream, but Mattie couldn't get any at the market this morning."

They were in the sitting room at the house on Dumaine Street. The small walnut teatable between them was exquisitely inlaid with patterns of flowers and butterflies.

"Delicious!" Prosper announced after his first sip. "I shall have to get Delphine to make some for me."

Carrie put the silver pot back on the tray. "Prosper," she said, "I've been meaning to talk to you about the silver here at the house. Abby Morrison told me that General Butler has ordered that it be confiscated. Shouldn't this, and the other pieces here, be hidden away in a safe place?"

Prosper's expressive eyebrows rose. "It is quite true about the confiscation order, but"—he paused for a moment as if considering his coffeecup—"you are overlooking one thing, *ma chère*."

"And what is that?" Carrie asked, puzzled.

"The Northerners claim that they are fighting the war to

alleviate the plight of the Negro, among other things. The Yankee officials here hold people of color in a favored light. They would touch nothing in this house.''

"Oh," she said, embarrassed, "I should have realized."

"It is quite all right." He grinned. "It is one of the few times that my ancestry has proven to be an advantage. And one must take what advantage one can when dealing with the likes of General Butler."

His matter-of-factness put Carrie at ease again. "I suppose so," she said.

He sipped at his coffee, again nodded his approval. His waxed mustache was glossy in the light spilling through the French doors from the sun-drenched courtyard. He took up his cup and went to look out at Susannah, who was leaning toward a big macaw in a wicker cage hung in the shade of a vine-covered lattice. The bird had been left, at Susannah's request, when Prosper moved his things to the apartment above his salon.

"Tell me," he asked heartily, "is Susannah enjoying her stay in the city?"

"Oh, very much," Carrie said, sighing as she came to stand beside him, looking out at her sister who was fetchingly attired in a morning dress of pale green muslin.

"Captain Canfield?" Prosper said knowingly.

"He is very attentive. It worries me."

"Do you have reason for that?" The dark eyes were filled with immediate concern.

"She's so young . . . And he's a very attractive man."

"Are you sure," Prosper said gently, "that you are not being overly protective of your little sister? She has reached an age when she is sure to attract the attention of men. And are you," he teased, that twinkle in his eye once again, "such an old engaged woman that you have forgotten?"

Carrie laughed. "Perhaps you're right. But if Leroy Tate arranges a loan for me, I'll be going back to Kingston's Landing as soon as possible. I had planned to leave Suzy here with the Morrisons . . . but maybe I should take her back with me."

Prosper shook his head, frowned. "I think that it would be unwise for either of you to go back now. I heard that another plantation upriver was looted and burned only recently. It was said to be by jayhawkers."

"What place was it?" she said anxiously.

Prosper shook his head. "It was owned by some people named Demanche, I believe."

Carrie sighed. "I know the place. It's up above the Gayerre plantation." She turned back into the room to pace nervously. "All the same," she said stubbornly, "if I can get the money, I have to get my crop in."

"You cannot plant a crop until spring," Prosper pointed out calmly. "At least remain here in New Orleans until then. I am sure it is what your father would wish you to do."

"Oh, Prosper . . . I don't know. There are things that need to be seen to at home."

"Benjamin and Chloe are very capable."

"Yes, they are. But we're imposing on you here. I wouldn't want to continue to do that."

"*Imposing?* How can you say such a thing! It has been my intention to move back to the apartment above the salon for some time now. And if you weren't here, this house would simply be closed, and forlorn, and sad." He cocked one dark eyebrow at her. "Promise me that you will consider very carefully staying on here until spring. Promise . . ." he coaxed.

She smiled in spite of herself and gave in. "Very well, I promise that I will think about it very carefully. And meanwhile I will wonder how I can ever repay you, my dear Prosper, for all your kindness to Suzy and me."

"Now let me think." He put a long finger up to his face and narrowed his eyes as if in deep contemplation. "I have it!" he burst out, grinning. "You can come to tea! Next Thursday afternoon."

"Oh, Prosper . . ."

He sobered. "You know, that is really a very good idea. My Jeanette and I used to have people in to tea on Thursdays. It was lovely."

As he talked about the old days, Carrie noticed the lines that seemed a little deeper in his face, the strongly etched furrows from nose to mouth. And for the first time, she caught the glint of a silver hair or two among the dark ones.

"You loved her very much, didn't you?" she said. The words just seemed to come of their own volition, and for a moment she was afraid that she had presumed too far. But then he turned to her, the usually twinkling eyes filled with an old pain.

"I adored her," he said. Then he smiled, and the pain receded. "That is one of the reasons it would be so nice to have Thursday afternoon teas again. It would remind me of her, and I love being reminded of my Jeanette."

He began to walk back and forth as he talked, his jaunty self once again. "You can bring Susannah . . . and even her Captain Canfield if he would care to come." He shrugged. "The color line is very rigid where social gatherings are concerned, though Jeanette and I used to entertain some of the cream of Creole aristocracy at our teas. Pupils of mine. Of course, we would not have been welcome in their homes. It was always understood. I shall never forget how shocked the guests were to see Jeanette and me at the ball that your father gave to celebrate your brother George Pierre's birth. Adam was not daunted in the least, but we left after paying our respects."

Prosper had said it all without the slightest self-pity, but Carrie suddenly caught a glimpse of what it would be like to be a person of color and be discriminated against because of it.

"I'm sorry," she said softly.

"Oh, do not be." There was a look of surprise on his face. "I have had an extraordinarily rich and full life."

He stood there with a quiet dignity, and she realized that what he'd said was true.

"Now," he went on, "as I said, if Canfield wishes to come, by all means bring him. I shall see what I think of him as a suitor for Susannah. And"—his eyes flashed with a new thought—"I have taken on a pupil or two recently. I might invite one of them to join us."

"I thought your retirement was definite," Carrie chided.

"Well . . ." he hedged, "I shouldn't want my bones to get creaky from inactivity. I am not ready to give up and sit in a rocking chair yet."

Carrie laughed.

"Perhaps," he said, "you would consent to act as the hostess on Thursday?"

"I would love to."

"Splendid!" He placed his empty cup on the tea tray. "Then with that settled, I shall stop and say goodbye to Susannah and then be on my way. Until Thursday, *ma petite*."

Abby Morrison greeted Carrie at the front door, her face strained and set, her eyes red from weeping.

"Mother Morrison! I came as quickly as I could! As soon as old Thomas gave me your message!" Carrie gripped the older woman's hands in hers as a terrible thought crossed her mind. "It's not J. D.? Have you heard something about J. D.?"

"No, no," Abby was quick to reassure her. "Forgive me for frightening you so. I just felt the need to talk to someone . . . and you, Carrie, have always been so sensible, so mature for your age. Sometimes I forget that you're only a young girl."

"I'm glad you sent for me," Carrie assured her quickly. "But what is it? What's wrong?"

They stood in the front hallway with its waxed floorboards and tall case clock. The house girl, on a low stool, was polishing the brass wall lamps with a cloth. Abby cast a furtive look toward her.

"Come, let's go out onto the gallery," she said. "It's cooler out there."

Carrie followed along, unable to imagine what had put Abby into such a state. It was shortly after noon, and the sun was high, bearing down mercilessly from a glassy blue sky. Abby, her shoulders stiffly erect, led the way to the far end of the verandah where a magnolia shaded cypress chairs cushioned with sun-faded, pink-flowered pillows.

"Honestly," Abby said as they sat down, "Seth keeps telling me that I mustn't talk in front of her. We always used to talk . . ." Her lips trembled. "I don't understand any of it. I walk into my house, and it's the same. The shops along Royal Street haven't changed. Jackson Square hasn't changed. But there are gunboats out there on the river . . . and soldiers everywhere . . . and I can't talk in front of my own house slave anymore . . . I can't use my silver."

"Mother Morrison, what's happened?" Carrie stopped her.

She turned pale blue eyes to Carrie. "Seth has been summoned to appear at General Butler's headquarters on Monday morning.''

"Whatever for?"

"We're not sure. He thinks it's about the loyalty oath.'' Abby plucked nervously at the carved ivory pin at her throat. "He's not the only one who's been ordered to appear. Many of his friends and acquaintances got the same summons. Mack Carter, who owns the big dry goods store on Chartres Street. Leroy Tate. Bradley Cunningham. Brother Brighton from the church. Even poor old Ephraim Skaggs. He owns the tobacco factory, you know.''

Carried nodded.

"All this loyalty oath business started a while back. I think it was about July. It was another of Butler's orders.''

"I know. You told me.''

Abby went on as if she hadn't heard her. "Order #41, I believe he called it. He has numbers for everything. Anyway, it directed all New Orleans citizens to take an oath of allegiance to the United States Government. Went on and on about not forcing anyone to do something that was such a *privilege*.'' Her mouth drew down scornfully. "We thought it was the same kind of harassment as the 'Woman Order.' No one could believe that he would actually enforce it.''

"And how do you know that he's going to now?'' Carrie said.

"Have you seen today's *Times*?''

Carrie shook her head. She had thought she would stop on her way to Prosper's tea this afternoon and get the *Picayune*.

"It says that General Butler has ordered that anyone not complying with the order by the end of September must register with the military government—''

"The end of September! That's only three weeks away,'' Carrie interrupted.

Abby nodded, looked steadily at her. "And they must present a list of everything they own, every possession.'' Her underlip trembled again. "What do you think that means, Carrie?''

"I don't know,'' Carrie said slowly, wishing she could say something comforting. "Maybe it *is* just more harassment.''

"Perhaps they'll send us to Ship Island,'' Abby said, her voice rising slightly.

"No," Carrie said firmly. "Now you're jumping to conclusions, Mother Morrison. They surely can't put everyone in New Orleans on Ship Island. Wait until Monday. See what they tell Mr. Morrison. We'll know more after that." Carrie's voice deliberately held more reassurance than she felt. In truth, she was wondering how far the Yankee general would go. Would he dare to imprison people or confiscate their properties because they wouldn't swear to a false oath? Surely even the Yankees wouldn't do that.

She looked away to hide the anger she felt, let her eyes follow the line of flowers along the verandah wall and move beyond to the herb garden and the gently rounded clumps of sweet shrub. There in the still, hot air, a cold unease gripped her. How could she doubt the lengths they would go to? She was almost certain that Yankees had killed Uncle Etienne, no matter what Rance Stewart had said. She'd seen that flash of blue, seen the Yankee cap.

"I hate them," Abby said. "Hate them all. But I hate General Butler most." She lowered her voice. "Some of the women I know say they take his pictures from the newspapers and put them in the bottom of their chamber pots."

She leaned her head back against the pillow and closed her eyes. The lids were nearly translucent. "I wish," she said, "that Beau hadn't gone out of town just now. He's so clever. He would know what to do."

Carrie didn't answer. Despite the shade, she could feel the fine perspiration bead along her upper lip, dampen the hollow between her breasts. A fat yellow bee buzzed from one creamy magnolia blossom to another. And Abby's voice came again, small, almost detached from her.

"I'm frightened, Carrie."

Carrie's fingers clenched, nails digging into the soft flesh of her palms. "I know. I am, too. But we must never let them know that. Never give in to them, no matter what they do. We must show them what Southern women are made of."

They were quiet for a moment, the buzzing of the bee audible. From somewhere in back of the house, Penelope called to old Thomas to fetch in some wood for the cookstove.

"You're right, of course," Abby said. "But all the same" —she managed a half-smile—"I'll be glad when this war is over."

Hair pinned high, Carrie stepped into the copper tub Mattie had prepared for her and sank down into the cool water. "Oh, Mattie, it's wonderful." She sighed, slipping down as far as she could, feeling that delicious coolness rise above her rosy pink nipples, splashing water lightly against her throat and face.

"Yes, Miss Carrie. Nothin' better on a hot day."

Mattie picked up Carrie's discarded clothing and carried it away. Carrie leaned her head against the high copper back of the tub and closed her eyes. The curtains were drawn at her bedroom windows, which lent a soft light and a quietness to the room, but Abby Morrison's disturbing news nagged at her.

Poor Abby. Carrie could see her still, see the nervous fingering of the pin at her throat, hear that helpless and bewildered trembling in her voice.

Fortunately she'd had a meeting of the ladies' sewing circle at the church to attend this afternoon. That would help take her mind off it for the time being. And Susannah, who had gotten so caught up in patriotic fervor since meeting Beau Canfield, had sent her regrets for Prosper's tea party and elected to go along with Abby to sew for the Confederate boys at the front.

Carrie sighed once again and wished she'd had Lafitte stop off for a newspaper on her way home from the Morrisons'. How serious was this loyalty oath business? she wondered. From what Abby had said, only very influential men had been ordered to appear on Monday. Seth owned the distillery. Leroy Tate was one of the leading bankers. What did it all mean? Would the Yankees dare try to force loyalty oaths on the people of New Orleans? And if they did, what would be the penalties for those who refused?

Mattie came back into the room with a bar of lavender-scented soap, and Carrie lathered herself while the Negro girl laid out fresh stockings, pantalettes, and a camisole.

"Don't be hurryin' now," Mattie said. "Ain't no use takin' a cool bath if you goin' to hurry and get yourself all hot again."

"No, I won't," Carrie said, "but I don't want to be late."

She rinsed herself thoroughly and then stepped out of the tub into the big white towel that Mattie held for her.

"Oh, Mattie," she said plaintively, her morning with Abby still on her mind. "I don't know why this wretched war had to be."

"I don't neither, Miss Carrie. But Solomon says that nothin' ain't ever goin' to be the same again."

Solomon was a great, strapping young Negro who belonged to the Marchands next door and was obviously taken with Mattie. And it seemed Mattie was not exactly discouraging his attentions.

"Well, with all due respect to Solomon, Mattie, I hope he's wrong," Carrie said.

"Yes, Miss," Mattie said dutifully.

Carrie dusted her smooth body with talcum powder, then slipped into her stockings and underwear and pulled on a pair of white kid, flat-heeled slippers.

"What dress you aimin' to wear, Miss Carrie?" Mattie asked.

"The lavender. I think it will be cooler."

Mattie brought the dress from the armoire and helped her into it, sliding it down over Carrie's wide crinoline and then fastening the hooks in back.

Carrie looked at herself in the mirror. The dress was one that Madame Louisa had refurbished for her, the material a delicate lawn of a light violet color. The skirt was flounced and ruffled, and Madame Louisa had caught it up here and there with small purple velvet bows. The tightly fitted bodice, which was cut rather low, was now joined to fine, cream-colored lace that swept up to Carrie's throat and was gathered to a purple neckband.

The effect was lovely, and Mattie clucked her approval as she pulled the pins from Carrie's hair and swept the brush through the shining chestnut length. She caught the tresses high on either side with combs and twisted the remaining cascade into a large flat coil at the back of her head. A tiny sprig of silk violets tucked just above one ear completed the coiffure.

Carrie looked at her reflection and drew a long sigh.

"What's the matter, Miss Carrie? Ain't I done your hair to suit you?"

"Oh, it's not that, Mattie. I was just thinking that I shouldn't have spent any money at the dressmaker's. Though"—she moved this way and that, and the skirt swirled about her—"it is pretty, isn't it?"

Mattie grinned. "It sure is. Besides, Miss Carrie, you know what Mama says. What's done is done, and they ain't no use worryin' about it."

Carrie pursed her lips, took a deep breath, and touched a drop of lavender water behind each ear. "You're right, Mattie." She laughed. "Have Lafitte bring the buggy around."

And as the girl sped away, Carrie resolved that at least for the rest of the afternoon, she would put all thoughts of money and loyalty oaths from her. She had promised Prosper to act as hostess, and it did seem a small thing to do for someone who had done so much for Suzy and her. She not only intended to go to the tea, she was determined to make it a grand success for Prosper's sake. Even if it turned out that only the two of them were there.

Prosper's salon was located on Conti Street a couple of blocks from the levee, and once there, Carrie said to Lafitte: "Monsieur Durant will see me home." And he touched his hat and clucked at the mare.

Carrie lowered her ruffled parasol and extended her hand to the ornate iron railing of the stairs that led up to the spacious apartment above the salon. Her foot was already on the bottom step when she heard the faint but unmistakable sound of metal on metal and a second later, the ebullient shout of Prosper Durant coming from the lower level. She smiled. He must still be with his pupil.

A closer inspection revealed that the big green door to the fencing salon was slightly ajar. She nudged it farther open and, encouraged by the sound of Prosper's voice, followed the narrow corridor to the first door on the right.

"Good! Good! Excellent! Give more play to the arm," Prosper shouted over the clang of steel.

After the dimness of the corridor, Carrie had to let her eyes adjust to the light that poured into the room from many windows and reflected off the highly polished surface of the wooden floor. It was a large open space, with swords of various kinds in a rack along one wall. Mirrors lined another.

Her eyes focused after a moment on Prosper and his pupil who were dressed in tight white pants and shirts with heavy pads to protect their chests, wire masks over their faces. The pupil was a big man, more than a head taller than Prosper, and yet he moved with surprising ease and grace.

Their feet, encased in light, rubber-soled shoes, made slight slapping sounds as they advanced and retreated, parried and thrust. Carrie could hear the sound of their breathing.

"Good movement!" Prosper sang out. "Again . . ." And the big man pressed, forcing Prosper slowly backward step by step, the clash of metal ringing with each blow. But in a moment, Prosper deftly twirled the end of his foil to turn his opponent's blade aside and in an instant had slipped the tip in to bend harmlessly against the wide, padded chest.

The big man shouted out in defeat, and they both laughed uproariously, their deep, masculine voices filling the place, bouncing off the walls.

"You are good, my friend! And getting better with each session!" Prosper was saying, but Carrie was staring at his pupil, caught by the sound of his laughter . . . that certain timbre in his voice.

She peered across the room at him, trying to see beneath the mask. There was something in that slim waist and broad chest tugging at her memory, something in the way he moved . . . that sureness.

She felt a sudden wild desire to turn and run back along the hallway, but it was too late. They had already seen her.

"Oh, *ma petite* . . . here you are! *Mon Dieu*, we have quite forgotten the time!" Prosper slipped his mask off. "Can you forgive us? Come, come, I want you to meet my friend and pupil. He is going to have tea with us today."

Carrie saw the man hesitate for just the barest instant and then follow Prosper. She stood as if she had lost the power to move as they traversed the short distance, and then as they drew abreast of her, the big man tucked his foil under one arm and pulled the wire mask back over the dark, thick head of hair and away. To her absolute horror, she found herself looking up into the clear gray eyes of Rance Stewart.

9

ALONE IN THE SOLARIUM WITH ITS PLANTS AND AIRY, CANE-backed furniture, Carrie paced nervously, her palms damp, her mind racing. To find Rance Stewart here at Prosper's was the last thing she had ever expected. And yet not quite twenty minutes ago she had looked up into those gray eyes as he'd drawled, "Well, Carrie . . . Miss Kingston . . . It's a pleasure to see you again." And Prosper had looked in astonishment from one to the other.

Had Rance known that she would be here? She couldn't tell. There had been that half-smile on his face, the quizzical slant of the eyebrows. What was sure, she told herself firmly, was that he was the last man on earth she ever wanted to see again. She hated him. There was no way she could ever forgive him.

She had been sorely tempted to make some excuse and leave, but she couldn't bring herself to do that to Prosper. She would simply have to see this through somehow. And at least she'd had this time to compose herself while the two of them freshened up and changed.

She heard them coming now and stopped her pacing, hurried over to stand beside a lovely potted fern that stood atop a reeded pedestal as if she'd been admiring the feathery fronds all along.

"*Ma chère*, I hope we did not keep you waiting too long." Prosper was once again his dapper self in a brocaded silk waist-coat and ruffled shirt, the cuffs of which showed to just the right degree beneath his jacket sleeves.

"Not at all. It's very pleasant here," Carrie said.

In spite of herself her eyes moved to Rance who was in full

120

dress uniform, dark blue frock coat, belted and sashed, brass buttons gleaming. The wide insignia straps at his shoulders had two gold-embroidered bars, to signify his captain's rank. His dark thick hair, neatly brushed, curled slightly at his sideburns and about his ears, as if still damp from washing. And as his eyes returned her gaze, there was a certain warmth in them, an unconcealed pleasure at seeing her again.

"I cannot believe it," Prosper said, as he pulled the bellcord for Delphine. "That the two of you should know each other." He lifted his hands palms upward and rolled his eyes heavenward. "Life is indeed surprising."

"Indeed," Rance said in that deep, resonant voice.

"I do hope that you made a good impression on your visit to Kingston's Landing," Prosper teased.

Carrie hesitated for only the barest second. "Captain Stewart behaved exactly as one would expect an officer and gentleman of the Union Army to behave."

Though Prosper seemed to miss the dryness in her voice, Rance lowered his head to stroke at the thick mustache. When he lifted his eyes to hers once again, she could not read them. Was it amusement she saw there? Or regret? The truth was, it did not matter to her, she told herself primly. All she wanted was to get this over with and never have to see Rance Stewart again.

"Sit down, sit down." Prosper shooed the two of them before him, and as they approached the white, cane-backed couch and the circle of chairs, Rance stepped aside to let her pass, and for a moment they were very close together. She caught a whiff of bay rum and a clean, man smell, and for some strange reason her knees started to tremble. She sat down quickly on the nearest turquoise cushion and made a great show of straightening the pretty flounces of her wide skirt.

Rance and Prosper sat in the chairs opposite her just as Delphine entered carrying a large tray, which she placed on the low table between them.

"Thank you, Delphine. That will be all for now," Prosper said.

Carrie surveyed the tray before her. "*Callas,*" she said as she saw the plate of delicate rice cookies. "I didn't think you could get them now. Mattie hasn't been able to find any."

Prosper grinned. "I have my sources."

There were other delicacies on the tray, small hot crab cakes, pecan-stuffed dates, and crisp pastries called palmettoes because they were shaped like the leaf of that plant. Carrie fixed a small plate for each of them and then poured the fragrant tea into thin china cups, grateful that she could keep her hands from trembling and that she could pass Rance his with hardly a glance.

"Too bad"—Prosper sampled a date, wiping his fingers carefully on the tiny linen napkin—"that Susannah could not come."

"How is Suzy?" Rance said.

"She's quite well," Carrie retorted, stirring her tea vigorously and feeling a decided resentment at his use of her sister's first name.

"You must give her my best," he said.

Carrie nodded coldly.

"Perhaps she can make it next week, and you could see her then, Rance," Prosper said, to Carrie's dismay. "Her gentleman friend may have returned to New Orleans by then."

"Gentleman friend?" Rance grinned. "So one of the local boys has fallen victim to Suzy's charm. I'm not at all surprised. She's a most endearing young woman."

"Hardly a local boy," Prosper put in. "The gentleman in question is one Beau Canfield who—"

"Canfield?" Rance cut him off, and there was something in his manner that caught Carrie's attention at once.

"Do you know him?" she asked.

"Not really," he answered slowly. "I've met him briefly. It's . . . just that the gentleman does seem a trifle sophisticated for a girl as young as Suzy. Though that's not for me to say, is it?"

"No." Carrie bridled. "It certainly is not! I happen to be delighted that Captain Canfield is calling on Suzy. He's . . . he's an extraordinary man!" She might have said more except for Prosper, who was regarding her with a slightly puzzled look.

She passed the cookies, though they hadn't finished the ones on their plates. Prosper tactfully changed the subject.

"I must tell you, Carrie, how I came to take Rance as a pupil." He launched into an account of their first meeting at the salon.

"I couldn't turn him down," he said finally. "He is remarkably good. The best big man I ever taught. Usually a smaller man has the edge, can move faster. But Rance . . .'' His eyes lit with approval. "It is a joy to work with him.''

"And how,'' Carrie asked in her politest voice, "did you happen to come to Prosper, Captain Stewart?''

He put his cup down, leaned back comfortably. "I've always been interested in fencing, Miss Kingston.'' There was a hint of amusement in his eyes as they conversed in such a proper and formal manner. "As a boy in Charleston, I took lessons. And then later when I spent some time in France, I studied there. However, I had always heard about the great Prosper Durant of New Orleans. When I found myself here, it seemed an opportunity too good to pass up, and I persuaded him to take me as a pupil.''

"Actually,'' Prosper said, eyes twinkling, "it was flattery such as that that persuaded me to come out of retirement.''

They launched into a discussion of the decline in interest for the ancient art, and all the while Carrie was conscious of Rance's eyes on her from time to time. She could almost feel his gaze as it lingered for a moment on the small tendrils of dark hair that had escaped to curl about her cheeks, or on the tightly fitted bodice of her gown. She was suddenly aware of the shadowy cleft between her breasts, which she was sure could be glimpsed through the fine lace. She wished fervently that she had worn the apricot silk with its high, opaque neckline . . . even if it would have been too warm.

She had all but lost track of the conversation when she realized that Prosper was speaking to her.

"Rance is formidable with the saber.'' He seemed to be explaining some earlier point. "His size and strength, not to mention skill, give him a great advantage.''

Rance chuckled. "It is a skill for which there's very little demand these days, I'm afraid. But I do like the challenge, the sheer power of it . . . unlike the French and Creoles who seem to prefer the épée and the foil. It may have something to do with my English forebears. Or with the fact that I'm an American. Are we not viewed by the rest of the world as aggressive? Perhaps even crude?''

He leaned forward and held his cup for Carrie to fill again.

"Forgive us, Miss Kingston," he said. "At times I'm afraid we men forget that such talk is boring to a lady."

"On the contrary," Carrie said, her eyes meeting his stonily. "I found that part about Americans particularly interesting." She replaced the teapot on the tray. "I have never found Southern gentlemen crude. Or perhaps I should change that to . . . only a few." When she saw the sudden tightening along his jawline, the cold darkening of the gray eyes, she knew that she was speaking recklessly, but she rushed ahead. "On the other hand, would you not agree that your General Butler seems to fit your description? He is certainly crude and aggressive . . . among other things."

"That is a view that many New Orleanians would share," Rance answered, rigidly controlled.

"And you, Captain Stewart," she pressed, "what is your view of the general?"

The steaming cup of tea, which Rance had not yet touched, was lowered to the tray. "As I told you once before, Miss Kingston, I am a soldier. I follow orders. General Butler is not accountable to me."

"Perhaps not," she said quickly, "but since you are his aide, can you possibly tell me why a group of leading businessmen have been summoned to appear before him on Monday? Seth Morrison, the father of my fiancé, is one of them."

Rance's head came up slightly. "Fiancé?"

"Yes." She looked directly at him and somehow felt a kind of satisfaction.

She found that her hand was trembling and put her cup down quickly, and in doing so saw Prosper's face, saw that quizzical, rather pleased expression, as if he'd just made some astonishing discovery. Annoyed with herself and with both men, she rose from the couch, moved to the lush potted ferns, and reached a hand out to the delicate blue blossoms of a lobelia that trailed from a hanging basket.

Rance seemed to have found his voice again and went on as if nothing had happened. "I don't know why Mr. Morrison and the others have been asked to appear on Monday. I am not the only one on General Butler's staff . . . and I'm certainly not privy to everything he does. But I would like to assure you, Miss Kingston, that though I may fulfill my duties as a soldier, I take no pleasure in whatever hardships the citizens of New Orleans have suffered as a result of the occupation.''

There was an awkward silence, which Prosper broke. ''Well, well,'' he said, ''I do believe that we should direct our conversation to a lighter subject. Do you not agree?''

And they did. They spoke of *callas*, and the French Market, and the opulence of the steamboats in prewar days. But finally Rance looked at his watch and rose.

''I regret I must leave,'' he said, ''but I have duty this evening.''

''Oh, too bad,'' Prosper said. ''We must do it again.''

''I would like that very much. It's been a pleasure.'' His eyes rested on Carrie for a moment. ''I have a hat around here someplace,'' he said.

Prosper pulled the bellcord. ''Delphine will bring it.'' But after a few moments and a second ring of the bell, Prosper opined that Delphine must have stepped out onto the back gallery for a moment. ''I shall get it myself. It will only take me a moment.'' And Carrie and Rance were left alone.

Avoiding his eyes, she rose nervously and went to toy once again with the lobelia, her back to him.

''Did you know I would be here?'' she asked after what seemed a long silence.

''No, I didn't. Prosper merely said that some friends of his were coming. I was as surprised as you were. But . . .'' he hesitated, ''I'd be lying if I said that I didn't welcome the opportunity to see you again.''

Carrie bit her lip, said nothing. And then suddenly she heard the sound of his boots as he moved toward her, felt him grasp her firmly and swing her around to face him.

She gasped, turning her face away, and yet somehow could not move as long as his hands were on her bare arms. She could feel each finger, could feel the strength of them, leashed for the moment.

A strange tremor pulsed through her, all the way to her toes, as he let go of one arm and gently cupped a hand beneath her chin, tilting her face back until she found herself looking up into those handsome features, the fine straight nose above that thick and dark mustache, the deep cleft mark in his chin. His eyes caught and held hers, though she willed herself to look away.

"I want you to know, Carrie," he said softly, earnestly, "that I never meant to harm you that night. Let me try to prove that to you."

For a moment she was all but mesmerized by the sound of his voice and those incredibly clear gray eyes looking into hers, by the smell of him, that clean man smell. And then, with a will born of desperation, she yanked her arm free and stepped back from him.

"I'll thank you never to mention that night to me again!" she said, her voice low and as brittle as ice.

He looked at her a long moment, and she tried to still the trembling deep within her.

"Very well," he said finally. "If that's what you wish."

Prosper had seen Rance Stewart out and now returned to sit opposite Carrie. "Well," he said, those black eyes dancing, mustache ends curled to jaunty points, "I do not know when I have enjoyed anything so much!"

"Yes. It was very nice," Carrie said, trying to meet his enthusiasm and failing miserably. Her hands were clasped tightly in her lap.

Prosper peered at her, and the smile on his face turned into one of apology. "I should have told you in advance who my pupil was. Forgive me. But I had no idea that the two of you had already met."

"It's quite all right."

He regarded her closely. "Would you like more tea? I shall have Delphine make a fresh pot."

"Thank you, no. But it was very good."

Prosper nodded and, with that enormous energy that always seemed present, rose and went to the wide windows to look out on the tiny garden below. "This afternoon made me think of your father. He used to come here often, you know. And later on, your *maman*."

Carrie nodded.

"I suppose that I should have mentioned before that one of my guests would be a Union officer. But in the old days"—he turned to her, and his eyes were alight with memories—"there was always an unlikely assortment of people at our teas. People who did not always fit socially on the outside. And yet it never seemed to matter here."

"But, Prosper . . . He's a Yankee!" The protest burst from her.

Prosper's eyebrows rose. "Oh?" he said. "I had always thought Charleston to be a part of the South."

Carrie drew a deep breath but remained silent. She was beginning to fear that she had revealed too much already.

Prosper sat across from her once again, and when he spoke, his voice was gentle and fatherly, but quite firm. "Rance Stewart is a Southerner who chose to fight with the North. He made that decision after long and painful searching of his deepest beliefs. And it has cost him dearly, *ma petite*. I have come to know him well these past months, and I would stake my life that he is a man of honor and decency. There are such men on both sides, you know."

"That . . . is a high recommendation," she said carefully, toying with one of the ribbons on her skirt. She wondered how honorable Prosper would think Rance Stewart if he knew what had happened that night at Kingston's Landing. But he would never know. No one must ever know.

"This is my land, too," he said gently. "My city. And I certainly did not welcome a conquering army. Though," he chuckled, "I may well be better suited to withstand the vicissitudes of history. My Negro ancestors were bought and sold and sent far from home, while my Creole forebears have known many flags. I am sure there must be elderly Creoles who still refuse allegiance to the American government and await the day when France reclaims her rightful property." Prosper laughed, and Carrie smiled in spite of herself.

"However," he sobered, "if you are truly offended by the presence of Rance Stewart, I shall not invite him to our teas again."

It was a tempting offer, but after all Prosper's kindnesses, she could not, she told herself, tell him whom he might invite to his own home. Besides, far too much had been said already, and if

127

Prosper entertained any suspicion about Rance and her, she wanted to lay it to rest once and for all.

"Oh, please," she said lightly, "I was simply surprised to find Captain Stewart here. I had not expected a Yankee officer. But I would have to admit that he is . . . an interesting man. It is unimportant one way or the other. By all means, have him again if you wish."

10

RANCE STEWART KNOCKED LIGHTLY AT THE TALL, PANELED OAK door of General Benjamin Butler's office and at the muffled "Come in," entered quietly to find the general, back turned, looking out the windows to the street below.

"Here are the papers you asked for, sir."

"Good, good. Put them on the desk there."

Rance put them on the oversized mahogany desk, which had been confiscated from the office of the elegant St. Charles Hotel.

"Is there anything else I can do for you, sir?"

"Yes. Hand me one of those cigars from the box there. Have one yourself if you like, Captain Stewart." He turned back into the room and settled himself in the big wing chair in the corner, his coat's double row of brass buttons straining over the considerable paunch. "Ah, it's been a damned satisfying morning, Captain," he said. His rather long, graying hair hung limply about his ears, the balding top of his head pink as a baby's in the light from the window.

"Is that so, sir?" Rance handed the general his cigar, then struck a sulphur match and held it while the older man puffed out clouds of white smoke.

When the cigar was glowing, General Butler waved him away. "Aren't you going to have one?" he demanded.

"Thank you, sir, not now."

"Well, then sit . . . sit."

It was in the nature of a command, and Rance winced inwardly. The general was in a talkative mood, and he knew from past experience that this was not always the easiest part of his duty.

"Had a dozen of the high muck-a-mucks of the city in this morning." Butler was already off and relishing his story as Rance reluctantly seated himself in the straight-backed chair nearby. "Old Skaggs . . . tobacco factory, you know. And Cunningham—heads one of the top brokerage firms. Seth Morrison and Leroy Tate. You know them, don't you?"

"Yes, sir. I know who they are," Rance said carefully, remembering what Carrie had told him at Prosper's on Thursday.

"Several others. So-called key men here. Oh, some of them were trying to brave it out. Seth Morrison faced me right down, the cocky little bastard. Said to me, 'I have a son in the Confederate Army, sir. Under the circumstances, I could not in conscience take a loyalty oath to the Union, or try to persuade others to do so.' Well, we'll see." Butler grinned. "Once he finds his tail in a crack, he just might change his tune."

He leaned back and puffed, his small eyes narrowed at the smoke. "The gentry are a worthless lot, so far as I can see, for all their airs. They have danced to a tune of their liking all these years, Rance, my boy, but now it's time to pay the fiddler. And some of them may find the cost damned high."

"Yes, sir," Rance said, trying to keep his face impassive.

Butler leaned forward suddenly. "By God, I keep forgetting. You're of that class yourself, aren't you, Stewart? But at least you"—he pointed his cigar—"had the good sense to choose the winning side. I'll have to say that for you. I was telling Major Barlow about you the other day. Good man, I said."

"Thank you, sir." Rance was thinking about Carrie, remembering the look on her face when she'd asked him if he knew why Seth Morrison had been summoned to General Butler's office. It was then that she had casually dropped the news about her fiancé. That must be the son Morrison had spoken of.

She had never mentioned a fiancé when he was at Kingston's

Landing. Never a word, goddammit. She might at least have said something. He wasn't in the habit of taking other men's women. Damn! It exploded inside him. Why couldn't he stop thinking about her?

Butler's great, snorting laugh resounded through the room, jarring Rance from his thoughts. "I tell you, Stewart, I had old Skaggs scared shitless," he was saying. "I made it clear to them that no less than the United States Congress demands that a loyalty oath be taken by penitent rebels before they are taken back into the good graces of the United States Government. And I told them they'd do well to spread the word.

"I'll tell you, Stewart"—he leaned forward and jabbed the air with the thick, black cigar—"they weren't a bit cocky when they left!"

Rance could feel the muscles in his jawline tighten into knots, but he steeled himself to say nothing. He had enlisted in the Union Army because he believed passionately that the Union must be preserved, whatever the cost. But he could hardly bear General Butler's gloating over the Southerners' humiliation. Fortunately he knew that there were better men in the Union Army, better officers. He had served under some of them.

"I don't understand these people, Stewart. Even the women are hellcats. Pullin' their skirts aside as they pass a soldier of the United States in the street. As if he was a pile of horse shit or something too revolting to risk brushing their petticoats against." Butler emitted an explosive sound of disgust and puffed harder on his cigar.

"Some of the women have shown a clear resentment of our presence here, sir," Rance said. "Though perhaps—"

"Did you hear what happened last week?" Butler cut him off. "A corporal was walking along Chartres Street after dark when a chamber pot was emptied on him from an upstairs window. He reported it at once, and a patrol was sent immediately to apprehend the guilty party, but with it being pitch dark and all, and the poor corporal being half-blinded by that filth, he wasn't able to point out the exact house."

Butler chewed at the end of his cigar, his face flushed with anger. "It was one of those 'genteel Southern ladies,' I know it was. And if I could find out which one, I'd send her down to

Ship Island for a spell. Let her load a few sandbags, and maybe she'd learn how to mind her manners!''

"I did hear about the incident, sir. It was . . . unfortunate." The whole thing struck Rance as ridiculous, and certainly not worth the hubbub it had created.

"Christ," Butler shook his head, "these people don't know when they're better off. This city has never been so clean. Looked like a pig sty when we arrived, but now I've got squads out cleaning the streets every day. Now we're giving them a chance to come back into the fold. It's a privilege to take an oath of loyalty to the United States of America!''

Rance was remembering Carrie and that lovely proud spirit of hers. She would probably die before anyone could *force* her to take such an oath.

"General Butler . . ."

"Yes?"

"Sir . . ." Rance cursed himself for a fool, knew that he was about to break his own rules. "Sir, with all due respect, the people here have great pride. It has not been easy for them to accept the occupation. Might it not be better to give them more time before pressing the loyalty oath? A few months, even, might make the difference."

General Butler straightened up in his chair and looked at Rance in amazement. "Captain Stewart, you are forgetting what we're here for! To secure and restore this area of the South to the United States of America!''

"Yes, sir," Rance said reluctantly.

"Oh, no. Don't think we can get soft with them, Stewart. They must be taught a lesson." He ground out the stub of his cigar. "Now let's get back to work. We have this damnable rebellion to put down! Right, Stewart?'' He chuckled.

"Yes, sir," Rance said, standing up immediately.

"Oh, Stewart"—the general wheezed audibly as he got to his feet—"before you go . . . Did you know that Major Barlow's wife and daughter arrived in New Orleans last week?''

"I believe I did hear something about that, sir."

"Yes. They came down by steamboat. Accompanied by two of our warships, of course. Got a few shells lobbed at them at

Vicksburg. Damned Johnny Rebs. Grant'll have them out of there by spring.

"Well, anyway," he went on, "my brother Jackson is having a large party at his home this evening, and Major Barlow and his womenfolk plan to attend. I suggested to him that you might like to escort his daughter."

"Well, sir, I—"

"She's a damned pretty girl, Stewart," Butler said, and there was a twinkle in those small, pouched eyes. "If I was thirty years younger . . ."

It was clear that the general was not giving him any room to say no. Besides, Rance thought, maybe a little relaxation was exactly what he needed. And for once, General Butler was right. Rance had seen Nora Barlow riding in a carriage with her father along Royal Street a few days after her arrival, and she *was* a damned pretty girl!

"Oh, how lovely!" Abby Morrison said, looking down from her box seat to the main floor of the theater where elegantly attired people moved toward their seats. "It seems so long since I've been to the Opera House."

Despite the attempt at enthusiasm, Carrie thought she could detect that note of strain that had been in Abby's voice so much lately. And though Seth Morrison smiled and reached over to pat his wife's hand, there had been about him an air of worried preoccupation for over a week, ever since his appearance before General Butler. He had tried to make light of the meeting, but Abby had confided to Carrie that she'd awakened several times in the dead of night to find him downstairs pacing the length of the library.

But now they were seated in a box at the sumptuous French Opera House at Bourbon and Toulouse Streets, with its brilliantly lit crystal chandeliers and deep red carpets. Musical sounds floated from the pit as the musicians started to tune up their instruments.

Susannah, in one of her prettiest new gowns, sat slightly in front of and to the right of Carrie; Beau Canfield, who had just returned to the city and was their host for the evening, beside her. "Oh, it's so exciting!" she said, her voice quivering with sheer pleasure. "You're just a darling, Beau! To do this!"

"Indeed you are, Beau Canfield," Abby put in. "It was very thoughtful of you."

"Not at all," Beau said quickly, his handsome profile emphasized in the reflected light, blond hair gleaming. "What man could resist sharing a box with three such lovely ladies? Don't you agree, Seth?"

Seth nodded as Beau, flawlessly dressed and sporting a large sapphire stickpin, leaned closer to whisper something for Susannah's ear alone. The girl giggled and blushed a deep pink.

Abby was leaning forward to survey the audience and pointing out a few familiar faces.

"Here, dear lady," Beau said, pulling a small, slim pair of opera glasses out of his jacket pocket and passing them to her, "do use these. You can see how lovely the ladies' gowns are."

Abby smiled her thanks and lifted the mother-of-pearl-covered glasses to her eyes, adjusting the button. "Oh, these are wonderful," she said, slowly sweeping the lower floor and the boxes and the crowded balconies above. "But," she added, a tart note creeping into her voice, "I never thought I would live to see so many blue coats in the French Opera House!"

Carrie agreed silently. One Yankee officer was just entering the box across the way, seeing his lady to her chair. He was tall and broad in the chest, and even at this distance, Carrie could discern a certain easy sureness about his bearing. He turned his head, and she caught an impression of a long, lean jawline, and suddenly the muscles just above her stomach gave a convulsive little flutter. It was Rance.

Fingers interlocked tightly, she tried not to stare. A quick look toward Susannah told her that her sister was still so engrossed in Beau Canfield that she hadn't realized who was occupying the box opposite them. And for that, she supposed, she should be grateful, since Suzy seemed to have no sense at all about Rance Stewart. That had certainly been apparent last week at Prosper's.

Susannah had accompanied her to tea on Thursday and, when she found Rance there, had practically squealed in delight, much to Carrie's disapproval. The two of them had greeted each other like long lost friends, Rance behaving for all the world like an

133

indulgent and doting older brother, admiring her new dress and telling her that she had indeed grown up since she'd come to New Orleans.

The only good thing about it was, if Rance and Suzy spent most of the time chattering away to each other, she didn't have to concern herself with him, and she hadn't. She'd managed to avoid him almost completely, had spent the afternoon talking with Prosper and his other guest, young Pierre Leblanche, who was of a fine old Creole family and a pupil of Prosper's.

All in all, it had not been as terrible as the first time there with Rance. That was the secret, she had decided. She'd just have to see that lots of people were invited, and then she would not have to endure him except on the most superficial basis.

But now she found her eyes going back again and again to the box across the way. She couldn't make out the features of the woman beside him, but could see that she was very fair and dressed in a gown of a brilliant peacock-blue color. Rance leaned toward her as if he were saying something, and suddenly, unbidden, the memory of that clean, sharp manly smell of him came to Carrie, and she looked away, feeling a quick stab of anger.

How dare he? How dare any of these Yankees come here tonight? Hadn't they done enough with their guns and their orders and their threats? Must they crowd into the theaters and restaurants, parade along the banquettes . . . they and their women?

"Carrie . . ." She jumped as she heard the sound of Abby's voice. "Carrie, wouldn't you like to use the glasses for a minute? Here, take them."

Abby held out the opera glasses to her, and for an instant Carrie's fingers itched for them. She could just casually turn them toward the box, could see what kind of whey-faced girl Rance chose to squire around . . . when he wasn't busy trespassing or taking advantage of helpless women.

She resisted the impulse. "No, thank you," she said.

"Oh, go ahead," Abby insisted, but the musicians were striking up a lively tune, the house lights were being lowered, and an expectant hush had fallen over the audience. The massive red curtains swept apart slowly.

The program for the evening was one of the lighter musicals presented at the Opera House from time to time. Performed by an English touring company, it was arch and witty and delightfully funny, and Carrie found herself laughing along with the rest of the audience and enjoying it thoroughly . . . though more than once she found her eyes straying from the stage to the box across the way. She could just make out the two figures who occupied it.

The time passed quickly, and soon it was intermission. Susannah was smiling and pink-cheeked.

"Oh, it's simply wonderful!" she said. "Didn't you just love it, Carrie?"

"Yes. It's very good," Carrie agreed.

"Come," Beau said, "let's walk out into the foyer. It is warm in here. Perhaps we can have some punch."

"That would be lovely," Abby said.

Carrie followed along with the others after taking a quick look toward Rance to see him in lively conversation with the young lady beside him. Good, she thought, let him stay put there, and she wouldn't have to worry about running into him.

They joined the other patrons moving along the corridor behind the loges, down the stairs, and into the large and magnificent foyer. Huge crystal chandeliers glittered with a gemlike brilliance and were reflected in the mirrors around the walls.

Beau and Seth brought punch, which was being served by white-jacketed Negroes. Carrie sipped at hers. A business acquaintance of Seth's came up to speak to them, and after the introductions, the two men drew away and spoke in low tones. From their sober expressions, Carrie couldn't help but wonder if they were discussing the loyalty oath. Beau and Susannah had drifted away together.

"Abby, dear . . . I didn't know you were here."

Carrie and Abby turned to find Geraldine Brighton, formidable in brown silk bombazine, her thin gray hair pulled back into a severe and tiny knot at the back of her head. Her niece Cissy, a woman well past the prime of life, accompanied her. Carrie noted the family resemblance, the pale eyelashes and the rabbity look of all the Brightons.

135

"You, child"—Geraldine fastened Carrie with those faintly pink eyes—"I don't believe I saw you in church last Sunday."

"No, ma'am," Carrie said. "I wasn't feeling well. I had a headache."

"If I recall correctly," Cissy said, "your Mama used to miss church half the time when she was your age. I know because we grew up together. She would come up with more excuses." She laughed archly, her pinched little chin growing even more pointy.

"Well, it's a wonder to me," Geraldine said, giving a passing Yankee officer a cold stare, "that we don't all have headaches constantly the way things are now."

"How is Brother Brighton?" Abby asked politely. "I heard he wasn't feeling well."

"Papa's not good. Not good at all," Cissy answered. "It's all this loyalty oath business. As pastor of First Presbyterian, the Yankees are pressuring him to influence the congregation."

"The poor man is beside himself," Geraldine agreed.

Before Abby could comment, Cissy lifted her head to look across the foyer and tugged at her aunt's arm. "Howard is looking for us," she said, and Carrie saw Cissy's portly, balding husband beckoning impatiently.

"All right, all right. That man always wants something," Geraldine said sourly to Abby. "I'll see you at the sewing circle. Why don't you come, too?" she said to Carrie.

"Perhaps," Carrie smiled, forcing her lips into a pleasant curve.

Abby watched the two women go. "I've never been able to warm to either of those women," she said.

Carrie laughed. "Mama couldn't stand Cissy Brighton. She said it often."

Seth was still talking to his business friend, and Beau and Susannah seemed lost in conversation a short distance away. A white-jacketed waiter passed, and Carrie and Abby put their empty punch cups back on his tray. People were beginning to drift back inside the theater, climb the stairs.

"Carrie . . ."

As she heard the deep and familiar voice behind her, Carrie froze for an instant, groaning inwardly, aware of a look of blank amazement on Abby Morrison's face. Taking a deep breath, she steeled herself and turned to see Rance Stewart standing there, the young woman beside him.

"Captain Stewart," she said coolly, "what a surprise."

"Yes, isn't it." He grinned, his teeth white and even beneath the dark mustache, the gray eyes betraying a certain amusement at her tone. "Miss Kingston," he said, "may I present Miss Nora Barlow."

"How do you do?" the girl said politely in her flat Northern accent.

Carrie returned the greeting, noting the small nose and delicate brows, the pale blond hair gleaming like silk, parted in the middle and pulled back to a cluster of curls at the nape of her neck. The blue gown she wore was in the latest fashion, with the widest hoops that Carrie had ever seen, and the bodice swept low to bare milky white shoulders and the swelling tops of her small breasts.

Carrie was irritably aware of her own dress. It was the one she'd entertained Rance in that night at Kingston's Landing, and she'd thought then that it was bewitching, but now it seemed provincial and outdated beside Miss Barlow's. She was sure its cream color paled to insignificance beside the brilliant peacock blue. Not that it mattered in the least, she assured herself quickly. Let this Yankee girl deck herself out however she wanted.

She realized suddenly that Abby, who had managed to close her mouth, was looking at her expectantly. "Oh, do forgive me," she said hastily. "Captain Stewart and . . . Miss Barlow, Mrs. Morrison."

"It's a pleasure to meet you, Mrs. Morrison." Rance smiled down at Abby, the brass buttons along his dresscoat gleaming in the gaslight. "I've heard of your husband."

"Is that so?" Abby said.

"And are you ladies enjoying the program?" Nora Barlow asked sweetly, though Carrie detected icy appraisal in the blue eyes as they flickered over her, then glanced to the handsome, ramrod-straight officer who stood beside her.

"Very much," Carrie said. She returned Nora Barlow's questioning gaze steadily, her head very high. The other woman was the first to look away.

"Good," she said. "So are we."

The four of them stood there awkwardly, Rance the only one who seemed at ease.

"Rance, dear," Nora Barlow touched her pale fingers lightly to the dark blue sleeve, "just so we won't miss a minute of it, I do believe we'd better go back in. They'll be starting soon."

"Certainly," he said. He inclined his head to Abby. "Mrs. Morrison, it's been a pleasure. Carrie . . ."

Nora Barlow tucked her hand into the crook of Rance's elbow, favoring them with a dazzling smile, and drew him along. Carrie deliberately turned her back on the retreating couple and found that Abby was staring at her.

"For heaven's sake," the older woman said, "who is he? And how does a Yankee come to talk like that?"

"He's the officer who quartered his men at Kingston's Landing overnight," Carrie said shortly. "You remember. I told you about that."

"Well, you didn't tell me that he talked like a Southerner! And I declare, I've never been so surprised in my life to have a Yankee come right up and speak to you!"

Susannah came over to them just at that moment. "Yankee?" she said. "What Yankee?"

"This Yankee just came right up to us," Abby explained. "I believe you said his name is Stewart." She turned to Carrie for confirmation.

"Rance?" Susannah's face lit up. "Rance is here?" Her eyes swept the foyer eagerly, but when she failed to see him, she turned back to Abby. "Oh, Rance is not really a Yankee," she said, grinning. "He's a good friend of ours."

"Oh, for heaven's sake, Suzy," Carrie hissed, her hands clenched tightly at her sides, "he's not only a Yankee, he's worse! He's a turncoat in that uniform! A traitor to the South!" And with that, she turned on her heel and marched toward the stairs.

11

"WELL, I AIN'T NEVER SEEN SUCH SHIFTLESS, NO-COUNT niggers!" Mattie stopped dead still in the middle of the banquette and stood, arms akimbo, as she watched a half-dozen Negroes in Yankee uniforms clatter past on horses. One of them swept his cap off and gave her a toothy grin.

Carrie stood beside the Negro girl and looked after the horsemen, no longer surprised at seeing such sights in the streets of New Orleans. The Union Army was glad to take whatever recruits it could get, including runaway slaves.

Mattie righted the wicker basket that she had almost dropped, and she and Carrie fell into step once again.

"Solomon, he says that one of these days they goin' to be whole regiments of nigger soldiers, Miss Carrie, but I don't know. I don't believe Mama'd think too much of it."

Carrie sighed. "She probably wouldn't, Mattie." Carrie thought of Chloe and the rigid protocol by which she regulated her own life and the lives of those around her. As strict as any *grande dame*, Chloe believed that there was correct behavior and there was incorrect behavior, and the two were clearly divided.

It was mid-morning and still cool, the sun partially obscured by fat, white clouds that drifted lazily. A Negro woman wearing a brilliant red- and white-flowered tignon scoured the steps of a house they were passing, scrub brush flying, the sharp smell of lye soap pungent in the air.

"Bonjou', Missy," she called out, bobbing her head at Carrie and grinning at Mattie.

139

They returned the greeting and continued on their way along Dumaine Street, headed toward the French Market, which was only a few blocks from the house.

"I hope I can find some eggplants fit to buy today," Mattie said. "They didn't have none yesterday. Lordy, I can remember when I was little and Mama used to take me along with her to the market, and it seemed like to me they had everything in the world there, Miss Carrie. But now . . ." She shrugged and swung her hips so that her bright pink skirt swayed. "Seems like nothin' ain't like it used to be."

"No, it isn't, Mattie." Carrie thought of the last two days, which she'd spent at the Morrisons' helping Abby make a list of all their household possessions, right down to the last linen towel, the last counterpane. The deadline for taking the loyalty oath was fast approaching, and the newspapers had made clear once again that those who refused to take it must report to the Provost Marshal and register as enemies of the government, presenting at that time a complete inventory of all their possessions, personal and otherwise. Abby had even been forced to list her wedding ring.

"Seth says it doesn't mean anything," she'd insisted, tight-lipped and drawn. "He says it's just another way for Butler to harass us." But Carrie wasn't so sure.

Rumors circulated that some of the leading businessmen had given way under the pressure and had already taken the oath. Men eyed each other in the streets and wondered. Those who had sworn to hold out were bitterly opposed to those who would betray their consciences. Though when Seth had said he knew for a fact that Ephraim Skaggs had already taken the oath, he could only shake his head in sadness for the sick old man.

"For the first time," Abby confided privately to Carrie, "I'm glad that J. D. isn't here. I only pray he's still safe and well in Vicksburg and that they can hold out. I wouldn't want him here to be arrested or anything . . ." She'd let her voice trail off and looked forlornly away from the china cabinet where they'd been making a list of the contents.

"No one is going to be arrested, Mother Morrison." Carrie had tried to comfort her. "What good would it do to arrest everyone? The military government would end up looking like fools.''

But Carrie was still disturbed enough that she'd felt the need of a long walk this morning to clear her head and had decided to come along with Mattie on her daily trek, past the old Creole houses with their walled gardens and lovely iron-lace gates and fences.

"Solomon says," Mattie was still chattering away, "that Mr. Lincoln goin' to come down here and set all the slaves free. Do you think that's a fact, Miss Carrie?''

"I don't think so, Mattie. And I believe that Solomon would do well to be more careful about what he says. His master, Monsieur Marchand, might not take kindly to such statements.''

"I done told him that, Miss Carrie. Sometimes I get down-right scared for him 'cause I don't want his master to whip him or nothin'.''

Carrie smiled at the Negro girl. "You like him, don't you?''

Mattie caught her full, ripe underlip between strong white teeth, her eyes laughing. "Yes, Miss Carrie.''

"Well, don't worry too much. Solomon's probably just repeating some things he's heard. Things are unsettled for everyone now, Mattie.''

"Yes, Miss Carrie.''

Up ahead, they could see the old French Market with its long stretch of tiled roof held up by gray, weathered pillars. Open on all sides, it was like a honeycomb with all its many stalls: vegetable and fruit peddlers, small stands beribboned with strings of garlic and bright red peppers, carts piled high with cabbages, baskets of dates and figs, counters where nothing was sold but shrimp or live crabs packed in damp moss. On any given day, skinned rabbits might hang from hooks or fat chickens poke their heads from between the slats of weathered coops and cluck to passers-by. And in the middle of it all, there were flower stalls and tiny, hideaway places where one might sit on a stool and have a steaming hot cup of coffee laced with chicory and a *beignet*. Though now with sugar in such short supply, the delicious hot doughnuts were not always available.

As they came closer, the smell of ripe peaches was heavy in the air, intermingled with bananas and mangoes and the less

141

pleasant smells of meat scraps, crayfish, and potatoes rotting in a nearby gunnysack.

They stopped at a stall where Mattie examined some okra and finally purchased some to go in her basket.

"You got any eggplant?" she demanded.

"No eggplant," the fat Negro man with a strong West Indian accent answered. "Tomorrow . . . maybee . . ." He grinned broadly and leaned down to give half a peeled peach to the plump baby girl who sat in a stained fruit basket beside him, her wisps of kinky hair tied up with lengths of multi-colored strings, her big brown eyes darting curiously.

They moved along to another stall where Mattie was soon arguing heatedly with a Cajun woman about the price of vanilla beans.

"I think I'll just walk along," Carrie told her. "I'll meet you at the other end."

And she strolled on, beginning to feel the closeness in the air here under the market roof as the clouds thinned and the sun began to bear down. She had worn her hair tied back loosely with a white ribbon, which she retied now to draw some of the heavy strands back away from her face. She could feel the fine film of perspiration between her breasts and at the nape of her neck. She was glad that the morning dress she was wearing, which was of white lawn with a tiny blue flower print, had a wide low neckline and puffed sleeves that bared her arms to above the elbows. She carried her big leghorn straw hat.

An elegantly dressed old Creole gentleman swept off his hat and said, *"Bon jour."* And a huge old Negro woman, ensconced in her chair behind her fruit bins, orange skirt billowing tentlike about her, fanned herself with a palmetto leaf and smiled broadly at Carrie.

She walked on to where strings of fish, freshly caught that morning and kept in large tubs of river water, gleamed with a silver iridescence. Two solemn-faced nuns, their headresses white and stiff with starch, leaned over to inspect them with a fixed concentration, while a white-kerchiefed cook pointed out to the seller the two large blue crabs she had decided upon.

Carrie could see the flower stalls down the way and she headed toward them, remembering that her mother had always said the first place Papa had taken her was to the French Market where they had had coffee and *callas* and Papa had bought her a white rose. Molly Gallagher Kingston always added that they'd lingered longer than they should have and gotten back home so late her parents had been quite upset with her. Perhaps, Carrie thought, they had walked right along here where she was walking now. Mama would have been so pretty back then . . . and Papa so handsome.

She was so lost in thought that she didn't see the booted foot stretched carelessly out in the aisle and came very near to pitching headlong across it, catching herself just in time.

She swung around, more than a little angry, and eyed the offender, a blue-clad soldier sprawled on an upturned box, his blouse partially unbuttoned, his hat askew. For an instant he looked up at her, a stupefied expression on his homely face, and then he scrambled to his feet rather unsteadily. She caught the distinct odor of whiskey on his breath.

"Well, well . . . jist look at you!" He grinned out of a face that had a nose too long and a mouth too wide and was fairly covered with freckles. His red hair stuck out from under his cap in fiery tufts. "You're jist the lady I been lookin' for." He planted himself in front of her, swaying slightly.

"Harley . . . !"

Carrie heard the flat, nasal twang and realized that it came from a second Yankee soldier who'd been stretched out nearby on a pile of potato sacks and had now gained his feet. Clutching at his cap, which had nearly fallen off in the process, he came purposefully toward them, his step only a shade or so steadier than the first one.

"Looky here, Billy . . . looky what I done found us!" the one called Harley chortled. Carrie found herself trapped, with a masonry pillar and stacks of empty bushel baskets at her back, the grinning soldier blocking her way in front.

"Stand aside, if you please!" she snapped, but the man only gave out a huge guffaw that sent gusts of liquored breath into her face.

"Now, Harley"—the second soldier had arrived and started to tug at his friend's arm—"don't be botherin' this lady now. He didn't mean nothin', Miss. Me and him was drinkin' a little last night . . . that's all.'' He was tall and stringy and badly in need of a shave.

"Leave off," Harley jerked his arm away. "I jist want a kiss from this pretty little thing. Ain't she the prettiest thing we've seen since we come here, Billy?"

Carrie looked around frantically. The only other person who was in a position to see what was happening was a thin and broken-toothed woman behind the flower stall. She looked away nervously as if she didn't know what to do against the Yankee soldiers and would just as soon not be involved in it. The place buzzed with sound, the haggling sometimes high-pitched, even shrill. Carrie wasn't sure if anyone would pay any attention to her even if she called out. She must, she decided, try her best to bluff her way past this lout.

"Get out of my way!" she said in her most imperious tone, drawing herself up as tall as she could. But she could feel the nervous perspiration at the hollows of her throat, beneath her armpits, and she felt as if the thin material of her dress was plastered to her breasts, outlining their fullness.

Harley grinned at her tone and let his eyes wander where they would, the homely face working with a kind of hunger.

"A kiss," he said again. "Jist one little, bitty kiss. The general hisself said that you was supposed to be nice to us."

"Come on, Harley." The other soldier was still trying to persuade his friend. "You're gonna git us both in trouble for sure."

"One kiss . . ." The red-haired soldier leaned closer, touched her shoulder. Carrie was almost suffocating with the foul, whiskey breath, the sour odor of him. She felt a mixture of panic and anger rise within her.

"Get away from me, you ignorant, bluebelly Yankee!" she shouted, and in desperation planted her hands right in the middle of his chest and gave him a hard shove.

He staggered backward a step or two but righted himself and was reaching out for her again when his friend caught him from behind and started pulling him away.

"Leave her alone now, Harley . . . Dammit, leave the lady alone!"

But Carrie didn't wait to hear any more. She saw her chance

to get between them and the pillar, and she slipped past, trembling, half-stumbling as she looked back over her shoulder to see if they were following after her . . . right into two strong arms and a broad chest.

She gave an involuntary little cry, looked up into Rance Stewart's face, and instinctively clung to him.

"Carrie . . . Good Lord, what is it? What—'' He stopped as he saw the two scuffling soldiers. " 'Ten'hut!'' he barked, and the two men jerked apart and to attention at once.

The red-haired soldier's cap was lying in the dust; his nose was running. The other one had lost two buttons from his blouse.

"What's happened here, Carrie?'' Rance asked gently. "Did either of these men bother you?''

She bit at her lip. "They . . . he . . . wouldn't let me pass,'' she said. "He demanded that I give him . . .''

"Give him what?'' Rance prodded, leaning his head down closer so that her answer could be for him alone.

"A . . . a kiss,'' she said softly, blushing a deep pink. She realized that she was still clinging to him, his arm still around her waist. She reminded herself sternly of who he was and quickly stepped away. But not so far that he didn't still have one hand resting firmly, protectively, at her back. She made no move to dislodge it.

"Just what did you men think you were about?'' Rance demanded, his face like a thundercloud.

The two men were still standing at rigid attention. "Guess we got a little drunk last night, Captain,'' the one called Billy said. "We didn't mean no harm, sir.''

"That man wasn't responsible, Rance,'' Carrie spoke up quickly. "In fact . . . he tried to help.''

"Cap'n,'' the red-haired soldier whined, his Adam's apple pumping, "I wasn't goin' to hurt her none. The general hisself said they was supposed to be nice to us. Ain't that right, sir? I was jist askin' her to be nice.''

Carrie saw the muscles in Rance's jaw clench. "General Butler's Order #28 never had as its intention that ladies be annoyed or insulted in the street. You understand that, soldier?''

"Yes, sir.''

"What are your names?''

145

"Private Harley H. Kincaid, sir. Fourth Wisconsin. Assigned to orderly duty at the hospital, sir."

"Private Billy T. Woolcott. Fourth Wisconsin. Orderly duty at the hospital, sir."

"Very well. You men report at once to your sergeant of the day and tell him that you will be receiving orders directly from me. Perhaps a month of loading sandbags and working on the levees will give you ample time to reflect on the correct way to treat a lady, Kincaid. And you, Woolcott, should know that a soldier does not appear in public half-drunk and greatly in need of a shave. I'll deal with the two of you later. For now you're dismissed. Be on your way." Rance's voice was clipped and brooked no more talk.

"Yes, sir." They both saluted as smartly as they could, given the state of their disarray, and sped away, the one called Billy grumbling under his breath and giving Harley sour looks over his shoulder. The lady behind the flower stall was grinning, her broken tooth showing.

Carrie was beginning to feel very foolish now that the whole thing was over. Worse than that, she was remembering with great embarrassment how she had clung to Rance Stewart. Of all people, he had to be the one to come by just at a time when she was frightened, vulnerable.

"Feeling better?" He looked down at her, that full, strong mouth curving in a warm smile. She couldn't seem to help letting her gaze linger for a moment on his face, taking in that strong line of his jaw, the cleft chin, the clear gray eyes. The thick, dark hair was revealed as he removed his black felt Hardee hat. Almost of their own volition her eyes moved back to his mouth, and she could suddenly feel it on hers as it had been that night, could remember the hot, sweet surge that had gone through her whole body as he'd kissed her . . . and more, could remember that urgent and traitorous clamor in her blood when his hands had moved over her naked body, his long legs twined with hers, that man part of him demanding, swollen, pressed against her.

She felt amost faint with the enormity of the images in her mind. She jerked her chin up and tried to assume a carefully formal demeanor. "I'm quite all right now . . . Captain Stewart," she added deliberately. "And I certainly"—she managed to avoid looking into his eyes—"want to thank you for all your assistance. It was very kind of you."

"Not at all. My buggy is nearby. I'll take you home," he said.

She was quite literally backing away from him now. "That won't be necessary. I'm really all right now."

"Carrie . . . wait. I insist on driving you home. You shouldn't be out on the streets alone."

"No, no. Thank you again."

She went from him blindly, not watching where she was going or hearing anything for a few moments. Then she knew that she was out of the market and walking hurriedly along a banquette.

The sun was bearing down, and her skirts felt heavy and hot. She had lost her hat someplace back at the market, but she didn't care.

After a little while she was vaguely aware of the sound of a horse's hooves clopping along the cobblestone street beside her, aware of the sound of oiled wheels.

"Carrie . . ."

She heard Rance's voice and turned, horrified to see him there in a small high-wheeled buggy, moving slowly, deliberately, along the street beside her. She never missed a step, just faced forward again and walked steadfastly on.

"Carrie, will you get in the buggy and let me take you home?" he called.

"Thank you, no. I'm perfectly all right," she said, and tried to walk faster, though the hot sun was making that difficult.

The buggy seemed to set its pace to hers, the horse moving doggedly along, the sound of its hooves making an irritating rhythm in her ear. A stout, matronly woman in green silk taffeta grasped her small boy's hand firmly and looked in bewilderment from Carrie to Rance and back to Carrie again, who was doing her best to ignore him.

"Will you just get in the buggy, Carrie?" Rance called once the stout lady and her son were past.

"No," Carrie snapped and stopped for a moment to put her hands on her hips. "Will you just go away and leave me alone, Rance Stewart?"

"No," he said. "I'm going to follow you until you get in this buggy. No matter how long it takes."

She saw that he was laughing at her now. She stamped her foot in a fine fury and stalked forward once again, sure that he was enjoying this whole thing. An old Negro nanny leaned from a second-story balcony to watch them pass, and across the street on the banquette, two tall-hatted gentlemen getting out of their carriage stopped still and gave Carrie and the following buggy puzzled stares.

She stole a look sideways at Rance and to her chagrin saw that he was still grinning as he kept the horse to its careful pace. He looked cool and comfortable and maddeningly handsome up there on the buggy seat with its overhanging fringed top. While she, on the other hand, must look a mess! Her ribbon had loosened, and she could feel her hair curling damply about her face. There was a fine sheen of perspiration along her throat, on her arms.

She made one final effort to outlast him, but her step was slowing in the punishing sun, and only a moment before she had remembered Mattie. She'd left her back there at the French Market; the poor girl must be looking for her frantically.

She stopped suddenly and got some small satisfaction from the fact that he hadn't anticipated her move. The buggy went on for several paces before he hauled the horse to a standstill in front of the walled ground of the old Ursuline convent on Chartres Street.

Rance swung down easily from the buggy and came round to her, the big straw hat she thought she'd lost in his hand. "Your hat, Miss Kingston," he said, a teasing grin on his face.

She glared at him, jammed the hat down on her head, and let him help her up into the buggy. In a minute he was beside her and clucking to the horse.

"If you would take me back to the market, please," she said imperiously. And then, somewhat sheepishly: "Mattie is waiting for me there."

He was trying to keep a straight face. "The market it is," he said, bringing the reins lightly down on the back of the big roan gelding.

Carrie tied the ribbons of her hat beneath her chin, looking straight ahead with her mouth set stubbornly. "This was totally

unnecessary," she said. "And you had everyone staring at us."
She refused even to look at him.

"Sorry," he said.

"And," she fumed, "while I appreciate your assistance back
there, I assure you that I would have been perfectly all right
without you. After all," she sputtered, "they . . . they were
nothing but a pair of bluebelly louts!"

Rance could contain himself no longer. He threw back his
head and roared with laughter so that passers-by were once more
turning to stare. The driver of a mule-drawn dray turned on his
seat and raised a grubby hand, laughing right along with Rance.

"Will you stop that?" Carrie said, furious.

Rance gasped and wiped at his eyes, finally brought his mirth
under control. "You know," he said, still catching his breath,
"I think you're right. Five more minutes and you'd have had
them yelling for help."

He laughed again, but this time it was merely a deep chuckle,
and though Carrie set her mouth firmly and struggled against it,
she couldn't hold it back, and she burst into laughter herself,
finally turning to look at him, her guard down for the moment.

"I do thank you," she said.

The gray eyes held hers. "It was my pleasure. And," he
sobered, "I'm deeply sorry that you were bothered in any way
by a Union soldier. I can assure you that they'll be dealt with in
the proper manner."

"I was a little nervous," she admitted, and then at once
regretted having said it. She must be careful to keep Rance
Stewart at a distance in every way. He confused her. She had to
keep reminding herself that she despised him. "Did you and
Miss Barlow enjoy the theater the other evening?" she asked
abruptly.

"Very much."

There was a silence.

"Miss Barlow is . . . new to New Orleans?" she asked
finally.

"Yes. Nora is the daughter of Major Kenneth Barlow, and she
and her mother came down to be with him. I believe they're
originally from Illinois."

"How nice," she said, remembering the sleek blond hair, the

stunning gown. She found herself angry again. It wasn't enough, she thought, to be invaded by Yankees. Now their harsh-voiced women in elegant clothes and fancy rigs must be put up with, too. It was as if they intended to make the humiliation of Southern women more complete.

But it wouldn't be this way forever. It was clear, even from the Butler-controlled papers, that the tide had turned. An attempt to capture the Confederate capital at Richmond had been a failure. General Lee and Stonewall Jackson had soundly defeated the Yankees and captured a Federal supply base at Manassas, sending General Pope scurrying back to Washington. And early in September, Lee and his army had actually crossed the Potomac, taking the war into Northern territory for the first time.

The day would come, sooner than the Yankees thought, when Confederate troops would come marching in to reclaim New Orleans. Then it would be General Butler fleeing north to safety, she comforted herself. And Miss Nora Barlow and her father the major would be going right along with him.

They had reached the far end of the French Market, and Carrie suddenly spied Mattie, talking excitedly to a wizened old flower peddler who carried his wares in a huge, flat basket hung round his neck by a strap. She was gesturing broadly, obviously upset.

"There she is," Carrie said, and Rance pulled the buggy closer and called to the Negro girl, who turned to them, a relieved smile spreading across her pretty face.

"Oh, Miss Carrie . . ." she said, coming at a run, her full basket swaying awkwardly, pink skirt billowing. "I didn't see you no place! I didn't know where in the world you had gone off to!"

"Get in, Mattie," Rance said, reaching down for the basket.

"Good day, Cap'n Stewart," she said. She hesitated, then swung herself up easily and perched on a small jumpseat toward the rear, all the time looking from him to Carrie who sat, stiff and proper, on the seat as far from him as she could get.

Rance slapped the reins down.

"I live just a few blocks from here," Carrie said.

"I know."

She looked at him in surprise.

"Prosper told me," he said.

The stylish buggy traversed the distance quickly, and soon they were pulling up in front of the house with its high-walled privacy. Rance handed the market basket down, and Mattie took it, throwing a last speculative look at the two of them before she disappeared through the small iron gate that led into the courtyard.

Rance held up his arms, and Carrie let him assist her to the banquette, terribly aware of his hands at her waist, on her arm. She stood there not knowing what to say to him. Though she had been concerned about her disheveled appearance, she actually had never looked more beautiful. Her cheeks were pink, her eyes wonderfully golden in the sunlight. The wide-brimmed leghorn hat framed her face perfectly, the dark chestnut hair curling about her cheeks in the humid air.

"I want to thank you again," she said finally, her voice very formal.

He inclined his head. "I'm just glad I happened along at the right time." He waited as if he thought she might ask him in, then took her elbow in his hand and walked her the few short paces to the gate.

"Will I see you at Prosper's on Thursday?" he asked, his eyes holding hers.

"I . . . I don't know," she said. "I've been helping Abby Morrison with"—she seized on it, used it as a weapon against him—"with the listing of her possessions for the Provost Marshal."

"The loyalty oath," he said, and there was a certain darkening of his eyes.

"Yes," she said defiantly. "General Butler's loyalty oath. What will happen to the people who refuse to take it?"

"I don't know, Carrie," he said slowly. And for a moment she could sense his anguish, sense how torn he was to see his people defeated, his land invaded . . . no matter how deeply he felt that he must fight on the other side.

"And what about me?" She assumed a certain bravado, even managed a half-smile. "Will I be asked to take this oath?"

"I don't think so. You're a woman. And you don't own property in New Orleans."

"Ah, but how long before the good general turns his attention to the plantations upriver?"

Rance regarded her steadily for a long moment. "I don't know that either, Carrie.'' There was a painful honesty in his voice. It created an intimacy between them that left her breathless.

"I . . . I must go in," she said, desperate to get away.

"Will I see you at Prosper's?" he asked again.

"Perhaps. I . . . I really can't say. Thank you again . . ." And with that she fled through the gate and closed it behind her.

Instead of turning into the covered front entranceway of the house, she went into the courtyard with its pale pink bricks and flower beds. It was cool after the street. The plum tree cast its delicate shade. Tubs of blooming roses and nicotiana perfumed the air. And Carrie sat down on a delicately scrolled iron bench, weak and trembling.

How could she ever, even for a moment, she asked herself, forget who Rance Stewart was, what he'd done? It was all because she'd been so disturbed over that terrible experience at the market. It would have unsettled anyone.

The Yankee captain could be deceptively charming when he wanted to be. Hadn't he taken in Prosper? And Suzy would follow him around like a puppy dog if she had the chance.

Even if she could forgive that night—and she couldn't—she must never forget that Paul Gayerre had said he'd heard a Yankee officer who spoke with a Southern accent when he was hiding in the house at his plantation. That could have been no one but Rance. And that had been three days before Uncle Etienne was killed, Maisonfleur burned, seven days before Rance had shown up at Kingston's Landing.

No matter what he'd said, there was no way she could be positively sure that he hadn't been responsible . . . not positively sure. And yet even thinking that made a strange ache in her chest, which she could not, would not explain.

12

CARRIE SAT LOOKING OUT THROUGH THE FRENCH DOORS TO THE sun-drenched courtyard, waiting for Mattie to bring her tea and thinking of Abby Morrison's hands. She had spent the morning with her future mother-in-law and couldn't get those pale, thin fingers out of her mind. They had moved constantly, plucking nervously at nonexistent threads, smoothing at hair that was perfect, twisting helplessly in her lap. The deadline for taking the loyalty oath was only days away now. And it was clear that there would be no last minute reprieve.

With Lee's crossing into Maryland, an unspoken but almost palpable hope had flared briefly, only to fade with news of his defeat along the banks of a creek called Antietam. The newspapers had reported it fully. A set of written orders had somehow fallen into Union hands and been taken to McClellan, the commanding general of the Union troops, who at once saw his advantage and attacked. And though Lee's trusted and brave Stonewall Jackson hastened back from a successful raid on Harpers Ferry, the battle was still the bloodiest and costliest thus far in the war. When that long day had ended, nearly twelve-thousand Rebel soldiers lay dead or wounded, and that many or more on the Union side. With the coming of morning, McClellan's troops were too exhausted to strike again, and Lee started his battered army back to Virginia to bind up its wounds.

The news was greeted with a quiet despair in New Orleans. So many Southern boys had been lost . . . and there would be no last minute rescue. The dilemma of the loyalty oath must be faced.

It had been announced that those lost to the privilege of

swearing allegiance to their rightful government would not be allowed to hold city or state office, practice law, work as a notary or a sheriff. They could not collect a debt, sell a piece of property, or leave the city. And there was still the matter of the lists of possessions that must be submitted to the Provost Marshal and the unspoken threat that implied.

Men, tight-lipped and drawn, locked themselves in their studies and drank, or walked in lonely contemplation along the levee, or gathered in back rooms to commiserate with one another and enter into discussions . . . sometimes heated.

It was only a matter of time until the South won the war, some argued. Why should they risk losing everything? And would they really be dishonoring themselves if they swore falsely to an oath that had been forced upon them? There were others who answered that question with unwavering scorn, who vowed to stand fast. Seth Morrison was among them.

Abby had told Carrie that Seth was hardly ever at home now. And when he was, it was to bluster that everything would be all right. The military government would not dare enforce the penalties it threatened.

Carrie rose from her chair and shook her head, running her fingertips lightly along her temples. There was so much to think about it sometimes made her head hurt.

Beau was at sea again and Suzy was clearly worried about him. Certainly not without reason. Though Beau insisted on treating it lightly, to repeatedly run the blockade into Charleston was terribly dangerous. Still, the medicines and surgical supplies were desperately needed. There was nothing to do but pray that it would all go well and he would return safely.

Carrie had insisted that Suzy attend Prosper's tea the Thursday before, hoping it would take her mind off Beau. Carrie herself had pleaded a slight indisposition. After the buggy ride home from the market, she had determined to avoid Rance Stewart . . . even at the risk of hurting Prosper.

The pain in her head throbbed dully. She would have her tea and try to put it all from her mind.

She glanced at the small gilt clock atop the mantel. Where *was* her tea? It must have been a good twenty minutes since she sent Mattie to the kitchen for it. She started to call out and then ealized that the kitchen was too far toward the back of the house or Mattie to hear her. She pulled the bellcord in the corner and went back to stand and look out over the courtyard again, noting ow large the roses were, their blooms drooping forward as if hey were too heavy for the stems to hold them up. If it weren't o hot, she would love to take her tea out there.

She massaged her aching temples again and wished that she were back home at Kingston's Landing. She had gone to the bank just yesterday to see Leroy Tate about the money she needed to borrow, quite forgetting that he was as caught up in he loyalty oath dilemma as anyone else. She had found him preoccupied, though polite. He looked tired; there were grayish circles under his eyes, clearly visible beneath the lenses of his small round spectacles.

"I'll need more time, Miss Kingston," he had said, absently slipping his watch in and out of his pocket. "I've just been . . . so busy."

She had said to take whatever time he needed. The truth was, if he failed her, she didn't know where to turn next.

She walked the length of the room, glancing impatiently over her shoulder. Where *was* Mattie? Whatever could be keeping her so long?

She sighed and went out along the long hallway, the wide floorboards waxed to a soft sheen underfoot; past rooms of lovely old French furniture; past the formal parlor and the library with its shelves of leather-bound books and its great, soft armchairs; past the dining room and the butler's pantry. She could hear Mattie's throaty giggle coming from the kitchen.

As Carrie entered the room, she saw the girl standing in an enticing pose, one hip thrust out slightly, lips pursed. Her eyes, sparkling with laughter, were fixed on Solomon, the Marchands' man from next door. A subtle change in the black man's expression caused Mattie to swing around quickly, and as she caught sight of Carrie, to straighten up primly.

"Miss Carrie . . ."

"I've been waiting for my tea, Mattie," Carrie said quietly.

"Oh . . . yes, Miss Carrie. I got the water boilin' right here."
Flustered, Mattie grabbed a thick pot holder, snatched up the

steaming kettle, and began to pour water into the teapot on a nearby table.

"I rang a minute ago."

Mattie cast a sidelong glance at her mistress. "I'm sorry, Miss Carrie. I didn't hear the bell."

Solomon, tall and broad-shouldered, stood regarding the two of them, his dark face carefully impassive.

"Solomon." Carrie nodded.

"Good day, Miss Kingston." He was very dark, his skin the color of polished ebony, though it was clear from his features that some white blood must flow in his veins. His nose was slim and straight with nostrils that flared slightly above a mouth that was well-modeled, lips full but not thick.

Most slaves, unless they were longtime members of the household, did not look directly into the eyes of a white person overlong, but glanced up and then looked discreetly away unless they were spoken to again, but Solomon regarded Carrie directly, almost boldly, and she caught a glimpse of something in those black eyes, a kind of challenge only partly concealed, that made her feel somehow uncomfortable.

Mattie, all the while, was trying to get the sugar bowl and the cream pitcher onto the tray beside the teapot. "I'll bring this here right in to you, Miss Carrie," she said, as she quickly wiped up a few drops of milk that she'd spilled in her haste.

"I'll take it myself, Mattie," Carrie said, smiling in spite of herself. Clearly Mattie was smitten with Solomon.

"Yes, Miss Carrie. Thank you." Mattie brought the tray and handed it over. "Miss Carrie . . ." She hesitated, breathing a little fast, her full breasts straining against the plum-colored cotton bodice. "Miss Carrie, I done finished with my work in the house. And I won't have to start supper for a while. Will it be all right if I go walkin' long the river? Me and Solomon?"

Mattie waited, such a pleading in her soft brown eyes that whatever small misgivings Carrie had disappeared for the moment. "Of course," she said. "Go ahead, Mattie. I'm just going to have my tea, and I might rest a while later."

"Oh, thank you, Miss Carrie!" A wide smile broke across the girl's face. "I'll be back in plenty of time to fix supper. I promise I will."

Carrie took the tray back to the sitting room and had her tea by the French doors where a breeze wafted in from time to time. She was just finishing when she heard the clatter of hooves in the courtyard. Lafitte bringing Susannah back from her errands. Carrie had asked her to bring back a copy of the newspaper. She hoped Suzy hadn't forgotten.

In a moment, she heard her coming in through the main entrance. "Carrie . . ." her sister called, and there was an odd pitch to her voice.

"In here, Suzy."

Susannah burst into the room in a flurry of petticoats, newspaper in hand, curls trembling about her face. "Carrie, look!" she said. "I can't believe this!"

Quickly Carrie rose to take the outstretched paper and stared down at the banner headline that leaped up at her in bold black type: EMANCIPATION PROCLAMATION. And just beneath it: Lincoln Frees Slaves.

She drew in her breath and sat back down, trying to absorb the full meaning.

"Carrie, he can't do that, can he?" Susannah asked angrily. "Everybody is all upset! People on the streets are talking and waving the newspapers around! Why, one man was yelling that Lincoln is a baboon, and a Yankee soldier heard him and chased him up an alley!"

"Wait . . ." Carrie held up a restraining hand. "Let me read this." It was unbelievable. And yet so much had happened that had once seemed impossible. She bent over the paper.

Abby Morrison arrived, and Susannah went to show her in.

"My God, have you heard the news?" Abby's face was pale as she entered the sitting room. A wisp of hair trailed over one ear.

"I have it right here." Carrie held up the newspaper.

"I wanted to talk to Seth as soon as I heard," Abby said breathlessly, "but I'm not sure just where he is. I think he was going to be at one of the warehouses finishing his inventory today. He said not to hold up dinner for him, he'd be late. Lord," she moaned, "what's going to happen next?"

"I don't know," Carrie said, trying to stay calm. "Here

. . ." She took Abby's arm and guided her toward one of the white damask-covered chairs. "Do sit down, Mother Morrison."

Abby did as Carrie said, twisting the gold wedding band on her finger. "He can't do this! I don't believe he has the right to say that people's property no longer belongs to them!"

"Mother Morrison, listen," Carrie said. "Despite what this headline says, the whole text of the proclamation is here, and it seems to me that it only applies to the Confederate States. It specifically excludes any Confederate territory that has been captured by the Yankees, such as New Orleans. And it also excludes those slave states that are still in the Union."

Abby stared at her. "Only the Confederate States? But Lincoln has no power to enforce anything in the Confederate States now."

"Exactly," Carrie said. "It has to be a political move." The three exchanged looks. But there was a vague stirring at the back of Carrie's mind that this was only the beginning of something much bigger.

"Then it doesn't mean anything," Susannah said, a relieved look spreading over her pretty face.

Abby's brows were still knit, her eyes anxious. "I don't know. What about the Nigras? We've had so much trouble with them already because of the war. What will this do?"

Carrie shrugged. "The ones who wanted to run away have already done it."

Abby seemed only partially convinced, but Susannah, always eager to look at the best side of everything, assured the older woman that it would all be forgotten in a day or so.

"Suzy is probably right," Carrie said. "Now I'm going to make a fresh pot of tea, and we're all going to have some. And since Father Morrison won't be home for dinner, you must stay and eat with us."

Abby leaned back, her blue-veined hands, still for the moment, folded in her lap. "Oh, yes. Thank you. I'd like that."

Later, as it was growing dusky outside, Carrie went back to the kitchen to tell Mattie to set a place at the table for Abby. As she drew near, she was surprised to see that the lamps in the kitchen were not lit. There were no sounds of pots and pans clanging, no sound of Mattie's soft humming. And once in the room, it was clear that the fire in the big iron stove was nearly out.

Carrie stood quite still, the unthinkable possibility washing over her that the girl had run off. It would have been impossible to contemplate before today, before that headline had leaped up at her. But now she considered it for one full minute before rejecting it. Mattie wouldn't do that. She had simply forgotten the time.

Quickly Carrie lit the lamps, then took some wood from the woodbox and laid it in the stove door, poking up the few coals that were still glowing. She was bending over, watching intently, when Mattie rushed in through the back door.

"Mattie, you're late," Carrie said, turning.

The Negro girl had lost her kerchief, and her short hair curled like a cap about her well-shaped head. There were traces of tears on her cheeks and a tremulous smile on her lips.

"Mattie . . . Are you all right?" Carrie moved anxiously toward her.

"Miss Carrie . . ." Mattie said, her voice quivering, "Miss Carrie . . . Solomon says we goin' to be free!" She took a deep shuddering breath. "We heard the people talkin'. Solomon says Mist' Lincoln done it!"

Carrie stopped, stared at Mattie's familiar face, at the mixture of longing and disbelief and even fear that struggled there, and suddenly she needed to sit down. She walked slowly to the straight-backed oak chair and sank into it, her eyes still on the girl's face.

When they had been children, she remembered, Mattie, who was several years older, had carried her around and wiped her nose and scolded her like an older sister. Carrie remembered the many times she had climbed onto Mattie's lap, asked her questions, and hung on every word. And then, as they'd grown, somewhere in those years it had become apparent to both of them that, though she was younger, Carrie was the mistress and Mattie a slave, and their behavior had changed accordingly. It was the way of things and never questioned by either of them.

Until now.

Shaken, Carrie looked toward the stove. It was smoking slightly, and the fumes stung her nose. "I tried to fix the fire," she said, her voice hollow, as if it were someone else speaking.

"Yes, Miss Carrie," Mattie said, slipping back into her usual tone. "I'll see to it."

She went to the stove and put in another piece of wood, expertly shifted the coals around and gave the damper a deft twist. The smoking stopped as if by magic. She laid the iron poker across the woodbox and turned back to face Carrie.

"Is it true, Miss Carrie?" she said simply.

It took Carrie the longest time to answer. "I'm not sure . . . but I think it's not," she said. She wanted to cry, but she wasn't sure why.

Rance Stewart skillfully guided the big roan gelding through the crowded New Orleans streets, the wheels of his buggy clicking rhythmically over the cobblestones. He approached Jackson Square, the heart of the old city, with its venerable state and court buildings flanking the ancient, three-spired St. Louis Cathedral. The newer, red brick Pontalba buildings opposite the cathedral sported delicate, French-made iron balconies. Called the Place d'Armes in the early days, the once dusty parade ground was now green and lush with shrubs and flowers. In the center of the square stood a bronze statue of Andrew Jackson, the man who had saved New Orleans from the British in the War of 1812.

Rance clucked to his horse and skirted the square to continue on past St. Anne, heading toward Dumaine Street. The late morning air was growing ever more still and humid, the sky overlaid with great masses of light gray clouds.

There wasn't a lot of time. He still had to pack a few things and inform the stout Creole lady who owned the house on Bienville Street where he kept rooms that he would be away for a few weeks. And his departure time was only hours away.

General Butler had given him no advance notice; the general was anxious that his policies be defended in Washington as soon as possible. Apparently the British and the French ambassadors had protested Butler's high-handed methods in New Orleans, particularly his "Woman Order." New Orleans had always had strong ties with Europe and had once, of course, belonged to France.

Now President Lincoln, confronted with the ambassadors' outrage, was asking for a full explanation.

Rance made a wry face. That he should be the one called upon to defend Butler's policies was ironic, since he so often disagreed with them, privately of course. Butler surely could have sent someone with higher rank. Major Barlow would have been a likely candidate. But Rance was beginning to suspect that he had been chosen deliberately because of his Southern background. What would be a nicer touch than to have a Southerner present General Butler's defense?

He tugged at the reins and turned the buggy onto Dumaine Street.

One eyebrow slanted upward as a new thought occurred to him. Could Butler have somehow found out that his father and Mr. Lincoln had been old friends before the war? He gave a mirthless chuckle. The general was a manipulator. He would use any advantage to strengthen his position with the president. Still, it was doubtful that he knew.

He had been in a towering rage when Rance was summoned into his office early that morning. He had paced the length of the room and back again, his military sash accentuating his paunch, his small eyes bloodshot, the pouches beneath them heavier than ever.

"By God," he'd stormed, "it's time the tea-sippers and the froggies across the ocean learn that they are not running this country *or* the conduct of the war! That point must be gotten across to the president! Do you understand, Stewart?"

"Yes, sir."

"Tactfully, and with all due respect, of course."

"I understand, sir."

"I knew I could depend on you." He turned toward his desk, wheezing slightly, and took up the thick packet of papers encased in a leather binding. "I worked on this the whole damned night. Didn't sleep a wink. This tells the president in plain words how it is down here. Shows him you can't mollycoddle these people. And you must tell him, too, Stewart. Tell him of the insufferable insults borne by our brave soldiers."

There *were* two sides to it, Rance admitted to himself now as he drove along Dumaine Street. And he would present Butler's

side as well as he possibly could. Duty demanded that he do no
less. The man was his commanding officer. But he still wished
someone else had been chosen to go.

Coming abreast now of the house where Carrie and Susannah
lived, he pulled the horse over to the banquette and secured the
reins, then swung down to pull the iron ring outside the gate. He
could hear the faint clang of a bell somewhere within.

Through the delicate hand-wrought scrollwork, he could see
one corner of the courtyard, could see the bright purple blossoms
of a bougainvillea trailing along the far brick wall. A bird, which
sounded as if it might be a parrot, screeched noisily and then
quieted.

There was the sound of a door opening and footsteps, then
Mattie's dusky face, framed prettily in a blue and white kerchief,
broke into a big smile as she recognized him and edged the gate
ajar.

"Cap'n Stewart," she said. "Good day to you."

"Mattie, I've come to see Miss Susannah. Tell her that I'm
sorry to call unexpectedly, but I need to speak to her today."

"Miss Susannah ain't here, Cap'n. She gone with Miz Abby
to the sewin' circle."

"Oh, I see. Well, what about Miss Carrie, Mattie? Is she in?"

"Yes, sir, she is. Come right this way, Cap'n."

Rance entered and turned into the covered entranceway, following Mattie through the solid wooden door. Its shape a graceful arch, its dark green color was mellowed and soft, the once
black iron strap hinges pleasantly grayed. Inside the front entrance hall, there was the faint smell of flowers, and as his eyes
adjusted to the light, he saw a large bowl of roses atop an inlaid
walnut commode. Mattie took his hat.

"You can wait right in there, Cap'n." She gestured toward the
bright sitting room with its mint-green love seats and white
chairs.

Through the French doors, which were wide open to catch the
slightest breath of air, he saw the bird he'd heard earlier, a huge
macaw in a big wicker cage that hung in the shade, suspended
from a latticework frame covered with clematis. The colorful
creature edged along his perch and solemnly preened himself.

Rance could hear soft, female voices nearby, first Mattie's, then Carrie's. He couldn't quite make out what they were saying, except that he thought he heard Carrie say, "No."

He stepped out into the hall.

"Just tell Captain Stewart that I am indisposed and cannot possibly see him this morning." He heard Carrie's hushed command and in the next instant saw her come out of a doorway a short distance away and start toward the stairs.

"Carrie . . ."

Her hand was already outstretched to the banister, her slipper on the bottom step. She paused for the longest moment before she turned to face him. She was in a pale pink dress that bared her arms and throat and emphasized her slender waist. Her dark hair was caught back loosely with a matching pink ribbon.

As always, the sight of her disturbed him, caused his blood to quicken. He found his eyes straying to those magnificent breasts that he remembered so well, found himself thinking that only a layer or two of cloth hid them from him now.

He cleared his throat noisily and reminded himself why he had come. "Carrie, I do beg your pardon for coming uninvited. I'll only take up a few moments of your time."

She flushed slightly. It was obvious to both of them that he had heard what she'd said. "Really . . ." she stammered, "I . . . I am quite occupied this morning. I had not expected a caller."

"Only a minute. Please." He indicated the sitting room from which he'd just come, and after a moment's hesitation, she nodded and led the way.

"May I sit down?" he asked, gesturing to one of the big white chairs.

"Of course. Please do." But she stood, rigidly formal, so he remained standing also.

"I actually didn't come to see you, Carrie. I came to see Suzy, but Mattie tells me that she isn't here. You see, I had promised that I would take her to LeGallienne's Sweet Shop tomorrow afternoon and—"

Carrie's eyebrows arched, her eyes were cold. "You and Suzy?" she interrupted.

"Yes. We had talked about it at Prosper's last Thursday. That was the day that you weren't feeling well . . ." He paused, eyed her steadily, and the color in her cheeks deepened. "I do hope you're feeling better," he said.

"Yes, thank you," she said shortly.

"Anyway, she was saying that she missed going to the Sweet Shop since Beau Canfield is out of town again, and I volunteered."

"I see," Carrie said.

There was a moment's silence while he studied her. Whatever softening he had felt in her the last time they were together, that day when he'd driven her home from the market, was now gone. She was as distant and unforgiving as ever.

"Do you disapprove of my taking Suzy to the Sweet Shop?" he asked.

Her eyes avoided his. "I would prefer that my sister, who has a brother in the Confederate Army," she said pointedly, "were not seen about town with a Yankee."

"Isn't it possible that a Yankee could be a friend, Carrie?" he asked.

She refused to answer, kept her head turned away. "If I can finish my business here in New Orleans, I intend to take Suzy back to Kingston's Landing, and that will be an end to any problem."

He stood watching her, his eyes taking in the smooth skin of her throat where a small pulse beat visibly, the rosy hue of her cheeks, the full moist lips. "I would hate to have you go," he said very softly.

She stiffened and turned back at once, her face rigidly aloof now. "I do believe you've forgotten your promise to stay only a minute, Captain Stewart, and I have yet to figure out just why you've come," she added tartly.

Stung, he assumed a manner as formal as her own. "Forgive me," he said. "I simply came to tell Suzy that I am leaving for Washington within a few hours. I am carrying dispatches from General Butler to the president."

"The president?" she said.

"President Lincoln," he said deliberately. "Please tell Suzy that I regret I cannot keep our engagement for tomorrow afternoon and that I hope to see her again when I return."

"Very well. And perhaps, Captain, when you see Mr. Lincoln,

you can ask him something for me. Ask him how he presumes to free all the slaves in the Confederate States? One would think that if he were intending to set anyone free, it would be in those states that are still with the Union.''

They glared at each other for a long moment, and then Rance bowed stiffly.

''Until I see you again, Carrie . . .''

Mattie was waiting in the hall with his hat, her eyes apologetic as she showed him silently out the door and through the gate.

Still fuming, Carrie sat in the courtyard on the bench under the plum tree, leaning against the scrolled iron backrest and fanning furiously with her lace-edged handkerchief. How dare Rance Stewart intrude himself into their lives? she thought angrily. Just because Prosper had invited him to tea, did he think that he had the right to be taking Suzy around?

Unable to sit still, she jumped up and walked along the far wall where tendrils of ivy crept upward, in some places nearly covering the old bricks. Yankees! she thought scornfully. Would the day never come when they would be rid of them? How she wished that the war would just be over. J. D. would come home, and they'd get married. Everything would be simple and neat and decided. She would never again have to think of Rance Stewart. Not ever again in her whole life. . . .

She jumped as the bell sounded, and though she couldn't see the gate from where she was, she turned involuntarily in that direction.

If that were he . . . if that were Rance again. . . . She set her teeth and glared at the corner of the house as if she could see right through it to the gate and as the bell sounded again, stamped her foot and gave her head a toss, rehearsing in her head all the things she would say to him if he had dared to come back.

Mattie had left only minutes before to go to the market. She had forgotten something that she needed for the stew she was making for dinner. And Lafitte had driven Susannah and Abby to their sewing circle meeting, so there was no one but Carrie to answer.

She steeled herself as she went around the corner of the house and along the narrow walkway to the front. She would be coldly polite, but she would send him packing in no uncertain terms.

She came determinedly up to the scrolled gate and stopped still, a glad cry escaping her. "Beau!"

He was standing on the banquette, obviously safe and sound, looking splendid as always in a fawn-colored suit, walking stick in hand. A cocky grin marked his face as he swept off the tall hat. "Good afternoon, Carrie," he said, sunlight burnishing strands of curling blond hair.

"When did you get back?" she asked, throwing open the gate.

"Only this morning. I came as soon as I could. I do hope I'm not intruding."

"Not at all. Do come in," Carrie said. "Though I'm afraid you're going to be disappointed. Suzy has gone to the sewing circle meeting with Abby Morrison this afternoon."

"She's out? That is too bad."

Carrie closed the gate behind him and he followed her back along the walkway. "I'm sure," she said over her shoulder, "she'll be sorry that she wasn't here to greet you. Come, we'll go in this way." They passed through the French doors and into the sitting room.

"I confess," he said, "that I hadn't expected that you would answer the bell personally, Carrie. To what do I owe the honor?"

Carrie laughed. "No one else is here." It occurred to her that it was quite improper to invite a gentleman into the house when she was there alone. But it wasn't every day that a gentleman returned from a dangerous mission. "And," she explained, "I happened to be in the courtyard when you rang."

The sitting room seemed delightfully cool after the heat of the sun.

"Here," Carrie said, "let me take your hat and stick." She took them into the hall and put them on the walnut commode by the bowl of roses, then returned to find him sitting comfortably on one of the silk-covered love seats, one arm stretched casually across the carved rosewood trim of the back.

"Would you like some tea, Beau? Or a glass of lemonade? I believe Mattie made some before she left."

"No, nothing." He grinned at her. "I'd like only to be allowed to sit here and enjoy looking at your beautiful face."

"Beau . . ." she chided. She was always a little flustered by his flattery.

She sat down in the chair opposite him. "Very well," she said, "if you don't want lemonade, you must tell me all about the trip."

"I'm happy to say it was successful," he said.

"No trouble?"

"Not the least bit."

"I don't believe you'd tell us if there were. At least tell me about Charleston," she prompted.

He took out one of his thin black cigars. "May I?" he asked.

"Of course."

He lit the cigar, inhaling deeply and blowing the white smoke away from her. "I think the people of Charleston realize now that the North won't back down easily. I heard very little in the way of bravado during this latest trip. They're settling in. And determined that we win. However long it takes."

"Did you tell them how things are here in New Orleans?"

"Yes. They're distressed about the loyalty oath business. I also," he chuckled, "told a group of gentlemen that the ladies here are much prettier than their counterparts in Charleston. I don't believe they appreciated it."

"Beau," Carrie laughed at him in spite of herself, "you are never serious."

"Oh, but I am," he said, and there was a subtle change in his eyes, almost as if he were quietly contemplating a private joke.

Carrie got up and brought him an ashtray from the cabinet and then began to rearrange the flowers in a vase on the mahogany card table against the wall. "I'm really sorry Suzy wasn't here to welcome you home."

"Yes, it's too bad. But perhaps a blessing in disguise."

"Oh?" Carrie's hand stayed as she repositioned a huge yellow zinnia.

"I've been wanting to talk with you for some time now."

"What about?" she asked, her back still turned to him. She felt a flood of misgiving. Surely he wasn't going to ask for Suzy's hand. She was still practically a child. She was much too young to get married, and even if she weren't, George Pierre would have to give his consent, and there was no possibility of that in the foreseeable future.

"Would you stop fiddling around with those flowers, Carrie?"

She heard him get up and come to stand behind her. "What is it you wish to speak to me about?" She turned to face him squarely. The ruffles of his shirtfront were crisp and perfect. He wore a carved carnelian stickpin in his cravat.

"Before I left the city," the dark eyes met hers boldly, "Susannah told me that you were trying, unsuccessfully, to borrow enough money to put Kingston's Landing back into production."

Taken by surprise, Carrie could only look at him for a moment. She laughed nervously. "Perhaps I should tell Suzy that I don't appreciate her discussing my private affairs."

"Oh, but in this case"—he grinned—"it was exactly the right thing to do. You see, I believe that I can help you."

"You do?" She couldn't help but seize upon it eagerly. "You know someone who might be willing to make such a loan?"

"I do indeed." He lowered his head slightly, gazing out at her from those deep-set eyes that seemed so dark for the fair skin and hair. "Under the right circumstances."

"I . . . I'd be willing to pay a fair return on the money once my sugar was sold," she said. "If I could just meet with this person . . . Could you tell me who it is?"

He stood there watching her, a strange smile playing about his lips. "Me," he said.

"You?"

"I would be willing to . . . make an arrangement with you." He took a step closer to her, and Carrie found herself backed against the table.

"Excuse me, please," she said stiffly, and tried to slip past him.

He blocked her way. The pungent odor of his very expensive cologne assailed her nostrils.

"You forget yourself, Beau!"

He moved a pace away, laughing at her all the while. "All right . . . all right."

He stepped into the hallway and returned at once with his hat and stick. "Think it over," he said coolly. "We can discuss terms anytime, but you need to get the money by spring if you're going to get the crop in. And it is a shame to let such a magnificent plantation lie there wasting.

"Besides"—his eyes narrowed—"Other things can happen. Worse things. Did you know that one of the neighboring places up there has been confiscated by the government?"

Carrie's fingers clenched. "What place?" she said.

"The one across the river from Kingston's Landing. I believe they said it was the Gayerre plantation."

"I don't believe you!" she flared.

He shrugged. "It's a matter of public record. It was abandoned, and the government acted in a quite legal manner to claim it."

He walked over to the French doors and turned back. "Think about it, Carrie. It's entirely up to you. And take all the time you please. Just remember, I have friends in high places. I can be a great deal of help to you when it comes to Kingston's Landing."

She stood there, too stunned by what he had just told her to speak. As she watched, he put the tall hat atop his head, touched the brim of it lightly with the tip of his walking stick, and with a mocking grin on his face, walked through the doors.

13

RANCE STEWART REPOSITIONED HIS BIG FRAME ON THE HARD, straight-backed chair and again looked about the crowded anteroom of the executive office at the people who waited there to see the president. Three bewhiskered gentlemen conversed in low tones in a quiet corner and occasionally passed some kind of graph from one to the other. A rotund, florid-faced fellow tugged at his graying mustache and tapped his foot impatiently, as he had done for the entire thirty minutes he'd been there. Across from Rance, a man in overalls dozed, slumping sideways in his chair, his mouth slightly open. Next to him a small boy, who was kept under tight control by his tired-eyed mother, couldn't seem to decide which fascinated him more, the softly snoring sleeper who gave every appearance that he might list right out of the chair and onto the floor, or Rance's full dress uniform with its shiny brass buttons and smartly tied sash, his dress sword in the scabbard at his side.

Rance had arrived in Washington the evening before and taken a room at Willard's Hotel on Fourteenth Street. After a good night's sleep and a hearty breakfast of steak and fried oysters served to him by a smiling, apple-cheeked girl, he had come at once to the Executive Mansion which, with its outbuildings and kitchen gardens, looked not unlike a thriving and busy Southern plantation house. An iron fence with large gateways bordered the front, and people could be seen traversing the lawns to wherever they happened to be going. Paths had been worn through the grass. A ripe, rank smell wafted on the breeze from time to time, emanating from the marshes at the lower end of that tract of land that lay just south and was known as the President's Park.

Inside the mansion, Rance had found sightseers wandering at will on the lower floor, gawking at the glistening chandeliers, dirtying the flowered carpets with dusty boots. Bonneted ladies paused to admire their reflections in the huge mirrors, and more than one turned to cast discreetly admiring glances at the tall and handsome officer who strode past, but Rance didn't notice. His mind was entirely on the business ahead, and he proceeded at once up the main staircase to the rooms on the east end of the second floor where executive affairs were conducted.

The doorkeeper had accepted his credentials and disappeared into the inner office only to return minutes later with a message from the president. He would see Captain Stewart as soon as possible. At the moment, he was closeted with Mr. Seward, the Secretary of State.

That had been more than an hour ago, and now Rance tried once again to find a sitting position that would make a hard chair seem more comfortable. Though, in truth, he preferred the hard chair of the anteroom to the prospect of presenting General Butler's case to the president.

He had wrestled with it since he'd first been informed of his mission by General Butler, and each time he had come to the same conclusion. His duty was clear. He was a soldier in the Army of the United States; he was there representing his commanding officer, and he must represent him well.

He thought of that last day in New Orleans, the rush to get everything done before leaving, and Carrie was suddenly there in his mind. She had been lovely in that pink dress, her eyes golden in the light, her mouth so kissable that it had caused an ache inside him to keep his hands off her.

Jesus, would he never be able to get that night, or her, out of his mind? He should be thinking of Nora Barlow, who certainly didn't hide the fact that she welcomed his attentions. Instead all he seemed to be able to think about was Carrie Kingston, who did nothing but spit fire at him whenever he got near her.

But, God, she was magnificent! Like no other female he had ever seen. Every inch a woman . . . beautiful. And yet proud and courageous, too. None of the vapors for her. He remembered that first time he'd seen her. That day at Kingston's Landing. Holding her ground and ordering Hagerty to put Mattie down, "At once!"

There was no way to forget her. And yet there was nothing to suggest that she would ever forgive him for what had happened between them that night, no matter how many times he apologized to her, no matter how many times he tried to make amends. And, he reminded himself sternly, she was engaged to marry this fellow Morrison. He mustn't forget that.

Still . . . the memory of her body was burned into him, irrevocably. The memory had all too often sent him riding in the dead of night to a certain shuttered house on Bourbon Street where there were several discreet and skilled ladies, any one of whom could relieve his feverish desire . . . at least for the moment. But there was always another night, always the memory of Kingston's Landing and Carrie . . . always Carrie.

"Captain Stewart?"

Startled, Rance realized that the doorkeeper was standing before him with a somewhat annoyed look on his face.

"I *said* the president will see you now, Captain Stewart."

"Thank you," Rance replied crisply to hide his embarrassment. He quickly gathered up his leather-bound sheaf of papers and allowed himself to be ushered through the door and into the president's office.

His eyes swept the room, which was large and bright and furnished with one large desk, a small writing desk, two cupboards, several chairs, a small table or two, and what appeared to be a map rack. The carpet was patterned in small squares, alternately light and dark, with flowers in the center of each one. The president himself, in a black frock coat that seemed slightly short on that lanky stretch of frame, stood in front of one of the two windows. Their heavy draperies were drawn back by tasseled cords, ornate cornices above. Mr. Lincoln was leaning forward to look out, shoulders stooped beneath the rumpled jacket, but he straightened and turned at once to greet his visitor.

"Rance . . ." he said warmly, coming forward, outsized hand extended.

"Mr. President . . ." Rance saluted smartly and then took the profferred hand.

"Relax." The gaunt face broke into a smile that lit those cavernous eyes. "I was looking out the window and admiring the day. It'd be just right to go fishin', a day like today. Be nice if the two of us could just go off and do that."

"Yes, sir." Rance grinned.

"Seems to me I remember a time when you and your daddy and me did that very thing. Do you recall it? You weren't much higher'n my knee then."

"Yes, sir, I remember it very well."

"Sit down, sit down." President Lincoln gestured to the chair opposite the bigger desk and then settled himself into the tall-backed chair behind it. "And how is your father?"

"I . . . I don't know, sir," Rance said. "I hope he's well."

Mr. Lincoln sighed. "He still hasn't forgiven you for choosing to fight for the Union?"

"No, sir."

The president leaned his head back for a moment and was quiet, his eyes infinitely sad. "This war . . . the costs have been heavy, Rance. And will no doubt grow heavier."

"Yes, sir." Rance thought of the day he'd announced his decision, remembered that stony turning away. It had been inconceivable to his father that any Southerner could fight against the Confederacy. Rance had managed to send letters several times, but there had never been a reply.

"Well," the president said, perhaps sensing that he had touched a raw nerve, "it will not always be so. Let us pray that once the war is ended the bitterness will be put aside."

He shuffled the papers on his desk top and made a clear space in front of him. "Now let's see what you have there . . ." He held out his hand for the leather-bound packet, which Rance quickly passed to him. After untying the laces that secured it, he scanned down the first page.

"Ah, yes . . . General Butler's report." He shoved it aside. "I'll read it later. Right now, I want you to tell me what you think of the situation."

Rance tried to remember his carefully rehearsed speech. "Mr. President," he said, "General Butler is a man of great military capability and certainly a man who displays the fiercest loyalty to the Union."

"I know that," the president said. "He has served his country well in the past. But he's stirred up a hornet's nest with this 'Woman Order' thing, Rance. The French are hopping mad over it. What in heaven's name prompted that whole business?"

"Well, sir, it was not totally without cause. The women of New Orleans were not too happy to see Yankee soldiers in the streets. And," he added, grinning in spite of himself, "Southern women are not exactly shy about showing their disapproval. Especially if they feel they're right about something."

Lincoln chuckled, nodding that big head slowly. "You don't have to tell me. Mrs. Lincoln, bless her, is from the South. Kentucky born, you know. As I was, but my family moved away early on."

"Yes, sir."

The president sobered. "But was there any real harm done by these ladies of New Orleans?"

"Sir, General Butler felt very strongly that any actions or attitudes that insulted or demeaned a United States soldier could not be tolerated."

"But *harm*, Rance? Actual harm done?"

Rance took a deep breath. "General Butler felt that there had been sufficient provocation to warrant Order #28. And it was certainly the duty of the general to take such action as he deemed necessary to keep the peace once the military government assumed control of the city."

"You're not answering my questions, Rance." The voice was gently chiding, and Mr. Lincoln's eyes probed from beneath those hooded brows. "I want to know what *you* think."

Rance hesitated for a moment, but then plunged ahead stubbornly. "As the lowest ranking aide to the general, Mr. President, I am not always in a position to make a correct judgment about such matters. I confess I was surprised that an officer of higher rank was not chosen to carry the general's report to you, sir, but I'm sure the report—"

"You were sent because I requested you." Lincoln cut him off. And while Rance sat there stunned, the president leaned forward, elbows on the desk before him. "I've known you since you were a boy, Rance. I needed someone I could trust to tell me what is going on down there."

"Mr. President, the general . . ." Rance began but stopped, unable to continue under those eyes that seemed to see right through him.

"The wounds inflicted on the nation by this war will be terrible," the president said, a deep current of sadness running through his voice. "Perhaps so terrible that neither you nor I will ever live to see them healed. It is my job and my wish to keep those wounds to the minimum that is possible, without jeopardizing that ultimate duty . . . to keep the Union whole. I cannot do that unless I have *all* the facts before I make decisions in any given situation."

"I understand that, sir," Rance said. He studied the face of the man before him, the face so many people seemed to find ugly. He didn't. He had always seen in those craggy features not only a wisdom but a genuine gentleness that was rooted in strength rather than weakness, as if it came from the very rocks and the land itself.

"It's commendable, Captain," Mr. Lincoln went on, "that you feel a duty to defend your commanding officer—and he may well deserve your defense. But I'd like you to remember that in this case, your first duty is to the country . . . and to me.''

The eyes of the two men locked, Rance sitting rigidly erect, the president with his shoulders rounding slightly, his big hands lying relaxed on the desk before him. Finally Rance nodded.

"Yes, sir, Mr. President,'' he said.

And for the better part of the next hour, he answered the president's questions as honestly as he could, all the time trying to be scrupulously fair to General Butler. They not only discussed the "Woman Order,'' but also a full range of other matters that had to do with the military occupation of New Orleans. And when Mr. Lincoln brought up the matter of profiteering, Rance told him what he knew but hastened to add that, though it was common knowledge that Jackson Butler had made a great deal of money out of the war, there was no evidence at all that the general had any part in it.

"But in your opinion, Rance, would it be possible for General Butler to be unaware of his brother's activities?'' the president asked.

Rance considered his answer for a long moment, then shook his head. "In my opinion, it would not be possible, Mr. President.''

Mr. Lincoln seemed lost in thought, his head hunched forward, chin resting on one of those big, knobby-jointed hands.

"Tell me of the people,'' he straightened up and broke the silence. "What would you say their main grievance is at this time?''

"The loyalty oath,'' Rance answered without hesitation.

"Ah, the loyalty oath . . .'' The president got up from the desk, paced to the window, and stood looking out again. "The gentlemen of the Congress were determined to pass it, but I've had reservations.''

"It's been my feeling, Mr. President—'' Rance broke off, fearing that he had overstepped himself.

Mr. Lincoln turned toward him, smiled. "Yes . . . go on.''

"I . . . I was just going to say, sir, that I thought it would have been better to give them a little more time before a loyalty oath was forced upon them. But, Mr. President, you must remember that I am, after all, a Southerner myself, and I can't find it easy to see my own people so defeated—no matter how compelling the circumstance, no matter how strongly I feel about the Union cause.''

"I would be surprised if it were otherwise, Rance." The president came back to the desk. "General Butler has required the oath? It's an accomplished fact then?''

"Yes, sir. The general set a deadline, and it is now passed . . . since I left New Orleans.''

The president grunted, the sound coming from deep within his chest. "Then it can't be helped. The United States government must not appear to our Rebel countrymen to be less than steadfast. That might lead to even worse things.''

He picked up the leather-bound pages from the desk. "I'll study General Butler's report carefully, and then I may have some more questions for you.''

Rance rose at once.

"Plan to stay on in Washington at least for the next few days," Mr. Lincoln said.

"Yes, sir.''

The president held out his hand and once again clasped Rance's warmly. "It's been a pleasure to see you again, Rance.''

"Thank you, Mr. President," Rance said. "May I say, sir, how deeply grieved I was to learn of the death of your son, Willie.''

The president nodded his head, the underlying sadness that never seemed far away flooding his eyes. "It's been hard for his mother and me.''

"Please give Mrs. Lincoln my condolences, and my very best wishes.''

The president grasped Rance's shoulder. "Why don't you come and take supper with us this evening? I'm sure Mrs. Lincoln will remember you and be pleased to see you again. Besides, it occurs to me that you might be able to give me some information on a subject I've been turning over in my mind lately.

"I'm told that there is a whole class of people in New Orleans, free people of Negro blood who are intelligent and well-educated . . . men of the arts, the professions.''

"That's correct, sir.''

"You've observed this yourself?"

Rance nodded. "As a matter of fact, Mr, President, such a man is a very good friend of mine. His name is Prosper Durant, and he is a fencing master of world renown. He was educated in Paris and is not only a man of intellect but of great honor and integrity." Rance grinned. "I confess that he can not only beat me with a sword, but he is formidable in our philosophical discussions. And I'll not be so foolhardy as to attempt a chess game with him again."

The president smiled thoughtfully. "Once this war is ended," he mused, almost to himself, "our Negro people must not only be free, they must be brought to full citizenship . . . must be given the franchise. What better place to start than with these remarkable people of color in New Orleans?"

He recovered himself, returned his full attention to Rance. "You will come to supper, won't you?" he said.

"It'll be my pleasure, sir."

"Very good. And, Rance," the president added, his eyes suddenly clouding, "it might be just as well not to mention Willie to Mrs. Lincoln. Even though it's been some months now . . . it's still very difficult for her."

"I understand, Mr. President," Rance said.

That great, craggy face smiled the gentle and sad smile, but the eyes were distant once again, already reflecting the weight of the days and months to come. "Until then," he said absently.

14

CARRIE SHIFTED HER RUFFLED PARASOL TO SHIELD HER EYES from the sun and watched the lush green lawns and clipped hedges that slipped quickly past as Lafitte drove her along the St. Charles Road toward the Morrisons' house, the trim mare moving easily, her flanks gleaming in the mid-morning sunlight.

Carrie had stopped off at the bank to see Leroy Tate, and though he still had no good news for her, she found him much more relaxed than the last time she'd called on him. She wondered if he'd given in and taken the loyalty oath. It was suspected that a great many people had. When that tremendous pressure had been brought to bear, they simply hadn't been able to withstand it and had mustered up whatever excuses they could to justify themselves and flocked to pledge their allegiance.

She was terribly proud of the Morrisons because they'd resisted. J. D. would be proud of them, too, Carrie thought, if he knew. It was clear, though, that the whole wretched business had taken a terrible toll on Abby, who had grown noticeably thinner, the once rounded chin sharp and angular, the oval shape to her eyelids more pronounced.

It had been two weeks since the deadline, since Seth had had to turn in his list of possessions and register with the Provost Marshal as an enemy of the state, and nothing had happened.

"You *see*," Seth had crowed just the other night at dinner, "I told you it was a tempest in a teapot! I knew Butler wouldn't have the nerve to take action against those of us who wouldn't give in to his demands!"

178

Beau Canfield, there also, had lifted his glass to that, his knowing eyes seeking Carrie's.

She had felt vaguely uncomfortable in his presence since the day of his visit. His manner had been admittedly disturbing. She had longed to discuss the offer he had made with the Morrisons but had drawn back because they were so preoccupied by the loyalty oath. It hardly seemed the time to ask their advice. And certainly not the time to question them about a man they obviously doted on.

Once, when his name had come up, she had been close, just on the verge of talking to Abby when that poor woman had launched into a litany of praise for Beau and added that she didn't know how she and Seth would have gotten through these terrible days of the occupation if they hadn't had him to rely upon. He had almost, she said, taken the place of a son until their own J. D. could come back to them.

Carrie had decided almost immediately against mentioning the incident to Suzy. She'd been so unsettled by the events of the day, however, by Rance's visit and then Beau's unexpected behavior, that she'd ended up soundly berating her sister for agreeing to go to LeGallienne's Sweet Shop with Rance Stewart. They had had a terrible argument, which had ended with Susannah running upstairs in tears.

Later when Carrie went up to make amends, Susannah had stood white-faced, her lips quivering but those green eyes determined. "I am not a child," she announced firmly, "and I will not be told who I may see and who I may not see! Besides, Carrie, Rance is not the least bit interested in me *that* way. You're the one he's crazy about. Can't you see that?"

Taken aback, Carrie had made her stumbling apology once again and then retreated to her own room where she'd lain on the bed and stared, dry-eyed, at the ceiling.

She almost wished that she had talked to Suzy about Beau that day. Small things had begun to nag at her. Beau's expensive clothes. His jeweled stickpins and cuff links and ivory-headed walking sticks. Even Prosper, who had always been something of a dandy, was beginning to look a little worn about the collar, a little frayed about the cuffs. No respectable Southerner she knew, except Beau Canfield, had any money these days.

But perhaps she was making something out of nothing, she chided herself. It was certainly true that he had to dress well if he were to continue to fool the Yankees into believing that he was a Union sympathizer. It was a pose that was necessary if he were to continue his aid to the Confederacy. She felt disloyal every time she entertained those vague misgivings. And there was no denying that her sister would be furious if she ever voiced them.

Lost in her thoughts, she was surprised to discover that they'd turned into the Morrisons' drive and now approached the front of the two-story, red-brick house with its wide front porch and vine-filled lattices. Bringing the horse to a smart stop, Lafitte came round to help her down and then, after seeing her safely up on the porch, drove on toward the back where he knew that old Thomas would be. The two men often passed the time with a game of craps on the stable floor.

Penelope, her head bound up in a crisp, white kerchief, greeted Carrie with a smile, her long-fingered hands gesturing down the hall. "The Mistress in the back sittin' room, Miss Carrie."

Carrie handed over her parasol and went to find Abby diligently working at still another woolen scarf, though she must have made a trunkful of them by now and there seemed little chance that they would ever be delivered to the Confederate boys for whom they were intended.

"Carrie . . ." she said, "you're just in time to have coffee with me. Will you bring us some, please, Penelope?"

"Yes, ma'am," the girl said and sped away.

But Carrie had hardly seated herself, had hardly had a chance to admire the fine stitching of the scarf when there came an insistent clanging of the bell.

"Good heavens," Abby said, "I wonder who that could be? I wasn't expecting anyone but you. It could be Miss Esther Beauchamp. She always rings that way." Abby laughed. "Just because she's deaf, she thinks everyone is."

They could hear Penelope's footsteps as she went down the hall, and then, with a growing concern, Carrie heard the sound of strange male voices followed by the stamp of booted feet on the wide floorboards.

Abby had dropped her knitting, and the ball of yarn rolled slowly across the floor unnoticed as the two women exchanged looks and stood just in time to see the blue-clad form of a Yankee soldier fill the doorway.

Hat in hand, the young lieutenant bowed awkwardly, his sun-bleached hair reminding Carrie of J. D.'s. "My apologies for disturbing you, ladies," he said. "This is the home of Mr. Seth Morrison?"

"Why . . . why, yes," Abby answered, her voice cracking slightly, her face gone quite pale.

"You are Mrs. Morrison?"

Abby nodded.

"And you, Miss?"

"This is Miss Kingston," Abby said quickly before Carrie could speak. "My son's fiancée."

The young soldier's pale blue eyes flickered over Carrie with a not-quite-hidden admiration, and then, cheeks reddening, back to Abby. "I'm sorry, ma'am. I have my orders," he said.

"What kind of orders?" Carrie demanded.

The lieutenant fiddled with his hat, clearly embarrassed. "If you ladies will just stay right here . . . I assure you that no harm will come to anyone in the household."

He turned away, and Carrie saw him nod to the other half-dozen or so soldiers in the hallway who set off in different directions, their heavy boots once again clumping noisily.

"Oh, Carrie . . ." Abby whispered. Her hands were clenched, the knuckles white as bone.

Throwing her a look that tried to be reassuring, Carrie followed after the officer.

"Lieutenant," Carrie called, "I demand to know your business."

Confronted by that imperious tone, by the golden eyes that seemed to blaze fire at him, he retreated a step, but then stood fast. "I . . . I'm simply following orders, Miss Kingston," he stammered.

"What orders?"

His cheeks burning now, he shifted his eyes away from hers and wished to heaven that he had never been sent on this detail. "I have a list . . . of certain items that are to be . . . must be confiscated for military purposes," he finished lamely.

"Confiscated?" she said.

"Yes, Miss." It was only after a long moment that he dared to look at her again.

She stood there staring at him, well-drawn, dark brows lifted in scorn, mouth curved contemptuously. "Confiscated, Lieutenant? Don't you mean *stolen*?"

Sweat popped out, glistened along his upper lip. He could not meet her eyes. "I . . . I'm sorry, Miss," he said and turned abruptly away to leave Carrie standing in the hallway.

As she turned to go back into the sitting room, she spied Penelope huddled against the far wall, half-hidden behind the tall grandfather clock. She beckoned, and the girl came at once, her narrow face pinched.

"I told them they got to wait, Miss Carrie," she said, as if she feared someone might blame her for this intrusion of uniforms and rough boots. "They didn't pay no attention to me. Just walked right past me, Miss Carrie."

"I know, Penelope. You come along with me."

They went back into the sitting room to find Abby weeping soundlessly, tears splashing slowly down her cheeks.

"They . . . they're going to take some things," Carrie said. She had never felt so helpless.

Abby bit at her lip, nodded. "I know," she managed to get out. "I heard."

The awful, silent weeping continued, and Carrie felt a blazing anger scorch through her. "You stay here with your mistress," she said to Penelope, and she swept back out into the hallway again, drawing her skirts aside as a burly soldier came out of the parlor with a small rosewood table hefted to his shoulder.

She managed to choke back a stinging rebuke and continued on to find the lieutenant in the dining room. He took one look at her, ducked his head, and busied himself examining the china in the cabinet.

She looked at that boyish profile. Honey, she thought, might get her more than vinegar. At least it was worth a try. "Lieutenant . . ." she said in as pleasant a voice as she could muster, "Lieutenant, I just know there's been some mistake."

"I wish that were so, Miss Kingston," he said, clearly struggling not to be dazzled by the smile that she turned on him.

"But surely," she coaxed, "you could delay this until the

matter has been reviewed by some higher official. Mr. Seth Morrison is a man of some importance in New Orleans.''

The young lieutenant squirmed. ''My orders are clear,'' he said reluctantly. ''They were issued by the Provost Marshal's office, Miss Kingston.''

''Even so . . .''

''I'm sorry,'' he said, his blue eyes young and miserable.

She wanted to stamp her foot and order him and his men from the house, but she didn't allow herself to unleash her temper.

He began to examine the contents of the china cabinet once again. Surely, she thought frantically, there was something she could do, someone she could appeal to. If Rance were back from Washington. . . .

Something inside her hardened. Never! She would never ask him for anything. It was his army that was doing this terrible thing. And he was every bit as bad as they were. Worse. *He* was a Southerner.

The lieutenant closed the cabinet doors. ''I really can't tell you, Miss Kingston, how much I regret all this,'' he mumbled and then fled the room as if he would get away from her accusing presence, but Carrie was not going to let him off that easily.

She followed right along after him, was at his side when he directed his men to remove the grandfather clock and load it in the waiting wagon.

''Careful with it,'' he said, trying his best to pretend that she wasn't there.

Her outrage growing by the minute, she watched them carry out a lovely marble-topped credenza and after that, the big mirror that hung in the hallway.

Upstairs, she couldn't hold back a bitter protest as she saw a rough soldier searching through a chest of drawers, pawing over Abby's delicate lace handkerchiefs and intimate garments. ''Lieutenant,'' she cried, ''surely this isn't necessary! I cannot believe that even a Yankee soldier would have so little respect for . . . for privacy,'' she sputtered. She could feel her cheeks burn, but the young lieutenant's face had gone an even deeper red.

"Once again you have my apologies, Miss Kingston. But our orders are to search for contraband."

"Contraband? That's ridiculous! What kind of contraband?" she demanded.

He moved nervously from one foot to the other. "Don't you think, Miss Kingston," he said plaintively, "that it would be best if you stayed with Mrs. Morrison downstairs? We'll be about this as quickly as possible and then take our leave."

Carrie ignored that and turned away only to see a skinny soldier straining to lift a trunk near the foot of the bed. She recognized it as the one that held Abby's silver in its false bottom. "Lieutenant," she spoke up quickly, "does the Union Army need to steal quilts and coverlets now?"

"Quilts?" he said.

"That trunk." She pointed to the boy. "If there's a cold spell, the Morrisons won't even have any covers."

"Simpson . . ."

The young soldier turned, sweating in the airless upstairs heat, struggling with the weight of the trunk. "Yes, sir?"

"Did you look through the contents of that trunk?"

"Yes, sir. Just bedclothes."

"Put it back."

Carrie drew a hidden sigh of relief, thankful that the boy didn't seem bright enough to figure out that the trunk was too heavy to hold just bedclothes. "Thank you, Lieutenant," she got out sweetly, though every word grated. To think, she fumed, that she would have to thank him for not stealing the Morrisons' property!

Back downstairs, she was able to persuade him to leave the chairs, most of the tables, and the lamps in the parlor. They took the love seats, the fine china vases on the mantel, and the mahogany secretary.

Out in back, old Thomas looked on helplessly as two young geldings were led out of the stables, leaving only an aging mare. But when the soldiers tried to lay hands on the mare and the rig in which Carrie had come, Lafitte ensconced himself with all his dignity on the seat and refused to be budged. When news of the ruckus reached the house, Carrie went storming out, the lieutenant right behind her.

"How dare you do this?" she burst out, unable to contain her anger any longer. She shoved her way right past the three soldiers surrounding Lafitte. "Stand back!" she demanded, her blue-checked skirt belling out about her, her lace-edged bodice showing a fine expanse of creamy neck and shoulders. "You have no authority to harass this man! He happens to be my servant! And this buggy," she raged on, "and this horse do not belong to the Morrisons, they—"

"Miss Kingston"—the lieutenant tried to calm her—"I assure you it's all a misunderstanding. No one is going to harass or harm—"

"Let me tell you, Lieutenant," she cut him off. The soldiers were nudging one another and trying to keep from grinning. "If any attempt is made to take this horse or this buggy, you are going to be in a great deal of trouble!" Her voice was quivering she was so angry, her hands planted firmly on her hips. Her hair had come loose from its pins and curled about her face.

"Carmichael . . . Jones," the lieutenant barked, "all of you men go around to the front and see that the wagons are securely lashed down. We'll be leaving now." He was sweating profusely, his uniform blouse showing dark stains at his back and sleeves, but he turned to Carrie and bowed rather formally.

"May I escort you back to the house, Miss Kingston?" he said.

"Thank you, no." She stood there with her head high, all the contempt she felt for him and his general clear in her face.

"I . . . I'm sorry, Miss," he said, and turned and walked stiffly away.

Before she went back into the house to poor Abby, she looked up at Lafitte, still on his seat, cool and unruffled in his black suit, and gave him a nod of approval. He returned the smallest grin.

"I think you should reconsider and take the oath."

Beau Canfield's words brought a gasp from Carrie, but she quickly clamped her lips together and waited silently for Seth Morrison to reject the suggestion in no uncertain terms.

He lifted his eyes without moving his head, which was hunched forward as if it were too heavy for him to hold up any longer. "I can't do that," he said, his voice flat and tired, like an old man's. And yet there was something in it, that slightest questioning of his own statement that caused Abby to turn her pale face to him and stare. Susannah and Carrie exchanged looks.

They were in the scantily furnished parlor. Some straight chairs had been brought in from the dining room to take the place of the love seats, and the bare floor beneath them showed a large, lighter area where the rug had been.

It had been three days since the Union foray into the house, two days since the army guard had gone up outside of Seth's distillery. It had been confiscated in the name of the Union, and no one, they said politely, could go in or out without General Butler's express permission. When Seth had tried to see Butler, he had been told that the general was too busy to see him.

"I couldn't do that," Seth said again. "I couldn't take the oath."

"Why not?" Beau rejoined. He stood with the shaft of light from the wall lamp etching that perfect profile. His hair curled softly about his ears, gleamed down the long sideburns. His usual elegant attire seemed to make the stripped house look all the more impoverished.

"Because I would be swearing to a lie," Seth answered him. "Because I would be betraying my own son who is even now trying to hold out at Vicksburg."

"I cannot believe," Beau leaned casually against the empty mantelpiece, "that J. D. would want this dear lady, his mother, to have all her lovely things taken from her. And as to lying, consider to whom you would be lying. You must learn to *use* the enemy, Seth. As I have. In the interest of the Confederacy, of course."

"The state of my finances is hardly vital to the Confederacy," Seth protested. "This only concerns a matter of honor."

"On the other hand," Beau parried, "there would be no great aid to the Confederate cause in letting a valuable piece of property go to the Yankees, would there?"

Seth considered that in silence.

"And have *you* then found it expedient to take the oath?" Carrie asked Beau.

"No," he said coolly, "but I would, without hesitation, if the occasion demanded it."

"You just don't understand, Carrie," Susannah rushed to defend him. "Beau would do whatever was necessary to help the Confederacy. No matter what." She beamed at him, dimples showing, and Beau acknowledged her admiration with a suitably modest smile.

Seth rose to pace the room, his footsteps loud and hollow in the all-but-empty room. "Even if . . . I could bring myself to consider such a thing," he said, as much to himself as to them, "it's too late. The deadline has passed. My business has been confiscated . . ."

"Perhaps not," said Beau. "A word from me in the right ear . . ."

Seth looked at him, torn, uncertain. "You could do that? You could get my business back?"

Beau nodded. "In order to pursue my endeavors on behalf of the Confederacy, I've had to, as you know, work my way into the good graces of certain Yankee officers. I think I could do it. You'd simply have to take the oath. It needn't mean anything."

Seth shook his head slowly, clearly fighting against the temptation. "No . . . no," he said. "It's out of the question. I couldn't do it."

Beau shrugged. "It's up to you, of course," he said. "It would seem a pity if one day soon the Confederate Army marches victoriously into New Orleans . . . just too late to save you from losing everything. Once your property is sold to someone else it'll be too late."

Seth just sat there looking at his wife, who was like a ghost, pale and silent.

Carrie wanted to cry out to them not to even consider Beau's offer, but she bit the words back. She had to ask herself how firm her principles would be if Kingston's Landing were at stake. What if she were confronted with the choice of losing it or swearing allegiance to the Union? Might she not be willing to do it? After all, she had been willing to give herself to Rance Stewart to keep it safe.

She realized that Beau Canfield's eyes were on her, dark and

187

glittering, almost as if he knew what she were thinking. Dear God, what was he up to?

"I . . . I'll go ask Penelope to make some coffee," she said, and fled the room, glad to be free of that heavy, stifling atmosphere.

The kitchen was probably the least changed place in the house. The soldiers had turned everything upside down in their search for valuables, but except for sifting through the flour bin and a thorough perusal of the jars of dried beans and other staples, they had pretty much left the kitchen intact.

Penelope was nowhere to be seen so Carrie made the coffee herself and, while it was brewing, went into the dining room and began to prepare a tray with cups and saucers.

Though it was well past the dinner hour, the evening had brought no relief from the weather, which was unusually hot for so late in the year. The air hung still and heavy. Carrie had pulled her hair high up on her head and anchored it in a simple twist so it would be cooler, but she could feel the damp, hot tendrils at the back of her neck, around her temples. She smoothed it with long, tapered fingers.

"I like it that way."

Beau's voice caused Carrie almost to tip over the china coffeepot that she had just set on the tray. She turned to see his grin, those slender nostrils pinching in ever so slightly.

"Your hair . . . I like it that way," he repeated.

"What are you up to, Beau?" she demanded briskly.

"Up to?" His eyes assumed an amused innocence.

"What game are you playing with the Morrisons?"

He spread his fingers in a gesture of openness. "Game? Me?" And then his brows lowered, and he fastened her with those hot, dark eyes, the smile suddenly gone. "Perhaps," he said, "I want you to see that I can do just what I say I can, Carrie. Perhaps I want to show you that I can get Seth's distillery back for him, that a word from me . . ."

She turned away from him, but he went on relentlessly.

"I can make it possible for you to get Kingston's Landing into production again. And I can keep it safe from the Yankees." His voice was as smooth as silk, like a web wrapping around her. She fought back an unreasoning panic.

"Your offer was . . . certainly generous, Beau. But for me to accept money . . . a . . . a loan," she stammered, "from a young man who is not a relative would be entirely beyond the proprieties."

"Proprieties?" He laughed. "Fortunately such nonsense has been swept away by the war."

"No." She shook her head. "I . . . I simply couldn't do it."

She took up the tray and started toward the door but as she drew near he grasped her arm lightly and looked down at her, his smile unreadable, his teeth white and even in the gaslight.

"You'll come to me, Carrie," he said softly. "Sooner or later, you'll come."

She stood there for a moment, dark lashes heavy over the golden eyes, ripe mouth trembling in spite of her. Then she said, "I . . . I must go, Beau. The coffee will be ready."

It was eight days before Seth Morrison decided to take the oath, eight days of shuffling about the strangely bare house. It was as if he had some dreadful illness that had aged him twenty years in a week. There were deep, new lines about his eyes, slack pouches of skin along his jawline.

He had always been a busy man, vigorous and hard working so that Abby had, many years before, gotten used to being alone much of the time. But during those eight days they were together constantly. Though they were silent for hours at a time, looking over at each other infrequently and then only to move their eyes quickly away, as if each saw in the other too much pain to contemplate, at other times they talked hesitantly about nothing, as if they were fearful of crossing some dreadful line that mustn't be crossed. Then finally, one bright afternoon, the sunlight pouring into the sitting room where they sat because no one had thought to close the drapes against it, Abby suddenly turned to Seth and took his hand in hers, the thin, blue-veined fingers grasping his as tightly as she could.

To her horror, she saw tears well in his eyes before he dashed them away with his free hand. She moved closer to him on the old couch that the soldiers hadn't wanted, moved into the circle of his arm and laid her head against his shoulder.

"What should I do, Abby?" he said after a long moment, his

voice thin and stretched. He had been so certain that the military government would not dare to do anything, at most impose a fine. That would have been difficult for him to pay, but he would have paid it somehow. But this . . . he had never once considered that he might lose everything that he'd worked for his whole life.

Abby curled closer to him, crying softly into his shoulder. It had been a long time since he'd held her, and she hadn't known how much she'd missed it until now.

"What should I do, Abby?" he asked again. "How could I ever look J. D. in the face again if I took that oath?"

Abby clung to him. "But, Seth, Beau says that's what J. D. would *want* us to do."

That afternoon, he sent for Beau, and two days later Seth Morrison swore his allegiance to the government of the United States.

Nothing was quite as it had been before. Though the guard was removed from the distillery gates and the warehouses, Seth found that countless barrels of his best whiskey had been carted away, and several batches of fermenting mash had been ruined because they hadn't been tended properly. Some of the things taken from the house were brought back. The love seats, the secretary, the clock, among other things. The missing pieces, Beau explained, had been sold at one of the frequent auctions about town and were lost forever.

"Well, I think they did exactly the right thing," Susannah declared, following Beau's lead. "After all, they have the business back, don't they? Why let the Yankees have it over some old oath?"

Carrie remained silent, torn between her understanding of why they had done it and her basic inability to accept any surrender to the Yankees.

Rance Stewart was back in New Orleans. Carrie saw him riding in his high-wheeled buggy, Nora Barlow beside him, her pale blond hair gleaming in the sunlight, tilting her face up to his and smiling possessively. There were new gold-embroidered oak leaves on his shoulder straps.

One week later *The Picayune* reported that General Benjamin

F. Butler, having faithfully discharged his duties as commanding general of the occupation forces, was being relieved of that command and reassigned, and that General Nathaniel Banks would assume that position early in December.

𝒮 15 ℚ

"**J**USTICE!" CARRIE LOOKED INTO THE FAMILIAR, DARK FACE of the man who had once been her father's overseer, for many years acknowledged to be the best in the Delta, and felt an overwhelming rush of affection for him and a stab of longing for Kingston's Landing. "Justice, how good to see you! Come, you must sit down. Are you hungry? Mattie will fix you something."

The house girl, who had just shown Justice in, nodded in quick agreement.

"Thank you, no, Miss Carrie. My wife, Tana, packed me a bucket of food—chicken and fried green tomatoes and cake. I stopped a spell by the river before I come on into town." He stood with his feet planted wide apart despite the rheumatism that plagued him, the stocky body and the thick arms and legs still muscular.

"And what of Kingston's Landing?" Carrie said. "I sent Lafitte up with some supplies about three weeks ago, and everything was fine then."

"Everything goin' along just like usual. Benjamin and Chloe are seein' to things. Chloe said to tell you you was to stay down here as long as you want to. They be all right."

"No sign of Yankees or jayhawkers?"

Justice shrugged. "I've seen a few soldiers. Patrolin' along

191

the river mostly. They ain't bothered nobody. They come by the house one day, and me and Tana drew 'em up some water from the well.''

They were still standing in the hall, and Carrie gestured toward the library. "Let's go in here where we can talk." She turned to the Negro girl. "Mattie, maybe you could bring us some coffee in a little while.''

"Yes, Miss Carrie," Mattie said.

"Remind me, before I leave," Justice said to her, "your mama sent some stuff by me for you. And some soap she said was special for you, Miss Carrie.''

They settled into the library, Justice easing his stiff leg out in front of him as he sank awkwardly into the big horsehair-covered chair. Carrie sat in the chair opposite.

"It's good to see someone from upriver, Justice. I'm homesick.''

He chuckled softly. "Knowin' you, Miss Carrie, I figured you would be.''

Carrie grinned. There was no way to remember her childhood, the old days at Kingston's Landing, without Justice. While other plantations up and down the river had to make do with run-of-the-mill overseers, almost always white and sometimes less than efficient, the black man who sat before her had become a legend among the planters . . . as much so as Adam Kingston himself. Together, year after year, they had produced the highest yields per acre and made the finest sugar in the Delta. Carrie was flooded with memories of the two of them, standing side by side in the hot sugar house, riding stirrup to stirrup over the vast fields of Kingston's Landing.

"Did you come down to the city on business, Justice?" she asked him now.

He drew a finger down an old scar on his cheek, the mark scarcely more than a pale pencil line in the dark skin. "I needed to buy a few things," he said carefully, and Carrie knew at once that there was something else.

She waited.

"I got sad news, Miss Carrie," he said finally. "Mist' Paul Gayerre dead.''

Carrie felt that sudden catch in her throat. "Oh, no . . .

when? How do you know?'' she asked, hoping that there might be some mistake.

"You remember their man Pompey?" At Carrie's nod, Justice continued. "Miss Aurore sent him down from Natchez with this letter for you." Justice took an envelope from his coat pocket. "Pompey told us that Mist' Paul was killed in the war."

Carrie took the letter and looked down on the delicate slant of Aurore Gayerre's handwriting. She slid her finger beneath the seal.

"Want me to wait outside, Miss Carrie?" Justice said quickly.

"No, no, Justice. You stay right there. Just give me a minute." She took out the single sheet of paper and read.

> Dear Carrie,
>
> It is difficult to write this letter. My dearest Paul was killed several weeks ago while he was on a regular patrol near Vicksburg. His commanding officer was kind enough to send his things to me here in Natchez, and the men with him at the time of his death sent letters to assure me that he did not suffer but was killed instantly. I am trying to accept this bravely, as he would want me to, and to draw some comfort from the fact that he got to see his son before he died. At least we were able to share those few hours together.
>
> I felt a need to write this because he told me of the kindness extended to him by you, and your sister Susannah, and your uncle, Monsieur Moreau. He related to me how you and your family put yourselves in jeopardy to shelter him. I shall always be grateful to you for that.
>
> My strength is in the knowledge that he believed passionately in the cause of the South and was willing, if necessary, to die for it. My hope is in the certainty that once this terrible war is over, I shall bring Paul's son back home where he belongs.
>
> Until then, God go with you and yours, Carrie.

Carrie looked down at the letter, deeply moved. She closed her eyes for a moment, and there behind her lids she could see

Paul Gayerre's face as he had looked on that night he'd left for Natchez, those fine, dark, Creole features outlined in the moonlight. She could still see his smile. "Do not worry," he had said. "I know the country better than they do."

She sighed and put the letter in her lap. "He was killed while out on patrol," she said to Justice. "Apparently he died at once."

Justice shook his head. "I am surely sorry."

A new thought nagged at Carrie. "Justice," she said, "I heard that the Gayerre place has been confiscated by the Yankee government. I don't know if that's true or not."

Justice looked away and then back to her. "It's true, Miss Carrie. I seen the signs myself. Posted around on the place. I think the soldiers that come by my place for water was the ones that put them up."

Carrie felt her fingers clench helplessly. "That place belongs to Aurore . . . and to Paul Gayerre's son. It's not right!"

Justice nodded, and they were quiet for a long moment, both of their thoughts in the same direction.

"I can't risk the Yankees taking Kingston's Landing." It was the first time Carrie had been able to say it out loud. The words shook her. "I *have* to get it back into production! I have to get a crop planted in the spring!"

Justice looked at her thoughtfully. "How you figurin' on doin' that, Miss Carrie? They ain't no hands left on the place."

"There are plenty of Negroes here in New Orleans who are willing to hire out to work. Most of them are runaways, but the military government doesn't care. Why should they when their own president, Mr. Lincoln himself—" She stopped the rush of words. She had been uncomfortable about the slave question since that day in the kitchen. The look on Mattie's face had made her know that nothing was as simple as she had once thought.

Still, hadn't it been the way of things since long before she was born? She clung to the fabric of the life she had always known, though it seemed to tear a little further with each passing day.

Justice's dark and calloused thumb moved back and forth against the palm of his hand with a barely audible sound. "I was a slave once, Miss Carrie,'' he said, as if he knew what she were thinking, '' 'til your daddy set me free. I know what it does to a man to be a slave. I know why all them men run off when they got the chance.''

Carrie looked deep into those black eyes, saw the glitter of old pain, old wounds. She was caught there for a moment, unable to speak.

"So," Justice went on finally, made it easy for her, "you're goin' to hire a crew, Miss Carrie?"

"Yes. If I can get the money." She was honest with him.

"Money?" Justice sounded surprised. No one knew better than he that Adam Kingston had been one of the richest men in the state. "Mist' Adam's money . . . ?"

Carrie shook her head. "Not much left."

Justice grunted. "Well . . ." he said slowly, "the bank should be willing—"

"I've been to see Leroy Tate, and he's doing what he can. Right now I must admit that doesn't seem too hopeful. But I'm going to get the money, Justice," Carrie said, her voice laced with determination. "Somehow I'll get it. And get the crop in. I'll have to hire a good sugarmaker once cutting time comes . . . someone who can oversee the grinding and the boiling of the syrup. I can handle the rest of it, but I'll need someone who can take charge of the sugar house operation."

"No cause to hire nobody. You got me, Miss Carrie."

Carrie looked up in surprise. "You?" she said.

Justice grinned. "Ain't no better sugarmaker from here to Barbados," he said.

"I know that . . . but, Justice," she stammered, "your rheumatism and—" She stopped, just sat there close to tears.

"I don't guess a little rheumatism's goin' to slow me down all that much."

Carrie remembered the times when she'd seen him wince with the pain in his leg when he thought no one was looking. "You'd do that for me . . . for us?" she said, fighting back the hot rising in her throat.

He looked at her steadily. "Me and your daddy was together a lot of years. If I can do anything to help his children, then I just guess I will."

*   *   *

As the weeks passed, Carrie's pressing problem, the matter of borrowing enough money to get the crop in and see it through the season, continued to plague her. Leroy Tate had all but said that it was hopeless, though he was far too kind to give her an outright "No." He was unaccustomed to dealing with females in such matters and reluctant to speak in the plain terms he would have used with a man in the same situation. Lord, he thought often, the war had turned everything upside down. Nothing in the world was like it used to be . . . or ought to be.

The weather turned cool and rainy, and there were nights when Carrie lay awake, staring at the dark shadows that stretched across the bedroom ceiling, listening to the pelting rain against the rooftop or the far-off, lonesome howling of a dog. What would she do? How would she ever get the money? But she had to . . . had to.

And in those sleepless hours, Beau Canfield's handsome face came to her more than she cared to admit, came to her smiling that knowing smile, the deep-set dark eyes so confident, so sure . . . And his words would echo inside her head. *You'll come to me, Carrie. Sooner or later, you'll come. I can make it possible for you to get Kingston's Landing into production again*. And she would turn her face into the pillow. There had to be another way. And she would find it. Somehow.

Christmas was a dreary affair. The community had been torn by the loyalty oath, men forced to choose up sides in a game they hadn't wanted to play. The obvious hardship thrust upon those who had not betrayed their convictions was a constant reminder to others of lesser strength, or more sense, depending upon who was discussing it. But one thing was clear—property had been confiscated, businesses claimed, careers interrupted. The Carter Dry Goods Store was closed. Bradley Cunningham had lost his brokerage firm. Some of the Morrisons' friends had had to seek shelter with their more fortunate relatives.

But Abby seemed almost her old self again, bustling about the house and telling everyone else what to do. If she missed those pieces of furniture that she had never gotten back, she didn't mention it. She was determined that the holidays would be celebrated as they always had been. She hoarded eggs for a

Christmas cake, and when Carrie found some glacéed fruits and dried currants at the market and took them over, Abby climbed down from the stool where she'd been hanging up greenery and clapped her hands like a child.

Seth was a different story, though. Seth was haunted by the knowledge that he had surrendered his principles in the hour of his greatest testing. It was always there in his eyes, no matter what he was talking about or to whom he was speaking. Sometimes, right in the middle of a sentence, he would suddenly stop still and look away as if he were quite alone.

"He'll be fine," Abby insisted, "just as soon as he gets the business back on its feet again."

The first week in January, there was a notice in the *Times* that a public auction would be held on the fifteenth to dispose of certain properties and equipment that had been legally claimed by the United States government. The Gayerre plantation was listed.

"It's so unjust," Carrie wailed to Abby. "Poor Aurore thinks she has a home to come back to after the war, and the Yankees are just stealing it from her!"

"I know. It's terrible," Abby agreed.

"And I thought General Banks was supposed to be so much better than Butler."

"They say he is," Abby said. "At least he doesn't let his relatives come down here and steal us blind right under his own nose."

"A skunk is a skunk, and a Yankee's a Yankee," Carrie said.

She thought briefly about attending the auction, but Abby talked her out of it. "It's no place for a lady," she said. "All those men, probably most of them Yankees, with their coarse talk and their cigar smoke." Carrie took Abby's advice. Anyway, there was nothing, she told herself, that she could do to help.

But on the morning of the sixteenth, Abby arrived at the house on Dumaine Street just as Carrie was coming down to breakfast. She took one look at the older woman and knew that something unusual had happened. Abby's graying blond hair was smoothly done in its usual chignon. Her green-checked taffeta dress, though beginning to wear slightly about the collar and cuffs, was spotless and neatly pressed. But there was a certain questioning in her eyes, an uncertainty about the mouth as she pinched her lips inward.

Mattie served muffins and coffee in the sitting room, and once the girl had left the room, Carrie looked steadily at Abby. "What is it, Mother Morrison? What's wrong?"

"Nothing's wrong," Abby said quickly, almost defensively. "I just . . . found out who bought the Gayerre plantation."

"Who?"

"Beau."

It was an instant before Carrie realized that she had sloshed coffee over the side of her cup, and she set it quickly back on the tray before them. "Beau . . ." she said, her voice hardly more than a whisper. "*Beau Canfield?*" she demanded.

Abby nodded, those blue eyes beneath their oval lids slightly defensive and more than a little bewildered.

Carrie got to her feet and paced the length of the room and back, her skirts rustling softly. Her face had gone pale with anger. "How dare he? How dare he do that?"

"I admit to being surprised myself at first." Abby's tone was placating. "But once you think about it, Carrie, you'll come to the same conclusion that Seth and I did."

"And what was that?"

"That there was no real reason why he shouldn't buy it."

"No reason?" Carrie whirled to face her future mother-in-law. "Mother Morrison, how can you say that? Think of Aurore!"

"I know, Carrie." Abby tried to soothe her. "I *have* thought of her. But at the same time, it would have done Aurore Gayerre no good at all for Beau to refrain from taking advantage of a good business opportunity. If he hadn't bought it, one of those Yankee upstarts would have, and wouldn't that have been worse? At least a Southerner has it."

"Oh?" Carrie threw up her hands in disgust. "I don't know that it's any better! How could he bring himself to take advantage of the injustice done to Aurore and her son? And how is it, Mother Morrison, that he has so much money when no one else has any?"

Abby looked shocked. "Carrie, whatever do you mean? I don't see how you could possibly question Beau's motives after all he's done, after all the times he's risked his very life! I know Beau! Know him as well as I know J. D.!''

Abby stirred her coffee vigorously, her mouth set in a nearly straight line. "I may as well tell you now, Carrie"—her tone was half-apologetic, half-defiant—"Seth has signed over half of the distillery to Beau. He's made him a full partner."

Carrie stared, hard put to believe what she'd just heard. "Oh, my God . . . But why?" she said.

"Because we just didn't have the money to keep it going any longer. We were going to lose it. Surely"—her voice had taken on a pleading tone—"it's better to have half of the distillery than nothing?"

Carrie sat down, suddenly tired. She sighed, wondered why she hadn't talked to Abby about Beau before. Was it, she tortured herself, because in some deep and secret place within her she was afraid that she might one day go to him in order to save Kingston's Landing?

"Isn't it?" Abby prodded, and Carrie jumped at the sound of her voice.

"Isn't it what?"

"Better to have half than nothing?" Abby Morrison's lips trembled noticeably, and Carrie put her hand out to her, but she couldn't answer.

Carrie touched the tip of her riding crop lightly to Juno's flank and turned the mare toward Jackson Square, laughing out loud with the sheer joy of being on horseback again.

She had missed Majestic and her daily rides dreadfully, and Prosper, hearing her say something of the kind, offered to let her use his favorite riding mare each morning, since he was busy with classes anyway.

She had ridden out along the road to Bayou St. John and back, all the way out to the famous "duelling oaks" beneath whose ancient branches so many young men had settled their differences and defended their honor against insults, real or imagined. It was a pleasant day, the rainy months over, the sun and sky brilliant, and now as she approached the square, she was aware that it was almost too warm for her old, plum-colored velvet riding habit which she had dug out of the depths of her armoire. After all, it would soon be February.

That thought caused her smile to fade. She should be planting now. The earth was warming and waiting, ready for the seed cane. But the money still eluded her.

Leroy Tate had finally told her flatly that there was no way she could borrow the money through any bank or private source that he knew about in New Orleans. He had assured her that he'd left no stone unturned. There was simply no money available for loans. And things were worse than ever what with the hardships caused by confiscations and business closings as a result of the loyalty oath penalties. There had been at least twenty people, he said, who had come to him desperate to borrow money. And there was none to be had.

She had to find some way . . . she had to. The Yankees must not have any excuse to take Kingston's Landing from her, as the Gayerre plantation and several others had been taken on one flimsy pretext after another. It might legally belong to George Pierre, but in her heart it was hers. She could feel the land in her very bones, in her blood, and she would let no one take it from her.

Besides, if she didn't get it back on a producing level again soon, how were she and Susannah going to live? She couldn't very well impose on the Morrisons, even though her betrothal to J. D. might give her that right. They were having too hard a time themselves to take on any additional burdens. One good sugar crop, as scarce as it was, and she and Susannah would be secure again for a long time if she was careful with the money . . . and she would be.

There had to be some acceptable way to raise the funds she needed. She closed her eyes for a long moment, then catching her underlip between those small, even teeth, gave her head a defiant toss. It was a wonderful day. And she was *not* going to spend it agonizing over her problems. She was not going to think about it again this morning, she promised herself.

Approaching the square, she dismounted and led Juno along under the canopy of shade fashioned by the interlacing tree limbs overhead. People bustled about, and an old man in a purple shirt sat on a sunny bench and sketched the green trees and lawns of Jackson Square. The three spires of the cathedral rose against the azure sky, and a priest from the mellowed old church hurried along, his black soutane flowing about his long legs, his beads swinging at his sides.

She was aware of a delicious smell wafting toward her, and her eye fell on a wizened black man hunkered down outside the ironwork fence that bordered the square. His woolly gray head nodded to passers-by, tallow-palmed hands gesturing gracefully to the bucket before him, which was filled with steaming, whole roasted sweet potatoes.

"Sweet . . . yams! Sweeeet . . . po-ta-toes!" he sang out. And as Carrie watched, a rangy Union soldier stopped to buy one. The old Negro deftly scooped out a fat potato, skin roasted to a dark, orangey-brown, and tucked it into a piece of oiled paper. The soldier walked away, eating contentedly.

Carrie's stomach growled. She had left the house without stopping to eat breakfast, and now she realized that she was famished.

"How much?" she asked the Negro on an impulse.

"Two pennies, Missy," he held up a couple of gnarled fingers. "Fresh . . . hot. See ashes in the bottom to keep hot. Sweet and good, Missy."

He grinned as Carrie fished in the small reticule she carried looped over her wrist. She silently scolded herself for buying it, remembering that before the war a whole bushel of sweet potatoes could have been bought for little more, but she paid the money and eagerly accepted the succulent, hot potato.

She found a shady bench, which she hoped was not too visible to anyone passing by, and loosely fastening Juno's reins to a low branch, sat down and ate the potato right down to the last, sweet bit, licking the brown skin. It was delicious, and she giggled guiltily as she licked her fingers. Her mother and Chloe had always maintained that proper ladies did not eat anything in public, unless at an eating establishment and then only a small amount and with the most delicate manners possible.

She pulled a dainty, lace-edged handkerchief out of her reticule and was busily wiping her fingers when she heard a footstep behind her and turned quickly. She was appalled to find herself staring up into Beau Canfield's face.

"Carrie, my dear . . ." He swept off his tall hat, taking full advantage of her discomfiture, grinning down at her smugly, and eyeing the remains of her sweet potato. "If I had known you were here and hungry, I would have been delighted to take you out to a charming little place I know over on Toulouse Street and buy you an enormous breakfast. Or better yet"—his perfect eyebrows arched—"we could have gone to my rooms."

Carrie eyed him coldly. "No gentleman would suggest such a thing," she said.

"I stay there," he said, ignoring her and indicating one of the Pontalba buildings that flanked the square, "when I'm in town."

"Which isn't too terribly often now, is it?" she said sarcastically. "I suppose you've been busy with your new plantation." She hadn't seen him since his purchase of the Gayerre plantation and she made no effort to hide her disapproval.

He bared the white teeth. "It *is* nearly time for planting, isn't it?" He paused to let the words sink in. "But I've sent someone up to run the place for me. I doubt that plantation life would be to my liking. And besides, I shouldn't want to be away from your beautiful sister for so long."

If it was meant to bait Carrie, it did. She rose, amber eyes flashing. "Just be careful that you behave properly toward Suzy, Beau!" she burst out. "My sister and I are not entirely unprotected in the world! In my brother's absence we do have friends! And if you should in any way . . . harm her—"

"Harm her?" He chuckled. "I? My dear Carrie, however could you suggest such a thing?"

Shaking, Carrie shoved her handkerchief into her reticule and turned to leave, but he put out a hand to grasp her forearm.

"Oh, don't go yet," he said. "You and I have a lot to talk about."

She felt a thick rush of alarm at his touch. "No . . . we don't!" she cried and jerked her arm away. She pulled at the mare's bridle, which had become slightly tangled in the leafy twigs. Her cheeks were flushed; a small pulse beat at the base of her creamy throat. She felt his dark eyes move over her, pausing for a long moment at that point where the plum-colored velvet jacket plunged to a deep V and revealed a glimpse of the soft hollow between her full breasts.

"You look lovely in that color." His voice was silken.

She yanked the reins free, hauled the startled horse around, and was up onto the sidesaddle in an instant, but Beau caught the bridle and held the quivering horse firmly.

"Let go!" she demanded.

He laughed. She could see the white of his teeth and the dark pink of his tongue. "Your time is running out, my dear."

The mare had begun to whinny nervously as Carrie dug a heel into her sleek side, and she lunged as Carrie brought her riding crop down across Beau's shoulder to break his grasp on the bridle.

With a quick gasping breath, Carrie wheeled the horse around and galloped away, but not before she heard, with a shudder, his laughter echoing after her.

16

HIGH-WHEELED CARRIAGES AND DUSTY BLACK BUGGIES CLOGGED the narrow streets of New Orleans as they converged upon the docks. Drivers swore under their breaths, sweated, and inched along. Delicate, many-hued parasols dotted the levee and the streets that led to it as excited ladies in their bell-like crinolines, interspersed with dignified businessmen and half-grown boys, pressed toward the wharves. Whores from Gallatin Street, gamblers, and pimps rubbed elbows with free people of color, preachers, and white-wimpled nuns. New Orleans, especially the ladies of New Orleans, had been in a fever of anticipation since it had been learned barely a week before that almost three-hundred Confederate prisoners had been brought into the city and on this morning would be marched down to the docks and put aboard waiting Federal gunboats. They would then be taken to an agreed upon point where they would be exchanged for an equal number of Yankee captives.

Carrie, Susannah, and Abby had arrived early and had a good view of the waiting boats and that whole length of wharf that the line of blue-clad soldiers was keeping clear.

"Do you see them yet?" Susannah, lovely in pale pink, asked. She was peering anxiously down the quay toward a commotion of some sort. "Are they coming?"

"No," Carrie answered. She was taller and could see that it was only some women who had pressed too far forward and were being herded back by the soldiers.

"Oh, I do hope I'll be able to get close enough to give them these," Abby said, patting the paper-wrapped bundle that was tucked under one arm. Susannah had a similar but smaller package, and now she sighed.

"It's so warm already I don't think they're going to be able to use any of the things I made. What will they do with woolen mittens?" She brightened almost instantly. "But maybe they can use the havelocks. That'll keep the sun off their necks." She referred to the white cloth drape men sometimes fastened to their field caps to ward off the sun.

"Of course they can," Carrie said. "Besides, they're going North to be exchanged, and I'm sure it's still cold up there. I bet they'll be glad to have the scarves and things."

"Seth promised he'd meet us here," Abby said absently, standing on tiptoe to look back the way they had come. "Of course, he didn't know that we'd have to get out of the buggy and come the rest of the way on foot. I never dreamed . . ." Her voice trailed off.

"I don't know how he would ever find us in this crowd," Carrie said. She was wearing the yellow silk dress that Madame Louisa had refurbished last summer. Ecru lace peeked along the tops of the low-cut bodice and ruffled at the edges of the big, puffy sleeves. Her straw bonnet tied beneath her chin in a fetching yellow bow.

One of the Yankee soldiers, a lanky youth who stood only a few feet away in the line that faced the crowd, stole a look at her as he had been doing right along. Carrie had noticed him earlier because he looked hardly old enough to be in uniform, his cheeks boasting only a trace of blond fuzz. Now she turned in time to catch his admiring glance point blank, and that smooth and boyish face turned a deep strawberry red as he touched a respectful finger to his cap and looked quickly away.

"Oh, I do wish they'd hurry," Susannah said breathlessly.

There was some jostling right in back of them as two stout ladies maneuvered for a better position, applying their silk fans vigorously.

Carrie stood quietly, thinking of George Pierre and of J. D. For these young men they were waiting to see, the war would soon be over. They would give their word that they would no longer take up arms against the United States—as the Yankee prisoners would swear to fight no more against the Confederate States—and they would all be sent home. She wished George Pierre were coming home. Perhaps he could think of a way to get the money they needed for Kingston's Landing.

She took a deep breath, the smell of the riverfront strong in her nostrils. Old odors of tar and molasses and turpentine mingled with the sharp smells of rum from Jamaica and carefully rolled cigars from Cuba and the ripe smell of the river itself.

There was the constant hum of voices punctuated by bursts of laughter. From far down the way a soprano voice began to sing "Dixie," and soon everyone had joined in. The sun came out from behind a fat white cloud to shine on the flushed faces of earnest young wives and worried mothers, grim-faced fathers and open-mouthed, young sisters, brothers and cousins—hardly anyone there had escaped the weight of the war. One elderly man who had lost a son and a grandson stood with tears running down his weathered cheeks as he lifted his unsteady voice.

The sound swelled out over the mighty river, carried along on the breeze that whipped the muddy water into pale, cream-colored riffles, and along the wharf the line of Union soldiers stirred uneasily, but their officers remained impassive.

After "Dixie," someone struck up "Bonnie Blue Flag" and then "Jeff Davis Was A Gentleman," and the ladies waved their handkerchiefs, some of which, sharp-eyed Union officers observed, had the Rebel flag embroidered in one corner.

The songs were one thing, but the Confederate flag was

another. The Yankee officers signaled, and the men moved forward to confiscate the handkerchiefs, but the ladies were steadfast, shoving the offending bits of cloth down the tops of their bosoms or holding them behind their backs. There were shrieks of protest all around.

"How dare you, sir!"

"Stand back! No gentleman would dream . . .!"

One tall and skinny red-haired girl near Carrie staunchly threatened to eat hers rather than give it up.

"I wish I'd sewn one," Susannah said to Carrie, throwing a defiant look toward the nearest soldier. "I'd wave it right in his face!"

"Perhaps it's just as well that you didn't," Carrie said. She was beginning to grow uneasy about the turn this whole thing was taking. But just at that moment a great cheer went up far down the quay, and as everyone stood on tiptoe and craned their necks, it became apparent that the first of the Confederate prisoners were being moved up, under guard, to the waiting boats.

As the Rebels came into view, Carrie felt a hot swelling in her throat. She saw that they were wearing what remained of their Confederate uniforms, so tattered and stained that the familiar gray color was nearly unrecognizable. They marched in cadence, and as the front rank came abreast of her, she looked into faces that all seemed tired and worn, even the youngest among them, and yet as resounding cheers went up from the crowd, the dull eyes lit, and many a head tilted to a jaunty angle, many a hand waved.

There was a great surge of bodies, and Carrie could feel herself pushed forward as the line of Union soldiers stiffened to hold the crowd in check. She found herself shoved against the boyish Yankee she had noticed sometime earlier, and the youth's face reddened once again.

"Sorry, Miss," he muttered grimly, but he stood his ground.

One young prisoner, striding up the gangplank not far from where Carrie stood, turned to give a piercing Rebel yell, and the crowd went wild. The women wept and waved the handkerchiefs that had been in dispute only minutes before, and the men held their hats high. The cheers were deafening and defiant. They had been invaded and conquered, they had been impoverished, many of them had been coerced into swearing an allegiance they did not feel, but now they put their hearts into cries of support for their own brave soldiers in gray.

Carrie joined in the cheering as lustily as any of them, while she twisted as best she could so as not to be pressed up against the young soldier in front of her. But the surging of the crowd behind her was growing stronger. She realized with a touch of panic that Abby and her sister were no longer beside her. She looked frantically about only to catch sight of Suzy's pink bonnet as she darted forward to hand one of the Rebels her package. She was instantly pulled back by one of the Union soldiers, and Carrie lost sight of her in the crowd.

She strained to catch a glimpse of her again, or of Abby, but she was pinned in by the soldiers in front of her and the people straining forward around her. She had been carrying her yellow silk parasol closed at her side, and now it was knocked out of her hand and in the pushing and shoving, kicked away and trampled underfoot.

The Confederate prisoners had boarded the boats and been whisked away to quarters somewhere out of sight, and now more Yankees swarmed along the quay, some of them on horseback, hooves making a dreadful clatter amidst the shouts of the crowd.

Only a few feet away, a bottle landed on the wooden dock and smashed into glittering pieces, and Carrie was stunned to realize that the hostile crowd had begun to throw things at the Union troops. She caught sight of a rock and a broken piece of wood hurtling through the air. A skinny, rabbit-faced boy had hoisted himself up onto a wooden derrick, and Carrie saw him take aim and let fly with something.

Suddenly she felt a slight brush at her ear and almost at the same moment heard the soft grunt of the boy soldier. With a look of surprise, he crumpled slowly to the dock.

Carrie heard a small cry escape her own throat as she looked down at him and saw the gash above his eye, saw the bright red blood begin to ooze along the length of it. No one seemed to be paying any attention to him. The faces in the crowd were distorted and ugly, and the Union soldiers had their hands full.

She dropped instinctively to her knees beside him and turned his face gently toward her, her hands trembling. She was relieved to see that his eyes were open, though he looked slightly dazed. He tried to say something, which she couldn't quite understand.

His face nearly colorless, the blood flowing freely now, she searched in her reticule for her handkerchief and, once she had it, quickly pressed it against the wound and held it there while she brushed the pale, fine hair back out of his eyes with her free hand.

He blinked as his head cleared, and struggled as if to sit up. "Sorry . . . sorry, Miss," he mumbled, giving Carrie an embarrassed look as she pressed him back down.

"Just stay there for a minute," she said. "It's all right." She was struck by the fact that he had apologized to her because he was hurt, and she noted the good features, the wide forehead and firm, square jaw.

She could hear the stamp of a horse nearby, and she shifted to shield the young Yankee, her eyes still on him when suddenly she heard Rance Stewart's deep voice, felt his strong hand on her arm as he dropped down to her side.

"Damn it, I knew you'd be here today, Carrie!" he said to her. And then to the boy: "What's happened here, soldier?"

"He's been hurt, Rance," Carrie burst out. "Someone threw something . . . a rock, I think."

The boy, seeing the gold embroidered leaves on Rance's shoulder straps renewed his struggles to get up. "Major . . ." he said. But Rance pushed him back.

"Easy," he said. "Let me have a look at this."

Carrie obediently took her hand away from the handkerchief, and Rance carefully pulled the blood-soaked cloth back, giving Carrie a quick look as he saw what it was, his face so close to hers that her heart started to pound even faster than it had been before. She could see a fine sheen of perspiration on his forehead, see the strong shape of his mouth beneath the dark mustache.

He carefully probed the edges of the wound, and though the boy winced, it was apparent that the flow of blood was slackening to a slow ooze.

"There . . . that's not bad." Rance pressed the handkerchief back and, taking off his neckerchief, tied it firmly about the young man's head. "Think you can stand up, soldier?"

"Yes, sir, Major," the boy said, color coming back into his cheeks.

Carrie got to her feet as Rance gave a hand to the boy who, once upright, seemed steady enough.

"You'd better report to the infirmary and let them check that," Rance said. "They might want to sew you up. Do you think you can ride?"

"Yes, sir."

"Here, take my horse." Rance caught at the bridle of the roan gelding standing calmly amidst all the shouting and confusion. "I'll pick him up later at the hospital."

"Yes, sir. Thank you, sir. And you, Miss . . ." The boy cast Carrie a grateful look and then mounted the horse without too much difficulty. As an afterthought, he saluted Rance, awkwardly, because of the makeshift bandage around his head. Rance waved him on.

Carrie realized that they were virtually in the middle of a battle. Objects were still being thrown through the air, and women were shrieking as soldiers attempted to take handkerchiefs embroidered with the forbidden flag from them. There was pushing and shoving, and where she and Rance stood was only relatively clear because of the embattled line of blue-clad soldiers.

Rance grasped her arm and put himself between her and the crowd. "I've got to get you out of here," he said, beckoning to a ruddy-faced lieutenant nearby. "Riordan . . ." he called.

"Rance, I'm not going anyplace!" Carrie protested, pulling away. But she saw that hard, lean line of his jaw set as he firmly pulled her back.

"Would you just for once not be so damned obstinate!" he growled. "Artillery has been ordered in. General Banks is not going to allow this! You're going home!"

"But you don't understand," she cried. "Suzy's here! I've got to find her!"

"Suzy? Oh, good Lord . . .!" he said, looking out over the surging mass of people before them.

The lieutenant had come up and stood waiting expectantly.

"Lieutenant Riordan," Rance rapped out his order crisply, "I want you to escort this lady safely to her home."

"No . . ." Carrie said, but he paid no attention to her.

"There's a buggy down there at the end of the quay. Take it. I'll take full responsibility."

"No, Rance . . ."

He swung her around, a hand at each shoulder, and leaned forward to fasten her with those clear gray eyes. "Carrie, I'll find her. I'll find Suzy and bring her home. I promise."

She stared at him, and from the look on his face she had the uneasy feeling that if she refused to do as he said, he would have her picked up bodily and carried away. "Abby Morrison's with her," she said, as if it were one last protest.

He grinned. "I'll find her, too." He raised a hand to the lieutenant. "Show Miss Kingston every courtesy," Rance said. "You'll answer to me if any harm comes to her."

"Yes, sir, Major." The lieutenant saluted and offered Carrie his arm, shielding her from the crowd with his body.

"Stay with her until I get there," Rance said.

Carrie threw an anxious look back over her shoulder. "You'll find her?" she said, her amber eyes enormous, her pale face framed by the straw bonnet and bright yellow bow.

"I'll find her," he said, ducking as a bottle flew past his shoulder. "Now go!"

Carrie paced back and forth in the sitting room, looking anxiously through the French doors each time she passed them, into the courtyard where Lieutenant Riordan waited patiently in the shade. He had declined her invitation to come into the house.

Mattie stood by helplessly and shook her head. "Don't you be frettin' so, Miss Carrie. If Cap'n Stewart says he'll bring Miss Suzy home, then he will."

"It's 'major' now, Mattie," Carrie said absently. "*Major* Stewart." She took another turn of the room. "Oh, Mattie," she burst out, "I don't know why I let him talk me into leaving! I should have stayed right there . . ."

"Now, Miss Carrie," Mattie chided, "the way it sounds to me you didn't have no business stayin' there a-tall. Cap'n—I mean, Major Stewart can find Miss Suzy and Miz Morrison a whole lot better than you could have. And he can take care of 'em, that man can . . . once he finds 'em."

It was true, Carrie admitted to herself. If anyone could get Suzy and Abby safely out of that mob, it was Rance. She remembered how he had taken charge of the situation the moment she looked up to find him beside her on the dock.

"Why don't you let me fix you some tea, Miss Carrie?"

"No, thank you, Mattie. I'll just wait a while."

She glanced at the small china clock on the mantel. It had been nearly three quarters of an hour, and still she'd heard nothing. She sat down and forced herself to be still, her hands clasped in her lap, trying not to think of what might be happening now. But it was impossible.

The sounds of the crowd still rang in her ears; she could see the distorted faces yet, see all that rage and frustration. The Yankee boy was lucky that his wound hadn't been worse. A few stitches and he'd be all right. That's what Rance had said. But Suzy . . . Suzy could be hurt right now. Or Abby. Or even Rance. . . .

Carrie remembered him ducking as the big wine bottle sailed close to his head. He was still grinning and ordering her out of there . . . tall and broad-shouldered in that Yankee uniform, his black felt Hardee hat set at a jaunty angle.

She brought herself up sharply. Whatever was she doing worrying about Rance Stewart, she confronted herself angrily. But all the same, there was a cold, hard knot in her stomach, and she ducked her head so that Mattie couldn't see her face.

She got up quickly and started to pace once again, but she had only taken a few steps when the bell rang, and she whirled toward the courtyard to see Lieutenant Riordan heading down the path toward the gate. She hurried toward the front of the house, Mattie right behind her, only to give a sigh of relief as she saw Susannah coming through the front door with Rance and Abby Morrison right behind her.

"Suzy!" Carrie cried. "Are you all right?"

"I'm fine." Susannah grinned impishly. Her pink bonnet was gone, and her hair was a wild tangle of curls, her face smudged, but her green eyes sparkled with excitement. "I gave my package to one of the prisoners!"

Behind her Abby Morrison, pale-faced and limping slightly, leaned heavily on Rance's arm.

"Mother Morrison . . . you're hurt!" Carrie said.

"I just turned my ankle. But I could have been trampled to death!"

"Do you need a doctor?" Carrie asked.

"No. I just want to lie down for a while, please." Her voice quivered.

Mattie came forward. "Here, let me help you, Miz Morrison." She slipped a strong arm about Abby's waist to take her from Rance, and Susannah came to support her on the other side. "We'll just take you right upstairs," Mattie soothed, "and get you settled, and then I'll make you a good hot cup of tea."

"Can you manage?" Rance called after them.

"We doin' just fine, Major Stewart," Mattie said.

"Really . . . it was dreadful. I never expected . . . never dreamed . . . ." Abby was complaining with every step, almost as if to herself. "Someone should surely have to answer for this."

"Thanks, Rance," Susannah called over her shoulder. "I'll tell you all about it later, Carrie. After I get cleaned up and changed."

Carrie watched them for a moment and then turned back to Rance, who stood hat in hand, regarding her with that clear gaze of his, as calm and unruffled as if he'd just gone for an uneventful drive along the levee.

"Well . . ." she said, "I . . . I suppose I'd better thank you, too."

"That isn't necessary," he said.

Carrie's eyes were drawn to the dark hair that curled slightly about his ears, at his sideburns. "But . . . you brought Suzy safely home. And Abby." She suddenly felt very unsure of herself.

"I said I would."

"Well, I thank you anyway," she said stiffly, not wanting him to guess that there had been that moment when she was relieved to see that *he* was safe, too. "Could I get you something?" She gestured toward the sitting room. "I believe Prosper keeps some brandy in the wine cabinet."

He grinned, the laugh lines about his eyes deepening. "Now I do believe some brandy would be just the thing," he drawled. "I'll just go dismiss Lieutenant Riordan first."

"You can go through the French doors." Carrie took his hat, put it on the hall table, and then led the way into the sitting room. "I'll fix your brandy while you're seeing to that. And . . . if you would, Major," she called after him, consciously avoiding the use of his given name, "tell him again for me that I appreciate his courtesy and care." The words came grudgingly. She had not ever expected to be thanking Yankee soldiers for anything, but the man *had* behaved well in every respect, and she could do no less than acknowledge it.

He had paused at the open doors, turned back for a moment. "I'll do that," he said, a hint of amusement in those clear-as-quartz eyes, as if he knew exactly how much it cost her.

In Prosper's wine cabinet she found a bottle of fine old apricot brandy. She had it poured and waiting, along with a glass of pale, dry sherry for herself, by the time he returned.

His dark brows raised appreciatively as he took the glass and touched it to hers. "To a truce . . ." he said deliberately, and both of them remembered their last, stormy meeting in this very room, before his trip to Washington.

Carrie's head came up. Her dark chestnut hair was parted in the middle and cascaded from high-set tortoise-shell combs, her amber eyes glowing golden in the light through the French doors. A slight smile softened that strong mouth. "To a truce. At least a temporary one." She met his gaze and could feel the quickened beat of her pulse as he nodded.

"I'll settle for that," he said.

She drank too quickly, feeling an unaccustomed confusion, and was terrified for a moment that she was going to hiccup, but fortunately she didn't.

"Mmm . . . This is very good," Rance said, lifting the glass to study the potent liquid and then taking another sip. "I haven't had brandy like this since before the war."

"I'm glad you like it." She drank some more of the sherry, growing increasingly uncomfortable with him. He seemed to fill the room somehow, to dominate it, this tall, booted Southerner in his Yankee uniform. And she realized that those memories of the night they had been together were always there, threatening to surface whenever she was with him. Was it the same with him? she wondered. The thought filled her with an embarrassed dismay.

"Would you care to walk in the garden?" she asked, feeling the heat in her cheeks. "It should be very pleasant out there now."

"Certainly. May I take my drink?"

"Of course," she said, but she left her own on the table. She already felt a little light-headed with the half-glass she had consumed.

It was pleasant outside, and they walked along the path that bordered the old courtyard wall, the faded bricks furred with green mosses, tendrils of ivy curling thickly.

"Tell me what happened after I left," she said as they came to the shade of the two old magnolia trees toward the rear. Rance leaned against a low branch.

"More of what you saw," he said. "And then reinforcements arrived, and order was restored fairly quickly." He chuckled. "Some of the ladies were still determined not to give up their Confederate handkerchiefs. A half-dozen risked falling into the river to run across a wide plank to a fishing boat just getting ready to cast off. One of the officers hailed the fisherman, and the ladies were brought back, handkerchiefs and all."

Carrie bristled. "That flag means a lot to some of us, Major!"

"I know it does," he said gently.

She had expected an argument, and his reply caught her off guard. She didn't know what to say to him.

"Your handkerchief didn't have a flag on it," he said.

She looked away toward the rose beds and the stables on the other side. "No," she said finally.

"I know it didn't," he went on relentlessly, "because it was your handkerchief that was pressed against that boy's wound. You did that, Carrie—"

She turned back defensively. "Don't make anything of that, Rance Stewart! I would feel it was my responsibility to help anyone who was injured right in front of my eyes . . . *even*," she snapped, "a Yankee soldier!"

"All right . . ." He laughed, putting a hand up before him in mock surrender. "I give up."

He drank the rest of his brandy, watching her steadily with a growing heat in his eyes. She toyed with the magnolia leaves nearest to her, painfully aware of that masculine, sensual force that emanated from him, causing a response that shocked her to the very core. She had never thought to have such feelings for a man . . . any man, let alone Rance Stewart who was a traitor to his own people. Lord, she wailed silently, whatever was happening to her must not happen! He was a Yankee soldier, and he had taken advantage of her in the basest manner. He was the enemy. She mustn't ever forget that.

She plucked one of the shiny magnolia leaves and turned it nervously, running her fingertips along the smooth, waxy surface. "I haven't congratulated you on your promotion," she said.

He watched her silently with that direct and unsettling gaze, and she plunged ahead, almost desperately.

"I saw you in your buggy on Royal Street one day. Nora Barlow was with you . . ." Her voice trailed off as she realized he wasn't listening to her.

He put his empty glass on the low, flat branch beside him, and there was a tightening along his jaw. "You'll never forgive me for choosing to fight for the Union, will you, Carrie?" His voice was low and deep and seemed to resonate off some secret place inside her.

She turned her face away from him. "Does it matter?" It was barely a whisper.

"It does to me," he growled, and before she realized his intention, he had pulled her around to face him, his arms closing about her, and his mouth came down on hers. In that instant she no longer thought of North or South or what uniform he wore, she only knew that her legs had turned to weak and trembling things as the touch of him scorched through her.

His mouth, hard and firm and warm against her lips, moved hungrily, the roughness of his mustache scratching her face, the taste and smell of the brandy he had just drunk so heady it made her dizzy. His tongue thrust, demanded entrance. Suddenly she found her mouth open to his, and the sweet fire that surged through her licked at her nipples pressed against that muscular chest, flamed into a hot wanting ache between her legs.

He gave her no chance to resist . . . even if she'd wanted to. His arms were around her tightly, incredibly strong and sinewy from his constant practice with the saber, yet they stopped just short of hurting her.

"Carrie . . . Carrie," he murmured, and she could only gasp as his mouth claimed hers again. She was lost, conscious only of their two bodies molding together in the heat of desire, the memories of that night, which were burned into each of them forever, fanning the flame higher.

Her arms were up around his neck, her fingers twisted in his thick, dark hair, her hand moving across his shoulders to feel the hard muscles there. And she kissed him back with all her heart, uncaring of the consequences.

And then her hand found its way to the wide shoulder straps, felt the oak leaves of his rank, and a cold, wrenching reason drenched her. *Dear God, what was she doing!*

She pushed him away with a suddenness that sent him reeling back against the low branch of the magnolia tree, and snatching up her skirts, she fled toward the house, her legs trembling, her cheeks burning with disbelief.

"Carrie, wait . . . please!" Rance called, just as she slammed the French doors shut with a force that barely missed shattering the panes.

And there in the courtyard, he set his jaw and swore under his breath. "Goddamm it!" he said, not understanding that Carrie had run away from herself as much as from him.

General Nathaniel Banks had the front pages of three New Orleans newspapers spread out across his desk and stood perusing the headlines as Rance entered his office.

"Good morning, Major," the general said, the deep furrow between his brows smoothing somewhat as he looked up. He fingered the small tuft of dark whiskers that graced the center of his chin. "I see you have the report ready," he said.

"Yes, sir. A full accounting of the occurrences at the docks yesterday, General."

General Banks cleared a place on the desktop. "Just put it there. I'll get to it." He was a well-built, slim-waisted man, every inch the soldier and the gentleman, and now he strode restlessly back and forth, his carriage impeccably correct, his back straight as a rifle barrel. He turned back toward Rance, a wry grin belying that military stance.

"The ladies have made us look like idiots," he said. He

gestured toward the newspapers. "They're calling it the 'Battle of the Handkerchiefs.' "

"Yes, sir, I know, I've read them."

The general shook his head and came back to the desk. "There were a number of males in that crowd, too, were there not?"

"Yes, sir." Rance grinned. "It's just that the ladies of New Orleans can be so vocal."

"I'm finding that out." He looked down at the papers on his desk again and grunted. "So much for the loyalty oaths, Stewart. These people are still body and soul in the Confederate camp."

"I think that's true, sir. It's going to take time."

"I believe you're right." General Banks sat back in his desk chair and looked up at Rance. "And meanwhile we do our jobs . . . and hope we do them the right way."

"Yes, sir."

"I understand that there were no serious injuries yesterday."

"That's right, sir. Mainly a few cuts and bruises among the troops. All from flying objects. There were a few minor mishaps among the ladies. A sprained ankle or two. One woman gashed her arm when she fell on a broken bottle. She was taken to the hospital and stitched up, then escorted home."

"Very good," Banks said. He gathered up the newspapers before him. "Here, take these with you, Major. I've seen enough of them."

"Yes, sir." Rance paused when he had reached the door. "If you have no further need of me, sir, I'd like to take an hour or two off this afternoon to see to some personal business."

"By all means, Stewart. Take the afternoon if you wish. You've earned it after yesterday."

An hour later Rance stood outside the gate of the house on Dumaine Street, waiting for someone to answer the bell. He wanted to see Carrie, had hardly been able to think of anything else. He wasn't quite sure what he'd say to her, but he wanted to see her.

Mattie let him in and, moving smoothly and gracefully ahead of him, her full crimson skirt swishing audibly, showed him into the sitting room. "Seems like everything back to normal today," she grinned, her teeth white against the rich, chocolate skin.

"Old Thomas brought over word that Miz Morrison just fine this mornin', and Miss Suzy and one of the young ladies from the sewing circle went off to the Sweet Shop just like nothin' happened a-tall yesterday."

"I'm glad to hear that," Rance said.

"You just wait right here. I'll get Miss Carrie."

"Thank you, Mattie."

He waited, more nervous than he cared to admit, but he smiled as he looked out into the sun-drenched courtyard. What would her attitude be today? Would she come storming into the room, those amber eyes of hers flashing golden fire at him, that ready tongue of hers upbraiding him for daring to take such liberties? Or would she admit that there had been that moment when she'd pressed against him, when she'd answered his kiss with a fervor that even yet caused a slow, throbbing heat in his loins whenever he thought of it?

He wouldn't let her deny it. He would force her to acknowledge what had happened in the courtyard yesterday.

He paced back and forth, wondering what could be taking so long. And then he whirled toward the door as finally he heard footsteps in the hall.

To his disappointment, it was Mattie who entered the room, her eyes darting away from his and then back, an uncomfortable look on her face. In her hand she held the broad-brimmed felt hat that he had left behind yesterday.

"Major Stewart," she said, her voice soft and apologetic, "I guess Miss Carrie ain't feelin' too good today. She told me to give you this." She held out the hat, and he took it stiffly.

"Very well," he said reluctantly. It was clear that Carrie didn't want to face him. Should he insist? No, he decided. Best not to force things today.

He rolled the hat brim in his hand. "You tell your mistress that I hope she feels better. And that I'll call again tomorrow."

Mattie's eyes slid away, and the dusky cheek took on a slightly rosy flush.

"What is it, Mattie?" he asked.

She bit the full, ripe underlip, shook her head, clearly not wanting to say more.

"Tell me," he ordered curtly.

She sighed. "I'm sorry, Major Stewart." The slim dark fingers twisted together. "Miss Carrie says . . . she says she ain't never at home when you come."

The girl looked steadily at him, regret in her eyes, as he drew himself up and felt the first rush of icy anger engulf him. For a moment he was tempted to go upstairs and kick the goddamned door down, and then as his wounded pride began to sting, his anger deepened to a quiet rage and a desire to be gone.

He put his hand out to the unhappy girl's shoulder. "It's all right, Mattie," he said. "Don't bother to see me out. I know the way."

Muscles cording along his neck, his jaw set so tightly it hurt, he drove directly to the house on St. Anne where Major Barlow lived with his wife and daughter. Surrendering the reins to a stable boy, he was soon inside and waiting in the cool, marble-tiled foyer.

Feathery green asparagus ferns cascaded from ivory pedestals on either side of the stairway. A wall clock ticked ponderously, and it seemed only a minute before Nora was floating down the steps toward him, her delighted laughter echoing through the hall.

"Rance, darling!" She was in a gown of blue silk. It was her best color, and she knew it. A ribbon of the same color wound through the elaborate massing of pale blond curls at the back of her head. The delicate apricot flush that suffused her cheeks served to soften the sharp little chin. She extended a white and languorous hand to him. "What a lovely surprise!"

He looked into the depths of those blue eyes, saw there the subtle invitation he'd seen for some time now, and cursed himself for a fool for not having availed himself of it before. He'd had some stupid notion after that disastrous night with Carrie that he should stick to women whose business it was to satisfy a man. They took their money, and there were no tears, no recriminations, no blazing amber eyes to accuse him. . . .

He looked boldly at the milky-white tops of Nora's breasts swelling over the banding of blue lace, his gaze lingering there for a long moment before moving down the tight bodice to the trim little waist, and then back up to catch the look of triumph in her eyes. The apricot blush deepened.

"Mama will be so sorry she missed you," she said, running the tip of her pink tongue over her already wet lips. "It's too bad"—she lowered her long lashes—"that she'll be gone for the *whole* afternoon."

☙ 17 ❧

CARRIE TOOK ONE LOOK AT A TEARFUL MATTIE AND GROANED inwardly. Not today. Whatever it was, not today, she pleaded silently. She might just break, shatter into a thousand pieces. She could solve no more problems.

She did her best to focus on the crying girl. "What is it, Mattie? What's the matter?" she asked.

The Negro girl, eyes red from weeping, advanced into the library and hesitantly approached the desk where Carrie sat. A handkerchief was twisted to a sodden mass between her long, dark fingers.

"Here . . . sit down and tell me." Carrie pulled up the small mahogany sidechair nearby, brought it right up close so the two of them could sit face to face. Mattie sank into the seat.

"It's . . . it's Solomon, Miss Carrie," the girl got out.

"Solomon? What now?" There was always something with Solomon, Carrie thought irritably, but as Mattie's sobs began anew, she reached out a hand to comfort her. "Just tell me, Mattie. It won't do any good to cry."

"He done somethin' bad, Miss Carrie," Mattie burst out.

"What? What did he do?" Carrie prompted her.

Mattie caught her breath in small hiccups, her eyes wide, obviously afraid of what Carrie was going to think. "He turned in his master to the Yankees, Miss Carrie," she said in a voice so soft that Carrie could barely catch the words.

Carrie stared. "He did *what?* He turned in old Monsieur Marchand? For what?"

" 'Cause his master had some guns in the house. They was just old guns that he had from when he was young . . . like some of them that your Papa had, Miss Carrie."

"You mean dueling pistols?"

Mattie nodded.

"But, Mattie, why on earth would Solomon want to do that?" Carrie demanded.

Mattie ducked her head. " 'Cause . . . 'cause he want to be free, Miss Carrie."

Carrie's mind raced. She did remember hearing about some such order of the Yankees, that if a slave in a Confederate household revealed the presence of firearms there, he'd be set free. But surely that didn't mean a pair of old dueling pistols!

"I told him not to do it, Miss Carrie. I told him he oughtn't—"

"You *knew* about this?" Carrie cut her off. "You knew beforehand, and you didn't tell me!" She rose to her feet and stared accusingly at the hapless girl.

Mattie squeezed her eyes together, and tears oozed out of the corners. "Solomon said nothin' would happen to his master 'cause he's old! He said the Yankees wouldn't do nothin' to him!" She opened her eyes and turned her face up, her cheeks wet with tears. "He says he got to be free, Miss Carrie . . . no matter what!"

Carrie looked for a long moment into the brown eyes that were so filled with misery. She shook her head and walked over to the window that looked out on the courtyard. The heavy rose-colored draperies were pulled back, and she could see the far brick wall and a branch of the magnolia tree beside which she and Rance had stood only a couple of weeks before. She set her mouth in a tight line and turned back.

"Well, I'll see what I can find out about Monsieur Marchand," she said. "And I want you to stop crying . . . though it does you credit that you realize you did something very wrong by not telling me what Solomon was going to do. There might have been something we could have done to prevent this."

Mattie kept her eyes on the flowered carpet. "That ain't why I'm cryin', Miss Carrie," she said firmly. "Though, I'm sorry if you're disappointed with me. Ain't no way I could've told on Solomon."

Carrie stared at her in surprise. Mattie had always been obedient. "Then why?" Carrie asked sternly. "What are you crying about if it isn't that?"

" 'Cause Solomon's gone and I don't even know where he is." She collapsed in helpless sobbing. "I . . . I m-might not ever see him again. And . . . and I love him, Miss Carrie."

Carrie grabbed the sobbing girl by the shoulders and gave her a shake. "Stop that!" she said. "Solomon is nothing but trouble, and you're better off that he's gone!"

Mattie was so surprised by her mistress laying hands on her that she did stop crying and looked up sullenly, her underlip stuck out. "I love him," she said stubbornly.

"Mattie . . . you can't always trust your feelings," Carrie said, the words tumbling from her lips. "Feelings betray you. I know . . . I . . ." She stopped suddenly, before she revealed something that she could never admit to anyone . . . that her feelings for Rance Stewart were undeniable, despite the insanity of them. Thank God she had the good sense never to see him again if she could help it.

She let go of the girl, trembling from head to toe. Mattie looked at her, their eyes locking and holding for the longest time, and it was Carrie who looked away first.

"I'm sorry, Mattie," she said. "I guess it's not my best day. Come on. Let's go make some tea."

And later she lay across the bed in her room upstairs, the drapes drawn against the sun, the afternoon air still and close around her. Not a bird called or a dog barked in the heat of the day.

She hadn't handled that very well, she admitted to herself. Instead of being strong and saying all the right things to Mattie, she had almost broken down herself, had almost started to cry, too.

Dear God, would nothing ever be right again? Would her life ever be serene and orderly and predictable as it once had been?

Through the night she had lain awake in this very bed, her mind going in circles and always coming back to the same place. Her time had run out. If she didn't move now, it would be too late to get a crop planted this year. And she *had* to get that crop in. The money she and Suzy had would only last another six months, if they were frugal.

And God knew what the Yankees might decide to do if she didn't get her land into production again. She had only to think of the Gayerre plantation to feel the cold fingers of fear grip her.

Finally, when she had been through it all a hundred times, there was only one thing left . . . one person left . . . the one person in New Orleans who seemed to have any money. Beau Canfield. She had come to that again and again.

Now her stomach knotted, and she felt a strong rush of nausea. She no longer trusted him. She feared what he might demand of her once she was under an obligation to him. She had sent a note to him this morning and wished a hundred times since that she could recall it. But it had to be done. There was no other way. And she could handle him, she told herself stoutly.

She had told Lafitte to take the sealed envelope to Canfield's rooms. "A business matter," she'd explained to the old Negro. The one line written on the sheet of paper inside had said: *I would like to discuss the matter of a loan*.

She thought of the way her hand had trembled as she'd written it, and she rolled over on the hot feather mattress with its linen sheet, drew her knees up, and curled herself into a tight knot. She was in her pantalettes and camisole, and the thin cotton felt damp against her skin. After a few minutes, she drifted off to sleep from sheer exhaustion.

She awakened late in the afternoon to the sound of Suzy's laughter downstairs. She was soaked in perspiration, and lifting the heavy chestnut hair up off her neck, she got up and went to the washstand to pour water from the ironstone pitcher into the bowl beside it and then sponge off her face and arms. The water was stale and warm, but it was wet and would do until she could get Lafitte to bring up some cool water for a bath.

She heard footsteps along the hallway, and there was a light knock at the door.

"Who is it?" she called as she reached for the towel hanging on the washstand rod.

"It's me," Susannah answered, and before Carrie could say anything else her sister had bounced into the room and perched herself on the side of the rumpled bed.

"This note came for you while you were asleep," she said, holding out a square white envelope.

It was all Carrie could do to continue drying her arms.

"I don't know who it's from," Susannah went on teasingly. "A young boy brought it. Perhaps it's from some secret admirer!" She giggled.

Carrie's mouth was dry, but she kept her expression carefully level. "I'm sure I don't have any secret admirers." She reached for the envelope and stared down at her name, printed in black ink.

"Well, open it!" her sister urged. "It's not every day that you get such a mysterious message."

Carrie slid her finger beneath the seal and took out the single sheet of vellum, turning away slightly so her sister could not see what was written there.

The note was in script, convoluted and curling back upon itself, as insinuating, she thought, as its writer.

> Carrie, my dear;
> I knew that sooner or later you would see that only I can help you. My carriage will await you promptly at 8:00 this evening, outside the house and a few doors down so as not to attract any undo attention.
>
> B.

Somehow Carrie forced a smile to her lips.

"Nothing mysterious, Suzy honey. Leroy Tate and his wife want me to have dinner with them this evening."

"Oh," Susannah pouted, "but we're supposed to go to the Morrisons."

"That's right, isn't it. But you go ahead and make my apologies for me. This is . . . business. I think perhaps Mr. Tate has arranged for a loan for us. They're sending their carriage to pick me up later."

"All right," Susannah said. "It's too bad you have to spend such a boring evening." She dimpled. "I expect Beau will be at the Morrisons. Unless he's gone out of town again."

Carrie's heart felt stabbed through. She looked at her sister's face, so young and pretty and trusting, and she could hardly keep the tears back. Beau Canfield wouldn't be at the Morrisons this evening. That much was sure.

She turned away and pretended to busy herself at her dressing table.

Carrie sat on the rich plush seats of the carriage, her arms in close to her body, her skirts pulled in as near to her legs as her hoops would allow. Shadows cast by the corner gaslights moved across her face as they passed through an intersection, and the horses' hooves sounded hollow against the cobblestones.

She shivered as she thought of the man who sat up top driving. Thin to the point of emaciation, he had held the door of the carriage for her without a word, his eyes glittering in the long and sallow face that was hunched forward on an equally long and stringy neck. He was like a scrawny bird, she thought. A vulture. That was it. A deep shudder went through her body, and she peered out the window into the darkened street, trying to see where he was taking her.

She had fully expected to be driven to the Pontalba, where Beau lived, but the carriage had not gone anywhere near the square. Instead it had headed away from the river, and a few moments ago they had turned and she was sure the sign had said Rampart Street. But why on earth there?

Few people had not heard the whispered stories of the houses along Rampart Street and the beautiful women of color who inhabited them. *Plaçage*, the old system was called, in which wealthy Creole planters, and later Americans, Carrie supposed, had taken the dusky beauties and kept them as their mistresses . . . most of them housed along this infamous street of which most white women pretended to know nothing. She wondered briefly if her father had ever had such an arrangement. No, she answered her own question. Papa had adored Mama. Carrie was sure he had never kept another woman.

Curiosity overcame her for a moment, and she moved closer to the window to see what the houses on this notorious street looked like. She was surprised to see that they were neat and well-kept. She could make out the outlines of flower boxes and baskets of hanging ferns. Lights filtered through the shuttered and draped windows.

She drew back against the seat, and within minutes the carriage had lurched to a stop. She waited, hardly breathing, as she felt the shift, heard the creaking springs as the driver got down. After a moment the door swung open, and the man peered in at her, his nose big and hooked, beaklike. There was a sly grin on his face as he motioned her out.

She would not, she decided staunchly, give him the satisfaction of seeing how frightened she was. With a supreme effort, she climbed down from the carriage, her step firm, her chin high, ignoring the grimy claw he extended to her.

He laughed, a gurgling sound that seemed to rattle up and down the full length of that overlong throat. "Cap'n Canfield be waitin' for ye," he said. He jerked his head toward the house before which they had stopped, and Carrie turned to look.

It was very much like the other houses on the street, with long, narrow green shutters at the windows and a tiny porch. The moonlight revealed neat, well-kept flower beds on either side of the flagstone walk. Carrie could catch a whiff of verbena.

The driver was still standing there, regarding her with his head cocked to one side. She drew herself as tall as she could and made her way along the path and up onto the porch. She gave the bell ring a hesitant pull.

Expecting to see Beau Canfield, she could only stand and stare when the door was opened by a small, exquisite young woman attired in a richly embroidered velvet jacket of a deep wine color. The matching skirt had tiny, golden tassels about the bottom. Her elegant head, the beautifully coiffed dark hair wound through with strands of pearls, was carried high above a slender neck. The flawless skin, which held only the slightest tawny cast to betray her blood, stretched smoothly over high cheek bones that could have graced some ancient Egyptian queen.

Carrie swallowed, uncertain what to say. The woman's black-as-night eyes glittered with hatred before the thick lashes swept down to hide it.

"Mademoiselle Kingston . . . do come in," the woman said, the calm and well-modulated tones hiding the volcano within.

Carrie stood rooted to the spot, stunned that the woman knew her name. "I . . . I . . ." she began, having no idea of what she intended to say, but it didn't matter because just at that moment

226

Beau Canfield swept through a draped archway into the small entrance hall, grinning.

"Carrie, my dear . . . I've been counting the minutes!"

He ushered her quickly through the hall and into the sitting room from which he'd just come, which seemed dark with mahogany woods and deep, jewel-toned fabrics, draperies and silk-covered cushions of ruby and amber and topaz. There were several lamps in brackets about the walls, and at the far end of the room, on a table set for two, there was a cluster of tall white candles.

Beau, in a dark green dressing coat, stood arrogantly in the center of the room, his eyes raking her from head to toe, a smile coming to his well-fleshed lips. "You look lovely," he said.

Carrie could see herself in the full-length mirror on the wall in back of him, her hair caught back loosely with combs, the lamplight bringing out the rich chestnut tones. She had worn her lavender dress, and the purple band at her throat merely accentuated how pale her face was. The mirror was too far away for her to see, but she could feel the pulse that throbbed steadily in her throat, feel the dampened palms and the cold, hard knot at the pit of her stomach. Dear God . . . what had she gotten herself into? But she couldn't leave. What other choices did she have?

"The first thing we must do," Beau grinned, "is make you more comfortable, my dear. Monique . . ." He lifted his hand, and the woman who had been standing in the archway glided away, her silk slippers soft against polished wooden floors.

Beau circled Carrie slowly, an amused and triumphant look in the dark eyes. "Aren't you even going to say good evening, Carrie?"

"I . . . I'm sorry," she said, her lips so stiff it was difficult to get the words out. "I just hadn't expected . . . I mean, I thought we would be meeting in your rooms."

His lips thinned out, edged back over his teeth. "Oh, but this is ever so much better. Don't you like my little hideaway? I can't tell you how—delightful—I have found this place to be. But come . . . this is what you need." He turned to the nearby cabinet with its decanter and tray, poured two small crystal glasses almost to the rim with a dark liquid, then held out one of them to Carrie.

"I really think it would be best if we got right to the matter of a loan." She ignored the glass and did her best to sound business-like and matter-of-fact. "We should put it in writing. That way . . . we will both understand one another. The arrangements for repayment . . ." her voice cracked, "the amount of interest—"

His laughter cut her off. "There's plenty of time, Carrie. I assure you we will get to . . . the arrangements." Again, he proffered the crystal glass.

She was on the point of refusing, then thought better of it. She took it and drank too fast, amber eyes widening as the fiery brandy burned its way down her throat. She gasped for air and coughed while Beau looked on in arrogant amusement.

The woman, Monique, came back into the room with a long silk dressing gown over her arm.

"Ah, here we are," Beau said, "You'll be much more comfortable in that, Carrie." He indicated the sapphire-blue garment. "You may go into the bedroom to change. Monique will assist you."

"Certainly not!" Carrie said firmly. "I am quite comfortable as I am, thank you." She set her soft lips in a hard line, and Beau Canfield eyed her narrowly.

He turned to the woman. "Is dinner ready?"

She nodded, gesturing toward the serving cart with its covered silver dishes. "All ready," she said. "The food is hot. The wine is chilled."

"Good. Carrie, you must join me. Monique has worked so hard."

He took the silk gown from the woman. "I think it's been far too long since you've visited your mother," he said to her, his voice like velvet but somehow chilling. "I'm sure she'll be pleased to see you. Jenkins is waiting."

Carrie caught the slight stiffening of the woman's slim body. There was a glint of tears before Monique quickly turned her face away. "Very well," she said, her words barely audible, and she stayed poised there for an instant, lovely with her long sloping shoulders and magnificent tawny skin. Her slippers then made their silken sounds, and in a moment Carrie heard the front door open and close.

She wanted to run after her, to call her back. It was as if the woman had been some protection to her while she was present.

In one gulp, Beau drank down the rest of his brandy and set the glass down hard on the table. "Now, Carrie," he said, turning those dark eyes toward her, "let's stop playing games." With a quick movement he tossed the gown to her, and instinctively she put out a hand to catch it. "I wish you to put this on before we dine. Will you go into the bedroom and see to it? Or," his voice dropped, "shall I do it for you? Right here and now."

She took a step backward, terrified, and then after a long moment, shrugged. "I'll put it on," she said. What difference did it make what she was wearing while they ate?

She went into a bedroom dominated by an oversized bed that was made up with a rich red satin coverlet. A single lamp cast its soft glow across the shimmering material, and Carrie turned away, could hardly bear to look at the place. She knew now the price Beau Canfield would exact for helping her.

Her fingers trembled as she undid the buttons and ribbons and let her dress fall in a heap about her ankles, then quickly she untied the tapes of her crinoline and stepped out of the wide, horsehair-padded hoops. She pulled the gown on over her pantalettes and camisole.

There was an oval mirror over the dressing table, and she saw that the foamy lace of her camisole peeked out over the top of the gown. She tucked it down out of sight and looked at herself for a long moment. The garment was lovely, cut wide at the neck to curve and plunge to the lowest possible point between her breasts. The silk molded to her, blue as the deepest sapphire, the color making her eyes look golden in her pale face. If only she were wearing it for someone else . . . Rance.

She jerked herself around, furious with herself that she had even thought of him, and head high, marched back into the sitting room.

"Beautiful!" Beau said, turning from the table as she came in. Wine bottle in hand, he slowly looked her up and down.

She made no reply to that but looked past him to the table and saw that he had readied everything while she was out of the room. Plates of delicate white fish smothered in a light cream sauce waited, and alongside them were saucers of buttery crescent-shaped rolls and tiny ramekins of green peas. With mocking gallantry Beau bowed and held out her chair. She could not escape him.

A part of her wanted to scream, to demand that he stop this charade and get on with what he wanted to do, get it over with. But she weakly took her place at the table.

Though she tried to eat, she found that she could hardly swallow so she pushed the food around and tried to pretend, all the while watching Beau watch her. He seemed to enjoy his dinner immensely, eating fastidiously, cutting the fish into small pieces and taking his time with it.

The candlelight burnished the curly blond hair, which contrary to fashion he wore rather short and close to his head, and highlighted the perfection of his features. Too perfect, Carrie thought. Like a Greek mask, sensual and cruel. And suddenly, unbidden, Rance was there in her mind's eye . . . the hard leanness of his jaw, the clefted chin, the rough masculinity of all the parts of his face that, put together, were so pleasing.

She quickly took a sip of her wine.

"More?" Beau indicated the decanter.

"No, thank you," she said.

"Coffee then?" He reached for the heavy silver pot on the nearby serving table and poured a thin stream of the steaming brew into the small china cup beside her plate.

She stirred it with a delicate spoon, unable to raise the cup to her lips because her hands had begun to tremble so.

Beau lowered the perfectly arched brows and regarded her for a long moment. "I don't believe you're the least bit interested in dinner, Carrie."

She was on her feet quickly as he rose and came around the table toward her. "Wait . . .!" she said, instinctively backing away.

"Wait? For what?" he said coolly, grinning. He grasped her forearm and pulled her closer to him.

"I said, *wait!*" she repeated imperiously.

He didn't release her but paused as they were. "All right. What is it?" he said, still amused.

Carrie's chin came up, though her heart was pounding at a

sickening pace. "What proof do I have that you will keep your part of the bargain once I have kept mine?" she demanded.

He stared at her for a moment and then threw his head back and laughed, the sound abrasive in the stillness. "My God, you're every bit the hellcat I thought you were! A challenge! That's what I like, Carrie! A woman who will stand toe to toe and challenge me!" He released her and strode over to a small desk deep in the shadow along the far wall. In a moment he was back with a packet of bills in his hand. He threw it down on the table.

"There," he said. "That's a thousand dollars. Count it if you wish. And," he added, "as long as you are my mistress, you'll have whatever you need whenever you need it. If you please me . . ."

Carrie was staring at the money, a deep revulsion flooding through her.

She picked up the packet and heard Beau's triumphant chuckle. There was a slick, oily feel to the greenbacks, as if they had passed through a great many dirty hands. She remembered the first time she had heard the word "whore" . . . whispered, the way young females always passed that secret knowledge to one another.

All the reasons she had for coming here suddenly seemed far away. And she knew that something deeper was involved, deeper even than her love for Kingston's Landing . . . the core of herself, her very being was involved.

She could not allow herself to be used by this man—by any man—for money. She wasn't sure why it had been different when she'd given herself to Rance . . . but it had.

She put the money back on the table. She would face him down. "I'm sorry, Beau," she said calmly. "I can't do this. I'd like to go home, please."

He stared as if he hadn't heard correctly, and then his eyes narrowed and his mouth hardened to an ugly line. "I've overestimated you, Carrie," he said. "I didn't believe you were foolish enough to think you could back out now." Before she could guess his intention, his hand shot out to catch her wrist in a grip of steel.

"Have a care, Beau!" she gasped. "I don't think that even

the Yankee courts would condone rape! I shall go to General Banks himself if you don't release me at once!'' Though her legs were trembling so she was afraid she would fall, Carrie stared defiantly up into the dark eyes of Beau Canfield, usually so cool, but now burning with a black fire. His laugh chilled her to the bone.

"Rape?" he said softly. "Rape in a house on *Rampart Street* . . . to which you came voluntarily? A fact to which my driver can attest. Who would believe you, Carrie?''

She tried to pull free, but it was no use. He swung her to him, and the pressure of his lips was against hers, though she fought and kicked at him. His mouth, soft and wet and revolting, ground against hers until his teeth forced her lips apart. His tongue defiled her, thrusting, choking her until she moaned with the nausea that assailed her.

Beau misread the sound for one of pleasure and drew back for an instant to grin at her. "I'll take you here first . . . here on the floor," he said. "And afterward . . . in the bedroom.''

He was offguard, and she wrenched one hand free and raked her nails down the length of his cheek. "Let me go!'' she screamed. "I loathe you . . . despise you!''

The words goaded him to a frenzy, the tracks down his face beginning to turn a deep, dark red. "I'm going to use you until I'm ready to quit . . . and by that time, Carrie, you'll be begging me for more . . . the way all women do!''

She let out a wail before his mouth came down on hers again, and this time he was like a wild man, his free hand pulling the silk dressing gown aside and tearing at her camisole until her breasts were bared to his bruising fingers. She tried to scream, but his tongue was thrusting into her mouth.

With a stout push from him, she felt herself crashing backwards to the floor, and to her horror he came down on top of her, his rigid member within his trousers thrusting against her. Her mouth was free of his now, and she would have screamed, but she needed every ounce of strength to fight him as he tore at her pantalettes. Then the buttons and fabric gave way right down the length of her smooth, taut-skinned belly to the triangle of soft, dark hair between her legs.

"Oh, God . . .'' she moaned, "no . . . please, no!'' But his hand was working frantically at his crotch to free himself, and his mouth was sucking at her breast.

In a haze of horror and pain, she could see that they were on the floor beside the serving cart, and looking up, she saw the heavy, silver coffee pot right there at the edge. A desperate hope flared.

With a cunning born of absolute despair, she suddenly stopped struggling and went limp. Beau gave a roar of triumph and renewed his assault upon her, his mouth slack as he finally pulled his engorged member free of his trousers. But at that instant, she felt a loosening of his hold, and she lunged for the pot, twisting her body cruelly in the effort to get it.

With a great cry, her fingers closed about the wooden handle, and she turned, the lower part of her still in Beau's embrace, to bring the heavy coffee pot crashing down against the top of his head. He gave one grunt and rolled off her.

She collapsed there on the floor, gasping for breath. Dear God, had she killed him?

When she could bring herself to look, she got to her feet and surveyed the scene before her. The pot had gone careening across the floor, spilling coffee in its wake, and Beau was lying on his side, his arms flung out before him. She bent over the crumpled form. He seemed to be breathing normally. That must mean that he was only knocked out. And if that were true, he might come to at any moment.

Panic seized her once again. She had to get out of this house! Right now!

She looked down at her nearly naked body and with numb fingers secured her torn pantalettes as best she could—the camisole was a lost cause. And then she clutched the silk dressing gown back around her and fastened the buttons, most of which were still there. Though she was trembling violently, she ran with feverish haste into the bedroom, snatched up her dress and reticule, and sped back through the hall and out the door, terrified that she'd heard a sound from Beau. She had reached the street before she realized that she was without one of her slippers, but there was no way that she was going back for it.

She ran along the darkened street, hoping against hope that she was going the right way. What if Jenkins came along? What if Beau . . .? She stopped herself from thinking, just clutched her dress to her and ran as hard as she could, her breath coming in ragged gasps, her stocking already shredded against the cobblestones.

The houses she passed were all closely shuttered and as quiet as the tombs in St. Louis Cemetery. She dared not go to any one of them to ask for help. She didn't know what kind of reception she might get.

Her breath came harder, and pain stabbed at her side, but she continued to run and in a moment saw the lights of an intersection ahead.

She approached cautiously, conscious of the picture she presented, running along the street in a torn dressing gown, one shoe off, grimly holding onto her dress. There was a street sign that said: TOULOUSE STREET. Yes, she decided. She would go that way.

Running along the banquette, she came abreast of a lighted doorway, but when she heard the rough voices of men raised in a drinking song, she ran on, only to stop dead as a horse came from the alleyway beside the building. The man atop the animal was obviously far gone in his cups and leaning forward muttering curses. She pressed back against the building and gave silent thanks that the moon had gone behind a cloud barely a moment before.

The rider safely past her, she continued on, this time more cautiously, beginning to despair of ever getting home, when suddenly she heard the creak of a carriage coming slowly along the street behind her.

She ducked into a dark doorway and waited while the sway-backed old horse plodded nearer. And then her heart gave a great leap as she realized that the wobbly-wheeled, broken-springed conveyance lurching along the dark street was a hackney. She could have wept, she was so glad to see it.

She limped into the middle of the cobblestone street, waving her arms frantically, and the fat Negro in the driver's seat, who had been softly singing an old gombo tune to himself, hauled the horse to a stop and looked down at her with wide and disbelieving eyes.

"Take me to Dumaine Street, please," she said, starting around the side of the disreputable-looking cab to the door.

The Negro held up a hand to stop her and shook his head slowly, eyeing her warily as if she were an apparition. "Sorry, Missy . . . sorry . . ." he said, belatedly remembering to remove the battered and stained top hat from his head. "No more work tonight. My woman is waiting with supper. No more . . . no more . . ."

"Oh, please . . ." Carrie begged, "I . . . I . . ." She cast about for the right words and then gave up on trying to offer an explanation for her present sorry state. "I must get home," she said. "I'll pay you very well . . ."

The round eyes in the man's dark, plump face wavered ever so slightly at the mention of money, and Carrie pressed her advantage. "I'll make it worth your while. I promise . . ." she said, and waited anxiously for a long moment.

He cocked his head to one side and peered at her, then gave a resigned grunt and clapped his hat back atop his head. "Dumaine Street, Missy?" he said.

"Oh, yes . . . thank you!" Carrie breathed a sigh of relief, gave him the number, then quickly climbed into the musty interior and sank gratefully back against the threadbare and dank seat. No carriage had ever seemed so luxurious to her before.

Carrie awoke with a start, sitting bolt upright in bed before she realized that bright morning sunlight was streaming through her windows and she was safe in her bed at the house on Dumaine Street. Slowly she lay back again, resting her head against the big square pillows, conscious of her bruised and aching body. Besides the blue marks, there were scrapes on each elbow and a shallow cut on her right foot from running barefoot on the cobblestones. She had cleaned it last night once she'd reached her room.

She closed her eyes and moaned, wondering how she could have been so foolish as to put herself at the mercy of a man like Beau Canfield . . . even to save Kingston's Landing. And there *was* that still hanging over her. But she wouldn't think about it now. Thank God that she had been able to get back home and into the house last night . . . and no one the wiser.

As it was, the hackney driver was probably beaming over his last run of the evening since Carrie had given him all the money she had in her reticule, which was probably more than the man had made with all his other fares of the day put together. His wife was undoubtedly delighted with the blue silk dressing gown Carrie had left in the carriage—she had drawn the window drapes as soon as she entered the broken-down old cab and, slipping out of the dressing gown, wiggled into her own dress as quickly as she could. And Beau, besides having a monstrous headache and a lump on his forehead, would have a ruffled petticoat and a set of hoops lying in a heap on his bedroom floor this morning. All in all a small price to pay for remaining relatively unscathed, she thought. She shuddered as she remembered every awful minute in that house.

Now what on earth was she going to do about Suzy? She had to find a way to keep her safe from Beau. But she would think about it for a few days, make sure that she didn't do or say the wrong thing. Suzy was so headstrong.

She sat up, putting her legs over the side of the bed and wincing at the soreness. A hot bath, that was what she needed. A steaming bath to soak away some of the pain of pulled muscles and bruises. But she'd have to be careful that Mattie didn't see any of the black and blue marks on her. She didn't want anyone to guess that she'd not been at the Tates' house last night.

Mattie proved to be easy to handle since she was still red-eyed from weeping over Solomon. So much so that in the afternoon, Carrie sent for Prosper, and he promised to see what he could find out.

He returned the following day with news of Monsieur Marchand. "It seems that Solomon was right about at least one thing," he said. "The Yankee authorities *did* take Monsieur Marchand's age into consideration and released him with a warning. He and Madame Marchand are recovering at their niece's house. I understand they will be back home in a few days."

Mattie, who was serving coffee to Carrie and Prosper in the sitting room, turned her eyes toward the dapper little fencing master and waited anxiously, her usually pretty face pinched and drawn under the bright purple kerchief.

Carrie spoke up quickly. "Mattie . . . that is, *we* would like to know if you've learned anything of Solomon's whereabouts."

"I'm afraid I haven't," he said gently. "I did find out that he was issued his manumission papers through the Provost Court, but they didn't have an address for him. I will keep trying, Mattie. I promise."

Mattie nodded solemnly, shoulders drooping. "Thank you, Mist' Prosper," she said and, eyes on the floor, turned to walk dejectedly from the room.

Prosper leaned back in his chair and sighed. "Poor girl. The pain of love can indeed be excruciating," he said.

"I suppose so," Carrie said. "And from Mattie's behavior now, I'm afraid that things had gone much farther than I'd supposed. Still . . . I can't help believing that she's better off that he's gone."

Prosper's expressive eyebrows rose. "Who can tell that for another?" he challenged, but immediately he grinned. "However, that is not really what I'm here to discuss."

"Oh?"

"No." He ran his fingertip along the gleaming waxed curl of his mustache. "I am here to discuss money."

"Money?" Carrie said, puzzled.

"Yes, I think it is time we spoke of certain facts. I have seen you try and fail to get a loan to put in a crop at Kingston's Landing. And, *ma chère*, I have seen your lovely face grow sadder and more worried all the time." He took a sip of his coffee. "Susannah tells me that you had dinner at the Tates' home a night or two ago."

Carrie resisted the urge to squirm in her chair. Instead she sedately straightened the cuff of the long-sleeved white shirtwaist, which hid the deep purple bruises on her arms. "Yes," she said cautiously.

"And I am assuming that nothing has come of that or you would have told me."

"That's . . . that's right," Carrie said, avoiding Prosper's eyes.

"I am sure that in all this time you have wondered why your Papa's old friend, Prosper Durant, the fencing master of world renown''—his black eyes twinkled—"has not come forward to offer financial aid.''

"Oh, no, Prosper. I never . . .''

He waved her to silence. "The truth, *ma chère,* is that I was a man of some wealth at the start of the war. But like the fox who outsmarts himself, I had most of my money in gold—believing it to be the safest specie—and when the bankers sent all the gold out of the city to keep it from falling into the hands of the Yankees . . . alas, mine went right along with the rest.'' He laughed, shrugging away the misfortune.

"But,'' he continued, "I have gone over my funds carefully, and while I know this amount is small for your needs, I wish you to have it.'' He took a piece of paper from his inside coat pocket and passed it to Carrie.

She stared down at the bank draft in the amount of two-thousand dollars. "Prosper . . .'' she gasped, "I . . . I don't understand.''

"I wish there were more,'' he said. "Can you manage a crop on so little?''

"Why . . . why I think I could . . .'' she stammered, still stunned by this unexpected turn of events. "But, Prosper, I can't take this from you. Especially after what you've just told me.''

"Of course you can. I will have it no other way. Besides, you would not presume to dictate to your elders, would you?'' he teased.

Carrie held the draft tightly, fighting back the tears. "Certainly not one so dear,'' she said, her voice cracking. "But you might need this yourself. Are you sure . . . ?''

"Positive.''

She sat there, almost past words. "I'll pay back every cent,'' she said finally as the reality of it hit her and the swelling in her throat threatened to overwhelm her.

Dear God, when she thought of what she had almost done. . . .

But now she had the money, thanks to Prosper. And she could take Suzy and go home . . . home to Kingston's Landing.

18

THE SUN WAS LOW IN THE SKY, BANDING THE WESTERN HORIZON
with a deep pink that shaded down to violet and finally
to rich plum. The silvery wisps of moss that trailed from
overhanging branches along the main drive up to Kingston's
Landing were bathed with a hint of lavender in the failing light.
Bone-tired herself, Carrie gave Majestic an appreciative pat on
the neck and let the chestnut gelding go at his own plodding
pace. It had been a long day for both of them.

She had left Justice only a few minutes before, back at the
river landing, and they had stopped to talk for a moment before
he continued on along the river road toward his own farm just
north of Kingston's Landing. His land had, in fact, once been a
part of the plantation, but years ago Adam Kingston had sold the
thirty-five acres to Justice, and the black man and his wife Tana
had lived there ever since.

Carrie was still basking in the warmth of the Negro's parting
words: "I do believe you would've made one fine overseer
yourself, Miss Carrie." High praise, she thought, from someone
who had been the best. But she knew that she could never have
done it without Justice's help. He came over several times a
week to help. And of course, Prosper had been invaluable before
she left New Orleans. He had helped her find and hire the hands
she needed to work the place.

She grinned to herself now, weary as she was. In her mind's
eye she could see the acreage south along the river where they'd
worked today, see the rich green shoots of cane, lusty as the
ground from which they grew. She had done it. With the help of

dear Prosper and Justice, she had gotten her crop in. And it was healthy and growing.

The house was visible up ahead now, Kingston's Landing, its mellowed beauty set off by the gnarled old magnolia trees. Shadows crept across the galleries, cast the guillotine windows into dark relief. The purple bougainvillea blossoms that trailed along the upper railings looked almost black in the rapidly failing light.

As Carrie drew nearer, she pulled the horse up and just sat for a moment, soaking it all in, feeling that surge of love she always did, so sharp and sweet that it caused her throat to tighten. Papa had always done that, she remembered, had always stopped for a moment and just looked at the house, as if it were his favorite sight in all the world.

The paint was beginning to peel on the front columns; one of the dark green shutters in front had a loose hinge and was sagging slightly. She would see that it all was fixed . . . everything put to rights just as soon as she could spare enough men from the fields.

There was always so much to be done . . . and not enough hands. Besides, the men she'd hired were forever sneaking off for a chew of tobacco or a nap under a shade tree. Justice said they had to prove to themselves that they were no longer slaves. She was forever hunting them down and getting them back to work, sometimes working right alongside them herself to keep them on the job. There were times Carrie wanted to fire them all, but she didn't. She couldn't keep going off to New Orleans and hiring a new crew every week.

She sighed now and, taking off the big straw hat that protected her face from the sun throughout the day, turned Majestic toward the stables where Benjamin waited.

"See that he gets a good rubdown, Benjamin," she said.

"I surely will, Miss Carrie." Benjamin rubbed an affectionate hand over the dusty flank, and the gelding whinnied softly at the prospect of food and his comfortable stall.

Carrie walked along the path back to the house, gardenia bushes on either side filling the twilight with their sweet fragrance. The sun was almost down now, sending final orange fingers of light through the deep purple of the western sky. She cut through the garden and crossed the gallery to enter the house through the sitting-room doors. Susannah was there, working on a dainty bit of embroidery by the light of a tall, pink-globed lamp on the table beside her, that rosebud mouth set into a decided pout.

"Well," she said, throwing the embroidery hoop aside as she caught sight of her sister, "it's about time! Chloe said we couldn't eat until you got here. And I'm starving!"

"I'm sorry, Suzy," Carrie said. "I had some last minute things to do."

Susannah looked Carrie up and down, her pretty face clouding with disdain. "Honestly, Carrie . . . would you just look at yourself?"

Carrie, battered straw hat in hand, looked down at the stout cotton shirtwaist and the dusty and worn riding skirt and boots that had become her work uniform. Certainly crinolines were impossible to work in, and she had found the riding skirts to be the best solution. Chloe kept the three Carrie had washed and clean, but a few hours in the fields and she was grimy again. She knew that her hair ribbon had come loose and that her hair was tangled and as dusty as the rest of her.

"I know, honey. I look a sight!" She grinned, trying to coax Susannah into a better mood. "I'll just go get cleaned up and then we'll eat. It won't take long."

But Susannah had spent a long and boring day, wondering why Beau Canfield had neither come himself nor sent a message in the weeks since Carrie had dragged her back to Kingston's Landing, and her vexation was not to be soothed so easily. "I don't know what's gotten into you," she railed. "Out working from sunup to sundown . . . like any common fieldhand!"

Carrie bit back a stinging retort and turned to go to her bath when she saw Chloe in the doorway, her face like a thundercloud.

"Seems to me," the Negress said to Susannah, "that a certain Miss Somebody would be mighty glad to have a sister what works so hard to take care of ever'body. I just guess Miss Carrie would like to sit around in the cool of the gallery doin' nothin' but a little stitchin' all day!"

Slave or not, Chloe had been like a second mother to all the Kingston children, and when she spoke, they still listened. Susannah squirmed uncomfortably in her chair under the stern, dark eyes and reluctantly gave in. "You're right, Chloe," she mumbled. "I . . . I'm sorry, Carrie. It's just been such a long day. And I hate it here! I don't know why we can't stay in New Orleans!"

Carrie and Chloe exchanged looks. Both Susannah and Mattie had been less than pleased to come back to the plantation—Mattie because she felt that Solomon would not know how to find her there—and neither of them had exactly hidden their feelings of discontent.

"I'll be ready for dinner shortly," Carrie said, and to acknowledge her sister's apology, she touched Susannah's shoulder lightly as she turned toward the doorway. "Did Lafitte get back from New Orleans yet?" she asked Chloe.

"Yes, Miss Carrie. Come back about an hour ago. And he got ever'thing you sent him for. Brought back a letter from Miz Morrison, too. And some newspapers."

"I still don't see why I couldn't have gone in with him," Susannah was muttering. "Even if he was driving right back, I could have stayed with the Morrisons, and he could have come back to get me in a week or so."

Carrie shook her head and almost turned back, but instead sighed and went on down the hallway toward the back of the house and her waiting bath.

After dinner, Carrie went into the study and settled herself in the big leather chair, exhausted after the long day but determined to read Abby's letter and at least glance over the newspapers that Lafitte had brought back with him before she went up to bed. She slid her finger under the seal, and taking out the closely covered page, scanned down it. The Morrisons had gotten word that their daughter Melissa had been safely delivered of a healthy son the day before Christmas. The rest of the letter was taken up with Abby's concern for J. D. at Vicksburg now that Grant was tightening the noose about that strategically placed city.

Carrie was worried herself. Grant had been devising stategies to storm the almost inpregnable defenses of the Confederates for months. Twice he had mounted major attacks only to be driven back by the heavy Rebel fortifications along the bluffs above the river. And now it was said that Lincoln was pressing for a victory, which would not only remove the last obstacle to Union supremacy of the entire Mississippi, but would bolster flagging

Northern spirits after their stinging defeat by Lee at Fredricksburg in December and again only recently at Chancellorsville.

The last victory had cost the South dearly. The irreplaceable General Stonewall Jackson had been lost, shot mistakenly by his own troops in the confusion of the battle, it was reported. Jackson had not only been Lee's "strong right arm," he had been a symbol of victory for the South since early in the war.

Carrie sighed and turned to the paper to see that Grant had finally given up on a direct attack on Vicksburg and had entrenched his men, vowing to starve the Rebels out no matter how long it took. She read it with a growing fear for George Pierre and J.D., but tried to reassure herself. No one was stronger or braver than their own Confederate soldiers. If there was any way possible, they would prevent the Yankees from capturing the city. And she could only pray that her brother and J.D. would come through it safely.

She leaned back in her chair and closed her eyes wearily, feeling the cool night air that wafted through the window. Despite her worry, the newspaper slipped from her hand before long to the mellowed old carpet as, exhausted, she drifted off to sleep.

It was an hour later when Chloe came in to see if Carrie wanted some tea. She stood looking down at the tired, young face, saw how the freshly washed hair curled about cheeks that showed a smattering of golden freckles now, despite all the efforts to protect that delicate skin from the sun.

Carrie frowned slightly in her sleep, and the old Negress shook her head sadly. "Lord, lord," she said softly, "but this child is tryin' to carry the world on her back."

After a moment, she put out a gentle hand to rouse Carrie and sent her upstairs to bed.

It started as a gentle rain, which Carrie welcomed since the weather had been dry for the past few weeks. She watched it from the south gallery and welcomed a day off from the grinding schedule that had become her custom since her return to Kingston's Landing. But by the second day, the skies had turned leaden, the rain coming down relentlessly all through that day and into a third, and Carrie watched with an ever more worried eye. If it kept on like this for much longer, the system of drainage ditches might be unable to handle the overflow and the crop could be damaged.

It would stop soon, she told herself. By tomorrow the sun would come out, and the delta land would steam, rich and fertile and lushly green. All the same, after lunch she had Benjamin saddle up for her, and over Chloe's protests, she rode out in the downpour, wearing an old rubber blanket with a slit for her head over her other clothes. Heedless of the pounding rain, which soon soaked through her straw hat and dripped down the neck of the "gum blanket," as the men called the rubber wraps, she rode directly to the south acreage.

The drainage ditches were carrying water away but seemed a trifle high, which either meant that they were clogging up with weeds and loose debris or the bayous themselves were rising fast. And that, she thought, could be a real possibility since the levees up and down the river had been damaged in places by troop movements and in many cases not repaired because of landowners who were absent or dead, or because their labor force had all run off.

Carrie looked out over the rows of growing cane, and her mouth assumed a determined line. She would keep those ditches open and flowing no matter what she had to do.

She turned Majestic and had started back resolutely when she saw Justice up ahead of her on horseback. He was draped in the same kind of rain blanket she was, and he wore his shapeless, faded felt hat low on his head. Beads of water glistened on his dark face as she drew abreast of him.

"Justice . . . I think we should get the men out here," she shouted.

He nodded, water draining in a stream from the sodden brim of his hat. "I guess it won't hurt," he said. "I've been in the fields up above . . . along the river. The ditches are high." A frown creased the dark brow, ridged between his eyebrows. "I'm worried about the bayous, Miss Carrie. If they start rising, the fields might flood. Ain't nothin' to do but get out then. And that cane will drown and rot sure as the world."

Carrie looked out over the cane rows. "That's not going to happen," she said stubbornly.

Justice gave her a wry grin. "I'll take half the men and go up above. You stay down here with the others. There ain't a whole lot we can do, though, besides keep the ditches open . . . and pray that it don't rain much more."

They routed the workers out of their cabins in the quarters, and after seeing that they were outfitted with rubber blankets and picks and shovels and axes from the work shed, they divided into two groups, as Justice had suggested, and each set off in opposite directions.

Carrie rode Majestic, and the men followed along in mule-drawn wagons, the lead wagon driven by Big Josephus—a man, who by virtue of his size and temperament, had assumed the position of gang boss. He was black as ink and had a large gap in the front of his mouth where he'd had a tooth knocked out in a fight one time. When they reached the edge of the field, he started shouting orders.

"Space you'selves out! Lot o' ground to cover here! Make sure they ain't nothin' cloggin' up them ditches!" He turned to Carrie with his gap-toothed grin. "I know cane, Miss Carrie. We don't want no water standin' on these here plants if we can help it."

Carrie threw him a look of gratitude. He was one man who had always done a full day's work for his pay.

For the next two hours the rain continued to fall, and the men watched for the least sign of a clog in the drainage ditches. Carrie herself got down from Majestic at times to chop away at a clump of coco grass or a high spot that was keeping a row from draining properly. She itched under the rubber wrap and sweated, rivulets of perspiration and rain intermingling on her face and neck, her hair hanging wet and heavy under her soaked straw hat. Her boots and the bottom part of her riding skirt were caked with mud.

Benjamin brought out big pots of steaming coffee and rich, thick gumbo, which the men drank out of graniteware cups. The crews took turns coming back to eat and rest for a few minutes.

Late in the afternoon, the rain slackened and then stopped altogether, and the sodden clouds even broke a little. Big Josephus grinned and at a signal from Carrie sang out for the men to come in. The cry was echoed again and again as it passed to the far reaches of the fields.

245

Relieved and hoping against hope that the sun would come out the next morning and the clouds blow away, Carrie went to bed early and slept restlessly until just past midnight when she was awakened by the hammering of rain against the roof.

She got up, lit the lamp, and dressed as quickly as she could, then went to look out her window at the dark sheets of water pouring down. Not a hint of a star nor a glimmer of the moon could be seen, only the swollen black sky. Oh, God, she wailed silently, the cane had to be all right. If this had happened later, when the plants were bigger, stronger, there would have been less chance of them washing out.

There was a light knock at her door, and Chloe came padding in, her old felt slippers soft against the floor, her faded robe tucked around her. "I knew you'd be up, honey," she said, her lined face filled with concern, her nearsighted eyes soft and warm.

"I can't lose it, Chloe! I can't lose this crop!" Carrie burst out, her voice edged with despair.

"I know, honey," Chloe said calmly.

Together they waited and watched, sometimes going into the hallway and opening the door that led onto the upper gallery to stare out at the torrential downpour. Finally dawn came, though the sky was still so dark and the leaden sheets of rain so heavy everything seemed gray and dim. It was as if all the color had washed out of the world.

"I'm going out to the fields, Chloe. To see how bad it is."

"Miss Carrie, no . . . You ain't got one bit of business out in them fields now. Ain't nothin' anybody can do now except wait." Chloe's words fell on air since Carrie was already halfway down the stairs. The Negress, twisting her hands and muttering under her breath, followed after her as fast as she could, slippers flapping.

Benjamin was waiting downstairs. "Justice back in the warming kitchen, Miss Carrie," he said. And Carrie hurried back there.

"Justice . . . How bad is it?"

Justice stood near the back door with a cup of hot coffee in his hand, water puddling at his feet from his soaked clothing. "The road along the river is still open, Miss Carrie, but the water's comin' up fast in the bayous. They ain't no way to get into the fields."

Carrie turned away, distraught, at the same time realizing that Justice had come through this weather to help her. "Tana?" she asked.

"Tana's all right. Her cousin's visitin' for a few days. And our place is on high ground. Ain't never flooded that high."

"Let me pour you a cup of coffee, Miss Carrie," Chloe said. She had come up behind Carrie and was standing in the hall doorway.

"No," Carrie said. "I have to get out there and see for myself. Benjamin, saddle Majestic for me."

"Miss Carrie," Chloe scolded, "didn't I just say you don't have a bit of business out there. You goin' to catch your death, get soaked through to the skin. And besides, if the water comin' up, they ain't a thing in the world you can do about it."

Justice could see by the look on Carrie's face that nothing was going to stop her from going, and he held up a hand to Chloe. "I'll go with her, Chloe," he said quietly.

"I'll go, too," Benjamin added.

They got down to the stables with no more difficulty than getting soaked through, and Benjamin saddled up a strong and placid mule for himself while Justice saddled Majestic for Carrie. Then the three of them rode out, the driving sheets of rain causing the animals to twitch their ears and whinny.

The drive leading to the landing was still fairly firm with its mixture of soil and gravel, and the river road was naturally paved with the small broken shells that had washed up on the banks over countless years. The river itself was swift and dark; pieces of tree limbs swept past, twisting in the rushing water.

"It's not too bad along here," Justice shouted above the roar of the muddy current. "But I don't think the road is passable back to the fields."

"I'm going to try," Carrie shouted back. She turned Majestic's head and started him down the narrower road that led to the cane. She was facing the wind, and she lowered her head against the stinging rain. The horse beneath her whinnied his protest.

She had gone scarcely twenty yards before Majestic began to

flounder, and after only a few feet more the gelding stumbled and almost went down in the deep mud.

"Whoa, boy . . . whoa," she said, and swung down from the saddle, determined to go on if she had to walk. But with her first steps she went into the soft mud almost to her knees, and as she slogged on, half-blinded by the rain lashing at her, she lost her balance and fell headlong into the deep and slimy ooze, turning her head just in time to keep from getting a mouthful.

She was sitting up and trying to wipe the mud from the side of her face by the time the two men reached her, and while Justice grabbed the trembling gelding by the bridle and started to lead him back, Benjamin scooped Carrie up in his still powerful arms and carried her as if she were a baby back to the hard road bed where he set her gently on her feet.

Justice grasped her by the shoulders, his dark eyes boring into hers. "There ain't nothin' we can do, Miss Carrie! You see that now?"

She nodded miserably, mud-covered and shivering. She could feel the mud caked in her hair, feel it rimming her ear. It clung to her clothes and weighed her down, oozing into her boots. But none of that mattered. She had lost the crop, and she knew it.

Justice helped her back into her saddle, and the three of them started back. The tears streaming down Carrie's cheeks mingled with the driving rain.

It was still hard for Carrie to accept . . . even though she was a planter's daughter and knew as well as anyone what the vagaries of weather could do to a crop. Still, it was difficult to believe that all that work and care—and money—had been wiped out in a single night.

It had been days before the flood waters receded back into the bayous and more than a week before the fields dried out enough that she could get into them. She found what she knew she would find. What little cane hadn't washed out lay rotting in the bright sunlight.

Now, ten days later, she sat out on the gallery, looking over the garden where sweet william and pinks and impatiens bloomed in lush profusion. The roses had never looked better. The herb garden at the far end was green and pungent. All of the teeming growth was spread out before her as if to mock her.

Susannah came out onto the verandah, daintily nibbling at one of Chloe's oatmeal cookies. She plopped herself down on the green cypress bench and cast a baleful eye at Carrie who was in the wide cypress swing at the end of the verandah.

"You didn't come in for lunch," she said petulantly.

"Sorry, honey. I just wasn't hungry."

Susannah finished off the cookie and licked the last crumb from her fingertips, her slippered foot tapping impatiently all the while. "Honestly, Carrie," she exploded finally, "I've never seen so much carrying on over an old cane crop anyway! I'm halfway glad it flooded out! Maybe now we can go back down to New Orleans and *both* cheer up a little!"

Anger propelled Carrie to her feet. "Don't you understand," she flared, "that we are going to run out of money if I don't get this place producing soon!"

Susannah stared at her a moment and then shrugged. "I'm sure the Morrisons would take care of us until—"

"The Morrisons can hardly take care of themselves!" Carrie cut her off. "Didn't you see that when we were there last?"

"Well, then . . . George Pierre will be coming home," Susannah said defiantly.

Carrie turned away in quiet despair. When *would* George Pierre be coming home? she wondered. Would this awful war ever be over? She could have told her sister that it was George Pierre's mismanagement that had gotten them into the straits they were in. But she couldn't do that. She loved her brother, and she knew that he had done the best he could. He had tried so hard to take Papa's place.

Susannah's voice came from behind Carrie, small and contrite. "I didn't mean to make you mad, Carrie. I'm really sorry about the cane."

Carrie turned back to look into her sister's pretty face, which at the moment was downcast, the rosebud mouth trembling noticeably. She had never been able to stay angry at Suzy for very long, and this time was no exception. "It's all right, honey." Slowly she grinned and held out her arms, and the two girls hugged each other soundly.

Susannah was at once all smiles again, dimpling and rosy. "Oh, Carrie," she said, "I really do mean it. I truly *am* sorry about the crop. But since it's ruined . . . I mean, there's nothing to keep us here. Couldn't we go back down to town for a while?"

Carrie sighed and looked out over the garden once again. She was right back where she'd started except that she now owed Prosper the part of the two-thousand dollars she'd used. There was certainly no way to raise any money here on the plantation. If there was any chance of a loan, it was in New Orleans. Maybe things had changed. Maybe Leroy Tate had come up with something by now.

She realized that Susannah was waiting for her answer eagerly, almost standing on tiptoe, her eyes shining with anticipation. So young, Carrie thought. So very young. All thoughts of money and crops and the war were a million miles away from her. She felt a rush of love for her little sister. She must do everything she could to keep it that way.

It didn't occur to her that she herself was only two years older than Susannah. She just reached out to take Suzy's hand in hers. "Yes," she said finally, "I guess we'll go back to New Orleans for a while."

☙ 19 ☙

"**G**UESS WHO I SAW THIS AFTERNOON? RIGHT OUTSIDE OF LeGallienne's Sweet Shop." Susannah bounced into the kitchen of the house on Dumaine Street where Carrie was arranging a vase of roses and Mattie was bent over the stove to inspect a black iron skillet full of frying chicken.

Carrie snipped off the stem end of a large pink rose and turned to her sister, hoping that it wasn't Beau Canfield whom she'd seen. Luckily, he had been out of town when they'd arrived a week ago, and Carrie hoped fervently that he still was. It would put off a little longer the confrontation she would have to have with Susannah upon his return.

"Well . . ." Susannah prodded her, "don't you want to know?"

"Of course." Carrie grinned. "Who did you see?"

"Rance Stewart," Susannah announced.

Carrie quickly turned back to the flowers, jamming the rose hard into the vase. "That's nice," she said, her voice carefully level.

"And you'll never guess," Susannah went chattering on. "I was really surprised."

"Surprised about what?" Carrie said carefully.

"He's engaged to be married. He and that Yankee girl . . . Nora Barlow. She was with him."

Carrie's hand froze in midair, and the pit of her stomach seemed to drop away. Engaged? Rance was going to *marry* that whey-faced Yankee!

She realized that Mattie had straightened and was looking at her. She pretended to be preoccupied with the flowers, grabbing another rose from the basket on the table beside her, clipping the end of it so quickly that she cut it much too short.

"Rance introduced me. And, Carrie, you should have seen her," Susannah rushed on breathlessly. "Her clothes were *beautiful!*" She hugged herself, her eyes half-closed, lips slightly parted and smiling as she envisioned the well-dressed Yankee girl once again. "Yards and yards of pink watered silk. And her hat, Carrie . . . the most fashionable hat I've ever seen! Just the tiniest little thing right here on top her head." Susannah demonstrated. "And all covered with the softest, pinkest feathers—"

"Miss Carrie . . . look what you've done!" Mattie interrupted, and Carrie looked down to see the bright red drop of blood trace its way down her thumb and splash onto the well-worn surface of the kitchen table.

"You've stuck yourself, Carrie," Susannah said. "How did you do that?"

"Here," Mattie said, and quickly dipped some warm water from the back of the stove into a graniteware basin and brought it to the table to wash out the small wound.

"It's nothing, Mattie," Carrie protested.

"Better it be washed out," Mattie insisted. "The thorns on the roses are extra big this year, it seems like." She eyed Carrie who looked away quickly.

"Well, anyway," Susannah went on, "Nora Barlow's clothes were just adorable. And I asked Rance when the wedding was, and he said in the fall. It's really *so* romantic. I wish I were getting married this fall."

"Thank heaven you're not," Carrie snapped. Her thumb throbbed dully, and she looked down at the small puncture that had turned purplish and still oozed blood. The thorn had gone quite deep.

"Let me tie that up for you," Mattie said.

"No." Carrie pulled her hand away. "It's all right, thank you, Mattie."

Susannah had seated herself in a chair across from where Carrie stood, and she propped her elbows on the table and looked earnestly up at her sister. "I guess I was surprised," she said, "because . . ." She stopped and began again. "Well, I know that you're going to marry J. D. But there were times when I thought that Rance . . . that you . . ."

Carrie's head came up, and she shot Susannah a stern glance. "Don't be ridiculous, Suzy! I'm sure Major Stewart and his Yankee bride will be perfect for each other!" She picked up the vase of roses, though there were still some blossoms in the basket. "I think this is enough," she said briskly. "I'll just take them into the sitting room."

But alone in the coolness of the front hallway, Carrie stopped and sank back against the wall, closing her eyes and clutching the vase to her. It was wonderful, she told herself. Wonderful that Rance was going to marry that girl. At least he would be out of *her* life. And that was certainly all that she had ever wanted. But the dull aching in her thumb seemed to have spread to her whole body, throbbed with every beat of her heart.

*   *   *

In the days that followed, Carrie stayed as busy as possible. It was not, she decided, too early to start seeking a loan for next spring's crop. She went to see Leroy Tate at the bank, and Simpson, the old clerk out front, showed her right in.

"I don't know, Miss Kingston." The banker stroked his heavy-jawed face thoughtfully once she had explained her predicament. "It's bad here for everyone except the army people and the confounded profiteers. General Banks has cut some of that out, I'll say that for him. But when you come right down to it, I guess there's no way in the world to stop it in wartime."

"But you'll keep trying to manage a loan for me, won't you, Mr. Tate?" Carrie pleaded. "I must have the money by spring."

"I'll do my best," he promised.

At least Carrie had enough to live on into the next year, if she was careful. Prosper had not only refused to take back what was left of the money he'd given her, but insisted that it had been a gift, not a loan. Still, she intended to pay it back . . . no matter how long it took her.

A good deal of her time was spent with Abby Morrison as the two of them watched and waited for news of Vicksburg. As June ended and the summer heat settled firmly upon New Orleans, Carrie could only wonder how long those gallant men upriver could hold out against the far greater numbers of Grant's Yankees. She feared for George Pierre and J.D., but managed to keep up a good front for Abby's benefit.

Now she sat in the library and read the days headlines once again. Though it was nearly eleven, there was no thought of going to bed yet; the news was too disturbing. *UNION VICTORY EXPECTED AT VICKSBURG SOON.*

"Bet you worryin' again, Miss Carrie. 'Bout Mist' George Pierre and Mist' J. D.," Mattie's voice came softly from the doorway.

Carrie looked up to see the Negro girl in her nightgown and pink-flowered cotton wrapper, her sleek head bared to show her close-cropped curly hair. "Come in, Mattie." Carrie sighed and put the paper aside. "They've been under siege for weeks now. I don't know how they can hold out much longer. The garrison must be running out of food . . . medicine . . . ."

"I tell you what, Miss Carrie," Mattie advanced into the

room, "I grew up watchin' them two boys, and they goin' to be all right. I guarantee that. Ain't no Yankee goin' to mess with them."

Carrie smiled in spite of herself. "You sound like Chloe," she said.

Mattie giggled softly and went to straighten a book that was out of line on the shelf nearest her. "If Mama was here, she'd say you needed some hot tea to put you to sleep."

"Maybe I do," Carrie said listlessly. "Is Suzy already in bed?"

"For more'n an hour now."

Carrie saw how the gaslight fell across Mattie's face to show the fine bone structure and highlight the beautifully shaped head. There was, she suddenly realized, a kind of glow about the girl that hadn't been there for a long time.

"Mattie," she asked suddenly, "have you seen Solomon?"

The lithe figure stiffened. There was a long moment before she answered. "Yes, Miss Carrie," she said finally and turned back to face her mistress with only partially hidden defiance.

Carrie took a deep breath. "I don't think you should," she said firmly. "The man is nothing but trouble, Mattie. Surely you can see that?"

The big brown eyes flashed. "Are you sayin' I can't see him, Miss Carrie?" Mattie demanded. And the room suddenly seemed very still as the two of them confronted one another.

Carrie wanted to say exactly that, that Mattie was not to see Solomon again. But for the first time in her life, she wondered if she had the right to say such a thing to Mattie, no matter that they were mistress and slave. And if she did say it, was it possible that Mattie might disobey her? It would have been unthinkable even a year ago. But so much had happened . . . so much had changed.

Their eyes were locked together, Carrie struggling to find the right words, when they were interrupted by Lafitte's measured tread along the hallway.

"Miss Carrie . . ." he said softly from the doorway, his long face unnaturally grave, "Benjamin is here. He came in through the carriageway in the back. He must speak with you at once."

Carrie hardly waited for Lafitte to get the words out before she was hurrying along with him to the kitchen, Mattie following along, the matter of Solomon forgotten for the moment.

"Benjamin . . ." Carrie burst out as she saw the big black man. "Benjamin, what is it? Is something wrong?"

Benjamin twisted his felt hat in his hands, his broad face set into a worried frown. "I used the pass you wrote out for me to get through the soldier's lines outside of town, Miss Carrie." He took an anxious step forward. "Ain't nobody else can hear us, can they?"

"No. Tell me what's happened."

"Is Mama all right?" Mattie put in.

Benjamin gave a quick nod to his daughter, along with a look of warning for her impertinence in speaking up so freely at such a time. "Miss Carrie," he spoke in a hushed voice, "Mist' George Pierre's at home, and he bad hurt. Mist' J. D. done brung him."

"Oh, my God!" Carrie felt almost faint as the words hit her. "He's been wounded?"

Benjamin nodded sadly.

"But he's alive, Benjamin?" she whispered. "George Pierre *is* alive?"

"Yes, Miss Carrie." The dark eyes avoided hers, dropped to the kitchen floor. "When I left . . . he was alive."

Carrie pressed her knuckles into her lips. Dear God . . . She wouldn't let herself think it, pushed it from her head. She must think what to do. She mustn't make any mistakes now.

She stiffened her back and made her voice steady. "Mattie, fix Benjamin something to eat. And you, Lafitte . . . go upstairs and wake Miss Suzy. Tell her to come down here at once. Hurry now, both of you."

They both moved quickly to do her bidding, and after another word or two with Benjamin, she went upstairs herself, passing Lafitte who was knocking at Susannah's door, and straight into her own bedroom where she hurriedly threw a few things into a small valise.

After a couple of minutes, she could hear Suzy's grumbling, and when she came out of her bedroom, bag in hand, she saw her sister standing in the hallway, heavy-eyed, hair tousled from sleep, her blue muslin wrapper buttoned right up to the throat.

"Carrie, why on earth did you tell Lafitte to wake me?" she complained irritably. "I was sound asleep!"

"Suzy, come downstairs. George Pierre is badly hurt, and J. D.'s brought him to Kingston's Landing. I must go home tonight."

Shocked into full wakefulness, Susannah hurried along after Carrie. "But when did all this happen? How do you know?" she called out, but Carrie just motioned her on to the kitchen.

"Benjamin . . ." Susannah said. The black man was just washing down some cold ham and corn bread with a glass of buttermilk.

"Miss Suzy . . ."

"Now listen to me, all of you," Carrie interrupted. "Just as soon as Benjamin is finished eating, he and I are going to start back to Kingston's Landing."

"I'll go, too," Susannah put in. "I want to be with George Pierre."

"No," Carrie said. "George Pierre's safety will depend on the three of you here. If the Yankees had any idea . . . There mustn't be a hint to anyone about what's happened."

"But Abby will want to know," Susannah protested. "Especially if J. D.'s there."

"We can't let her know, honey. Don't you see? The more people who know, the greater the danger for both J.D. and George Pierre. If Abby knew, she'd insist on going along . . . maybe Seth would, too. We can't risk it."

Susannah regarded Carrie with a look that said she was only half-convinced.

"Please, honey," Carrie put a hand out to her, "trust me. You mustn't breathe a word to anyone. Promise . . ."

Susannah hesitated for a moment, then gave in reluctantly. "All right," she said.

"Good." Carrie draped a shawl over the waiting valise. As hot as it was, she certainly wouldn't need the wrap for warmth, but it might keep some of the mosquitoes off her as they drove near the river. "Now"—she turned back to her sister, and to Mattie and Lafitte who stood waiting for their instructions—"the hardest part will be to convince everyone that nothing is out of the ordinary here. Do everything that you always do. And whatever happens, try to keep anyone from knowing that I'm away."

"But, Carrie," Susannah said, "we're supposed to go to dinner at the Morrisons tomorrow night. What can I tell them?"

"Just give them my regrets and say that I've developed a terrible headache and decided to spend the evening in bed."

"But what if Abby comes by one day?"

"Tell her I've gone to the market. Or the dressmaker's. Or to visit Prosper. Tell her anything. Make up some excuse. Remember"—Carrie's eyes swept the three of them—"not a word to anyone. I'm depending on all of you."

Benjamin finished his buttermilk and put the glass on the table, then looked expectantly at Carrie.

"Ready, Benjamin?" she asked him.

"Yes, Miss Carrie."

Carrie hugged Susannah quickly. "I wish you could go with me, honey. I'll be back as soon as I can."

Carrie smothered a sob as she looked down at George Pierre lying there so flushed with fever, his long body thin beneath the linen sheet. She noted the fine Creole features, the sensitive mouth and delicately drawn brows. As a boy, he had looked like Papa, like Adam Kingston, but as he'd grown to manhood, it was the blood of his Creole mother that had finally put its stamp upon him, had given him the gentle dark eyes and the sculpted cheekbones that were highlighted by the lamplight now.

Eyelids closed, he moaned and twisted fitfully, and Carrie reached out to press him back to the pillow. "It's me, George Pierre," she told her brother softly. "It's Carrie. I'm here . . ."

She felt Chloe's strong arm slip around her. "He can't hear you, honey. I don't think he even knows he's home. He was like this when Mist' J. D. brought him."

Carrie had arrived only moments before. She had thrown aside her shawl and come directly upstairs to the bedroom where her brother lay, the single lamp on the nightstand casting long shadows across the ceiling. Now she pushed the dark hair back from his forehead, felt how his skin was burning with fever, and tears traced their way silently down her cheeks. She tried to stiffen her lower lip, which was trembling in spite of her.

"Is he . . . is he going to . . . ?" Her voice trailed off.

"Not if I have anything to say about it, he ain't," the black woman declared staunchly.

Carrie pulled out her handkerchief, dried her eyes, and wiped at her nose. "What can we do to help him?" she said, as matter-of-factly as she could.

Chloe drew back the sheet to show George Pierre's swollen and discolored leg. There was a large and vile-looking dark poultice bound around it just above the knee, and Carrie caught the faintly sweet smell of mortifying flesh.

"Long time ago," Chloe said as she checked the bandages, "there was an old woman that lived here name of Zsamelda."

Carrie narrowed her eyes. "I think I remember. She was crippled, wasn't she? Walked with a limp."

"That's the one."

"She died when I was just a little girl."

Carrie nodded and drew up the sheet. "She was a conjure woman, old Zsamelda was. She knew lots of things . . . secrets. She could put a spell on somebody if she want to. But she knew healin', too. And she taught me. Ain't nothin' better than this here poultice for drawin' out poisons. It's got leaves and herbs and . . . other things," Chloe said, her voice somehow distant.

They stood there looking down for a long moment at the young man on the bed who moaned softly. Several days growth of beard shadowed his chin.

"You must be tired to death, honey. Why don't you try to rest for a while?" Chloe said.

Carrie shook her head. "I couldn't," she said. "Besides, I bet you haven't had a wink of sleep yourself. You go, and I'll stay with him."

"I'm fine," Chloe said. She straightened the rumpled pillowcase, and her plump cheeks lifted in a smile. "I'll go make us some tea, Miss Carrie. We've still got a while to go before it gets daylight."

As she reached the door, Carrie stopped her. "Chloe . . . where's J. D.?"

"He's sleepin'. Down the hall."

Carrie nodded and turned back to her brother.

After that, the two women took turns sitting by George Pierre and taking short naps in the big chair in the corner. The house creaked, and the unconscious man moaned and tossed from time to time, babbling feverishly. Once Chloe went down to the kitchen and came back a short time later with a fresh poultice, a wet, steaming mass, almost black. Carrie couldn't begin to guess at its contents, she only knew that it gave off a strong funky odor, like rotting leaves and mold.

"Oh, dear God!" Carrie gasped as she saw the actual wound in George Pierre's thigh for the first time. It was as big as a man's fist and seemed to go right down to the bone. The edges were yellowed and oozing while the flesh around was a deep and angry purple.

"I think it's beginnin' to drain some," Chloe said soothingly.

"That won't burn him, will it?" Carrie asked as Chloe brought the still steaming poultice to the bed.

Chloe shook her head. "But we want it good and hot 'cause it does more good that way. And we got to put a new one on every few hours 'cause the old one loses its power."

George Pierre didn't even move when Chloe pressed the hot mass against his fearful wound. He just lay quietly for the moment, his lips slightly parted, his face flushed with the fever that burned through his body. Chloe quickly bound the poultice up with clean, soft strips of old bedsheets that she kept with her store of salves and ointments and other medical supplies for just such an emergency.

Her legs suddenly unsteady beneath her, Carrie went back to the chair in the corner and leaned her head back, vaguely aware of the ticking of the clock atop the walnut gentleman's chest. The shadows seemed to have grown longer across the ceiling, stretching out to strange shapes and patterns that made the room seem somehow unfamiliar. Far off, she heard an owl hoot, once, and then again.

She remembered how it had been when she and George Pierre were just youngsters and she had tagged along after her older brother, scrabbling furiously to try to catch up to him. What a little pest she must have been!

But there'd been those times when George Pierre would look back at her and grin in that grave way he had and then call to her. "Come on, Carrie," he'd say. And her heart would all but burst with love and pride that this brother six years her senior would wait for her.

Now she was calling to him. "Come on, George Pierre," she whispered so softly that even Chloe didn't hear her. "Come on . . . Don't die. Please don't die . . ."

Carrie started awake, her neck stiff and sore from the way it had been crooked against the chairback, and from the look of the sun coming in through the window, she realized that she must have slept for several hours. Her eyes swept to the bed to find Chloe dabbing a wet cloth gently against George Pierre's cracked lips.

"Chloe . . ." Carrie eased herself out of the chair and stretched, "you shouldn't have let me sleep so long. I didn't mean to."

Chloe turned back toward her and smiled, graying hair escaping in small wiry strands from her usually neat white kerchief.

"I would have woke you and sent you off to bed if I'd thought you'd go, honey. But I knew well as anything you wouldn't."

"Is he any better?" Carrie drew nearer to look anxiously at her brother. He seemed quieter, lying half-turned toward her, the smallest frown between those handsome, well-drawn brows.

"He ain't no worse," Chloe said. "And that's a good sign."

Benjamin came and stood in the doorway and asked about George Pierre. "I put you some hot water in your room, Miss Carrie," he added in a near whisper.

"Thank you, Benjamin," she said. "I'll just go get freshened up now. Then I'll make some coffee and come back to relieve you, Chloe. You've got to get some sleep yourself. You can't do George Pierre any good if you collapse. I'll stay with him."

She cast one more worried look toward her brother and then went down the hall to her own room where the familiarity of the poster bed, her walnut chest, and the pair of small oval flower prints on the wall between the windows gave her some comfort.

She would have loved a soaking bath, but decided against it. She'd just use the hot water that Benjamin had brought up for a sponge bath and then get back to George Pierre as quickly as possible.

She stripped out of the clothes she'd had on for so many hours and, catching her hair up with a ribbon, washed and rinsed herself piecemeal but thoroughly, then dried off with the big white towel that Benjamin had brought along with the soap and water. She retrieved clean stockings and pantalettes and a ruffled camisole from the valise she'd brought along, and once they were on, turned toward the big walnut wardrobe. She hadn't taken everything with her to New Orleans. There were still lightweight cotton frocks and a faded riding habit or two.

She chose a blue gingham dress, which was slightly worn but very comfortable, and didn't bother with her crinoline; she just wore a soft white cotton petticoat underneath. She was home, she told herself as she put her slippers on. She didn't have to worry about fashions here. She could dress as she pleased.

She had just finished brushing her hair and tying it back with a wide blue ribbon when she heard footsteps and a soft knock at her door. It must be Benjamin, she thought, as she called, "Yes . . . come in."

Still patting her hair into place, she could see the door swinging open in the mirror before her. Suddenly J. D. was standing there, his tall frame filling the opening. She gasped and stared at his image in the glass for a long moment before she whirled to face him.

He was noticeably thinner than the last time she'd seen him; his face was lean and seemed longer. But the eyes were the same bright blue, and there was still that cocky set to his head. He was dressed in faded army-issue trousers and a field blouse of light brown homespun. She had heard that some Confederate soldiers had to make do with such odd pieces of uniform.

As he stood grinning at her, she felt a sudden stab of guilt. She had all but forgotten him in her concern for George Pierre, hadn't even given him a thought this morning, and the sight of him in the mirror had been a jolting reminder that he was home. As if to make up for it, she took a quick step toward him. He opened his arms, and then he was beside her, sweeping her up in a bear hug.

"Carrie, honey . . ." His mouth found hers hungrily, and though she was still a little unprepared, she tried her best to kiss him back. This was the man she was going to marry, and she intended to welcome him properly.

When his tongue probed, hot and eager, she allowed it, but

with that he groaned and tightened his hold until she was sure that he'd crush her. Without her padded crinoline she could feel his rising manhood pressing against her. Instinctively she pushed against his chest with the palms of her hands and turned her face away, laughing to soften the action.

"Here, let me look at you," she said, stepping back a pace and smoothing back the wisps of hair that had escaped her ribbon.

"Let me look at *you*," he said, his breath coming fast, his face slightly flushed. "God, I'd forgotten just how pretty you are, Carrie Kingston!" He grabbed her hand and pulled her to him again.

"Wait," she said, "we haven't even had a chance to talk!"

"That's just the trouble," he growled. "I don't want to wait . . . or talk." He kissed her again, soundly, and she didn't protest, but slid her arms up around his neck and again kissed him back, wondering if she was doing it right. But when his hand slipped down the front of her bodice and found her breast, she pulled away.

"J.D.!" she chided.

"Sorry, honey." He grinned. "Sometimes I clean forget what an innocent little thing you are."

She looked away quickly. *Innocent?* Dear Lord, what would J.D. say if he knew that his intended was not innocent at all, but had climbed into bed with a Yankee! And if that night with Rance wasn't enough, whatever would he think about her ending up nearly naked in a house on Rampart Street? She felt her cheeks flame.

J. D. chuckled. "You sure are cute when you blush, honey!" he teased her, clearly thinking that he had brought the color to her cheeks.

"Tell me about this." She touched the sleeve of his homespun jacket to change the subject.

He shrugged. "That spanking new, gray broadcloth jacket I left New Orleans in met with an accident or two that left it a little the worse for wear. And when I put in for a new one, this is what I got. Most of us wear this now. The boys in butternut," he said jauntily. "If you see a man with a whole gray uniform, you almost *know* he's a conscript."

"George Pierre wears butternut, too?" she asked, sobering at the thought of her brother.

The smile faded from J.D.'s face as he nodded.

"Tell me what happened," Carrie said softly.

He moved to the window and looked out toward the sun-washed barns in the distance. Horses grazed in the near field, and farther away, sweetgum trees, ash, and live oaks seemed to quiver in the heat. He stood there for a long time before he spoke, so long that Carrie had begun to wonder if he'd heard her question.

"Grant and his boys have had us pinned down at Vicksburg for weeks now," he said finally.

"I know. It's been in the New Orleans papers."

"We held them off. Did it say that in the paper?" he asked almost defiantly.

Carrie smiled. "Yes."

"We could have held them off till hell froze if we had supplies. Food . . . equipment . . . medicine." He shrugged. "We dug into the hillside to avoid the shells and the sharpshooters. But you couldn't stay in those damned holes all the time. George Pierre took a minié ball in the leg."

A small sound of pain escaped Carrie. She could feel how difficult it was for J. D. to talk about it.

He ran a hand quickly through the thatch of sun-bleached hair. "The doctors dug it out, but after a couple of days . . ." He paused. "The surgeon said the leg would have to come off or . . . George Pierre would die."

"Oh, God!" Carrie whispered.

"He begged me not to let them do it, Carrie. Asked me to bring him home. So I bribed the orderly on duty and hauled him out of there. But"—his voice cracked slightly—"I swear to God I don't know if I did the right thing."

He turned back to her, anguish in his face, and Carrie ran to him and held him, leaning her head against his chest. They stood, arms around each other, swaying slowly from side to side. She could hear his heartbeat.

"I love you, Carrie, honey."

She hesitated only an instant. "And I love you," she said. She must. Couldn't she feel her heart swelling for him right now? Wasn't that love? "And you did what George Pierre wanted," she added. "You mustn't blame yourself."

He was silent, still greatly troubled. After a moment, Carrie hugged him hard and then stepped back and wiped her eyes. "How did you get past Grant's men?" she asked.

A wry grin twisted his mouth. "Who knows how to slip through the marshes and bayous better than a Louisiana boy?"

"Will you be in trouble with your superiors?"

J. D. snorted. "I doubt if they know I'm gone. The old man—General Pemberton—was discussing surrender terms when we left. It's probably done by now."

"Surrender?" Carrie stared at him. "Then you won't be going back?"

"Not likely! Not to be carted off to some Yankee prison!" He shook his head. "I'll be heading out of here tonight to find General Joe Johnston's boys and join up with them. Or maybe Kirby Smith's outfit." Catching sight of her woebegone expression, he reached out a hand to cup her chin gently.

"Don't look so discouraged, honey. Vicksburg's not the whole South. We'll still send the Yankees running back where they came from. You just watch!"

She managed a half-grin. "I just believe you will," she said.

Her face was still cupped in his hand, and he kissed her, his lips soft and undemanding on hers. She felt a sudden flood of guilt, but she wasn't sure why.

"I should go now," she said the moment he released her. "Chloe has to get some rest. She's exhausted. Maybe you could sit with George Pierre while I get some food cooked. Everyone must be starving."

"Sure," he said.

"And we can talk some more later, J. D. I can tell you all about your folks." He didn't know yet that Seth had given half of his plant away, she thought.

"Are they all right?" he asked anxiously.

"They're fine." She lied—Seth hadn't really been himself since he took the loyalty oath. "They got word that your sister Melissa has a baby boy," she added brightly.

"Hey, that's great! I'm an uncle!" He grinned, his blue eyes bright. The light coming in the window slanted across his wide forehead and slightly crooked nose. He had broken the nose in a fight when he was a boy.

She held out her hand to him. "Come on," she said, and as they turned to go, they saw Chloe standing in the open doorway, tears running down her cheeks.

Carrie stopped dead still. "Chloe . . . Oh, my God . . . Chloe!" Fear squeezed her heart, and then she realized that the black woman was smiling broadly through the tears.

"He ain't out of the woods yet . . . not by a long sight, he ain't. But Mist' George Pierre's fever done broke!" Chloe said. "Praise the good Lord!"

Beau Canfield watched as Susannah made her mouth into a perfect heart shape, and her tawny curls quivered. "Oh, Beau, I am *so* glad to see you again!" she said. "You can't imagine how terrible it was to be stuck for all those months up at Kingston's Landing. And if it hadn't been for the rain and the crop washing out and everything, we'd still be there. Honestly, I can't imagine why Carrie prefers living there to New Orleans."

"Nor can I," he said. His face molded itself into lines of concern as he took one of her small hands between his and leaned closer to her—actions that set her blushing and quivering all the more.

They were on the verandah at the Morrisons' house, and the cool night air was welcome after the stuffy interior and the starchy meal they'd just shared with Seth and Abby. The moon, butter-ripe and full, lay just above the dark shadows of the live oak trees, and stars pierced the inky sky with glittering points of light.

Beau had just returned from a long and most successful trip, first sailing up the Atlantic coast to the North where he'd put in at Baltimore and New York to unload cotton and turpentine. Then, after some suitable diversions ashore, he'd come back down to run the blockade into Charleston and deliver outrageously priced quinine and other medicines to a Confederacy that needed them badly. Only moments before at the table he had allowed the Morrisons and Susannah to draw out the story of his daring defiance of the blockade to deliver medicines to those poor wounded boys in gray . . . all in the name of selfless patriotism.

That accounted for at least a part of the dewy-eyed look that Susannah was bestowing upon him at the moment.

Patriotism was for fools, he thought darkly. The back streets of Boston had taught him early that he must fight for nothing and no one except himself. The war had proven to be an enormous stroke of luck for him, as he was able to pass in and out of both camps with relative ease. Since he had grown up in the North, he understood the Yankees, knew how they thought. Yet the soft, Southern drawl which he now affected had not been too difficult for him since his father had been a Southerner—a white-trash overseer, thrown off one plantation after another, usually for drunkenness or petty theft.

Taylor Canfield had finally ended up in Boston, hanging around the gambling halls and taverns, scrabbling for a coin to buy himself a pint, while Beau's mother was spreading her legs for a half dollar in their cramped and foul smelling quarters above a tannery. He had not seen either of his parents since he was thirteen.

On that last day, the old man had started after him with the strap, as he'd done regularly since Beau could remember. But that time he didn't beat his son until the boy's back and legs were covered with angry red welts that would turn to deep purple bruises as the days passed. That time, Beau had suddenly realized that a spurt of adolescent growth had made him almost as tall as his father. He'd wrenched the leather strap out of the old bastard's hands and sent him thumping head first down the narrow stairway to the filthy alley below, his mother shrieking all the while. He had not even stayed to see if the old man was dead or alive.

He'd made his own way since then. Gambling and pimping, or anything else that came his way. Gradually, he had acquired the outward trappings of a gentleman. His activities now were mostly legal. Of course the Morrisons and the Kingstons would hardly approve if they knew the entire extent of his business dealings.

His eyes flickered over Susannah. He had decided to seduce her. It would be so ridiculously easy that it took all the fun out of it. He preferred women who presented a challenge. Still, she was undeniably a lovely little thing . . . and so young.

Taking her would hurt her sister, and he would do anything to hurt her sister. He was determined to teach Carrie a sound lesson for her behavior that night at the house on Rampart Street. He *would* have his revenge. He had vowed it after coming to, lying on the floor with his head throbbing as if a hammer were rapping away inside it. No one could make a fool of him.

He realized that Susannah was looking up at him questioningly, wondering at his long silence. "Forgive me, my dear," he said quickly. "I was thinking what a shame it is that your sister Carrie couldn't be here for dinner this evening. I had not had the pleasure of her company since before you went back to Kingston's Landing."

Susannah's green eyes moved away with the smallest evasive flicker, and withdrawing her hands from his, she began to twist one of the buttons on her pink silk bodice. "Yes," she said, "she had a terrible headache. It came about quite suddenly, and she decided it would be best if she just spent the evening in bed."

Like a hawk circling for prey, Beau noticed the slight nervousness, the almost rehearsed quality of her statement and swooped down on it. "I do hope it's nothing more than that." He watched her narrowly. "Perhaps I should stop by the house tomorrow afternoon."

"No!" Susannah said hastily. "I . . . I mean," she stammered, "she might not be entirely recovered from her headache."

"Of course. You're quite right," he said. He noticed that small beads of perspiration had appeared along that pretty little upper lip. Whatever was she hiding?

She took a step or two away, as if to look out over the moonlit grounds.

"My dear Susannah"—he came up behind her and put his hands lightly on her bare arms—"is anything wrong?"

"Wrong? No. What would be wrong?"

He turned her around slowly to face him. "I have dared to let myself believe that you and I have a most special relationship." His voice was low and soft.

"Oh, we *have*, Beau," she said earnestly.

"And I would hope that you would feel free to confide in me. Anything that concerns you, my dearest, is of the greatest concern to me."

Susannah's lovely young breasts were rising and falling rapidly, and the color in her cheeks had deepened. "Oh, Beau . . . you do know me so well . . ."

"I believe I do. Of course, I would never presume to pry."

"Oh, you're not, Beau." She clasped his hand, her fingers hot and slightly damp. "I mean there's nothing in my life that I wouldn't share with you. I trust you."

"You can't know how much that means to me," he said, and waited.

"Oh, Beau, I wanted to tell you from the first minute that I saw you tonight, but Carrie made me promise that I wouldn't tell the Morrisons. That's because no one must know, you understand." She took a deep breath. "Carrie isn't at home with a headache, Beau, she's at Kingston's Landing. Our brother, George Pierre, is there. He was badly wounded, and J. D. Morrison brought him home. You can see what might happen if the wrong people found out," Susannah said. She pressed her pretty little hand to her throat.

"Indeed I can."

"Oh, Beau"—her voice quivered timorously—"it's so wonderful to have someone you can trust completely."

And he smiled.

20

RANCE STEWART UNDID THE TOP TWO BUTTONS OF HIS JACKET, settled back in the chair, and nodded to the waiter as the fellow set a glass of brandy on the table before him. He tasted, rolled the fiery liquid over his tongue, and swallowed, smiling appreciatively.

Since he had only just arrived, he looked around the Bourbon Street establishment at the other patrons. An elderly Creole gentleman moved his hands expressively and spoke with a decided French accent to his equally ancient friend. The two of them puffed contentedly at their cigars.

On the wall opposite Rance, a mirror reflected the curving sweep of the mahogany bar and at the end of it, a doorway that led back to the gaming tables. From time to time the sound of male laughter or an occasional curse emerged.

Rance had spent the evening with the Barlows, he and Nora's father listening once again to the endless chatter of the women about the plans for the wedding. For the life of him, Rance couldn't understand why Nora and her mother felt such an urgency about deciding everything now when the wedding wasn't until the middle of October, but they both assured him that it was necessary. "I want everything to be perfect, darling," Nora purred every time he suggested that there was still plenty of time.

He had managed finally to steal her away to the gallery where he could kiss her properly. There had been a few delicious moments together and then Nora answered her mother's call to look at sketches for the bridesmaids dresses.

"Oh, you don't mind, do you, darling. There's just *so* much to see to yet."

He had surrendered to the ladies and made his goodbyes early.

Now, he caught sight of a young captain he knew coming out of the gaming room, the uniformed reflection caught in the mirror, and he turned in his chair to greet him. "Will . . ." he called, and the young man stiffened to attention as he saw a superior officer.

Rance waved an easy hand at him. "Relax. Come have a drink with me."

Young Will Catton hesitated, grinned, his reddish sidewhiskers bristling. "That's too good an offer to pass up, Major Stewart. I'll have one, gladly. Though I shouldn't." He slid into the chair. "I should be at home sleeping. I have an early detail tomorrow."

Rance raised a hand to gain the waiter's attention. "Early detail, eh?" he said. "That's too bad. It's been a long time since

I got really drunk, Captain. I thought you and I might just tie one on tonight.''

Catton laughed. ''It'd be an honor and a pleasure any other time, sir.''

The waiter took their order, a whiskey for Catton and another brandy for Rance. The drinks were there before they could exchange more than a few words.

Rance watched as Catton tossed off half his whiskey, narrowed his eyes, and gave a slow wink. ''Good stuff,'' he said.

Rance grunted. ''It's why I come here. Some of the drink around town will kill you.''

Catton smiled, nodded.

''So you have early duty tomorrow?''

''Afraid so. I'm stuck with taking a detail upriver.''

Rance sipped his brandy. ''It's beautiful country. You'll probably enjoy it.''

''Probably will at that. It's just . . .'' Catton hesitated.

''We're at ease here, Will. Forget about rank tonight.''

A slight frown creased Catton's forehead. ''I . . . I'm just not crazy about the assignment, Rance.''

Rance shrugged. ''In war we all have to do things we'd rather not.''

''I suppose so. And I'll follow my orders, even though I confess that I'll feel sorry as hell for the poor devil if he's up there.''

''What poor devil?'' Rance asked.

Catton swirled the whiskey left in his glass and gazed into the amber depths. ''Somebody—I don't know who—leaked word that a Rebel officer is hiding out at his plantation upriver. The informant said he was wounded pretty bad. My orders are to take a detail of men up there and arrest him.'' He shook his head and looked at Rance over the rim of his glass. ''I'll do what has to be done. Though I must admit it'd be more to my liking to face a sound man head on.''

Rance nodded. ''But the rules that most of us live by are suspended in wartime, Will. And there's not a hell of a lot that any of us can do about it.''

''Guess that's a fact.'' Catton tossed down the last of his drink and drew a deep breath, his sandy mustache glistening with a drop or two of whiskey. "So, I'll be on my way to this Kingston's Landing by sunup."

Luckily he was pushing back his chair and didn't see Rance's head come up. "Kingston's Landing?"

"Yes. That's the place. The fellow's name is Kingston. George something or other Kingston. Old line family up there, I understand. They say his daddy was one of the real powers around here in the old days." He retrieved his hat from the chair and inclined his head, a grin splitting his face and making his sidewhiskers bristle all the more. "Thanks for the whiskey, Major. And I'll hold you to that invitation to get drunk sometime soon."

Rance nodded, trying to keep his face impassive, his mind racing. "See you when you get back, Will," he said. But the moment the young captain was gone, Rance groaned beneath his breath and leaned forward over his drink. Jesus . . . Kingston's Landing! Carrie's brother! It had to be.

He wished that Catton had never mentioned it to him. There was nothing he could do, he told himself. But Carrie's face loomed up before him, those enormous eyes accusing as they had that night at Kingston's Landing.

He had not thought of her in months . . . not *really* thought of her . . . because, he owned up to himself, he hadn't allowed himself to. He couldn't risk it. He and Nora were going to be married, and there was no place in his life or his thoughts for a beautiful, golden-eyed girl who was as passionate a Rebel as he'd ever seen. And she had certainly made it all too clear that there was no room in hers for a Yankee.

"Damn!" He threw down enough money to cover his bill, clapped his hat on his head, and walked out of the place into the still, hot air of Bourbon Street where his big roan gelding waited patiently at the hitchrail.

The horse nickered softly as Rance swung up, saddle leather creaking. He turned the animal in the direction of Bienville Street and his rooms. A shiny black carriage with polished brass headlamps moved almost noiselessly over the cobblestones, a dignified old Negro on the driver's seat. Two soldiers walked a trifle unsteadily along the banquette. They paused near the corner gaslight where one of them draped his arm good-naturedly over the other's shoulder and began a mournful rendition of "All Quiet Along The Potomac." Rance hardly saw or heard them. His mind was filled with Carrie.

If it were true, if Kingston really was hiding out up at the plantation, did Carrie know about it? Of course she did. And, Jesus Christ, what would she be apt to do? She'd go up there. That's what she'd do.

He touched his heels to the horse's flanks and put the animal into a brisk trot. There wasn't a goddamned thing he could do about it, he told himself harshly. He was a major in the Army of the United States. There was no way he would do anything to warn a Rebel officer that his whereabouts were known. Not even a wounded one. Not even Carrie Kingston's brother. A man foolish enough to do that would be betraying his solemn oath, would be laying himself open to a court martial, perhaps even a firing squad.

Groaning, he hauled the horse back on its haunches, stopped dead still in the dark street. *He owed Carrie.* He owed her for that night. Maybe nothing could ever make up to her for it, but goddamn it, he would do this for her . . . He had to.

He wheeled the horse around and headed for the house on Dumaine Street where, at his insistent ringing of the bell, a sleepy-eyed Mattie answered the door, clutching her wrapper about her.

"Mattie, I need to see Miss Carrie at once!" he said.

There was an instant's hesitation. The girl's big brown eyes avoided his for a moment, then raised squarely to meet his gaze steadily. "Miss Carrie's not here, Major Stewart. She spendin' the night with one of the church ladies . . . from the sewin' circle."

Rance had stepped into the front hall, and now he saw Susannah coming down the stairs, her light brown curls tangled prettily. She, too, was in her night robe.

"Rance," she said, "I heard the bell."

"Suzy, forgive me. I had no idea it was so late . . . and I wanted to see Carrie about something." He watched her closely as Susannah's eyes moved quickly to Mattie as if in appeal and then nervously back to him.

"Carrie?" she said. "Why, she . . . she . . ." Susannah was stammering when Mattie interrupted her smoothly.

"I done told Major Stewart how Miss Carrie's spendin' the night with Miss Gertrude Lawson from the sewin' circle, Miss Suzy."

"Oh, yes." Relief flooded Susannah's doll-like features. "It's really too bad that you missed her. Gertrude just insisted that Carrie come visit."

"Well"—Rance played the game—"I'm sorry that I came barging in here and disturbed you, Suzy."

"It's all right," she said."

"I'll say good night then. And I'll wait and see Carrie another time."

"Fine." Susannah relaxed visibly, smiling.

And moments later as the gate closed behind him, Rance slapped his hat against his thigh in frustration. She was up there, all right. Up there with her brother, just as he'd thought. The little fool! The *magnificent* little fool!

His eyes narrowed as he figured how long it would take him to get there. Luckily there was a full moon. Once he'd slipped past the road sentries he should be able to make good time. With a little luck he'd be there by two in the morning.

Carrie started awake, her heart leaping almost into her throat, it seemed, as she heard the pounding on the front door. She jumped out of bed and grabbed the green-flowered muslin wrapper that lay across the chair. She was just pulling it around her as she reached her brother's room where George Pierre, mending but still terribly weak, was trying to sit up.

She pressed him back to the pillow. "No one could possibly know that you're here," she whispered reassuringly. "Just stay very quiet."

The moonlight stealing through the window was enough to reveal the concern on his face, but he nodded. "Be careful, Carrie," he said. "You are not to get into any trouble because of me."

She smiled at him, put her finger against her lips, went out into the upstairs hallway, closing his door quietly behind her. The knocking had stopped, but she could hear voices downstairs—Chloe's and a deeper, masculine voice. She crept closer to the head of the stairs to listen and suddenly froze. *Dear God, it was Rance Stewart!*

"I know she's here, Chloe. I wish to see your mistress at once," he was saying.

"Ain't nobody here but Benjamin and me, suh . . . seein' after things. Miss Carrie been down in New Orleans for I don't know how many weeks now," Chloe replied coolly.

"I intend to see her, Chloe. Carrie!" he shouted. "I know you're up there! Come down or I'll come up!"

His big, deep voice beat against her. Good God, what was he doing here? Now of all times! With George Pierre in the house!

"Carrie!" His tone grew sharper, more insistent.

She could feel the clammy dampness of her palms. Could he have found out? Could he be here to arrest George Pierre?

"Carrie!"

With shaking fingers she made sure that her wrapper was completely buttoned and drew herself up. She would have to bluff it out somehow.

He saw her when she was part way down the stairs and in three strides was at the foot of the steps to meet her. "Carrie," he said, "I must speak with you."

"And what, Major Stewart," she said icily, "brings you to Kingston's Landing?"

His eyes bored into hers. "I might ask you the same thing, Miss Kingston," he drawled.

Not to be outdone, she stared right back at him. "Not that it's any of your business," she snapped, "but I came up to see that everything is running smoothly on the place. It is my intention to leave for New Orleans first thing in the morning."

"That isn't true, Carrie." His voice softened slightly. "You're here because—"

"Major Stewart." She cut him off. "How dare you burst in here in the middle of the night and tell me what is true and what is not! Do you have a troop of men at your back, as you did the first time that you intruded yourself into my home?" She saw the slight tightening about his eyes, the pull of a muscle along his jawline. There was a moment's silence before he spoke.

"Perhaps I deserve that, Carrie," he said finally. "But there's no time for it now. I know your brother's here."

Carrie's blood seemed to stop in her veins, but outwardly she didn't betray a thing. "George Pierre here? Wherever did you get that idea? I haven't seen my brother since—"

Rance's long legs took the stairs between them in an instant, and his fingers dug into her arms. "Carrie, listen to me! A Union patrol will be leaving New Orleans just before dawn! They're coming for your brother!"

Carrie could feel her face drain of color, but still she tried to bluff it out, her mind racing frantically to decide what to do. "I don't know what you're talking about!" she said defiantly. "Now, if you'll please leave, Major!"

"Carrie," he said, his voice low, compelling, "Carrie, I've not come here to harm you . . . or your brother. Trust me."

Those clear gray eyes held hers for a long moment, and she could feel the strength of his hands, feel her legs tremble. Could she? Could she dare trust George Pierre's life to Rance Stewart?

No! Dear Lord, he was a Yankee officer. He had made his choice, and he was for the Union heart and soul. To give aid to a Rebel soldier would be unthinkable for him. She tried to turn away from him, but he pulled her back, made her face him.

"Trust me, Carrie," he said again, and despite all her misgivings there was some deep-down response in her. Some instinct stronger than reason guided her. She felt her gaze waver under his and then nodded slowly.

"All right," she whispered. "I'll trust you, Rance."

"Good." He released her at once. "Where is he?" he asked.

She hesitated only a fraction of a second. "Up there," she indicated the second floor and at the same time caught the worried questioning in Chloe's eyes.

"He's wounded?"

Carrie nodded.

"How bad? Can he be moved?"

She caught her underlip between her teeth, frowned. "He's very weak," she said finally, "but we've got to hide him. I know that. There's a place, Rance . . . a cubbyhole that goes back under the rafters. You can get to it from the captain's walk."

"No." He ruled that out instantly. "I know the man who's commanding this patrol, and he not only follows orders, he's no fool. He'll check every inch of this house. Every board. Every mousehole."

"Then what?" Carrie asked, surprised at how easily they had fallen into this exchange.

"We have a little time. Is there anyplace where we could take him? Anyone that you'd trust to hide him?"

Carrie's eyes sought out Chloe's. "Justice . . ." It was almost as if the word passed between them at the same moment. "There's a man who was once my father's overseer." The words tumbled from Carrie's lips. "He has a place just north of the plantation boundary. He'll help us."

Rance nodded. "We'll need a wagon."

Carrie turned to Chloe. "Have Benjamin hitch up a wagon and put plenty of straw in it with quilts over the top to make the riding easier."

"Yes, Miss Carrie," Chloe said, apparently at least half-convinced that this tall Yankee officer had indeed come to help.

"And we'll need a fresh saddle horse for me and one for you. Have your people hide my horse in some far pasture," Rance said to Carrie. "Once we get your brother safely to this man Justice, we must ride back to New Orleans tonight. It's important that we both be seen there tomorrow."

"But I can't do that!" Carrie said. "That would leave Chloe and Benjamin here alone to face the soldiers!"

"I promise you no harm will come to them."

"But how can you promise such a thing?" Carrie demanded. "How do you know what might happen? Yankee soldiers haven't always conducted themselves properly in such situations. No, I'll stay here and meet them myself!"

Rance looked exasperated. "Carrie, that's the worst thing you could do! If they find you here, there'll be all the more reason to suspect that your brother is here someplace. They'll be determined to find him. On the other hand, if you're seen in New Orleans tomorrow, it should lay further speculation to rest."

"He's right, Miss Carrie," Chloe said. "Me and Benjamin be all right."

Carrie hesitated.

"I promise you nothing will happen to them," Rance said. "I know Will Catton. He'll search the place thoroughly, and when he finds that no one is here except the servants, he'll leave. Now you said you were going to trust me . . ."

"Oh, I don't know . . ." Carrie agonized.

"This way be the safest for Mist' George Pierre, Miss Carrie," Chloe said firmly. "I know what to say to them Yankees. I say, 'The mistress down in New Orleans. Ain't nobody here. The master been away fightin' in the war for the *longest* time.' "

Rance grinned. "That's just right, Chloe," he said. "I swear to you, Carrie, this is the best way to do it."

Carrie sighed. "All right."

Chloe nodded and started toward the back of the house. "I'll go get Benjamin up. That man could sleep through a cyclone!" she grumbled.

"And you and I had better get your brother ready," Rance said.

Carrie led the way upstairs to George Pierre's room. "It's all right," she reassured him as they entered.

She lit the lamp on the nightstand, and from the bed George Pierre Kingston looked up at them calmly, his dark eyes lingering on Rance's uniform, his fine-boned features pale from his long ordeal.

"Rest easy, Lieutenant," Rance said.

"This is Rance Stewart," Carrie explained to her brother. "He's . . . a friend." Her voice quivered slightly, and though she was looking at George Pierre, she knew that Rance had turned toward her at her words. "A Union patrol will be on its way here at dawn," she rushed on. "We're going to take you to Justice's place. You'll be safe there."

George Pierre looked at Rance steadily. "I don't quite understand, Major. You came here to warn us?"

Rance hesitated. "I guess I did," he said.

"Why?"

The two men stared at one another for a long moment before Rance finally answered. "I owe your sister a favor," he said.

Carrie broke in nervously. "We're wasting time."

"That we are," Rance said. "Why don't you go get whatever you need to take with you?" he said to Carrie. "And I'll get Lieutenant Kingston dressed."

In the muted light of the moon, the pair of mules plodded stolidly along the rutted river road, Rance doing his best to keep them on the smoothest areas possible, the wagon creaking with each turn of the wheels. Trees along the edge of the roadway made dark patches against the sky, and the water lapped softly at the shoreline. Two saddled horses were tied to the back of the wagon.

From her place on the driver's seat beside Rance, Carrie looked back anxiously at George Pierre. Though her brother kept telling her that he was all right, she could see the pasty color of his skin, see the beads of perspiration standing out on his face.

"Rance, pull up for a minute," she said.

He gave her a questioning look but hauled back on the reins. The moment the wagon came to a stop Carrie, outfitted in a riding habit, swung from the seat back into the wagonbed with relative ease.

"Be careful!" Rance said, and put out a hand to steady her, but she was already down beside George Pierre.

"Go ahead now," she said. "Keep to the river. I'll tell you where to turn."

With a gentle jolt, the pair of mules moved forward once again. Carrie took her handkerchief from her jacket pocket and wiped George Pierre's face.

He forced a smile. "I'm doing all right."

"I know you are." She took his hand and held it tightly, knowing full well that he was in pain. She had heard him groan softly when Rance and Benjamin carried him down the stairs and put him into the waiting wagon.

"The river is beautiful tonight," she said trying to distract him. He was lying too low in the wagon to see over the wooden sides. "The moon is making a path across it . . . all shimmery. It looks as if you could walk right over to the other side."

They rode in silence for a full minute or two.

"Remember when you and J. D. used to go fishing at night?" she said.

He nodded.

"I always wanted to go, but Mama wouldn't let me."

He smiled again but closed his eyes and winced as one of the wheels jolted over an unseen rock. Carrie heard Rance swear under his breath.

She checked George Pierre's leg and saw that there was some

278

dark seepage through the bandage and his pants leg. That meant the wound had pulled open. But, thank goodness, he didn't seem to be bleeding badly . . . not so far.

They reached a point where the river swung wide in a curve of breathtaking beauty, the moon highlighting the sweep of water, the far shoreline cast into darkness. Carrie leaned up in the wagon and spoke to Rance. "Just up ahead, there's a rough road that leads off to the right," she said. "Take that." She squeezed George Pierre's hand. "It won't be too long now."

The entrance to the road was badly overgrown, but Rance swung the mules into it, the wagon jolting even more along the rough and narrow roadbed. George Pierre kept his eyes closed, his mouth set in a tight, bloodless line. Carrie tried to cushion him as best she could.

It was the hardest part of the journey, but after nearly ten long minutes the wagon emerged into a clearing. Up ahead they saw a neat wooden house with a wide front porch. A thriving vegetable garden grew nearby, its borders defined by blooming flowers.

Rance swung down, and a pair of spotted hound dogs loped around the side of the house, baying frantically at the intruders. A moment later, a light appeared in one of the darkened windows.

Carrie called out to the dogs. "Patches . . . Lady . . . stop that!" The animals seemed to recognize her and halted their suspicious circling of the wagon. Tails wagging, they shifted into excited little yelps.

Rance helped her down, and the dogs darted in and out, wiggling their hindquarters and panting.

"Who is that out there?" Justice called from the doorway.

"It's me, Justice." Carrie went toward the porch as the black man walked out, pulling his faded suspender straps up over his shoulders as he came.

"Miss Carrie . . . what in the world?" Justice quickly took in Rance's uniform and the waiting wagon and then listened quietly as Carrie told him the situation.

"I hope I'm not asking too much, Justice. Will you help us?" she asked breathlessly.

For his answer, Justice headed toward the wagon, favoring his bad leg slightly, head thrust before those thick shoulders that had carried young George Pierre Kingston so often in years past. He nodded briefly to Rance, as suspicious as the hound dogs had been, and then swung up into the wagon to look down on the drawn-faced man.

"Mist' George Pierre . . ." he said, his voice cracking slightly. And George Pierre reached out his hand, and pale fingers intertwined with dark ones for a moment. Justice blinked once and turned his head sideways. "Let's get you into the house," he said.

Justice's wife, Tana, her pale, saffron skin and almost red hair betraying her share of white ancestors, had come to stand on the porch, a shawl wrapped loosely over her long, white nightgown.

"Get him right in here," she called to Justice, her thin features sharp with concern.

She went to ready the extra bed, bustling about like a skinny bird, as Rance and Justice carried the ashen-faced George Pierre inside. The moment he was deposited on the moss-filled mattress, she was ready with a knife to slit his left pant leg to mid-thigh.

Carrie hovered anxiously as Tana examined the oozing, angry-edged wound.

"All right . . . all right." The Negro woman clucked. "I'll just bind this up good with a clean cloth. Sleep's what you need, Mist' George Pierre, and I'm goin' to make you some tea directly. Got my own special herbs to go in it. Makes you sleep like a new baby."

George Pierre could only nod his head, a half-smile on his stiff lips.

"Are you sure he's all right?" Carrie asked.

Tana nodded, opening a small, rough chest nearby and delving into her hoard of clean linen rags.

"We need to start for New Orleans at once," Carrie said.

"You leave him to me, Miss Carrie. It sure won't be the first time I doctored up this boy."

"I won't forget this, Tana. Thank you," Carrie said, reaching out to the thin, strong arm of the woman.

She kissed George Pierre. "It's going to be fine," she said. "Just get well. I'll see you as soon as I can."

She left quickly, afraid that she might cry, and went into the front room of the small, well-kept house. The wide, bare floorboards had been scrubbed almost white. The large fireplace, constructed of flat riverstone, had a basket of flowers on the hearth, and the lemon-yellow curtains at the windows looked as if they'd been freshly washed and ironed. Rance and Justice stood awkwardly apart.

"We should leave right away, Carrie," Rance said. And when Carrie nodded, Justice jerked his head toward the front porch.

"I'd just like a word with you before you go, Miss Carrie."

She followed him out, and the porch was not so dark that she couldn't see the worried ridges along the familiar face.

"What about this Yankee major, Miss Carrie? You sure you can trust him?"

Carrie didn't hesitate. "He's risked a lot to warn us, Justice."

The Negro grunted, peered skeptically back through the open doorway toward Rance who stood waiting impatiently. "If you say so, Miss Carrie. Anyway"—he set his feet stubbornly wide—"you can rest easy 'cause I ain't lettin' nobody find Mist' George Pierre here. When I built this house for Tana and me, I put in a special hiding place or two. I ain't never had to use them to this day. All the same, a black man learns to be cautious early on, Miss Carrie." He nodded his head, his dark eyes far away now. "A black man learns to be cautious."

21

THE AIR HAD COOLED AND FELT DAMPLY FRESH AGAINST RANCE'S cheek as a chorus of bullfrogs bellowed from the bayous. He maneuvered his horse around a fallen tree. Up ahead of him Carrie rode with ease, skillfully guiding her gelding to the high side of the spongy ground.

Though it made the going more difficult, they had decided to stay away from the commonly used roads near the river and travel back through the rougher bayou country in case the Union patrol had left New Orleans sooner than scheduled. "We sure as hell," Rance had said, "don't want to run smack into Will Catton and his men!"

Over his protests, Carrie had insisted on taking the lead, and before long Rance had admitted to himself that she knew exactly what she was doing. There were stretches that even in bright moonlight looked deceptively solid, innocently covered with long grasses, but in reality were watery morasses. Once, he hadn't followed her exactly but tried to cut across to an opposite point and found his horse in water up to its knees.

"It gets deeper," she called to him, laughing. "Back up."

He did, somewhat shame-faced, but with more than a little admiration for her skill. She seemed to sense such places and skirted them unerringly. And when Rance asked her how she did it, she confessed that when she was a child, her father had taken her along often when he rode the bayou country.

"Mama was always scolding him for taking me places she thought were unseemly for a little girl. I'm afraid Papa didn't pay any attention," she added with a grin. "When I was really young, he'd put me on the saddle in front of him, but when I was big enough to ride by myself, he gave me my own pony."

Now Rance watched her up ahead, noted the slim curve of her back, the wealth of chestnut hair, which seemed darker in the passing shadow of a tree. She turned just slightly in the saddle, and he caught a glimpse of the curve of her breast swelling gently against her riding jacket, marked the strong line of her brows, the maddeningly beautiful mouth.

Jesus, she might have been a little tomboy when she was a kid, but now—he narrowed his eyes—she was every inch a female. A woman to set a man's blood boiling if he weren't careful. And he'd already been burned in that flame, he reminded himself.

Why had he put himself in this position for her? He had betrayed the uniform he wore, put aside duty, commitment . . . Why?

He eased up in the saddle and stretched his muscles. He would ponder that question at length tomorrow. Right now he was not sorry. The Union cause would not be lost if one poor Rebel was allowed to heal his wounds in peace. And he did owe Carrie something.

Damn that night! The truth was, he would never be able to free himself of the memory of her. And if it hadn't happened, maybe Carrie would have been able to see him through other eyes. . . .

But, no, goddamn it! That was a fool's thinking. They were on different sides of a war, and she would never forgive him for that. For tonight, he had suspended the rules, but tomorrow the battle lines would be drawn again. He knew it, and so did she.

They had been riding for nearly two hours, and Rance took note of subtle changes in the night sky to the east, not yet a lightening but some small difference in coloring that warned that the dawn was not too far ahead. They would not reach New Orleans before daylight, but that just meant they would have to be more careful in slipping past the road sentries. It shouldn't prove too difficult.

He saw her stretch upward in her saddle, and from the way his own muscles ached he knew that she must be tired. She had had little sleep, and the ride had been hard, but there hadn't been a word of complaint from her. Nora would have delivered a litany of woes by now, he found himself thinking, and at once felt guilty for the comparison.

There was a small clearing in the underbrush ahead and he called to her. "Let's stop and rest here."

She threw a grateful look back at him. "Do we dare take the time?" she asked, obviously hoping that he would say yes.

"The horses need it." He grinned at her as he came abreast of her gelding and they both swung down, she before he had any chance to help her. She arched her back and put a hand up to the slender neck as he tethered the horses loosely at the edge of the clearing. "I'll fix us a place to sit," he said. He began to scoop up armfuls of dried grasses and pile them beside a large rotting log. It would make a good back rest.

"I'll help," Carrie said, bringing an armload.

Once they had enough, Rance covered the pile of brush with a blanket that had been tied behind his saddle, then stood back to survey the makeshift seat with a certain satisfaction.

"Miss Kingston . . ." he bowed with a flourish, "your couch."

"Major . . ." She replied in kind, though her cheeks colored slightly as if she didn't quite know how to handle such banter. She sank gratefully to the blanket.

"How is it?" he asked.

"Wonderful!"

He tried it out himself, leaning back against the log, stifling a groan of satisfaction as he realized how long it had been since he'd slept. His leg accidently brushed hers and she scooted over quickly, but not before a slow heat had begun to stir within him. Even with his trouser leg and her riding skirt to blur the contact, he could remember every line of those long legs, every curve, every sweet hollow.

"I . . . I haven't thanked you yet," she said. "And I do, Rance. My brother is very dear to me."

He nodded, still struggling with the desire he felt for her, but determined to carry on an ordinary conversation . . . anything to keep from pulling her into his arms as he wanted to do. "He was wounded at Vicksburg?" he asked.

She hesitated. "Yes," she said finally.

From the moment Rance had heard that George Pierre Kingston might be wounded and hiding out at Kingston's Landing, it occurred to him that he'd probably been at Vicksburg. It was the only major campaign within a suitable distance. And the irony was, if the word coming through to headquarters in New Orleans was correct, Grant and Pemberton had negotiated surrender terms that included releasing the Confederate prisoners on their own parole. Once they'd sworn not to pick up arms again against the Union, they would be sent home. It was unprecedented, but Grant had taken the responsibility for it.

However, since Kingston had left Vicksburg, he would not come under those terms but would be considered a fugitive Rebel by the Union Army. Rance didn't have the heart to tell Carrie that.

"And your fiancé?" he said instead. "Lieutenant Morrison? Is he there?"

She nervously smoothed the folds of her riding skirt and did not answer. He didn't press her. Morrison was almost certainly involved. A man so badly wounded could hardly have gotten to the plantation on his own. And if that were true, then Morrison would undoubtedly have taken off as soon as possible. The thought that he and Carrie had spent some time together stung him, but he reminded himself sternly that it was none of his business.

"It's lucky that you had a place where we could take your brother," he said. "I don't believe anyone would look for him there."

"The Kingston family has always been lucky to have Justice as a friend," she said.

Rance nodded.

"He's a remarkable man. My father said he was the best man who ever worked for him. Those times Papa was away, Justice ran the whole Kingston plantation."

They were quiet for a moment, Rance waving his hand at the hum of a mosquito.

"It's President Lincoln's plan to give such men as Justice and Prosper Durant full citizenship after the war," Rance said. "The vote . . . every right that any other man has."

Carrie's chin came up, and she turned to confront him. "Mr. Lincoln will have no authority to decide anything for the Confederate States of America after the war!" she said tartly.

He laughed in spite of himself. "Forgive me," he said. "I'd forgotten that the very name 'Lincoln' can set off an explosion when it's mentioned to a Rebel."

She softened. "He's not terribly popular," she admitted. "I've heard people call him a monster."

Rance shook his head. "He's the gentlest, the kindest man I've ever known."

"You know him personally? I mean before you were sent to Washington?"

"Long before. He and my father were close friends."

"Were?"

Rance looked away. "The war," he said, "has driven a wedge between a lot of people . . . friends . . . family."

She didn't speak for a moment and then her voice came, small and hesitant, "Between you and your father, Rance?"

He turned to find her looking at him with a kind of gentle

speculation, perhaps even sympathy, that unnerved him. "Yes," he said finally.

"I . . . I realize now," she confessed, "that it must have been terribly difficult for you."

Cicadas hummed and the deep bass of bullfrogs echoed from the bayous.

"It was hard," he admitted, suddenly remembering his father's gently seamed face, the shock of white hair.

"You quarreled?"

"Not exactly. I'd searched my conscience those weeks after South Carolina seceded and the other Southern states followed. I tried to explain to him that in spite of the differences between the North and South, I believed deeply that we must not tear the country apart. That the South *was* the country as much as the North. Jefferson. Washington. Patrick Henry. They were Southerners. Could we undo everything those men had done?" Rance shook his head. "He didn't listen. I suppose there was no way he could believe that a son of his would refuse to fight for the Southern cause.

"My brother had already enlisted with the Confederates. Father, despite his age, had dragged out his old rifle and was drilling with the Charleston militia. One day he called me into his study and asked me point blank when I was joining up. I had been trying to think of a way to tell him. Tell him that I had joined the army four days before. The Union Army."

He was quiet for a moment, wondering why he had told her all that. He had never spoken about it with anyone. He waited, half expecting her to lift that beautiful chin scornfully, the amber eyes going to ice as they had so often before. But she sat there quietly beside him, the moonlight catching in the chestnut hair, her face partly in shadow.

"And what was his reaction?"

Rance felt the tightening in his throat. "He walked from the room without a word."

"But surely . . ." Carrie's voice trailed off. "You haven't heard from him? Since then?"

"No. When my brother Brandon was killed . . . a cousin wrote to tell me." The words came hard and Rance leaned forward to brush some twigs off his pantleg, suddenly embarrassed that he had revealed so much.

"Oh, Rance . . ." she said softly. "I'm sorry . . ."

Her hand touched his for a brief instant and he felt the muscles along his arm ripple. He looked at her in surprise, their eyes holding for a long moment and then she shifted herself on the seat and smoothed her riding skirt nervously.

He reached for the canteen which he'd placed on the log behind them. "I don't know how we ever got on that subject." He tried to be casual. "Would you like a drink of water?"

"Yes, please."

He passed it to her and she tilted her head back to drink thirstily, laughing a little at the droplets of water that escaped and dripped onto her chin. She brushed them away with long, slender fingers, the nails faintly pink and oval. As she passed the canteen back to him she was careful that their hands didn't touch again, but all the same it was as if summer lightning crackled unseen between them.

He drank, conscious that she was watching, and he imagined that he could taste her, taste where her lips had been, taste the sweetness, and the hot wanting grew until he wasn't at all sure that he was going to be able to control the situation.

He recapped the canteen, angry with himself. Was he never going to learn his lesson where Carrie Kingston was concerned? She had more than made clear her feelings toward him.

"Jesus!" he swore softly, and then remembered himself. "I beg your pardon," he said stiffly.

"What is it?" she asked, her voice trembling, her eyes avoiding his now.

"Carrie, I . . . I . . ." He broke off, his head coming up as he heard the stamp of horses, several of them from the sound of it, coming through the underbrush. He looked at Carrie, pressing a finger to his lips as male voices drifted toward them on the night air.

"I be damned if I don't wish we'd stayed in Texas and not come back here," one of them growled.

"Me, too," a thin voice answered. "Ain't even nothin' 'round here to steal no more."

As the higher-pitched voice continued a whining litany of

complaint, Rance saw the two geldings tethered at the edge of the clearing begin to twitch their ears and toss their heads. "Here," he whispered, unsnapping the leather holster at his belt and passing the gun to Carrie. "If you should have to use this, you just pull back on the hammer, point it, and fire."

She nodded.

"Get over behind the log here. Lie flat and stay down." As she did as he said, he tossed the blanket after her and quietly pushed the grass aside so that it didn't look so deliberately put there.

With one final look to make sure she was out of sight, he hurried toward the tethered horses. He had to keep them quiet if he could. With a little luck, those men out there might just ride right on by. But if they didn't, he would at least be able to lead them away from Carrie.

He swore silently as the geldings stamped the soft earth, their sleek hides rippling. One of them lifted his ears and whinnied shrilly to the oncoming horses.

"Will you shut up, Cletus!" a deep voice boomed. "I heard something. Over this way!"

Rance made a grab for his rifle which was tied to the saddle, but before he could free it the excited gelding danced sideways. As he lunged again, he heard a quickening of the horses' hooves.

"Looky here! We got us a soldier boy!"

"Shit! A major! Get 'im!"

"Rance, look out!" He heard Carrie's warning cry and whirled to see her standing upright, holding the gun out in front of her. The lead horseman was half way across the clearing and bearing down on him fast, sawed-off shotgun in hand.

"Get down!" he shouted to Carrie, but his voice was lost in the roar as her pistol discharged. The bullet came so close to the lead rider that his faded blue cap flew off his head.

The man hauled his mount back on its haunches, his mouth dropping open as he saw Carrie. He gave a shrill yell, yanked his horse's head around, and clapped his heels against its flanks to lunge toward her.

Rance's fingers had closed about the stock of his rifle and he had it up instantly, his cheek pressed close, sighting down the blue barrel. His index finger squeezed. The rider was lifted right out of his saddle and slammed down against the ground to jerk once. The horse careened wildly away.

"Damn it, get down, Carrie!" Rance yelled. A bullet whined close by his ear and he dropped to one knee so that he'd make a smaller target. His sights fastened on a large man wearing a slouch hat and coming fast astride a big roan. Rance fired and the man clutched at his shoulder, the reins slipping free of his hands. But he managed to keep his seat as the roan veered away through the trees.

There were more of them, Rance counted at least three more, their horses crashing through the underbrush beyond the fringe of trees, but as he sent several shots their way, he heard them call a retreat.

"Let's get out of here!" one shouted.

"They got Cletus!"

"To hell with Cletus! Let's go!"

Hooves pounded, and when Rance was convinced that they really were heading away, he ran back across the clearing toward Carrie. She was still standing, her face drained of color, her eyes fastened on the crumpled form only a few feet away. He leaned the rifle against the log and took a quick look to assure himself that the man was dead, then turned to pull Carrie into his arms. She was trembling violently.

"It's all right . . . all right," he soothed. Her head was against his chest and he ran his hand along her hair. "It's all right, Carrie." She was still trembling and his own heart was beating rapidly as he held her close to him. He wanted to stay that way forever but he knew that they had to move out immediately.

He put a hand beneath her chin and lifted her face. "Can you ride?" His eyes searched hers. "We need to put some distance between them and us."

"Yes," she said, her voice stronger than he had expected.

"You're sure you're all right?"

She nodded.

He released her and bent down to retrieve the pistol which she'd dropped just before he'd come to her. He slid it into his holster, took up his rifle, then grabbed her hand. "Let's go," he said.

She pulled back stubbornly. "Wait." She had turned back to stare once again at the corpse on the ground. "I want that. Please, Rance . . ."

"What?" Baffled, Rance saw that she was pointing toward a ring on the dead man's hand. "You want that ring?"

"Yes, please . . . It belongs to me."

He wasn't going to waste time arguing, he reached down and stripped it off the man's finger. As he passed it to her, he saw that it was a signet ring. The initials were E. M. "Now for God's sake, let's go. They could be doubling back."

He gave her a hand up to the saddle and then swung up on his own horse. "Luckily, they were headed upriver. We'll just go the same way we were headed before."

They rode hard for nearly an hour, low hanging branches and silvery mosses brushing at them. The horses were lathered and winded. Rance could see that Carrie was totally exhausted. Though she went grimly ahead, she was slumping forward in the saddle. "Here," he called. "We'll stop here."

He swung down, took her horse's bridle and led it away from the rough trail back into a tight little thicket which shielded them completely from the path. The grass was deep and thick and formed a tiny hollow between the bushes and a cluster of trees.

He reached up for her, putting his hands at her waist and swinging her to the ground. She swayed and he pulled her against him, tipping her face up to examine the slight traces of tears that had come from sheer exhaustion. He ran a gentle finger beneath each damp eyelash.

She made no effort to move away from him and they stood that way for a long moment.

"Have I ever told you, Carrie Kingston, that you are one hell of a woman!" he growled.

There was a half smile on her lips and she closed her eyes, sighing, already half asleep as he lowered her into the deep and sweet smelling grass.

The horses had wandered a few steps away and were grazing contentedly. A thin rim of light was beginning to edge up at the horizon, and Rance took up a protective position near Carrie.

"Sleep . . ." he said aloud. "Rest now. I'll be right here."

*   *   *

Carrie stirred, rolled over, and felt herself come against a muscular, male shoulder. Her eyes started open as she jerked awake, crying out in terror.

"Carrie . . . Carrie, it's all right. It's me."

Rance lay stretched out beside her on the grass, his body between her and the opening formed by the thicket and the trees. He quickly reached a reassuring hand out to hers.

"Rance!" She gasped, looking into his gray eyes and sinking back with relief.

The sun was up but the thicket was cool, shaded by the thick branches. The air smelled fresh, redolent of honeysuckle.

"I . . . I've been asleep?" she said slowly, trying to remember everything that had happened.

He nodded.

She turned her head and looked around, beginning to recall their arrival here. "You watched me . . . all this time?"

"It's only been a couple of hours. You're beautiful when you sleep."

He was up on one elbow now, looking down into her face. She knew she should get up, that it was important that they get back to New Orleans at once, but somehow she seemed unable to move, though they were lying so close together they were almost touching.

"I . . . I thought that man was going to kill you. Back there in the clearing," she said softly.

"So you risked your life to save mine. How the hell did you ever learn to shoot like that?" His voice was husky.

"Papa taught me." It was a whisper now, because somehow their bodies had made contact. She could feel the whole length of him down her side . . . and she had never been more vulnerable.

Her defenses had been breached. All her lies to herself, all her justifications, her tirades against him had been shown up for the shams they were last night in the clearing when she'd thought he was going to be shot down in front of her. And now at his touch, desire scorched through her, startling and demanding. He had put his man's mark upon her that night at Kingston's Landing. Some deepest woman part of her was his forever.

The heat within her was mirrored in his eyes. He groaned, his fingers moving lightly over her lips, along her throat, tugging at the buttons of her shirtwaist. His mouth found hers and he kissed her hungrily, as if he were starving for the taste.

"Rance . . . Rance," she gasped between kisses. And then gave a little cry as her breasts came free to him.

He cupped them in his hands, bringing his head down to flick lightly at the nipples with his tongue, and then taking them into his mouth to suck, gently at first and then stronger. A sweet fire throbbed between her legs, caused her to moan and move her hips.

He was out of his shirt and now he stripped her riding skirt and pantalettes from her. "Carrie . . . Oh, Jesus, Carrie . . ." He was crouching above her, that strong face filling her eyes and her heart, his hands moving up her inner thighs to the soft patch of dark hair. "I've never stopped wanting you . . . not since that night."

He freed himself from his trousers and her legs opened. She was warm and wet to him, the pleasure so intense when he entered her that she cried out . . . and then again, and again as he stroked. He murmured words only some of which she could make out. "Carrie . . ." And "Jesus . . . sweet Jesus . . ."

She hadn't dreamed such pleasure existed, but it climbed higher still, until she could hardly bear it. She rose to meet his thrusts, her hair loose from its pins and flowing about her face.

"Carrie, you do want it . . . you do . . . as much as I . . . Say it. Tell me . . ."

"Yes . . . yes . . . yes!" she cried, the word turning into a wail as that deepest and secret place exploded within her, sending out waves of pure ecstasy that filled her, blinded her, left her deaf to everything except his own hoarse cry.

Hearts pounding still, breath coming rapidly, they clung to each other. "Carrie . . . my sweet Carrie," Rance said raggedly, his lips against her throat.

They lay that way for several long and lovely minutes. Carrie could hear the chirping of the birds again. The tree branch above her swayed slightly in the breeze.

Rance slid slowly, reluctantly, away from her and sat up to fix his trousers, then began to pull on his shirt.

Carrie suddenly felt very shy at her own nakedness and hurriedly donned her pantalettes and wiggled into her riding skirt. She was buttoning her blouse when Rance turned back to her.

His gray eyes searched hers tentatively. "Are you all right?" He put a gentle hand out to her cheek.

Very slowly, she smiled at him. "Oh, yes," she said.

He stood, pulling her up with him and into his arms, kissing her slowly and tenderly. She rested her face against his chest for a moment and then looked up at him.

"We should go now, shouldn't we," she said reluctantly.

He nodded.

It had been easy to slip back into the city unnoticed. The sentries they had skirted were engaged in a lively game of craps, and once they were closer in, Rance hailed the first hackney cab he saw. He fastened their horses to the rear before climbing into the closed carriage to join Carrie.

"We don't want anyone to see us. Not just yet," he said, as the rig gave a gentle lurch forward.

"Once you're at home," he went on, "you can sleep for a couple of hours, but then you must get up and go out. That's when I want you to make *sure* that you're seen. Go to the dressmaker's or to Madame LeGallienne's Sweet Shop, or both. I know you must be exhausted, but it's important to lay any suspicions to rest. Your presence in New Orleans should be firmly established just in case the Army should check. Can you manage it?"

"Yes," she said. "What about you?"

"I'll catch an hour or so of sleep, then arrive late at headquarters and plead that I went on a tearing drunk last night. Even once I'm shaved"—he ran a hand over the light shadow on his chin—"I should still look pretty convincing."

"Will you be in trouble?" she asked anxiously.

He shrugged. "I might get a dressing down from the general. That's all. If I'm lucky, he'll send me back home to sleep off my 'hangover.' "

Carrie looked away from him, fixed her eyes on the plush upholstery with its heavy cord trim around the windows and doors. The carriage rocked gently from side to side.

It seemed an eternity since she'd been awakened by the pounding on the front door at Kingston's Landing and had gone downstairs. So much had happened. Getting George Pierre to Justice's. The men in the clearing. Rance . . . Most of all, Rance. It would take her some time to sort it all out.

She reached into the pocket of her riding skirt and brought out the heavy signet ring that Rance had taken from the dead man's finger, turning it over in her hand to look closely at the intitials. "There's something I want tell you, Rance. Before we leave each other. This ring belonged to my Uncle Etienne. He was wearing it the day he was killed." She held it out for him to see. "I recognized it at once. I don't know how I could ever have thought that you . . . I should have known, should have realized . . ."

He put a finger to her lips, stopped the flow of words. "Hush," he said, "hush . . . I'm just so glad that you know the truth. God, Carrie, I never wanted you to think that I—" He broke off, staring at her, his finger still touching her lips, his eyes locked with hers.

His arms slipped around her and he kissed her. They held each other with a bittersweet pain and finally drew apart to ride silently.

After awhile, he pulled back the faded red curtain and looked out on the sunlit street. "It won't be long." He let the curtain fall back into place. "We'll be at your place soon." He was looking straight ahead but Carrie nodded.

"There is one thing," he turned toward her. "I found out something about Canfield that I think you ought to know. Because of Suzy."

"Tell me," she said.

"I saw some papers at headquarters. Papers that go back to General Butler's command. They show that Canfield and the general's brother, Jackson, were partners in the sale of some Texas beef to the government at what seemed outrageous prices. It's all perfectly legal, you understand. But I don't think it's very honorable. And I've often wondered why a man of Canfield's age isn't in uniform. On one side or the other. Perhaps I shouldn't have told you, but—"

"I'm glad you did," she cut him off. "I've . . . come to

realize, Rance, that Captain Canfield is not exactly what he seems. But don't worry. I intend to see that he doesn't hurt Suzy."

"I'm glad to hear you say that."

The carriage came to a gentle halt and in a moment the cabby was down and rapping at the door. "Here we be, sir. At the back of the house like you told me."

"Just a minute," Rance said.

He turned to Carrie, his face set into rigid lines. They looked at each other for a long moment, their eyes saying all the unsaid things. "Will you be all right?" he got out finally.

She nodded, her throat so full she didn't trust herself to speak.

"If . . . you ever need me . . ."

He didn't finish but Carrie nodded again. She could bear no more. She put a hand to touch his face and then she was down and out of the carriage before he could move or speak, fleeing through the back gate.

22

AFTER TWO DAYS, WHEN SHE COULD STAND THE WAITING NO longer, Carrie sent Lafitte up to Kingston's Landing to see what had happened. She was considerably relieved on his return to find that Rance had been right. The captain in charge of the patrol had simply searched the place thoroughly, and when he found no one but the servants there, offered his apologies and left. George Pierre was doing well at Justice's and probably would stay there for some time. He sent word that Carrie should stay in New Orleans so as not to arouse any suspicions.

Lafitte had brought Rance's horse back with him, and Carrie instructed him to deliver it discreetly. She had allowed herself a faint hope that Rance might send a note back, but he didn't.

It was best this way. She made herself face the pain of it squarely. She would hold the memory of him, of that brief and magic time together always. But it was a moment encapsulated, set apart. It could mean nothing now that they had picked up the threads of their lives again. Rance had committed himself to marry Nora Barlow. There was no way he could refuse to honor that commitment. And one day J. D. would come home . . .

It helped that back in New Orleans she found problems enough to occupy her. Abby Morrison, who'd been distraught with worry at the fall of Vicksburg, was now anxiously awaiting the arrival of J. D. under the terms of the surrender agreement. Carrie was torn between her natural inclination to tell his mother that he hadn't been taken prisoner at all, but was off to join up with Kirby Smith, and her determination to keep George Pierre safe from the authorities. Though her conscience hurt everytime she heard Abby making plans to celebrate J. D.'s return, she chose George Pierre's safety.

After all, *someone* had given the information to Yankee headquarters that George Pierre was at Kingston's Landing. She couldn't imagine how it had happened, but she knew that she wasn't going to take any chances. She had not even told Suzy about Rance's involvement or their moving George Pierre. In New Orleans, only she, Rance, and now Lafitte, who was sworn to secrecy, knew of George Pierre's true whereabouts, and she intended to keep it that way.

But Susannah herself was another problem. The moment that Carrie had dreaded had arrived. She had found out that Beau Canfield was back in New Orleans and Suzy was seeing him. There was no way she could let that go on. She had to tell her sister the truth about Beau.

It was a lovely summer morning, the air as sweet as baby's breath, and Carrie found Susannah sitting beneath the shade of the plum tree, staring balefully at the needle in her hand and the large mending basket on the bench beside her.

"I don't know why we have to mend this old underwear,"

Susannah complained as she caught sight of her sister. "Why can't we just get some new?"

"Because there isn't enough money," Carrie said patiently. "Everyone is having to make do these days. You see how Abby mends constantly."

Susannah sighed. "Maybe Mattie can do it."

"Mattie is at the market. Besides, Mattie has more than enough to keep her busy with the housework and cooking. Here . . . give me a needle and thread, and I'll help."

Susannah scooted over and made room for Carrie on the bench beside her, then gladly handed over a tattered pair of lace-edged pantalettes.

"Suzy, honey," Carrie began hesitantly as she applied her needle expertly to the worn garment, "I think you and I need to talk about something."

"Oh? What?"

Carrie steeled herself. "Beau Canfield."

"And what about Beau?" her sister asked, at once defensive.

"I heard he's back in New Orleans."

"That's right. As a matter of fact, he's taking me to the theater this evening."

Carrie tried to think of the right words to use. She had to make Susannah understand how dangerous the man was. "Suzy, honey . . . I've struggled with this for a long time now," she began, "about whether I should tell you the full truth about Beau. I drew back from it because I didn't want to hurt you . . . but now that he's back it's imperative that you know."

"That I know what?" Susannah asked, the rosebud mouth set into its stubborn line. "If you're going to start saying terrible things about Beau, you can just stop it! I see nothing wrong with the fact that he bought the Gayerre plantation. Someone was going to buy it. And I happen to think he's done the Morrisons a favor by buying half of the distillery. He's saved it for them."

"You could hardly call it buying," Carrie flared. "Seth just signed over half of it to him."

"In return for the money to keep it going!" Susannah countered.

Carrie looked at her little sister, and her heart squeezed with love and pity for her. She was infatuated with Canfield. It was obvious.

"I'm afraid it's more than that," Carrie said.

"Well, what is it?" Susannah put her needlework aside. "Just say it and get it over with!"

Carrie took a deep breath. "Beau Canfield is not what the Morrisons, or what you think he is," she said quietly. "I . . . I know that because of certain things . . . that have happened."

"What things?" Susannah demanded angrily.

Her mending forgotten now in her lap, Carrie looked away toward the beds of rose bushes and the sweet alyssum that edged the brick walkway. "While he was pretending to court you, he made advances toward me," she managed to get out and rushed ahead though she felt Susannah stiffen beside her. "He made . . . made proposals that no honorable man would have."

"I don't believe you!" Susannah's voice was high and quivering, and Carrie looked back to her sister. Her face had gone deathly pale.

"It's true," Carrie said. She knew that she couldn't stop now. "He told me that he would give me the money we needed for Kingston's Landing if . . . if I would become his mistress."

Susannah jumped to her feet and stood white-faced and gasping. "That's a lie!" She started toward the French doors, but Carrie caught her wrist and swung her around.

"It's not a lie, honey, and you're going to listen to this! He told me that if I would consent, no one would have to know . . . not you, not the Morrisons."

Susannah jerked her arm away, her green eyes enormous and filled with disbelief and anger. She shook her head slowly. "You would do anything . . . say anything to turn me against him, wouldn't you? I know you're lying because he loves *me*, Carrie. He's told me so."

"No . . . no, Suzy."

"You want him for yourself! It's been plain from the beginning!"

"That's not true! I despise him . . . and you will, too, once you wake up to what he really is!"

"I don't intend to listen to any more of this!" Susannah said coldly and turned again to leave the courtyard.

"Suzy!" Carrie couldn't hold back the words. "I forbid you to see Beau Canfield again!"

"Forbid?" Susannah jerked around. "You *forbid* me?" She was quivering with rage. "I am seventeen years old, Carrie! I'll do just as I please! And if you do anything to come between Beau and me . . . you'll be sorry!"

"Suzy . . . wait!" Carrie pleaded, but it was too late. Susannah had already turned her back and stormed into the house.

On July 16, just twelve short days after the surrender at Vicksburg, the steamboat *Imperial* arrived in New Orleans from St. Louis. It was the first commercial steamer to come down the river in over two years, and a huge crowd turned out to greet it, Yankee and Confederate alike, as if it were a holiday.

It was quite a sight after so long, the tall twin stacks puffing smoke as the gleaming white paddlewheeler slowly came in, multi-colored pennants, one with the name *Imperial* emblazoned on it, standing proudly on the breeze. There was a deafening cheer as the big steamer nudged in, engines coming to a shuddering stop, all three of its decks filled with waving, cheering people.

"Oh, it *is* wonderful, isn't it?" Abby said. She and Carrie had chosen a good spot on the levee and could see everything quite clearly. "I can get letters from Melissa now! Maybe she'll send us a daguerreotype of the baby," she went on, happier than Carrie had seen her in a long while.

"It's exciting," Carrie agreed, not having the heart to remind her that the fall of Vicksburg had brought this about. All around them Rebels of the staunchest order were cheering wildly, as if, just for today, they could put the war aside and welcome this gleaming white lady, could allow themselves to remember the old days when the curve of the river was always crowded with the floating and elegant "palaces" of the Mississippi, all snugged up close to the levee. This day seemed to promise a return to the past, and few of them could resist cheering.

"I do wish Susannah could have come along with us," Abby said.

Carrie kept her eyes on the canopied gangplank being slowly lowered into place. "I think she was going to drive over with Beau Canfield." The words were like knives in her throat. She had done everything she knew to reach her sister, but Suzy had met it all with stony resistance.

"How nice," Abby said. "I haven't seen them . . . but then this crowd is so enormous. Look there," she said, suddenly catching sight of Geraldine Brighton and her brother, the First Presbyterian's pastor, in the crowd. She waved. "Brother Brighton looks so old since the war started." She sighed. "Look at how his shoulders are stooped." But her attention was soon diverted as the passengers from the *Imperial* began pouring down the gangplank.

Carrie's eye was drawn to the first person ashore. A small man, he stepped down onto the dock with an easy swagger, gold tooth gleaming, his oiled hair as shiny as the tops of his patent-leather shoes. He took a quick and calculating look around him, and then disappeared into the press of people.

Though he was followed off the boat by solid-looking business-men in flowered waistcoats, drummers who carried their sample cases with them, and whole families who had come to be re-united with their Yankee soldier husbands and fathers, Carrie was nagged by the image of that first man. In a moment she realized why. There were others of that same stripe among the disembarking passengers, others with that same slick oiliness and frankly greedy expression about their eyes and mouths. And there were frowsy women with more than a hint of rouge on their cheeks and a hard brightness in their gazes.

The people of New Orleans had had to endure not only the hardships of war, but the avarice of men like Jackson Butler and Beau Canfield. And now that the river was open once again, the small-time opportunists, adventurers like those she had just seen, would pour in, anxious to get their share of the spoils. And though the sun was hot and bright, Carrie felt a sudden chill.

She would as soon have left right then, but Abby was so obviously enjoying herself that Carrie waited with her until most of the passengers had left the boat and only a few stragglers could be seen on deck.

Back in the house on Dumaine Street, she tried to dispel the gloomy feelings she had brought with her from the docks. With the French doors ajar, the sitting room was cool after the heat of the riverfront, and she and Abby relaxed while Mattie poured tea into delicate china cups and added thin slices of lemon.

"This is lovely," Abby said. "Tea is so expensive now I hardly ever have it anymore."

"I know," Carrie said, "but Mattie found these lemons in the market this morning, and the thought of tea and lemon was too tempting to pass up. She's going to make a pie from the rest of them. You and Seth must come and help us eat it."

Abby sighed blissfully, sipping her tea and leaning back comfortably in one of the big white overstuffed chairs. "This could make a person imagine that everything was right with the world," she said. "But I suppose it wouldn't be long before I remembered that we haven't heard anything yet from J. D. About coming home."

"It's too soon," Carrie said quickly, hoping that she sounded convincing.

"I suppose." Abby inhaled the fragrance of the hot tea, then took another sip. "I'm afraid he's going to be terribly shocked at how things have changed."

Carrie remembered how thin and worn J. D. had looked when she'd seen him at Kingston's Landing, remembered that somewhere deep in those blue eyes there seemed to be all the awful things of war he'd seen. "I'm sure that J. D. will expect some changes after two-and-a-half years," she reminded Abby gently.

"Of course," Abby agreed softly. "Perhaps I'm the one who has difficulty with the changes. It seems there's always something." She stirred her tea. "I suppose you've heard about the Nigra who's inciting all our house people to run off, haven't you?"

Mattie had just come into the room, and Carrie saw her almost drop the plate of biscuits she was carrying.

"No . . . I hadn't," Carrie said. The Negro girl kept her eyes carefully averted.

"Why, it's all over town," Abby went on. "They say the man lives in that shack community the Nigras have built near the old Congo Square. That's the area up above Rampart Street, you know, where the slaves used to sneak off in the old days to dance and make voodoo and Lord knows what other mischief."

"I know," Carrie said, trying to curb her impatience. "What about this man?"

"They say he's a great big buck . . . used to be a slave himself but claims he's free now. And he makes speeches every night about freedom and how Lincoln has set the slaves free already and all they have to do is walk away from their masters. Half the Nigras in town are slippin' away to listen to him. My Penelope was gone from her bed three times last week when I checked on her. And even old Thomas wasn't around when Seth needed him for something night before last. Lordy, I don't know what the world is coming to.''

"This man," Carrie asked quietly, "does he have a name?"

"They say he's called Solomon," Abby answered.

When Carrie looked toward her, Mattie was standing in the doorway, her face like a mask. "Will there be anything else, Miss Carrie?" she said tonelessly.

"No, Mattie," Carrie said. "That's all . . . for now."

But later when they were alone, Carrie confronted her. "Mattie, Mattie . . . I suppose you've known what he was doing all along!"

The girl eyed her, half-defiant, half-fearful. "Yes, Miss Carrie."

Carrie shook her head. "And you must know that he's doing nothing but stirring up trouble! For himself and everyone else!"

"Solomon believes what he doin' is right, Miss Carrie," Mattie pleaded. "He says the day's comin' soon when black people are *all* goin' to be free. Free to do whatever we want to do. He says we'll be able to go to school and learn things same as white people. That we'll be able to make money for our work and buy things . . . and decide for our ownselves what we want to do with our lives. He says we'll be able to do all the things that you can do, Miss Carrie!" Her voice had risen as she spoke, and now she stopped suddenly as if frightened by her own emotions.

Carrie stared at her, remembering what Rance had said Mr. Lincoln had planned for the Negroes if the North won the war. And an astonishing thought came unbidden to her mind. *Would it be so terrible?* After all, Papa had freed Justice.

She turned away quickly because she wasn't ready for Mattie to see what her face might reveal. "Mattie, you may be letting yourself in for a lot of heartache if you continue to see him!" she burst out.

There was a long silence, and then Mattie spoke, her voice

sounding older than her years. "That's the way of it sometimes when you love a man. Don't you know that, Miss Carrie?"

Carrie couldn't answer.

It was a gray and humid day in September when Carrie, alone in the house, heard the bell ring and went to find a tall, gaunt man waiting outside the gate. He leaned heavily on a stout hickory cane, his black slouch hat pulled low on his forehead. A dark, thick beard covered most of the rest of his face.

"Yes?" she called from the doorway.

There was something familiar in his chuckle, in the flash of white teeth. "I guess I'm pretty safe as long as my own sister doesn't recognize me."

Her hand flew to her mouth. "George Pierre . . ." she whispered, and immediately unlatched the gate and whisked him into the covered entrance and through the door . . . at least as fast as the pronounced limp would allow her brother to move, even with the help of the cane.

The door closed safely behind them, Carrie hugged him soundly. "George Pierre . . . my God, what are you doing here in New Orleans?" She scolded and laughed at the same time, taking the battered slouch hat from him and searching the thin, bearded face with her eyes.

He grinned, which relieved some of his drawn and hollow-eyed look. "After the way I just fooled you, I don't think I'm in too much danger. Not many people would recognize that cocky young pup who went off to win the war for the South damn near single-handedly! And I doubt very much if the Yankees would have any interest in a skinny fellow with a game leg . . . who's leaving New Orleans this evening anyway," he added, sobering.

"Leaving?"

He nodded.

"Where? Where are you going?" Carrie asked anxiously. "Surely you're not going to try to go back to the army?" It was a foolish question, and Carrie knew it the moment it was out of her mouth. She saw him glance down at his leg and then back to her.

He shook his head. "The war's over for me." Carrie had to fight back tears.

"Well, come on," she said brightly after a long moment, "let's go see what Mattie left in the kitchen to eat. I'm surprised," she teased him, "that Chloe and Tana between them haven't been able to fatten you up some."

She found a pot of soup rich with chicken and dumplings on the back of the stove and ladled out a huge bowlful, George Pierre protesting the size of it all the while. Biscuits were left over from lunch, and there were peaches in a basket by the table. Carrie sliced one, sprinkled it with some of their precious sugar and poured milk over it. She put everything, including a cup of hot coffee, on a tray, and they went into the sitting room where George Pierre began to devour the food as if he hadn't eaten for days.

Carrie watched approvingly and waited until he began to slow down before she started to ask questions.

"How *is* your leg now?" she wanted to know first.

He took a deep drink of coffee and swallowed. "About as well as it's ever going to be," he said quietly. "It still pains sometimes, but that will get less . . . at least that's what the doctor said yesterday."

"You risked going to a doctor? Here in New Orleans?"

George Pierre nodded. "You probably don't remember him. He's an old man now . . . a free person of color. His name is Baptiste Rambeau. Papa knew him and trusted him, said he saved his life once. Anyway"—he moved the teatable with his tray aside and leaned back in his chair—"he told me what I already knew. That I'll be walking like this for the rest of my life."

Pain filled Carrie until the look on her face must have betrayed her, and George Pierre leaned over and gave her hand a gentle squeeze.

"It's not so bad," he said, smiling ruefully, "when you consider that I might have been without it altogether. The army doctors wanted to amputate, you know."

Carrie nodded. "J. D. told me."

"Have you had any word from him?"

"No."

"Don't worry." George Pierre smiled. "He can take care of himself. He'll be all right."

He took out a slim, black cheroot and lit it, puffing white smoke. "I don't have a lot of money, but I bought myself a couple of these. I guess now is as good a time as any to smoke one. You don't mind, do you?"

"Of course not."

He looked down the length of it. "Haven't had one for a long time. Not since before the siege, I guess."

"How was it at Vicksburg?" she asked.

"Pretty bad near the end," he admitted. "The shelling was constant. Nobody was safe anyplace. And there was hardly any food at the last."

"I . . . I read in the newspapers that some people killed their mules . . . and ate them."

"It's over now." George Pierre looked at her with those gentle, dark Creole eyes. "No use thinking of it anymore."

"But the war . . . ." Carrie burst out. "We're going to win! Aren't we?"

The room seemed terribly quiet, and George Pierre slowly tapped the white ash of his cigar into a saucer. "Maybe," he said. "I'm not sure."

Carrie looked at him, too surprised to speak. It was the first time she had heard a Southerner express anything other than absolute certainty.

"The Yankee troops are better fed, better supplied, while our men are outnumbered and outgunned," he said bitterly. "Most of us have nothing better than old time smooth-bores . . . some of them flintlocks. We might as well be fighting back in the Revolutionary War. The Yankees have the latest repeating rifles."

He broke off as he saw how the harsh facts affected her. "But," he countered gently, "we have the best generals in the world. And there are no braver or better fighting men than those I've known in the Confederate Army. If that, and more determination than you ever saw, can win the war . . . then, yes, we'll win."

He leaned back in his chair, looked tired. "It's all up to other people now, Carrie. I've done what I could."

"I know," she said quickly, and they were quiet for a moment.

He puffed on his cigar. "Where's Suzy?" he asked finally.

"She's gone to spend the night with a friend of hers from the

305

sewing circle at church,'' Carrie answered, praying it was so. The way her sister had been acting lately, Carrie was never certain if she'd be where she said she'd be. There was always that awful possibility that she . . . that Beau . . .

"Carrie . . . she *is* all right, isn't she?"

She realized that George Pierre had asked her twice about their sister. "Oh, yes," she lied. "Suzy's just fine." There was no reason to worry him. Not when he could do nothing about it, she decided.

"I wish she'd been here. I wanted to say goodbye . . . to both of you. I'll have to go soon. I'll be sailing on the evening tide."

"Sailing?"

George Pierre nodded. "I'm going west, Carrie. I found this old merchant ship that runs down to Central America for bananas, and the captain has agreed to put me off in Texas. From there, I intend to go on overland . . . as far as California, maybe."

"But, George Pierre," Carrie pleaded, "why would you want to do that? Why don't you go back home to Kingston's Landing and stay there? The war can't last forever. And besides, if the Yankees knew that—" She stopped.

"If the Yankees knew that I've got a crippled leg and not much danger to anyone anymore," he finished for her, and then laughed at the woebegone expression on her face. "Carrie, honey . . . I need to go. There's nothing much for me here . . . no matter which side wins the war."

She tried to interrupt, but he held up his hand. "Let me finish. I never was any good at running the plantation. You know that better than anyone else. You're just too sweet and loving a sister to say it."

"That's not true . . ." she tried again, but George Pierre waved her to silence.

"It is true, and we both know it. It took me about five years to lose most of what Papa had built up. And I have no excuses. There were people who tried to help me. Justice tried, but no"—he laughed bitterly—"I had to run everything myself. Papa's agents in Philadelphia warned me against every single move I made." He took a deep breath.

"You were only a boy!" Carrie protested.

He nodded his head slowly. "But I'm not anymore. I'm a man

who has to try to find something he's good at." He grinned. "I always had a notion that I might like to teach . . . but I was never sure if Papa would approve."

Carrie thought of their father, thought of how strong and sure he had been, and how terribly hard it must have been for George Pierre to follow in those footsteps. Tears welled in her eyes.

"You are the best brother anyone ever had," she said slowly.

"Here now . . . no tears," he said, though his own eyes were suspiciously red. He reached into his inner coat pocket and brought out a piece of paper. "I want you to have this."

"What is it?"

"I've signed over Kingston's Landing to you, Carrie. And the truth is, it should have been left to you anyway."

Stunned, Carrie stared down at the paper he'd pressed into her hand. "George Pierre . . . I can't take this!"

"Of course you can. You have to," he said gently. "You're the one who loves Kingston's Landing as much as Papa did. You're the one who's like him, Carrie. If anybody can hang on to it . . . and make it pay again, you can, honey."

The tears started again, this time in earnest. Carrie couldn't hold them back. And with some difficulty, George Pierre hauled himself out of the chair, pulled her up, and hugged her to him for a long moment.

"All right," he said, wiping his hand across his face, "that's finished now." He set her from him. "I want you to thank Major Stewart for what he did. I don't quite know why he did it." He peered at her closely. "Is there something I should know, Carrie?"

"I don't understand," she hedged.

"About you and Major Stewart?"

"No. Of course not," she said softly. "He . . . he felt he owed Suzy and me a favor. That's all."

"It was a big favor." His eyes still searched her face, but he accepted it finally, nodded. "Will you be all right?" he asked.

"Yes." She grinned, her chin up, her head high, and he grinned back.

"I wish I had some money to give you." He hugged her again. "Kiss Suzy for me. I'll write as soon as I get settled."

𝒪 23 𝒪

ONCE GEORGE PIERRE WAS SAFELY OUT OF NEW ORLEANS, Carrie could tell Abby Morrison the truth about J.D.

"You mean," she stared at Carrie for a long moment, red blotches beginning to appear across her cheeks, "that J. D. was at Kingston's Landing and you didn't tell me?"

"Mother Morrison . . ." Carrie tried to explain. "The whole situation was just too dangerous."

"But I am J. D.'s mother."

"I know. And I'm sorry," Carrie said, feeling more than a little guilty. "Really I am. I did what I thought best at the time."

"But I could have gone up there with you! I could have *seen* him!"

"I understand how you feel." Carrie tried to soothe her. "And perhaps that is what I should have done. It just all happened so unexpectedly. There wasn't time to think very much about what to do."

"And you've kept it a secret all this time. You've let me believe that J. D. would soon be home," she accused.

Carrie sighed. "I was thinking of George Pierre's safety. Someone told the Yankees that he was up there. I still don't know who it was. I just couldn't take any chances at all. Please understand . . ."

But despite Carrie's best efforts, Abby remained only partially mollified, clinging to a quiet, martyred air until a couple of weeks later when something happened to turn her attention

308

elsewhere. She arrived at the house on Dumaine Street with handkerchief in hand and eyes reddened from crying.

"Penelope has run off!" she wailed. "She just took her clothes and sneaked off in the middle of the night! And it's all the fault of that Nigra, that Solomon! Somebody should *do* something about him!"

At his wife's insistence, Seth complained to the military authorities that his slave girl had run off, and he was told by a bored lieutenant that President Lincoln had set the slaves free.

"But captured territory was clearly exempted from that," Seth insisted.

The lieutenant shrugged. "A technicality." And he turned away to the next person in line before his desk.

Abby hurried right back to unload this latest tale of woe on Carrie. "I don't know what in the world I'll do about running the house!" she sobbed. "Seth says we can't even *buy* a girl now! Even if we had the money!"

Trying to hide her impatience, Carrie assured her that she and Susannah would be glad to help her out. But there were times now when she wanted to shake the woman. With everything else that had happened, housework did seem the last thing to worry about.

One thing was becoming clear though, there wasn't a Negro in New Orleans, and not many whites, who hadn't heard about Solomon now. And Carrie was sure that Mattie was going to him regularly.

Each evening after dinner, Mattie would appear dutifully in the doorway of the sitting room or the library or wherever Carrie happened to be. "Will you be needin' me for anything else, Miss Carrie?" she'd say. Carrie would shake her head no, and Mattie would go off, as if she were going to her room. But Carrie knew that if she checked it later, she'd find the room empty.

She was sure that Solomon was preaching the same things to Mattie that he did to all the others, and yet there didn't seem to be anything at all that she could do about it. She couldn't help but wonder how long it might be before she got up one morning to find that Mattie had left, too.

Meanwhile Susannah was as headstrong and defiant as ever.

Carrie could only pray that something would happen to show Susannah what kind of man Beau Canfield really was before it was too late.

There were times when Carrie wondered if things could get any worse, and then one day Mattie informed her that a Yankee soldier was downstairs demanding to see her.

"I ain't never seen him before, Miss Carrie. And he won't say what he wants."

The sergeant was plump and red-faced and stood sweating in the downstairs entrance hall. Mattie had shown her disdain by not showing him into the sitting room.

"Are you Miss Carrie Kingston?" he asked officially as Carrie reached the bottom of the stairs.

"Yes," she said.

He held out a white envelope. "I have a summons for you, Miss. From the Provost Marshal." And once she had taken the envelope, he clapped his hat back on his head, nodded curtly, and left.

Mattie hurried back from securing the gate to find Carrie still staring down at the envelope. "What is it, Miss Carrie?" she asked fearfully.

"I . . . I don't know, Mattie." Carrie summoned all her courage and opened it.

> You are hereby summoned to appear before this court at 2:00 o'clock in the afternoon, Wednesday, October 12th, to show cause why the plantation upriver of New Orleans, known as Kingston's Landing, which to all appearances has been abandoned by its owner, should not be confiscated by the United States government and thereby restored to full production in the best interests of the country.

It went on to say that if Carrie failed to make an appearance in court on the appointed day, the confiscation would be automatic and immediate, but she hardly saw that. At the first sentence, her legs had just seemed to give way, and she sat down on the stairs, clutching the summons to her.

310

"Oh, my God!" she said, rocking back and forth while Mattie bent over her anxiously.

General Banks fastened his favorite aide with his searching eyes. "Is it possible, Rance, that you are, uh,"—he paused delicately—"*involved* with this young woman?"

"No, sir," Rance said quickly, squirming inwardly.

The general leaned forward, his expression not without a certain understanding. "Rance, I may be your commanding officer, but I am also a man. If you have gotten yourself—"

"General Banks, Miss Kingston's reputation and conduct are above reproach," Rance said firmly. "She and her sister are friends of mine, nothing more."

"Well"—the general picked up the file on his desk—"since you are being married on Saturday to Colonel Barlow's lovely daughter, I'm glad to hear it."

"Yes, sir," Rance said.

"It seems this plantation, Kingston's Landing, came to our attention not too long ago when it was searched on the false information that the owner, a Rebel officer, was hiding out there. What was found, though, is that for all intents and purposes the place is abandoned. Only a few Negro servants there. I must say, Rance, I don't see anything improper in the Provost Court summons to Miss Kingston . . . or the pending confiscation."

"Sir, the Kingstons have been a family held in high regard for many years in this part of the country. I would not like to see any injustice done to them."

"Nor would I," General Banks reminded him mildly. "However, the country does need cotton and sugar. And you know as well as I that it's government policy to get these idle lands producing again as soon as possible. If at some future date the owner of this land can prove that he is a citizen in good standing of the United States, he can apply to be compensated for the land that was taken. We're not trying to steal anything. We're just trying to do what's best for the greatest amount of people in these most difficult times."

"But, General, I don't believe this plantation is really abandoned. Miss Kingston has plans for it. If you would just be present with me at that hearing this afternoon. If you'll just listen to what she has to say," Rance pleaded. "I would take it as a personal favor, sir."

The older man leaned back in his chair and folded his hands across the double row of brass buttons lining his blue jacket. "Very well, Major," he said. "I'll go along as an observer. But you are going to have to make the excuses to your bride-to-be when we're both late for her garden party this afternoon." He chuckled.

The garden party! Rance groaned inwardly. He had forgotten the damned thing! "Well"—he recovered quickly—"I'll make our excuses to Nora. I'm sure she'll understand, sir."

The general smiled. "I'll leave that task to you, Rance." He glanced at his watch. "I'll see you then in a little over an hour, Major."

"Thank you, sir," Rance said.

He went back to his own office, thinking of the garden party and wishing that it were some other day. He had had his fill of Nora's Yankee relatives, all of whom, it seemed, had descended on New Orleans for the wedding. Her long-toothed and equally long-winded Uncle Harry, fat Aunt Bertha, and numerous other relations whose names he could barely remember would simply have to begin the party without him or General Banks. After all, he reasoned, the hearing shouldn't take that long. He would send word to Nora and then explain when he got there.

He was just about to summon the sentry who stood outside his office when, to his chagrin, the door opened and Nora entered in a flurry of pale blue silk and cream-colored laces. "Rance, darling . . ." She came around the desk, arms outstretched. "I *told* the private it was all right," she said airily. The young soldier had followed her into the room and now stood red-faced and apologetic.

"It's all right, Tomkins," Rance said, and waved him away. "Nora . . ." He stood up. "This is a surprise." He leaned down and kissed her.

"What's the matter?" She drew back and looked at him, the tip of her close-fitting, little blue silk hat forming a widow's peak in the middle of her forehead, her pale blond hair gleaming and smooth on either side, done up in a cream-colored snood.

"Nothing . . . nothing at all," he said.

"Good!" She smiled. "I came to tell you that my Aunt Margaret arrived from Philadelphia this morning. And I am *so* glad that she could get here in time for the garden party this afternoon. She's my favorite aunt! And you'll *love* her, dearest. I just know you will!"

"That's uh . . . fine, Nora. I'm glad to hear it. But, honey . . . I'm afraid I'll have to be a little late to the party. General Banks and I have something that we must take care of. . ."

"Late?" Nora squared around to face him, pouting. "Why, Rance, I can't believe that General Banks would make you late for our very own party . . . and he the guest of honor! I just think I'll go speak to him at once!"

The determined set of her sharp little chin gave every evidence that she was preparing to do just that, and Rance grabbed her hand. "Nora . . . wait," he said. "I . . . I'm afraid that it's my fault, not General Banks's."

"Yours?" Her eyes had widened, and she stood regarding him incredulously.

"Yes. You see a matter of some importance has come up, and I have asked the general to look into it personally."

"Something more important than our party?" she demanded coldly. "My Aunt Margaret has just arrived, all the way from Philadelphia, and my cousin Millicent, and Uncle Harry . . . All our friends will be waiting. Just what is this *important matter*?"

Clearly this was not going well. "Now, Nora honey, don't be cross." Rance pulled her into his arms. "If it weren't important, I wouldn't think of being late. And I assure you, it won't be more than an hour . . ."

He tried to kiss her, but she disengaged herself. "I want to know what it is that's going to detain you, Rance," she said in a brittle tone that he was beginning to recognize. When Nora wasn't getting her way, she used that tone. And if she still didn't get it, she threw a tantrum of tears until she did.

He was beginning to grow impatient. "Nora," he said briskly, "a friend of mine has to appear in Provost Court this afternoon to show cause as to why her plantation should not be confiscated. I've asked General Banks to look into it."

"*Her* plantation? Who is this you're talking about?"

"Carrie Kingston."

Her delicate nostrils flared. "I might have known!" she cried. "I knew she was after you the first time I laid eyes on her!"

"Nora . . . don't be ridiculous."

"It's true! Do you think I'm some kind of fool! I saw the way she looked at you that night you introduced us at the theater!"

"Nora, I can assure you—"

"I will not stand for it, Rance!" Her lips began to quiver, and tears began to tremble on her lower lashes. "I will not be humiliated this way, with you traipsing off to pay attention to this girl practically on our very wedding day!"

"I'm not paying attention to anyone but you, Nora. Carrie and her sister are friends of mine. I would not like to see them treated unjustly. Carrie Kingston was . . . kind enough to give shelter to my men and me when we were caught upriver without food. She was very hospitable."

Nora stared at him, her face white, tears streaming down her cheeks now. "I just *bet* she was!"

She wasn't exactly keeping her voice down, and through the door, which was partially ajar, Rance could see Private Tomkins rigidly at attention, trying to pretend that he wasn't hearing any of it. With something like surprise, Rance suddenly realized how tired he was of her temper and tears . . . even of her flat Northern accent.

"I'm going to the hearing and that's final, Nora. I'll be along as soon as I can," he said quietly.

She stamped her foot and glared at him, so angry she stopped crying. "If you are not at that party on time, Rance Stewart," she hissed through those perfect little teeth, "you needn't come at all! To the party . . . *or* the wedding!"

There was a long silence in the room, Rance regarding her with a curious detachment. And then he gave her a stiff bow. "If that's the way you want it, Nora," he said.

The sergeant at the door jumped to attention as Rance and General Banks entered the courtroom, but the general motioned him at ease, and the two officers slipped unnoticed from the center aisle into a back bench.

It was a fairly large room, but there were few seats left since several cases were on the afternoon docket. The air was stuffy

314

and buzzed with soft conversations. Here and there paper fans were applied languidly.

Rance saw Carrie seated with the Morrisons up in the front row. Prosper Durant was directly behind her, and across the aisle Susannah sat with Beau Canfield.

Rance's gaze moved back to Carrie. Turned slightly sideways as she was, he could see the lovely white column of her neck, the determinedly brave set of her head, chin high. Her dark hair spilled from beneath a small straw bonnet that was trimmed with sprigs of violets on either side, and she was wearing the same lavender gown that she'd worn on the day that Prosper had first invited him to tea.

He found his eyes going back to her again and again.

Three officers sat at a long oak table down in front, facing the spectators. Rance recognized the middle one as the Chief Provost Marshal. He was Colonel Jeffrey Collins, a dour man with a reputation for doing his job to the letter. The other two were both majors with whom Rance had a nodding acquaintance. One of them had done some drinking with him one night. There were several desks along the back wall where clerks sat.

One of the clerks, a private with a shock of red hair, brought a sheaf of papers over to the table and placed it before Colonel Collins and then returned to his desk. The colonel perused the papers for a moment, then rapped his small gavel. The conversation faded to a shifting of boots and rustling of skirts.

He gravely recited the powers vested in the court by the government of the United States and then rapped his gavel once again and laid it on the table in front of him. "This court is in session," he said, "and will take up next the matter of the confiscation of the plantation known as Kingston's Landing."

As the colonel's voice droned on, giving the exact location of the plantation, Rance could see Susannah fidget in her seat, but Carrie had grown as still as if she'd been carved from marble.

"It was learned recently," Colonel Collins proceeded, "that for all intents and purposes, this piece of property has been abandoned by its owner, one"—he squinted at the page before him—"George Pierre Kingston. Given this fact, and unless some serious evidence to the contrary can be presented at this time, it is the judgment of this court that the property be confiscated in full conformity with the directives laid down under Section—''

''No! You can't do that!'' Carrie had come to life and was standing there confronting him.

Colonel Collins looked up, clearly startled. He had a rather long, aquiline nose, and he peered down the full length of it, appraising Carrie with an expression of mild annoyance. ''And may I ask, Miss, just who you might be?'' he said, and then rapped the gavel sharply at the buzz the outburst had produced among the spectators. ''Quiet!'' he snapped, and then turned his attention back to the young woman before him.

''I . . . I'm Carrie Kingston, sir. I am the sister of George Pierre Kingston.''

The colonel ran his hand over a balding head. ''Ah, yes . . .'' He searched among the papers before him and came up with the one he wanted. ''Since it was learned that Mr. Kingston had two sisters now residing in New Orleans, a summons was issued to you, the elder of the two, as a courtesy, Miss Kingston. This was in the event that you might have some information that this court does not, something that might affect the outcome of this hearing.''

''I do, sir,'' Carrie said. She stepped closer to the table. ''My brother is not the owner of Kingston's Landing. I am. And here is the proof.''

She took an envelope from her reticule and handed it to the colonel, who opened and read it, then looked up at her in some surprise.

''This appears to be a paper signed by your brother, transferring complete ownership of the plantation to you, Miss Kingston.''

''Yes, sir. It is.''

He rubbed the long nose. ''Do you know the whereabouts of your brother at this time, Miss Kingston?''

''No, sir,'' she said truthfully. ''I do not.''

The colonel had passed the paper to the officers on either side of him, and now he paused for a whispered conference before he turned back to Carrie who waited with her hands clasped rigidly in front of her.

''Miss Kingston, I'm afraid this paper is not acceptable to this court. It is neither witnessed nor dated. It could have been written by anyone.''

"But it was written by my brother!" Carrie burst out. "That's his signature. And I'm sure that that could be proven!''

Rance could see how pale she was. He wanted desperately to go up there and speak for her, but he knew it wouldn't do any good. He looked over at General Banks, who was watching with complete attention.

"Even if it could be proven," the colonel was saying, "I'm not sure that it would change the situation.'' His voice was not without sympathy. He would have had to be a stone to totally resist the appeal of this beautiful young woman who stood before him, golden eyes pleading. "I . . . I don't know how," he said gently, "a young woman such as yourself could possibly manage a plantation of this size and bring it to full production again."

"But I can!" Carrie insisted.

The colonel shook his head. "I don't see—"

"I can do it! I can!" She lifted her head high, eyes no longer pleading but blazing with amber fire. "That land belonged to my father, Adam Kingston. And now it belongs to me! Not all the Yankees in the world can take it from me!''

There was instant chaos in the courtroom and enough Rebels present that a cheer or two resounded to the rafters. Though Rance could see tears running down Carrie's white face, they were the proudest, bravest tears he'd ever seen. He ached for her. He turned to General Banks beside him. "General, if there's anything . . . .''

The colonel was pounding the table and demanding order, and in all the confusion no one seemed to notice as General Banks rose from his place in the back and strode briskly down the center aisle. And then Colonel Collins and the other officers caught sight of him and immediately stood to attention, while a gasp went through the crowd as they recognized the commanding general of New Orleans—a fine figure of a man in his scarlet sash, sword at his side.

"At ease, gentlemen," the general said quietly, though the room had fallen so still his voice was heard easily throughout. "I should like to ask this young lady a few questions if you don't mind, Colonel.''

"Yes, sir. Certainly, sir," Colonel Collins said and stepped aside so the general could take his place behind the table.

General Banks remained standing and smiled reassuringly at Carrie. "Miss Kingston, my name is Banks," he said.

"I know who you are, General," Carrie said in a clear, firm voice.

General Banks's eyes gleamed with a wry amusement. "I'm one of those Yankees you spoke of a moment ago," he said, and a titter rippled through the room. "But," he added, sobering, "I'm trying to help."

Carrie stared at him a long moment, as if taking the measure of him, and then nodded. "Thank you, General," she whispered. She was still so pale that Rance was afraid she might faint. He could hardly keep himself from going to her.

"Can you tell me why you are so sure, Miss Kingston, that you could operate this plantation, Kingston's Landing, if you had the chance?" General Banks asked.

"Because my father taught me about running a plantation, sir," Carrie answered without hesitation. "He was the best planter in Louisiana, and he taught me all I need to know. Besides, I've already shown that I can do it. I got a crop in last spring."

"This past spring?"

"Yes, sir."

"And what happened to this crop? I understood that the land is lying idle now?"

Carrie's white teeth nipped at her lower lip. "It was flooded out in May," she said reluctantly. "But that could happen to anyone!"

General Banks thought about that for a moment. "Yes . . . I suppose it could," he conceded. "And what of your plans for the future?"

"I have every intention of getting another crop in when planting time comes, General Banks." There was the least little bit of hope beginning to creep into Carrie's voice, but it was dashed by the general's next question.

"You have the necessary funds to do this? I know that the place is virtually abandoned, which means that you'll have to hire a sufficient work force . . . and also have enough to take care of other expenses until you can get your sugar made and to market.''

Carrie stood silently for a moment. "Well . . . no," she admitted finally. "Not right now, I don't. But I will have by the time I need it.''

"And how do you intend to raise this money?" the general pressed.

"I intend to borrow it," Carrie stated firmly.

General Banks fingered his chin whiskers and regarded her thoughtfully. The room was silent, every eye in the courtroom fastened on the beautiful young woman who had captured their hearts with her obvious courage and the imposing figure in blue, the commanding general of New Orleans who held her future in his hands. There was not the creak of a floorboard, not so much as a cough or a clearing of throat. Even the paper fans were motionless. And then the general gave his head a shake, and two deep creases appeared between his eyebrows.

"I would like very much to decide this matter in your favor, Miss Kingston," he said, "but at the same time, I must remember that I am sworn to my duty to uphold the laws and regulations of this government." There was a faint wash of sound through the onlookers, which the general ignored.

"Given the economic climate of New Orleans at this time," he went on, "it would surprise me very much if you were able to secure the necessary financing. However, I want to give you every opportunity. To that end, I am going to carry over this matter until tomorrow at this same time. If by then you can give me proof that you can indeed raise the money, I would recommend that the confiscation of this property be dropped. But I must tell you, Miss Kingston," he added reluctantly, "that if you cannot give such assurances at that time, I would be remiss in my duty if I did not allow this court to apply the same standards that it applies in any such case. You understand that, do you not?''

Rance saw Carrie hesitate, her hands rigid at her sides, but she met General Bank's eyes directly. "I understand, General," she said. "I'll be here.''

The Morrisons hurried after her as she turned and started down the center aisle. Prosper Durant brought up the rear, and farther back, Susannah came on the arm of Beau Canfield. But all eyes were on Carrie as she walked, white-faced but with her head high, her skirt making a soft rustle.

When she was almost to the door, she turned her head slightly and saw Rance. She hesitated just for an instant, those great amber eyes brimming with pain. But before he could make a move toward her, she turned her face away and was gone through the double doors.

Carrie lay on her bed and stared dry-eyed at the ceiling, one finger moving aimlessly back and forth against the patterned weave of the coverlet, which she hadn't even bothered to turn back. She had gone over it in her mind a hundred times. There was no way she could give General Banks the assurances he asked for; she had seen Leroy Tate only yesterday. She was going to lose Kingston's Landing tomorrow. The knowledge left her numb as if with a terrible injury; the full force of the pain would come later.

On their return from Provost Court, Susannah had stormed out of the house with Beau Canfield after Carrie made it clear that he wasn't welcome there. The Morrisons and Prosper Durant had gone away, understanding her request to be alone. And she had been on her bed ever since, eyes fastened on the cream-colored wallpaper above her, sometimes jumping up to pace restlessly. She hadn't even changed her clothes.

It was growing dark in the room now, and Carrie heard Mattie's soft knock. She couldn't bring herself to answer, but the girl came in anyway and set a tray on the nightstand by the bed.

"Thought you might like some dinner," Mattie said, her voice assuming a forced brightness as she lit the lamps and drew the thin white curtains.

Carrie shook her head. "I couldn't, Mattie. I couldn't touch it. Thanks anyway."

Mattie stood in the middle of the room, hands on hips, and looked at her mistress through worried eyes. "It ain't goin' to do a lick of good if you starve yourself to death, Miss Carrie."

"I won't starve, Mattie. I'm fine. Really."

"Well—" Mattie took up the rejected tray and sighed—"I'll be right down in my room if you need me. Right downstairs."

Carrie realized that Mattie was telling her she wouldn't leave the house tonight, she wouldn't go to meet Solomon. "Thank you, Mattie," she said softly. "I appreciate that."

Sometime later she forced herself to get undressed and into her nightgown, then returned to bed to go over it all in her mind again. "I've exhausted every possibility, Miss Kingston," Leroy Tate had told her sadly. "I don't know what to say." It buzzed in her head. That and the general's words: "If you cannot give such assurances . . . remiss in my duty . . ."

At last she dropped into a restless and febrile sleep only to start upright when she heard the knocking at her door, and an instant later Mattie's kerchief-bound head appeared.

"Mist' Prosper downstairs, Miss Carrie," the girl said.

"Prosper? Oh, no." Carrie moaned, coming fully awake now, her head throbbing dully. "I told him that I really didn't feel like being with anyone."

"He says it's real important."

Carrie sighed. Dear Prosper . . . She swung her legs over the side of the high bed. "All right, Mattie," she said reluctantly. "Tell him I'll be right down."

She pulled on her old pink-flowered wrapper and a few moments later entered the sitting room to find the fencing master waiting impatiently.

"*Ma chère,*" he said the moment he caught sight of her, "forgive me, but I must speak with you privately. At once!"

"Prosper . . . what is it?" It occurred to Carrie that he might be planning to offer her more money, but she knew he really didn't have it to spare.

"It is about a matter that requires the utmost discretion. There must be no possibility," he said, going to look out into the empty hallway and then closing the double doors tightly, "that what I am about to say to you could be overheard."

She watched him, thoroughly mystified. "Who would overhear us?" she said. "Mattie has gone back to her room. Lafitte is long since in his quarters. I don't think Suzy has even come home yet."

"Good!" he said. He began to pace nervously, fingering the watchchain that stretched across his wine-colored silk waistcoat. "I wish I knew what your father would have me do. I would have sworn on my honor, on my very *soul,* that I would never reveal—''

"Prosper, what on earth are you talking about?" Carrie demanded. As dear as he was to her, her head ached abominably, and she was in no mood for games.

"Carrie—" he took her hand and led her to one of the big, overstuffed chairs and then sat down himself in the one opposite her—"Carrie, I have searched my heart this night . . . and I have decided I must reveal something to you that I was sure I would carry with me to the grave."

From the gravity of his tone, Carrie realized at last that something very serious was involved. "Is it about Kingston's Landing?" she asked anxiously.

"In a way," he said quietly. "It is something that might enable you to keep the plantation . . . but at a cost. Perhaps a terrible cost." He looked away from her, as if suddenly reluctant to meet her eyes, but she leaned forward to grasp his arm.

"Oh, tell me, Prosper! If it's something that could save Kingston's Landing, you must tell me!"

He nodded, reluctance still evident in every line. "I will. Heaven help me, I will," he said.

He got up and walked to the French doors, looking out toward the courtyard, which was bathed in moonlight. "All his life," he began, "your father carried a secret, Carrie. A secret that only a few people knew. To the world, he was the son of the wealthy Barbados planter, George Kingston. He had been raised by that man and inherited his fortune. But the truth was—" he turned back to look at her—"Adam Kingston . . . your father . . . was the illegitimate son of Armand Moreau."

Carrie stared at him, trying to digest what he had just said. "Armand Moreau . . . Papa's father? But that can't be, Prosper. Armand Moreau was Uncle Etienne's father. Papa was married to Armand Moreau's daughter, Dominique, before he married Mama."

"*Foster* daughter, *ma chère.* Dominique was an orphan, a daughter of another old and prominent Creole family, but not really a Moreau."

Carrie's brows knitted as she was flooded with hazy memories. Faded images came to her mind of an old man in the cane-backed wheelchair . . . long ago. She could just barely remember him.

"Old Monsieur Moreau was Papa's father?" she said. "Then that means that Uncle Etienne was really Papa's brother!"

Prosper nodded. "His half-brother."

Carrie shook her head. "But I . . . I still don't see what this has to do with saving Kingston's Landing."

Prosper stood looking at her, his dark eyes brooding. "I do not know what it will mean to you, *ma chère*. And I know of no way to say it, except to say it." He moved his hands expressively. "Adam's mother, your grandmother, was a beautiful woman named Madeleine Tristesse."

"Yes . . .?"

"She was an octoroon."

There was a pause, like a skipped heartbeat. Then Carrie drew in her breath sharply, and Prosper turned away toward the French doors, allowing her this moment in privacy.

Thoughts clamored. She could hardly sort them out. Papa's mother had been an octoroon? Papa was a person of color? *She . . . was a person of color!*

She seemed unable to speak. This whole long day had been like a dream. A nightmare. And now Prosper was telling her she wasn't really who she'd thought she was. She rebelled at that immediately. She *was* Carrie Kingston . . . whoever, whatever Carrie Kingston was.

She was trembling violently, but suddenly saw why Prosper had revealed this long kept secret. "The authorities would not touch the property of a person of Negro blood," she said numbly.

Prosper turned back and nodded.

"Is there any proof . . . legal proof?"

"Besides my testimony, there is a letter."

She raised an unsteady hand to her face and tried to consider the consequences. It was very quiet in the room. Only one gas lamp cast long shadows against the far walls and the high ceiling. The light flickered now with a sudden shift of air, and the shadows moved.

"It is up to you, *ma chère*," Prosper said softly. "I could not have lived with myself had I kept this from you now. I know how much Kingston's Landing meant to your father. I know how much it means to you. But I also know what it means to be a person of color in this society."

There was a twisted smile on Prosper's face, his eyes infinitely sad, and Carrie's throat was so full that she couldn't speak.

"You alone must make the decision, *ma petite* Carrie. If you decide not to reveal this information, you and I shall carry the secret together, and it will never be mentioned again. If you decide otherwise . . ." He made her a bow in a fair imitation of his old self. "I am at your service, Mademoiselle Kingston."

◖ 24 ◗

THE AFTERNOON SESSION OF PROVOST COURT HAD SELDOM SEEN such a crowd. Word had gotten around that General Banks himself was presiding over the case of a spunky girl who was fighting to save her family plantation from confiscation, and so many people showed up that some had to be turned away. As it was, every seat was filled, and people stood along the sides and back, adding to the heat and confusion. The soldiers on duty kept the center aisle clear only with some difficulty.

General Banks was there on time and so was Carrie, but even when she heard her name called, she did not yet know what she was going to do. She had lain awake most of the night trying to sort it all out, and she had failed.

To please Mattie and Abby Morrison, she had forced down a little breakfast. And when it was time to get ready for what might be the most important hour of her life, she had dressed herself with great care, choosing an ivory-colored silk dress with big puffed sleeves to which Madame Louisa had added a swirl of lace to fall just below the elbows. She'd done her hair in a simple style, catching it back on either side with tortoise-shell combs, and instead of the bonnet she'd worn the day before, she wore the wide-brimmed leghorn straw hat. She wanted to look her very best today . . . no matter what happened.

There had been a stir when she entered. But now, as her name was called and she rose and stepped forward in clear view of everyone, there was an audible whispering. Women straightened their bonnets and looked at her with a grudging admiration. Men nudged each other and shook their heads, even dyed-in-the-wool Yankees agreeing that it was a shame indeed that such a lovely young girl would have to take on the whole Union Army by herself.

As for Carrie, she was aware that the Morrisons were out there and Prosper . . . and Susannah sitting stubbornly next to Beau Canfield. She wondered fleetingly if Rance was there. She had wanted to look for him, but hadn't let herself.

She realized, in a kind of numb detachment, that General Banks had asked her if she had been able to bring along the assurances that he'd asked for the day before.

"No, sir," she said in a voice that surprised her it was so clear, so solid. "I'm afraid I could not."

There was a buzz of whispers, and Colonel Collins rapped on the table and brought the room back to order.

General Banks hesitated, as if he were deeply reluctant to do what he must do. He cleared his throat noisily. "Miss Kingston," he said, "I want you to know that I am deeply sorry that . . ."

He continued on, and Carrie could hear his voice as if it were coming from far away, could see his mouth move, and she knew what he was going to say.

She could keep silent, and the Yankees would take Kingston's Landing, and she would do something . . . *something* . . . It was not the end of the world, she told herself.

But then as she heard him coming closer with each word, her throat closed, and a terrible urgency gripped her. Dear Lord, she could not lose it! She thought of the land and the river, of the house where she'd been born . . . It was a part of her as it had been a part of Papa!

She had to save it. Whatever the cost. The thought was so

clear and compelling she wondered why she'd ever considered anything else.

She turned instinctively to look back at Prosper. He was seated in the second row, impeccably dressed as always, his mustache waxed to stiff points, his plum-colored velvet waistcoat setting off the white ruffles of his shirtfront. He understood her look and smiled at her, nodding his head slowly.

Very sure now, she turned back to face whatever was ahead. "General Banks," she interrupted in a high, clear voice, "there is something else that I think you must be told, sir."

His eyebrows raised slightly, but he inclined his head. "Very well, Miss Kingston," he said, willing to give her every possible chance.

"I have recently learned certain facts," she began, "which I believe will have a great bearing on this matter, General. It is well-known in New Orleans that it is not the policy of the military government to interfere in any way with the property of a person . . ." —she hesitated only a moment—"of Negro blood."

There was dead silence in the courtroom except for a baby toward the rear who wailed thinly for a moment.

General Banks shifted his weight from one foot to the other. "That's true," he said, "though I don't see—"

"My grandmother," Carrie said in a voice that was not only steady but could be heard throughout, "was a woman named Madeleine Tristesse. She was an octoroon."

There was a moment when the whole room seemed to be paralyzed, then it erupted with sound and movement. People were turning to one another and shaking their heads in total disbelief. It was a trick, they said, a trick to fool the Yankees and keep the land. There was no way that this lovely young woman could possibly be touched, as the saying went, with the tar brush. There were some present who remembered Adam and Molly Kingston. "Preposterous!" one shouted.

"For God's sake, Carrie," Seth Morrison cried out, "don't tell such a damnable lie . . . even to keep the place!" It was more life than Seth had shown since he took the loyalty oath.

Carrie looked toward him and saw that Abby Morrison was leaning heavily on his arm, her handkerchief pressed to her eyes.

And then Carrie caught sight of Susannah's face, gone deathly pale, and the full awareness came, like a knife in her heart, that she would not be the only one affected by what she had revealed.

The uproar continued. Colonel Collins too stunned to even use his gavel. It was only after General Banks gestured that he remembered himself and brought the gavel down repeatedly. "Order . . . order!" he shouted again and again. "We will have order or this room will be cleared!"

It took a full minute or so, but finally the hearing could continue.

"Miss Kingston," General Banks said, his voice anxious, fatherly, "I realize that you are overwrought. If you would care to withdraw that last statement—"

"No, sir," Carrie said slowly. She knew that there was no going back, though her heart was breaking with the memory of Susannah's face. "There is a person here today who can corroborate the truth of what I've told you. Monsieur Prosper Durant. He is a man not without reputation in New Orleans and elsewhere, a fencing master of international renown. He was my father's dear friend . . . as he is mine."

Prosper had stood up, and General Banks beckoned him forward while all craned their necks to see.

"He's colored hisself!" someone hissed in a whisper that was loud enough to carry across the room.

The room was gaveled to silence as Carrie moved to stand proudly beside the man who had been such a friend always.

"You are Prosper Durant?" General Banks asked.

"I am," Prosper replied.

"And do you have information that . . . ."—he paused, then plunged ahead—"that would establish the truth of what Miss Kingston has just told us?"

Prosper made a small bow. "I believe I do." He reached into his inner coat pocket and drew forth a yellowed envelope, which he handed to General Banks. "This is a letter written to me by Adam Kingston a month before his death. In it, he speaks of a confidence he shared with me in the later years of our long friendship. He speaks of his mother, Madeleine Tristesse . . . and his closely kept secret . . . that he was, in fact, a person of mixed blood. In case of any doubt, I am sure his signature can be verified easily.

"There is one thing more that I would wish to say at this time . . . Adam Kingston was the finest man I ever knew."

Prosper had conducted himself with such dignity that the entire courtroom remained quiet throughout his statement and then waited, many of them on the edges of their seats, as General Banks took out the two pages and read through them quickly, pausing only once in the middle of the second page . . . obviously to read one passage a second time.

His face showed his distress as he folded the pages, returned them to their envelope, and gave them back to Prosper. "I thank you, Mr. Durant," he said and then turned to Carrie. "Under the circumstances . . . the confiscation proceedings are dropped, Miss Kingston. The plantation is yours. To do with as you please."

There was an embarrassed silence as the significance of the general's words hit them, and then from a far back corner a half-grown boy standing along the wall shouted out, "Shit . . . She ain't nothin' but a darky in all them fancy clothes!" To which his ruddy-faced friend standing next to him elbowed him hard in the stomach and a small scuffle broke out. The soldiers on guard rushed to stop it.

Heated discussions and raised voices were beginning to erupt around the room, but all Carrie could see was Seth Morrison bending over Abby who had fainted dead away. And then Susannah was there before her, Beau standing smug and triumphant beside her.

"You're a liar, Carrie!" Susannah screamed, her face twisted almost beyond recognition. "You and Prosper are liars! You'd say anything to keep that place . . . anything!" she shrieked. "*I hate you . . . hate you, Carrie!*" She beat at her sister with her small fists until Beau pulled her back.

General Banks stepped forward to shield Carrie and gestured to four soldiers just pushing through the rapidly filling center aisle. "Escort Miss Kingston and Mr. Durant out of here. See them safely to their homes," he said quietly.

Carrie thought she heard Rance calling to her just as they

reached a side door, and she hesitated, but the sergeant beside her took her arm and propelled her away.

Carrie watched the library clock nervously and tried to sip some of the coffee that Mattie had brought her. It had been hours, and Susannah still had not come home. Prosper had gone out to look for her.

Unable to sit quietly in the chair, Carrie put the coffee aside and got up to walk aimlessly around the room, past the shelves of leather-bound books, the tall mahogany secretary, and the tapestry-covered wingback chairs. Mattie had put a small bowl of roses on the tea table, and Carrie could catch their faint fragrance. Suzy liked roses. . . .

She sighed and went to the window. She could see part of the Marchand house, and past it to tiled rooftops, and farther still in the hazy blue sky, the faint outline of the three towering spires of the St. Louis Cathedral.

Restlessly she turned back into the room. How could she, she asked herself again, ever have forgotten that Susannah had a right to share in the decision of whether to reveal their true heritage? She hadn't even warned her. It was unforgivable, and she knew it.

She could still see Susannah's face, could still feel the impact of those small hands hammering at her shoulders and arms. Dear God, maybe Suzy was right! Perhaps she did treat her like a child. But she would try to make it all up to her somehow. She would try to explain.

She heard the bell. Could that be her? No. Suzy wouldn't ring. Perhaps it was Prosper. She hurried out into the hall to find Mattie showing Seth and Abby Morrison in.

They stopped as they saw her and stood awkwardly in the foyer, Seth tugging at his collar as if it were too tight and Abby licking at her lips, which looked suddenly puckered and old.

"We . . . we thought we should come," Abby said, and Carrie realized that it was the voice Abby would use in speaking to a stranger . . . someone to whom she owed a social obligation.

"That was good of you," Carrie said. Her face felt stiff. "Come into the sitting room. Can Mattie bring you some coffee?"

"No," Seth said, his tone unduly hearty, "we can't stay long.

There's a business matter . . . an acquaintance I—that is, we— have to see later.''

"Of course," Carrie said.

They sat uneasily in their chairs, Seth perched on the edge of his, waistcoat buttons straining. The silence seemed to get louder and louder.

"I don't suppose you've seen Suzy, have you?" Carrie asked, hoping that she might have gone to them.

"No . . . not since—" Abby broke off.

"Not since the hearing," Seth finished.

"Oh, Carrie," Abby burst out stiffly, "are you positive that—" Again she stopped in mid-sentence, and Carrie suddenly felt sorry for her.

"Yes, I am, Abby." It was the first time she'd ever called her by her given name, but neither of them noticed.

"Did you know this? Before?" Seth demanded, almost angrily.

"No," Carrie answered quietly. "I only learned last night."

"From that Prosper Durant," Abby said bitterly. "I never could see why your father . . . but—" She caught herself. "I suppose that they . . . found some things to share," she ended lamely, looking terribly embarrassed.

Again there was a silence, and Abby twisted her wedding ring on her finger. "We want to . . . do what we can, of course," she said, her eyes avoiding Carrie's, and Seth was already edging up out of the chair.

"Absolutely," he said in that falsely hearty voice. "We want you to know that you can depend on us . . . that's why we came. But—" he took out his watch and peered at it, and Carrie was strangely aware of the wild gray hairs that had sprung up in his eyebrows—"As I said, there's this business thing."

"I understand, Seth," she said. "I'll show you out."

They had reached the front door when Carrie stopped them. "There is one thing," she said slowly. "I would like you to keep this . . ." She slipped the gold ring with the three small emeralds off her finger and held it out to Abby.

J. D.'s parents exchanged quick glances, and then without a word, her eyes brimming with tears, Abby took the ring. Seth reached a hand out to Carrie's arm.

"I'm sorry it's like this," he said, his voice breaking,

and Carrie knew that he really meant it. "If you should need help . . ."

She nodded, and they left.

She wasn't sure how she felt. Surely not any great pain that she'd given J. D.'s ring back. Under the circumstances, it had seemed the right thing to do. Even if she weren't "touched by the tar brush," she knew that she didn't love J. D. . . . not the way you needed to love someone to marry him. What seemed more important right now was the way Seth and Abby had looked at her, as if searching for some dusky cast to her skin that they'd never noticed before, some clue that should have warned them.

How was she ever going to hang onto the fact that she was the same person she'd always been when everyone else saw her through different eyes? And poor little Suzy. Would Suzy ever be able to deal with that?

Prosper came back a short time later, but he'd had no luck. "I looked everywhere I knew to look," he said helplessly. "I went to all of the places that I have heard Suzy mention that she and Canfield go together. LeGallienne's and the confectioner's shop over on St. Anne. There is a tearoom on Royal. I went to his rooms in the Pontalba Building. I also learned of a house on Rampart Street . . ."

Carrie had been about to tell him that.

"No one was there," he went on. "But, *ma chère*, I am sure that she will be returning home shortly. Perhaps she just needs some time alone . . ." He gestured, palms upward.

Carrie went to her room to rest, but Prosper stayed, worried about her. And it was only a few minutes before he was knocking gently at her bedroom door.

"Just a minute," she called, sure this time that Suzy had at last come home. She hurriedly slipped her wrapper about her and opened the door eagerly.

"Rance Stewart is downstairs to see you, Carrie," Prosper said. He regarded her speculatively as her hand flew to her throat.

"No . . . no, tell him that I can't see anyone . . ." She said it instinctively.

"He is very insistent, Carrie. I don't know that he will accept a refusal."

"He'll have to," she said. Her mouth was quivering and tears were swelling in her throat. She fought them back.

Prosper frowned. "I wish you would see him."

"No!" she said firmly, shaking her head. "No!"

"Very well . . ." Prosper said reluctantly, "I shall tell him."

The moment she was alone, the tears that she had managed to hold at bay began. She threw herself across the bed and buried her face in the pillow, wanting desperately to run down the stairs and throw herself into Rance's arms.

She would not do that to him. He was going to be married to Nora Barlow this very weekend and she couldn't make demands on him now. It would only make it harder for him . . . and for her.

It was the next day before Carrie heard from Susannah. A note was brought to the house by a raggedy urchin who disappeared as soon as he'd handed it over to Mattie. It said:

> By the time you read this, I'll be far away at sea with Beau. We are to be married at our first port-of-call. I will truly never forgive you for what you've done, Carrie.
>
> Susannah

In those next days, Carrie read it again and again, always with the same anguish.

"She does not mean it," Prosper tried to comfort her. "You'll see."

But Carrie was terribly afraid that she'd lost her sister forever. And the knowledge that Suzy would be married to a man like Canfield was almost unbearable.

Toward the end of that next week, a message came from Leroy Tate that he would like to see her, and Carrie went to his office, but not without some trepidation. She had not been outside of the house much. She was simply not yet up to the stares and nudges and whispers that she had encountered even on a simple walk through the French Market. She dreaded having the banker greet her with that awkward embarrassment that seemed to come with her presence.

She needn't have worried. Leroy Tate ushered her into the office, smiling and resettling his spectacles on his nose. "You're looking splendid, Miss Kingston," he said, though Carrie knew that he was lying. She was thinner than she had been, and there were faint smudges beneath her eyes from the sleepless nights.

"Thank you, Mr. Tate," she said.

"Here . . . sit right here." He fussed over her and then settled himself in his chair behind the desk and tilted it back, a wry gleam in his eye. "I heard about the Provost Court affair," he said straightforwardly and without apology or embarrassment. He grinned. "By God," he said, "but it was good to see somebody take them on and win!"

He said it with such exuberance Carrie found herself smiling for the first time in days. And she wondered briefly if this man would have given in and signed the loyalty oath against his own convictions, as so many had felt they must.

"Actually," he said, clearing his throat and becoming more businesslike, "I believe I have some welcome news for you."

"Oh?"

"You may not be aware of this—" he shuffled through the papers on his desk and pulled out a sheet—"but there is a banking operation in New Orleans now, known as the Free Labor Bank. It was established only recently at the instigation and with the backing of the Federals. It is, Miss Kingston, for Negroes only." He said it without the slightest embarrassment and peered over his spectacles with a sly grin on his face.

"I took the liberty," he went on, "of investigating this for you, and I am certain that we can get you a loan through them . . . if you want it."

Carrie could hardly believe what she was hearing. "Oh, of course I want it!" she said eagerly. "But . . . are you sure that I—?"

"That you qualify?"

She nodded.

"Well, the law says that any person known to have any Negro blood, no matter how small, is legally a Negro. To my way of thinking, that's a foolish notion. But in this case, a silly law is working to your advantage, and you may as well make use of it.''

Carrie sat there for a moment, still not sure she could believe it. It seemed so ironic that she had been unable to get a penny before, but now that it was known that her grandmother had been an octoroon, she was going to get the money she needed.

"How long will it take to get it?" she asked. "If the weather is good, I'd like to plant as early in the year as possible."

"Anytime," Tate said. "I've made the arrangements, but you'll have to go to the bank to sign the initial papers, then the monies will be transferred here to me. I'll be happy to escort you over there if you like . . . any day but today. I have appointments right through the afternoon."

"Oh, that won't be necessary," Carrie said. "I'll get Prosper Durant to go with me."

"Very well. This is the man to see . . . and the address." He handed her the paper he had looked for earlier.

Carrie wanted to hug him. Not only because of the loan, but because he was the only person yet who hadn't treated her as if she had some dreadful disease. She started to thank him, but he waved it aside and walked her to the door as he always did.

"You know, Miss Kingston," he said, "I know I've said this before, but I want to say it again. My Uncle Rhymer thought the world of your daddy."

Carrie gave him her hand. "Thank you for saying it now, Mr. Tate," she said, her throat tightening.

Outside, Lafitte was waiting with the buggy, and as he helped her in, Carrie had a sudden impulse to go ahead to the Free Labor Bank at once. There was no use at all, she told herself, in putting it off until another day. The sooner she signed the papers, the sooner she'd get the money. She gave Lafitte the address, and he swung up and clucked to the horse.

The buggytop was up to shield her from the sun, but she still had a good view of the bustling streets as they rode along, the inevitable mule-drawn drays heading toward the riverfront with the wagons and carriages. A street peddler sang his wares. "Flo-wers . . . lovely flo-wers . . ." Carrie saw two pretty women with skin the color of rich caramel making their way across the street, and she heard them speaking gombo, that ripe patois, syllables round and smooth as melting butter.

Had Madeleine Tristesse ever spoken gombo? she wondered.

After a few blocks, Lafitte pulled the buggy up in front of a rundown-looking building with a wide, wooden covered porch in front. Green shades at the windows were all the way up. A Negro man in a straw hat leaned against one of the porch posts. Another sat with his back against the building wall, whittling a soft piece of wood. They eyed Carrie curiously.

"Would you like me to go inside with you, Miss Carrie?" Lafitte asked as he helped her down.

"No, thank you, Lafitte. You wait here," she said.

Inside it took a moment for her eyes to adjust. Even with the shades rolled all the way to the top of the windows, there still wasn't enough light with the porch overhang, and a gas lamp burned on a wall beside the desk at which a light-skinned Negro sat. Three Negro men and a woman sat waiting on a bench along the wall. They looked up in obvious surprise at the sight of Carrie, their faces settling into patterns of sullen wariness.

"Can I help you, Miss?" the man behind the desk asked.

"Yes," she said hesitantly, beginning to wonder if it had been such a good idea to come alone. She went to stand in front of him. "There are some papers here that I need to sign . . . for a loan," she added as he looked at her skeptically. "My name is Carrie Kingston."

"Umm," he grunted. He was heavy-lidded and deliberate, but he regarded her curiously. "I'll have to ask Mr. Mason," he said.

"Yes, that's the man I'm supposed to see," Carrie said quickly.

"He's with someone now." He jerked his head toward a closed door nearby. "Just have a seat."

Carrie went to the far end of the bench and sat down.

The minutes dragged by, and the silence in the room was deafening, not even the shifting of a boot or the scratch of a pen. Carrie could feel them all looking at her, but she sat there with her head high, looking straight toward the window. She could see Lafitte and the buggy through the streaked panes.

Before long the door opened, and a startlingly black man came out, papers clutched along with his hat against a yellow waistcoat. He cast a bemused look at Carrie and hurried out.

The man at the desk stepped to the door, which had been left partially ajar, exchanged a few quick and unintelligible words with whoever was in the office and then turned back.

"You can go in now, Miss Kingston," he said. Carrie heard a muttered curse from a disgruntled man who'd been waiting his turn. "You only have to sign a paper," the clerk added for his benefit, but the mutterings only increased, and Carrie fled through the doorway.

The office she entered was flooded with light from the windows, and a small fair man with thinning hair squinted at her from behind his desk. He didn't stand up.

"Mr. Mason?" she said.

He nodded perfunctorily. "You're the one Tate contacted me about," he said shortly. "If you'll sign here, and here," he indicated the places on the yellow sheets of paper, dipping a long pen into the inkwell and passing it to her.

She hesitated. "Shouldn't I read—"

"Look, do you want the loan or not?" he said. "There are people waiting out there."

She swallowed hard. "Yes," she said, "yes, I do." She signed quickly. "Mr. Tate didn't say how much money."

"It's written right there," Mason said.

She looked where he'd pointed and saw the figure $2,500. All right, she thought. She could make do with that.

"That's all that's needed," he said with a thin smile. "You can contact Mr. Tate and draw on the money within a day or so."

"Thank you," she said stiffly.

"Don't mention it." He was already shoving the papers into a file by his desk and reaching for something else.

She headed for the door, her lips pressed tightly together. She had never been treated quite that way before, as if she weren't a person worthy of direct attention, but she had the money. She could go home now . . . home to Kingston's Landing. And that was what she needed most.

She hurried into the dim waiting room and turned toward the door only to find her way blocked by the three men who had been sitting along the wall. They confronted her silently, spread out just enough so that she couldn't get past them on either side. The woman who still sat on the bench looked on impassively.

Carrie's heart started to pound as she looked into the hostile black faces, and she glanced nervously back toward the mulatto clerk, who seemed to have become terribly busy all of a sudden. He had his head bent low as if studying something in one of the desk drawers.

"Excuse me . . ." she said, but none of the men moved, and she caught the blazing anger, the resentment in their eyes. She could feel the sudden perspiration at the hollow of her neck, in her palms.

"I don't know what you doin' here, lady," the man in the middle said. His face was rough, a crescent-shaped scar curved above one eye.

Despite her fear, she was surprised to realize that she understood. To them, she was white, and she was not wanted in this place that was supposed to be *theirs* . . . a place that had taken them so long to get. She could feel the pent-up rage, the pain of a hundred years beating at her.

"I . . . I," she began, trying to think of what she could say to them, but suddenly the door was flung open behind them. Carrie looked up, and her breath came out in a small rush of air. Solomon stood there, his head barely clearing the doorframe, his face like some wonderfully carved piece of ebony.

He was dressed in a well-fitting gray suit, soft white shirt open at the collar, and he stood still for a moment, his eyes flickering from Carrie to the men and then back again. It was as if his presence had brought with it a kind of current into the room, and the woman on the bench moaned softly.

The three men, seeing who he was, made way for him quickly.

He moved in from the doorway, and his glance took in the mulatto at the desk, who was watching with rapt attention now, and the woman on the bench, and then came back to the three men who still stood in attitudes of sullen challenge.

He smiled. "Why don't you have a seat, brothers?" he said in that soft, deep voice of his, and after a long moment, one by one their eyes fell under his direct gaze, though not one of them moved toward the bench.

"Good day, Miss Kingston," Solomon said, as if nothing out of the ordinary were happening. "Are you on your way out?"

Carrie nodded. "Yes . . ." she finally managed.

He came slowly to stand beside her. "Then may I escort you?" he said, and offered his arm.

The air in the room seemed hot and heavy. She hesitated only a moment and then placed her hand in the powerful bend of his elbow, and together, with every eye on them, they walked to the door and onto the porch where the man in the straw hat and the whittler stared.

"Thank you," she whispered, her mouth dry as sawdust.

He made no reply, but she could feel that intensity that seemed to radiate from him, could feel the hard muscles ripple along his arm.

He took her all the way to the buggy and handed her up under the startled gaze of Lafitte, then he stood looking up at her, the dark fires burning in his eyes.

"I guess it's not easy for you, Miss Kingston," he said finally. "And I'm sorry for your trouble. But they—" his head tipped toward the place from which they'd just come—"have been niggers *all* their lives.

"Take her home, Lafitte," he said, and he brought his open hand down sharply against the horse's sleek flank.

What Carrie wanted desperately now was to get home to Kingston's Landing, and with most of the packing done, she expected to leave on the following day. She, Mattie, and Lafitte would take the afternoon packet upriver. But there was still one thing that she'd decided she must do before she left, and she had Lafitte drive her over to Prosper's.

He had just finished a class, and he made her comfortable in the solarium while he freshened up before they had coffee.

"I shall miss you, *ma chère* . . . but never fear, with the packets running again I shall be coming up often."

Carrie nodded. "And I'll have to come back down from time to time. There'll be bills to pay and supplies to get."

He took up the china pot and poured more coffee into each of their cups.

"However," Carrie said, as casually as she could, "before I

leave tomorrow there is one person I'd like to see. Do you think you could get a message to Rance Stewart that I'm leaving . . . and ask if he could call at the house?" She couldn't quite meet Prosper's eyes. "This evening . . . or in the morning would be fine."

She tried to be off-handed about it. She didn't want Prosper to guess how she had agonized over it. But she had finally decided that she couldn't leave New Orleans without seeing Rance . . . without thanking him for persuading General Banks to take an interest in her case. It hadn't taken her long to figure out that he had . . . and she was grateful.

"Of course," she added quickly, "if he's too busy . . ." She had started to say, "with his new wife," but she just couldn't get the words out. She made a great show of smoothing out the fingers of her white kid gloves on the seat beside her and glanced up to find Prosper looking at her in a very odd way.

"Carrie," he said quietly, "I'm afraid Rance has gone."

"Gone?" she said. "I don't understand." She tugged at the gloves again, her hands suddenly cold.

Prosper had the grace to look away and stir his coffee. "He was transferred. I do not know where he was sent. He was to report to Washington for his new orders."

"Oh . . . well," she said quickly, trying her best to hide her feelings, "I hadn't heard. I . . . I hope everything works out well for him." He was probably glad to go, she tortured herself. He had a new wife now, and he would want to put everything else behind him.

She managed to recover herself, and they spoke of other things, Carrie trying to find the words to thank Prosper for all he had done for her, he refusing to listen and assuring her that he would be over the next afternoon to see her off.

Carrie returned home to wander listlessly in the courtyard, stooping over a flower bed to pick a sprig of lemon verbena and inhale its fragrance. She thought of Rance . . . remembered his face, the clear gray eyes and the clefted chin. Her body remembered the feel of him, that wonderful, hard, man length of him.

She closed her eyes, and there was such an ache in her she didn't know if she could stand it. She'd been such a fool! If she hadn't behaved like an idiot in the beginning . . . before Nora.

But now he was gone, married and gone with his new wife . . . and it was too late.

"Miss Carrie . . ."

She jumped as she heard Mattie's voice, and she turned quickly, hoping her face hadn't given her away. "Yes, Mattie . . . what is it?"

"Miss Carrie, I . . . I got to talk with you."

Now that she looked closely, she could see that the girl had been crying, and she gestured toward the bench under the plum tree. "Come, let's sit down," she said. "Is something the matter?"

Mattie sat uncomfortably on the edge of the bench, her hands clasping and unclasping before her. "I don't know, Miss Carrie. I guess there is."

Carrie waited, Mattie rocking slightly, her hands still curled tightly in her lap.

"Solomon wants me to stay here with him," she said finally. "He says . . ."—Mattie looked off toward the old brick wall and the vines that trailed along it—"that nobody belongs to anybody anymore except their own selves, Miss Carrie."

They were quiet, and Mattie began to cry again, making small hiccupping sounds as the tears rolled slowly down her cheeks.

"Don't cry, Mattie," Carrie said, though she could feel a lump in her own throat threatening to choke her.

"I don't know what to do," Mattie cried. "He says . . . that you can't stop me."

"No," Carrie said softly, "I don't suppose I could."

"But if you tell me not to, Miss Carrie . . . I don't know if I can!" Mattie cried harder, and Carrie put her arms around her, trying to comfort her.

"Oh, Mattie . . . Mattie," she said, remembering how those men had made way for Solomon at the bank. There was a kind of power about him that was frightening. He was a natural leader . . . and heaven alone knew where that might take him. "He's unpredictable . . . dangerous!"

Mattie snuffed, nodded, smiling through her tears. "I know it," she said. "He's my man."

Carrie couldn't hold back her own tears any longer, and the two of them embraced again, both of them crying. There was a time, Carrie thought, when she would have felt she had the right answer to everything. Now she wasn't so sure anymore. She only knew that she had been fool enough to lose Rance . . . and she didn't want Mattie to make the same mistake.

"Then I just guess you better go to him," she said, and the two of them laughed and cried, hugging each other again, the way they had when they were little girls.

"Oh, Lord," Mattie said after a moment, wiping at her eyes, "what in the world are you goin' to tell Mama?"

Carrie took out her own handkerchief. "I'll make her understand," she promised.

𝒮 25 ⧫

CHLOE'S WORN FACE SET ITSELF INTO LINES OF DISBELIEF "What you mean, Mattie ain't comin' home, Miss Carrie? Who is this Solomon?" she demanded.

Carrie tried to explain about Solomon . . . that he was fast becoming the leader among the great numbers of slaves who had fled to the Yankees and freedom in New Orleans. She didn't add that he was currently preaching that those who had remained loyal should desert their masters now. It wouldn't have helped his cause with Chloe, who was as resistant to change as many a white Southerner.

"I don't like the sound of it," she grumbled. "When we ever goin' to see her again?"

"She'll be coming for visits. Chloe," she added gently, "she loves him."

"Lord, Lord . . ." Chloe wiped a tear away with the corner of her apron. "Miss Suzy run off with a scalawag, Mist' George

Pierre gone I don't know where, and Mattie takin' up with someone that don't know his place . . ." She shook her head sadly, but the misery reflected in her eyes seemed to lighten just slightly as she looked at Carrie. "Thank God *one* of my babies has come home," she said.

And as the days and weeks passed, Carrie began to know who she was again. She rode through the lush fields on Majestic, skirting the bayous where great flocks of birds fed and the waters teemed with fish and slow-moving turtles, the mudbanks thick with crayfish holes. She walked along the river, sometimes sitting for hours under the spreading limbs of one of the giant trees that clung to the edges of that mighty stream, feeling the power of the current and the richness of the land as if it were a part of her very bones.

Her only regret was Suzy. Other than that, she knew she had done the right thing. Whatever it cost her, she would pay. And the thing that sustained her most was the realization that some of the people she loved most were of Negro blood. Papa, Chloe, Prosper, Mattie. Society could, and would, put its own premium on her, but she would not let anyone make her ashamed of sharing the blood of such people. Whatever burden her father had carried, she could carry, too.

Prosper came for Christmas, and then in January Carrie went down to New Orleans briefly, accompanied by Justice. Together with Prosper, they hired the laborers she would need for the upcoming season.

While she was there, she ran into Seth Morrison on the street and learned the sad news that J. D. had been captured by the Federals and was in a prison camp somewhere in Ohio. She grieved over it. She might not be in love with J. D., but in many ways he had been like a brother to her.

She also went to see Mattie.

"Miss Carrie!" Mattie shrieked, her pretty face alight with pleasure. She ushered Carrie into the small, rough-lumber shack, which was one of many that had sprung up near the old Congo Square. The two rooms were scrubbed spotless. There was a chipped bowl of flowers on the table, and a makeshift bookcase in the corner held a dozen or so books. "Come right in here!"

she said, drawing Carrie to one of a pair of straight-backed chairs and quickly putting water on the stove for coffee.

Carrie only had to look at her to know that she was all right. There was a bloom about her, a contentment. She had stopped wearing the kerchief, that badge of servitude, and her close-cropped curls molded to the shape of her lovely head.

"Mattie, you're beautiful," Carrie said, and the girl's wide and generous mouth curved in a soft smile.

"If that's the truth," she said, "it's because I'm happy, Miss Carrie. Happy with Solomon . . . and happy doin' what we're doin'."

"Is he . . . doing well?"

"Oh, yes. More people come to him all the time. And they're listenin' when he tells them we got to be free, we got to learn, we got to work. We got to be ready 'cause someday our people goin' to vote . . . goin' to do everything anybody can. And"— her dark eyes sparkled—"I'm teachin' some of the children now."

"Teaching?"

Mattie nodded. "I'm showin' them how to read and write. Mist' Adam let me learn when I was little. And Solomon's so smart. He teaches me new things all the time."

They laughed together, and Mattie fixed coffee heavily laced with chicory to make it go farther, apologizing that there was no sugar. "Costs too much," she said.

They talked about home. Mattie wanted to know all about Chloe and Benjamin and promised to come for a visit before too long. "You tell them I will," she said.

"Do you need anything?" Carrie asked.

Mattie shook her head. "I got all in the world I want."

Back home, the weather remained good, and Carrie was pleased to get the planting started by the first of February. The hours were long and hard, but she still managed to keep up with the news of the rest of the country . . . though some of it was a week old by the time she read it. The packet stopped once a week to deliver the papers from New Orleans and whatever mail there was.

The pace of the war stepped up with spring. Lincoln named Ulysses S. Grant commanding general of all the Union Armies after his brilliant showing in the areas west of the Mississippi, and Grant promptly put one of his subordinates, William Tecumseh Sherman, in charge of the Western sector. It would be Sherman's job to go after Joe Johnston and his Rebs. Grant would take on Lee in Virginia.

And meanwhile the Confederates held. The tired and ragged legions—down to fat meat, crackers, and ground corn cobs for flour—held stubbornly, still determined to win.

One day toward the last of May when the sun was beginning to hint at the heat of the summer ahead, Carrie had come in for the noonday meal. Now she finished off her glass of cold buttermilk and went out onto the gallery nearest the garden to rest for a few more minutes before she went back out to the fields.

She sat in the old cypress swing hung from the ceiling beams, a faded pillow at her back, and thought with satisfaction of the morning's work. The cane was healthy and beautiful. With a little luck, Kingston's Landing would be sending good quality sugar down to New Orleans again come December.

She had gone at such a pace for weeks now that even taking this small time off in the middle of the day made her feel vaguely guilty. But she knew that Big Josephus would see to things.

Josephus had been eager to come back to work at Kingston's Landing when he'd learned that she needed hands again, and knowing his capabilities, Carrie made him her foreman. He was paid six dollars a month instead of the four that the others got. He had brought his woman along with him, as some of the others had. Some even had children, and the quarters were beginning to come to life again.

Carrie supplied them with salt meat, beans, and flour, and each of them had his own vegetable plot and kept his own chickens. There was always enough milk for everyone.

With a day off each week, Carrie felt that the working conditions were fair, and some of them did work hard and seemed dependable. But then suddenly a whole family would be gone one morning without notice or reason. It still infuriated her, though she was beginning to take it more in stride.

"They're provin' to themselves they're free men," Justice insisted.

"But they could at least give us some warning," Carrie argued.

"They'll learn that after a while." Justice had looked off toward the river, his eyes squinted in the sunlight. "It takes some gettin' used to bein' a slave. And I guess it takes some gettin' used to bein' free, too."

Maybe so, Carrie thought now as she leaned back in the swing and enjoyed the gentle breeze on her face. A lot of things took some getting used to.

Her attention was caught by the whinny of a horse toward the front of the house, and she got up and walked around the corner of the gallery, wondering if Justice had decided to ride over today after all.

She circled the sweet olive brushes and caught sight of a big bay horse and rider. The man was just swinging down, his back to her, and it wasn't until he turned that she realized who it was.

"My God . . ." she said, "J. D.!"

He dropped the reins and came to her, doffing his slouch hat and giving her an awkward kiss that almost missed her mouth, laughing. "Hello, Carrie," he said.

"You're back." She took in the civilian clothes, the dark brown jacket and white shirt open at the throat.

"Yeah." He grinned.

"When?"

He shrugged. "Oh, two, three weeks now. I . . . I had some catching up to do."

There was a small silence, which Carrie ended quickly. She smiled and nodded. "I'm sure," she said, trying her best to put him at ease.

She saw the deep lines around his eyes, the ridges from nose to mouth that hadn't been there before. He was very thin, and somehow the new tan didn't quite hide the pallor. "I heard you'd been captured," she said. "Seth said they'd gotten word that you were in a prison camp somewhere in Ohio. It must have been . . . terrible for you."

He looked back toward his horse as if he were checking on the animal and then finally back to Carrie again. "I got exchanged.

That's what's important, I guess. And damned lucky, too. They aren't making many exchanges anymore."

"You gave your parole?"

"Yeah, I did," he said after a moment. And Carrie caught a glimpse of things buried deep in those blue eyes that were too awful to talk about. She reached out and took his hand.

"I was sitting on the gallery by the garden," she said. "Come around with me, and I'll go see if Chloe has some more of that cold buttermilk left."

"Sounds good. I'll just go unsaddle my horse and put him in the barnlot, then I'll meet you there."

And a little later, as Carrie was putting the tray she'd prepared for J. D. on the old cypress table there on the gallery, she considered how greatly things had changed. Time was, not so long ago, when four or five young boys would have been around to take a visitor's horse immediately. And she, if she were greeting a guest, would have been in her best silk dress, maneuvering her hoop skirts through the doorways and serving lemonade sweet with sugar. And cookies.

She laughed softly, aware of her worn riding skirt and much mended shirtwaist, her rough hands.

"What's funny?" J. D. said, coming up on the gallery.

"Nothing," she said. "I'm just glad you're back home. And safe, J. D."

Benjamin had gone fishing, and there had been fried fish for lunch. Carrie had put some on a plate with potatoes and a piece of cold cornbread, but it was the buttermilk that J. D. went to first.

"Have you heard the news from the east," he asked, after he'd finished half of it. He turned his attention to the food and started to eat slowly.

"No."

"Grant has moved on Lee. They met in a place in northern Virginia called the Wilderness. They say it's a wild stretch of land covered over with second-growth timber and brush. It lasted for days. Lot of casualties on both sides."

Whenever Carrie learned of a battle now, a small cold finger of dread touched her, and she wondered if Rance might have been there. If only she could just know where he was, know that

346

he was safe. That would be enough. But Prosper had had no word from him.

With an effort, she brought herself back to what J. D. was saying.

"Jeb Stuart and his cavalry boys were covering Lee's flank. Stuart was killed."

"Oh, my . . ." was all Carrie could say. It had often been declared that the dashing Stuart and his men could make the Yankee cavalry look like ploughboys astride mules.

"It's a terrible loss for the Confederacy," J. D. said. "But Lee's still holding Grant off of Richmond. Grant's digging in . . . but Lee's holding."

He talked some more about the war, as if, Carrie thought, that would put a cushion between them, would delay for a little while longer the inevitable things they must say to one another.

"You didn't eat much," she said finally.

"No," he said ruefully. "I think I'm going to have to learn how again." He made a little gesture as if he'd meant it to be a joke. "Tell me, have you heard from George Pierre?"

Carrie nodded. She had gotten a letter from her brother no more than two weeks before. "He's in San Francisco," she said. "He's hoping to get a teaching position soon, but right now he's working in a dry goods store and is doing well."

J. D. shook his head. "George Pierre in California," he said. "It's hard to believe."

"Yes."

"You'll give me his address?"

"Of course," she said.

He got up, walked to the edge of the gallery, and leaned against one of the square, brick columns that supported the second-story gallery above, looking out over the garden and the stretch of land to the barns and the stable. His horse was grazing contentedly in the lot.

"How are your parents?" Carrie asked.

He shifted his position so that he could look at her, his back against the column now. "I guess they're as well as anyone else." There was a terrible sadness in his voice. "Pa can hardly get into his own distillery. The agent this . . . this Canfield left in charge has everything so tied up. Jesus, I don't know how they could ever have been so taken in! Canfield practically stole the place from them!"

"I know," Carrie said.

"I . . . I understand that Suzy ran off and married him." J. D. seemed embarrassed.

"It's true," Carrie said, fighting the quick tears that were always just beneath the surface when she thought about her sister. "She did that because of me . . . because of what I said in Provost Court. I'm sure your folks have told you everything."

Those shoulders, which had once been so broad and now, incomprehensibly, looked so fragile, hunched together. J. D. shoved his hands into his pockets and turned away again.

He was silent for a long time, that thick thatch of blond hair—perhaps the only thing about him that hadn't changed—ruffling gently in the breeze.

"Do you remember," he said finally, "that time we took a picnic basket and went over that way"—he pointed toward the river—"way down there beyond the sugar house and the mill? Let's see, we had chicken . . . chicken, was it? And cake. Chloe's burnt sugar cake."

"I remember," Carrie said.

He reached in his coat pocket and took out something, then came back and sat across from her, his hand held out. The emerald ring lay in his palm.

"I mean for you to have this . . . if you want it," he said.

They were quiet for a long moment. One of Justice's old hound dogs bayed in the distance. Carrie drew a long breath and shook her head slowly.

"No, J. D." Her voice was gentle. "It was right for me to give it back to your parents. And right for me to refuse it now."

"Carrie. It doesn't matter to me about . . . about—"

"J. D.," she interrupted, "there are laws that would make it impossible. Whites can't marry someone of color. Besides," she rushed on, knowing it was too easy to leave it at that, "I would have given the ring back even if I hadn't learned about Papa's mother."

His eyes narrowed. "Why?" he said, the muscles working along his thin jaw.

"Because I'd come to realize that I loved you like a brother . . . no other way."

He sat there silently absorbing that. Carrie could feel the pain in him, but she knew it was not without relief. And it was all right. She understood. She knew that it would take him a long time to come to terms with all that had happened to him. He needed no further complications now.

After a while, he put the ring back in his pocket and cocked his head to one side in a mannerism that reminded her of the old J. D. "Is there someone else, Carrie?" he asked, the blue eyes squinting ever so slightly, a deep ridge between his eyebrows.

She nodded.

He looked away. "Who is he?"

She didn't answer.

"Where is he?"

"I don't know," she said.

They were both quiet then, thinking their own private thoughts, and the breeze wafted the scent of lemon verbena from the garden.

"Listen," Carrie said, breaking the silence at last. "Why don't we ride out, and I'll show you all the work we've been doing? The cane is beautiful! Just like in the old days . . . except not as many acres," she cautioned him, laughing.

The stretched, tight lines of his face seemed to relax as he looked at her and smiled. "Yeah," he said. "I think I'd like that."

Carrie stretched out her toes to the end of the copper tub and delighted in the warm water, sliding down to let it lap at her breasts and the back of her neck. She didn't care if it got her hair wet. She was going to wash that anyway. But first she wanted to lose herself in this luxury and relax as she hadn't for weeks.

Since Lafitte and Benjamin were away in New Orleans getting supplies, she had carried the hot water herself all the way from the summer kitchen to the brick-floored bathroom in the back of the house, Chloe scolding throughout that it was too heavy for her. But it hadn't been. She had learned that she could do a great many things that she'd once thought she couldn't. And she was determined to enjoy this respite before the sugar making began.

Once the cutting started, there would be no time for anything as lovely as a long soak in the tub.

She had given the workers a few days off to be with their families, but everything was ready.

It was a complicated process, and the thought of trying it scared her a little. It would have been impossible without Justice. But he had made sugar for years with her father, and she knew that with his help, she could do it.

Once it began, the process would continue right through to the end, the furnaces going night and day without ceasing until the last batch had been struck and golden drops of molasses gathered in the cisterns under the hogsheads of draining sugar.

She smiled just thinking about it. Chloe could make cakes and pies to her heart's content. And molasses cookies.

She soaped herself leisurely all over, her hair, too, and then rinsed it carefully. She'd saved two full buckets of water just for that. Once she was finished, she stepped out onto a small cotton rug, pulling the plug in the bottom of the tub so that the water could run out and into the drain in the brick floor where it would be carried well away from the house into a gravel bed.

Dried off, she dressed quickly, wrapping her wet hair in a towel, and then went out to sit beneath the arbor that covered part of the walkway between the summer kitchen and the house to let the warm breeze dry the chestnut tresses. The sunlight was pleasantly dappled through the bougainvillea that trailed along the lattices above her, purple blossoms peeking through. A bee explored the violet depths of each flower, then flew away.

Her hair finally dry, she was brushing it carefully to get all the tangles out when Chloe came to the back door, waving excitedly.

"Mist' Prosper's out front!" she called. "Just pulled up in his carriage."

Surprised and delighted, Carrie quickly followed Chloe through the house, tying the errant tresses back with a ribbon as she went, her cheeks flushed a pretty pink.

"Prosper!" she burst out as she came through the doorway onto the wide front gallery. "What a pleasant surprise!"

Prosper had just gotten down from the driver's seat of the carriage, and he came with his bounding step up onto the gallery in an instant and enfolded Carrie in an exuberant hug. "Carrie . . . you look beautiful, *ma petite!* Simply beautiful!"

Carrie grinned at him. "Whyever did you bring that big old carriage?" she said. "Is something wrong with the buggy?"

His face sobered. "No," he said. "I thought the riding might be easier in this."

Carrie looked at him, puzzled. She had never known Prosper to be concerned about such things. "You're not ill, are you?" she asked anxiously.

"No, of course not. It is just that . . ." He hesitated as if he were trying to find the right words. "You will understand after—" His face set into serious lines. "There is someone in the carriage who would like to see you, *ma chère.*"

He took Carrie's arm and led her to the big black carriage. The window curtains were partially closed so that she still could not see inside, and her mind was racing with questions. Was it Abby? Had something happened to Seth . . . or J. D.? Rance? It seared through her, made her heart start to pound. No, of course not. Rance wouldn't wait inside the carriage like that.

Prosper opened the door and then stepped back, as if not wanting to intrude, and she peered into the dim interior, her eyes focusing on the pale, slight figure sitting in the far corner, slight except for the enormous pregnant belly, which could not be hidden even by her crinoline.

"Suzy . . ." she whispered. "Oh, my God . . . Suzy, honey . . ."

Susannah looked at Carrie solemnly out of eyes that seemed exhausted and dulled in the sallow face, the once bouncing curls hanging lifelessly. Her thin hands rested atop her stomach, white fingers twisting a handkerchief into endless knots. "Can I come home, Carrie?" she said in a voice that was flat and infinitely tired. "Can I please come home?"

Tears were streaming down Carrie's face, but she was laughing at the same time. "Oh, Suzy!" she cried. "Chloe, it's Suzy!" she called over her shoulder, and then she was climbing up into the carriage and hugging her sister again and again.

"Here, let's get you out of here and into the house," she said.

Prosper helped Susannah down, and Chloe, who'd been waiting impatiently, clasped Susannah's swollen body to her, enfolded her in those strong arms. "Thank the good Lord you done come home!"

It was clear that Susannah was very tired after the trip from New Orleans. Chloe bundled her off upstairs to her old room to get her undressed and tucked between cool, lavender-scented sheets, then came down the stairs grumbling to herself.

"Wish we had some tea. That be good for that child." But lacking that, she went off to make some rich chicken broth.

Carrie and Prosper spoke privately on the south gallery.

"Did she tell you anything?" Carrie asked him. "Where has she been all these months?"

"No." Prosper shook his head sadly. "She only said that someone, she would not say who, helped her to get back to New Orleans, and she came directly to me. I wanted her to see Baptiste Rambeau. He's the doctor who lives just down the block from the salon."

Carrie nodded.

"She refused. She insisted that all she wanted to do was come home."

In the days that followed, it almost broke Carrie's heart to see her little sister so silent and pale, walking through the house like a ghost. And it was touching to see how she tried to make herself useful. She was forever trying to help, even attempting things that were clearly too much for her in her condition. Chloe or Carrie were forever taking laundry baskets filled with clothes away from her or scolding her about being on her feet too long.

"You got to rest, and you got to eat more," Chloe chided. "You don't want to hurt that baby, do you?"

Susannah shook her head no.

She would talk very little about the things that had happened to her in the year she'd been away, except she did tell Carrie that she would have come home a lot sooner except that Beau wouldn't let her.

"There . . . was a woman," she said hesitantly. "She was with us. She didn't like me at first . . . but later Monique was good to me, Carrie."

Monique! Memories beat at Carrie of the night on Rampart Street and the exotic, beautiful Monique. She remembered the glint of tears in her eyes as Beau had sent her away. What it must have been like, Carrie thought, for poor little Suzy all these months . . . with Beau flaunting one woman to the other.

"Monique helped me," Susannah said. "She gave me enough money for passage back to New Orleans. I don't know what Beau might do to her if he ever found out."

"And were you . . ."—Carrie was reluctant to ask, but she needed to know—"were you and Beau married, Suzy?"

Susannah closed her eyes and leaned back in her chair, her face drained and looking far older than her eighteen years. "No," she whispered.

"Thank heaven!" Carrie said.

Susannah looked up at her in surprise, green eyes haunted. "But, Carrie," she said softly, "my baby . . . my baby won't have a name!"

"Oh, yes it will, Suzy," Carrie said. "That baby will be a Kingston!"

The greatest risk to a planter at cutting time was that the weather would turn unseasonably cold and ruin the cane in the fields before it could be cut and carted off to the mill. But October continued to be perfect, the breeze balmy, and the sun glinted off the cane knives as workers severed the thick cane stalks with one quick stroke. The blades whirred as they sliced through the air.

Carts waited at the edges of the fields, the horses plodding back and forth to deliver the cut cane to the mill where it was put through giant iron rollers to squeeze out the sweet juice. After removing the pith and rind, the juice was poured into the first of the big iron kettles—six feet across, it was called the *grande*— and the cooking began.

There were four kettles in all, and the syrup would be watched carefully and, at the proper stages, be ladled from one to the other in buckets swung on long poles until that moment when a batch, or "charge" was ready to be "struck," turned into shallow wooden tanks for granulation. It was a precarious time. If the charge was struck too soon or too late, the sugar could be ruined.

Justice had the last word on it. He would dip a long-handled wooden spoon into the bubbling mixture and draw it up, watching with an expert eye the way the golden syrup dripped back into the kettle, spinning a thread, and he would either shake his head or call out, "Strike it!" in which case a cheer would go up from the workers.

Big Josephus rode back and forth from the fields to the mill, checking, keeping the cane moving. Carrie was everywhere.

At first, she thought she would faint from the heat and the strong smell inside the sugar house, but after a few days she grew used to it. She even got used to the men working half-naked, stripped to the waist, cotton trousers cut off to mid-thigh.

The women from the quarters pitched in, making great pots of gumbo, skillets of cornbread, and fried side meat or chicken, which they brought right to the men wherever they were working. Sometimes when Carrie went outside the sugar house to check on the feeding of wood into the furnace or the pace of the grinding, she would find Susannah there with the other women, handing out graniteware cups of hot coffee or cold buttermilk.

"Suzy, honey," she'd scold, "you shouldn't be out here. You should be at home resting."

Susannah, her stomach enormous, her hair tied back to reveal the thinness of her small face, would brush aside her sister's objections. "I'm fine, Carrie," she'd say. "Really I am. I like helping. It gives me something to do."

But then one day, about two weeks into the grueling routine, Lafitte came into the sugar house, looking out of place in his worn black suit, making his way carefully among the sweating workers to find Carrie, who was standing with Justice at the last kettle.

"Miss Carrie." Lafitte stepped over the long-poled skimmer in his way. "Miss Carrie," he called again, raising his voice over the noise.

Carrie knew at once that only something important would have brought him. "Lafitte, what is it?"

"Miss Carrie, Chloe says you had better come. Miss Susannah's time . . ." He left the rest unsaid as Carrie gave a small cry and turned to Justice.

"Go," Justice said. "We'll manage here."

At the house, Carrie found Susannah in her room, pillows at her back propping her to a half-sitting position in the bed. She

354

was in a clean white cotton gown, her hair tied back with a pink ribbon. Carrie was struck by the tight, scared look about her eyes.

"You all right?" she asked anxiously.

Susannah nodded, and Chloe, who was hovering near the bed, gave Carrie a reassuring look.

"Her water broke about two hours back, Miss Carrie. But those pains are comin' right along. Goin' fast for a first baby. Looks like this child might be in a hurry to get in the world." Chloe grinned.

"What can I do to help?" Carrie asked. She had never witnessed a birth before and was a little frightened herself.

Before Chloe could answer, Susannah's body arched slightly, her head drawing back, breath sucking in audibly, and Chloe leaned over her, pulling back the light sheet and pressing a practiced hand to the distended abdomen. "That's good . . . good . . ." She nodded as the pain stretched out. "I think we goin' to have you start pushin' here before long, honey."

After what seemed a long time to Carrie, Susannah relaxed, her breath coming out in a rush. There was a fine sheen of perspiration on her face. Carrie went to the washstand in the corner, poured cool water from the pitcher into the bowl, and came back with a wet washcloth to pat over her sister's face.

"Oh, thank you," Susannah said, her voice still a little breathless from the pain. "That feels good."

"I'm goin' to go get some stuff we'll need," Chloe said. "You want anything, honey? How about a little sip of cold buttermilk?"

Susannah shook her head, and Chloe left the room.

Carrie sat on the side of the bed, the washcloth still in her hand. The room was hot, hardly a stirring of air coming through the open windows, and the stillness seemed almost unnatural after the constant noise of the sugar house, the clank of the mill as the rollers turned, the roar of the furnace.

"Carrie," Susannah said softly, "I'm scared."

Carrie clasped her sister's thin hand in hers and held it tightly. "I know," she said.

"But I want this baby. No matter who its father is."

There was something controlled in Susannah's soft voice. The

immature girl who had dimpled one minute and thrown temper
tantrums the next seemed gone forever, Carrie thought. And
there was something about that that broke her heart. Maybe Suzy
had needed to grow up, but the process had been so harsh, so
terrible for her that Carrie was afraid she'd never again be that
thoroughly captivating creature who had always endeared herself
to everyone.

"Oh, Suzy . . ." she burst out, near to tears, but she took a
firm grip on herself. This was no time for it. "Listen," she said,
"we all want this baby. And everything is going to be fine.
There's nobody any better than Chloe when it comes to babies.
She delivered *us!* Right here in this house."

A new pain seized Susannah, and she set her mouth in a thin
line, Carrie holding her hands until it was past.

They talked about the old days when Papa used to take them
all down to New Orleans on grand shopping sprees, and to the
confectioners' shops and the very best restaurants. And the pains
came intermittently, getting closer together with each one.

Carrie was relieved when Chloe came back, a whole washbasket
filled with linens on one hip, her doctoring satchel perched on
top.

"Pains comin' good?" she questioned as she put the basket on
the floor.

Susannah nodded, and just at that moment another one began.
Chloe attended closely, a pleased smile on her face as it ended.

"All right," she said. "I believe we about ready to get down
to some plain old hard work now, honey."

She pulled back the sheet to expose the lower part of Susannah's
body, and Carrie could see the bloody stains on the thick pad.

"Chloe?" she said.

"It's all right," the Negress reassured her. She quickly examined Susannah and then pulled the sheet back over the thin,
white legs. "Everything is just exactly the way it ought to be."

She took two large towels from the laundry basket and knotted
them securely to each of the head posts of the bed, bringing the
free ends to where Susannah could reach them. "There now,"
she said. "When the next pain comes, you hold on to these
'cause they goin' to help you to bear down. That's just what I

want you to do . . . bear down. We goin' to push that baby along with every pain now."

Susannah did as Chloe said, and in the next hour and a half, as the pains came harder and faster, great drops of sweat stood out on her face, and she moaned softly.

"Just hang on, Suzy, honey," Carrie encouraged her. "It won't be too much longer." She said that, though in reality she had no idea how much longer it would be, but Chloe nodded her head in agreement, and Carrie felt better.

"I'm thirsty," Susannah said. And Carrie poured a glass of water from the decanter on the nightstand and helped her drink, but in a moment another pain hit her, and her lips drew back as she arched upward.

"Push, honey . . . push hard . . . that's right," Chloe said as she bent over the bed, dark hands probing between Susannah's thighs as gently as she could, but the girl cried out and twisted, her hair, which had come loose from the ribbon, lying wet with sweat across the pillow case. "I know it hurts, honey . . . I know," Chloe crooned.

Carrie bit at her lip, hardly able to stand seeing her sister in so much pain. It was almost a relief for Chloe to send her for a bucket of hot water, which she had boiling in the summer kitchen.

"Best you hurry," Chloe called after her.

Carrie did.

It was stifling in the room when she returned. She could feel her own camisole clinging damply to her body, and once she'd put the bucket of steaming water by the washstand, she fanned Susannah with a linen towel, stopping now and again to bathe her face with cool water.

The pains were so close together now, there hardly seemed any respite from them, and Susannah gasped and panted as she arched upward once again.

Chloe pressed on the heaving abdomen, and her cry mingled with Susannah's. "I can see the baby's head! Oh, push hard, honey!"

"Suzy!" Carrie could hardly contain her excitement as she saw the crown of the baby's head clearly visible between

Susannah's legs. "Oh, Suzy, I wish you could see! You've almost done it!"

The contraction receded, and Susannah lay limp and panting. Then another seized her almost immediately, and as she gave a high, thin cry, the baby's head emerged. She hardly paused, but continued to pant, rising into a half-crouch to push, sweat streaming down her face.

"Take my hands," Carrie said. "I'll help you . . ."

Susannah's eyes rolled, her mouth opened in a wide grimace, and then she clamped her teeth shut to push, grunting with the effort, tugging mightily at Carrie's hands. A scream wrenched from her as Chloe skillfully freed one of the baby's shoulders, and then suddenly the slippery little body came through. Susannah gave one final cry, her breath coming out in a rush, and slumped back onto the pillow.

"Oh, Suzy!" Carrie said, unable to take her eyes from the blood-streaked baby.

"Look at this! Just look at this baby!" Chloe exulted as she pulled the baby up by its heels. But before she could give it the usual smack on the buttocks, the infant gave an outraged cry, which gave way to lusty howling, its tiny face red, its arms moving in and out. Chloe laughed happily as she laid it on its mother's belly. "We got us a little girl! Thank the good Lord!"

Susannah was leaning up to see the baby better, and tears were running down Carrie's cheeks. She was quite sure she had never seen anything so beautiful in her life. She turned to say something to Susannah and saw her sister smiling, her face transformed, her eyes shining as she looked down at her daughter. It was the first time Suzy had smiled since she came back.

After the afterbirth had passed, and both the baby and Susannah had been sponged off with warm water, and clean bed linens put beneath them, Carrie sat by the bed and watched her new niece in wonder. She lay in the crook of her mother's arm, wrapped in a soft blanket, the light fuzz of hair dry now, eyes closed. The tiny mouth pursed, and both Carrie and Susannah laughed with delight.

"Have you decided on a name for her?" Carrie asked.

"I think I have." With a gentle forefinger, Susannah nudged one of the tiny fists and watched it uncurl.

'What?''

"I'm going to call her Molly Caroline," Susannah said. "After Mama . . . and you, Carrie."

26

MOLLY CAROLINE WAS A HEALTHY AND BEAUTIFUL BABY. A deep dimple marked each chubby cheek, and she was angelic with her tawny ringlets and eyes that promised to be as green as her mother's. Everyone on the plantation agreed that she was precocious for five months old since she could already sit alone and clap her fat little hands on cue.

Carrie adored her niece, and now as she pressed a piece of seed potato into the soft rich earth of the vegetable garden, she looked down to the far end of the patch where the child sat on a quilt and played happily in the shade of a sweetgum tree. Susannah laid off rows with a hoe close by, turning now and again to smile at her daughter.

Carrie, down on her knees, covered the potato over, firming the dirt around it with her hands. It was good to see Susannah looking better. That pinched look was gone from her face, and she seemed a little more like her old self . . . though it was clear that she would never be that bubbly, young girl again. But she did delight in Molly Caroline. The child was the center of her life. And she seemed content now at Kingston's Landing.

Benjamin came along the row toward Carrie, a gunnysack filled with cut-up seed potatoes slung over his shoulder. He replenished the supply in her basket. "It's goin' pretty good,

Miss Carrie,'' he said, squinting down over the area they'd already planted. "Be some good eatin' here."

Carrie grinned at him.

He surveyed the entire plot. "With the early peas over there, do you want beans back that way?"

"I think so, Benjamin. Don't you?"

He nodded and went on down to where Molly Caroline sat, poking her gently in her round little belly with one dark finger, which made her squeal with pleasure. She loved everyone on the place, but Benjamin was a particular favorite since he would toss her high in the air and then cuddle her close to his big chest and sing to her in a deep, rich baritone.

Carrie watched for a minute as the child waved her arms and gurgled at Benjamin, who laughed, and to Molly Caroline's obvious enjoyment, he counted off the bare toes of one fat little foot, touching them each in turn. Then he went back to his task, getting down on his hands and knees to push potatoes into the rows that Susannah was laying off.

Carrie went back to her own work, enjoying the heat of the sun and the feel of the earth between her fingers. With the cane all planted and shooting up, she had a little free time to help with the garden. There was still a lot to do, though the green onions, the early salad greens, and the cabbages were already up. Chloe wanted sweet potatoes and okra. And it would soon be time for tomatoes. It was a lot of work, but at least they would be sure of eating. The vegetable patch, along with fish and shrimp from the river, and a little saltmeat and flour from town, would see them through.

Sometimes Carrie wondered if the bad times would ever end. Things went from bad to worse with the war. Only a few weeks after Molly Caroline's birth, the news had come that Sherman had burned Atlanta, and the whole South grieved. Atlanta . . . that beautiful city. Carrie remembered it. Her father had taken her along on a business trip once, long ago. She remembered gracious hotels and restaurants . . . and Peachtree Street. She could still see the carriages and beautifully dressed ladies and gentlemen.

Not content, the Union general had begun his march to the sea then, his army laying waste to everything in its path. More than sixty-thousand men spread fifty miles wide had ravaged the countryside all the way to Savannah and then up toward Charleston. The South had been gutted. And only the diehards believed that the Confederates could win now. Even though the gallant Lee and his ragtag army still held out against Grant.

Carrie thought of Rance more often than she wanted to. She remembered that his family plantation was near Charleston and wondered what had happened to it. But most of all, she wondered where he was . . . and she prayed to God that he was safe.

She would never see him again. She had accepted that. But it did not stop her from loving him. And there were times his face came to her so clearly it was as if he were right before her. There were times she would wake up in the dark heat of the night, imagining for a moment that she could feel his touch, memories torturing her.

She shook off those thoughts now, turning her face up to the sun and then looking off toward the barns and the river in the distance. She could see the edges of the south acreage, see the greening as the cane shoots pushed upward. This was her world and her life, and she loved it. Susannah and Molly Caroline were safe. She had sold her sugar crop and paid off most of her loans. Of course, she had just had to borrow more, but that was to be expected. She didn't ask any more than this.

Big Josephus, astride the sorrel gelding he favored, came plodding along the far end of the garden. He called a greeting to Carrie, and she walked down to talk to him.

"I got a crew out workin' on the drainage ditches, Miss Carrie, just in case we get some early hard rains. And we cultivatin' through the cane rows, keepin' one step ahead of that coco grass."

"That's fine, Josephus," Carrie said. She had come to depend a good deal on this big man.

"I thought, if it was all right with you, I'd put a few boys to fixin' on that barn roof today. I seen one hole in there you could run a man's hand through."

"That's a good idea," Carrie said. "And, as we can, we ought to see about repairing some of the cabins in the quarters. Bessie, Willie's woman, told me that her place is leaking now."

"I'll send somebody down there this afternoon."

Carrie had hardly gotten back to her place in the row when she looked up to see a rider emerge from a clump of sweetgum trees far to the left of her. The horse was coming at a brisk canter, and she straightened and squinted under the brim of her straw hat, trying to see who the well-dressed figure was. Could it be J. D.? she wondered.

She watched for a full minute, waiting until she could make out the features, and as she did, her heart froze in her chest. The man on the horse was Beau Canfield.

She looked quickly to where Susannah worked. She hadn't seen him. "Suzy . . ." Carrie called out. "Suzy, get Molly Caroline!"

Susannah looked up, puzzled. "What?"

"Get Molly Caroline!" Carrie repeated, and just at that moment Susannah saw Beau. The hoe dropped from her hand. Even at this distance, Carrie could see the look of pure hatred that spread over her sister's face before she ran to pick up the baby.

Benjamin was aware that something was wrong, and he raised up frowning, moving closer to Susannah and the baby, his dark eyes fastened on the approaching rider.

"Benjamin . . . get them back to the house," Carrie called as she placed herself between them and Beau.

Benjamin hesitated, torn between his desire to protect Susannah and the baby and his reluctance to leave Carrie alone.

"Benjamin, hurry!" Carrie urged him. And when he saw that Josephus was heading back towards Carrie, he took the baby from Susannah and put his free arm around her. They hurried in the direction of the house, disappearing behind the thicket of bushes and wild honeysuckle vines.

Carrie deliberately went out to meet Beau, her heart pounding, and as he drew closer, she could see that he was riding a fine-blooded Arabian. The horse danced to a stop right in front of her.

Beau swept off his hat, that familiar grin on his face. "Well, well," he drawled, looking her up and down, taking in the faded old riding skirt and the patched shirtwaist, the earth-ringed nails and the smudge of dirt on one cheek, "are you down grubbing in the soil with all the other darkies now, Carrie?"

She felt the edges of her teeth grind against one another, but let the barb go by. "What are you doing here, Beau?" she said shortly.

He smoothed the lapels of his perfectly tailored jacket, touched a hand to the black stock. She hadn't seen anyone dressed so well in a long time.

"Just paying a neighborly call," he said. "You surely haven't forgotten that we are neighbors!"

Carrie hadn't forgotten that he owned the Gayerre plantation, but she had never thought to see him here. An overseer had run the place for him from the beginning.

"I can hardly imagine you settling for the country life, Beau," she said.

"Oh, but it's so peaceful here away from the city. Besides, there are certain attractions . . . such as my child."

Carrie suddenly felt cold in the heat of the day, but she glared at him. "You'd do best to rid your mind of any such ideas," she said firmly.

Beau glanced at Josephus, who had just come up, swinging down from his horse to plant his feet apart wide and stand like a black oak tree just in back of Carrie.

"Can I help you, Miss Carrie?" he said.

"Stay right there," Carrie directed, and Beau laughed.

"Good Lord, Carrie . . . you act as if I meant you some harm. I've only come about the baby. Surely a father has some rights."

"Don't talk to me about rights! You have no rights where Molly Caroline is concerned, Beau!" Carrie cut him off quickly.

"A girl!" He grinned. "Tell me, Carrie . . . does she look like me or her mother?"

"No rights at all," Carrie continued. "You and Susannah were never married, thank God. And Molly Caroline's birth was recorded in New Orleans—father unnamed. She's a Kingston, Beau. Molly Caroline Kingston. And you have no claim to her, legal or otherwise. Now I suggest you get off this property. And don't ever set foot on Kingston's Landing again."

"Carrie . . ." he chided, "you don't mean that."

Carrie's chin was high, her eyes unflinching. "I never meant anything more."

"Come now. I'm sure that Susannah will be anxious to see me . . . even if you're not."

"Escort Mr. Canfield off the plantation, Josephus," Carrie said coldly.

For the first time, Beau's face showed his anger. His nostrils flared slightly, and there was a small muscle that moved beneath his eye. He looked the big Negro up and down slowly and at last made Carrie a mocking bow. "It seems that you have the advantage, Carrie," he said. "Do give Susannah my love."

And with that, he turned his horse around and put him into a trot. Josephus, throwing Carrie a look, sprang up on his gelding and followed after him.

Carrie watched the two riders and heard Josephus give the piercing whistle he used to call workers to him. Two men on horseback came across the far field to fall in with the foreman behind Beau.

It was only then that she hurried to the house to find Susannah all but hysterical, clutching Molly Caroline to her and crying in a way that had set the usually good-natured baby to howling. Chloe was trying her best to get Susannah to give the child to her.

"Suzy, he's gone!" Carrie assured her sister. "Now let Chloe take Molly Caroline. There . . ." she said to the sobbing, red-faced baby as Susannah finally relinquished her hold. Chloe hugged her close, patting her little bottom and making soothing sounds.

"Don't take your eyes off her!" Susannah pleaded as Chloe took the baby out of the room.

"Don't you worry, honey," Chloe called back. "Ain't nobody goin' to get this baby away from me!"

Susannah was still weeping uncontrollably, and Carrie put her arm around her. "Don't worry, Suzy. Josephus is putting him off the place. He can't hurt you here."

It was nearly an hour before Josephus reported back to the house. "We followed him to the ferry, Miss Carrie," he said. "We saw him get on."

"Thank you, Josephus. I want you to spread the word among the men. If Canfield should show up at any time, he's to be put off the place immediately."

Josephus nodded. "You can depend on it, Miss Carrie."

But no matter how much Carrie reassured her, Susannah wouldn't go outside the house or allow Molly Caroline to be taken out, until a week later when Justice brought word that Beau had gone back to New Orleans. Justice had made it his business to get friendly with Canfield's overseer.

"He said Mist' Canfield fussed and carried on. Said there wasn't nothin' to do up here. Said he didn't care if he never saw that place again, long as it kept on makin' him money."

Susannah finally was convinced and relaxed again.

The war ended in a small town in Virginia. The Confederates evacuated Richmond, and their president, Jefferson Davis, had fled, perhaps hoping still for some miracle. But it was only a matter of time before he would be captured by the Federals. The real end, and everyone knew it, was Lee's surrender at the Appomattox Court House.

It was there that the brave and gallant man stood straight and silver-haired, proud even in defeat, and General Ulysses S. Grant proved himself to be a man of wisdom and compassion when he allowed the Army of Northern Virginia to lay down its arms and go home in peace.

It was ended at last. The South had been defeated. And yet Carrie could feel only a numb kind of relief. The right and the wrong of it seemed blurred now. She felt no sharp emotions. Just a weary sadness that it had taken so long and cost so much.

Hard on the heels of Lee's surrender came the news of Abraham Lincoln's assassination. And as Carrie read of it, she remembered that night out in the bayous when Rance had spoken of the president.

". . . the gentlest, the kindest man I've ever known," Rance had said.

Wherever he was now, Carrie knew that Rance would be deeply saddened by this latest news.

In those next days and weeks, the long trek home began for gaunt-faced soldiers with burning eyes, who rode when they could, and if they couldn't, walked or limped or dared the power of the Mississippi on homemade rafts . . . anything to get home.

They were always hungry, and they would come, raggedy

homespun uniforms barely covering them, to knock gently at the door and ask in their soft Southern voices if a piece of cornbread or a cup of buttermilk might be spared.

Carrie instructed Chloe to feed every one who came to Kingston's Landing.

A few, she soon found, were not so gentlemanly. They would steal onto the place in the dead of night and carry off chickens and rip out whole plants from the vegetable garden. A cow was found butchered one morning, as much meat as could be carried hacked off. And since another of the cows had died of sickness, milk was not as plentiful as it had once been.

One soldier had frightened Susannah almost to death when she'd found him standing in the middle of the downstairs hall, just staring at her as she walked down the steps. The man had apologized profusely when her cries brought people running, explaining that he had knocked but hadn't received an answer and had thought that the house was deserted . . . as so many were.

All the same, Carrie got out one of her father's pistols and she and Justice taught Susannah and Chloe how to fire it.

The weather was unusually dry and hot, and Carrie watched the cane anxiously, putting in long hours and then sitting up late into the night poring over the books, trying to meet all her payments on time. It seemed there were always more expenses than she'd counted on.

"Lord, child," Chloe chided as she found her up past midnight hunched over the old desk in the study, "you can't get enough rest this way! You can't sit up all night and work all day, too!"

Carrie leaned back, rubbed her tired eyes, and stretched her neck. "What about you?" she laughed. "You're up. Did Molly Caroline wake you?"

Chloe shook her head. "Thought I'd see about Lafitte. He wasn't feeling good all day."

"Lafitte? He's ill?"

"Oh, he says he's all right. You know how he is. Won't let nobody do nothin' for him."

"Do you think I should go look in on him?" Carrie asked.

"I don't know, Miss Carrie. He can be the contrariest man,"

Chloe grumbled. "Worse than Benjamin. Said he was just *fine* and would appreciate a night's sleep."

Carrie smiled. "Well, in that case I'll speak to him in the morning before I leave the house.'

But that next day, for the first time in anyone's memory, Lafitte was too ill to get up, though he did keep saying that with just a few more minutes rest, he would be up and about his duties as usual.

"He's got a fever, Miss Carrie, and he's been coughin' all night. Benjamin and me could hear him in our room next door. And now he won't even take this medicine I brung in to him," Chloe complained as Carrie stopped in to see the ailing man.

"I shall be quite all right, Missy," he insisted, clearly put out with all the attention.

To his obvious embarrassment, Carrie felt his forehead. The skin was hot and dry, and almost immediately he started to cough, a hard wracking series that caused him to turn his face away to the wall.

Once the spasm had passed, Carrie patted his shoulder. "Now I want you to do what Chloe says, Lafitte," she said. "Do you promise me?"

His mouth set itself into a resigned grimace. "If you insist, Miss Carrie," he said, Chloe standing by with the medicine and looking triumphant.

"I do," Carrie said. "And I'll be back in to see you when I come in for lunch."

"I shall be up by then," he said stubbornly.

But he wasn't. In fact, Chloe met Carrie almost as soon as she was in the door with the news that he was worse.

"I don't like it a bit, Miss Carrie," she said. "He's burnin' up with fever. Got summer pneumonia and been walkin' around with it for a day or two, or I miss my guess. I don't like it."

Carrie took one look at the dull eyes that barely acknowledged her presence, listened for a moment to the raspy breathing, and motioned Chloe outside the bedroom, which was as neat and precise as Lafitte himself.

"I think we'd better send Benjamin for a doctor," she said.

Chloe nodded. "It won't hurt none. Though I'm doin' everything in the world that I know to do."

"I know you are, Chloe. Let's see . . . three hours there and three hours back at best, plus however long it takes Benjamin in town. Probably be eight hours before he can get back here. I'll tell him to go to Prosper. He'll get a doctor for us."

Once Carrie sent Benjamin on his way, she went back to Lafitte's room to help Chloe grease the sick man's chest with melted lard mixed with a little turpentine over which they applied a warm flannel. He didn't protest, and Carrie realized how very sick he was.

They reapplied the lard mixture and changed the flannels often in that long afternoon, and Chloe periodically dosed him with her own medicines, which she made with herbs and roots and other secret things . . . the ingredients and their exact proportions passed down from ancient high priestesses and conjure women. Sometimes Chloe's cures seemed almost miraculous. But now nothing seemed to help Lafitte.

When Susannah got Molly Caroline down for her nap, she came to sit by him and press his hand. He recognized her and smiled. Carrie remembered that Susannah had always been able to make Lafitte smile.

After that, he lapsed into a light sleep, fitful at first and then calmer. Susannah left the room with tears in her eyes.

"Call me if you need me," she said.

The light curtains at the window stirred gently with the hot breeze, and Carrie leaned back in her chair and thought about Lafitte. He had always been there, his presence as solid and dependable as the coming of summer or the flow of the river. And yet she had never really told him how much he meant to her. She would. As soon as he was better. She would also talk about the war's end and what it meant to him . . . and to Chloe and Benjamin. Perhaps she had put it off because she was afraid that she might lose them. And they were as much her family as Susannah and Molly Caroline . . . as much as George Pierre.

Feeling vaguely guilty about her procrastination, she broached the subject with Chloe now, explaining that she wanted to be sure that both she and Benjamin understood what it really meant. "You're free," she ended softly. "You could go anywhere you wanted . . . anytime. Though I don't know what I'd do without you."

Chloe peered over her nose at Carrie, her dark eyes half-laughing, half-scolding. "Now what would Benjamin and me want to do a thing like that for? Lordy no, honey. We ain't goin' no place." She shook her head as she bent over Lafitte and tested the warmth of the flannel.

Carrie sat silently for a moment, watching Chloe as she smoothed and straightened the pillow sham and the sheet beneath the sick man. "Do you think," Carrie said finally, "that he feels that way, too?"

"Lafitte?" Chloe raised up and smiled at Carrie, her plump cheeks lifting to deepen the wrinkles around her eyes. "Why, child . . . you couldn't run him off with a stick!"

Susannah brought in some food for the two of them and some hot broth for Lafitte, but when they tried to rouse him, he simply turned his face away, his breath coming hard.

Chloe and Carrie carried in steaming kettles of water and placed them near to the bed. "It'll help him breathe better," Chloe said.

But as evening fell and they lit the lamps in the room, it was clear that he had slipped into a coma, and though they still worked over him, changing the flannels on his chest and moistening his dry lips, his breathing grew more labored. His cheeks seemed to have sunken into the always thin face, and there was a peculiar gray look to the skin around his mouth and eyes.

Benjamin arrived about ten o'clock, Prosper and Dr. Baptiste Rambeau along with him. Rambeau bowed gravely to Carrie and Chloe, his curling hair silver in the lamplight, and then turned his attention immediately to the patient. After a few moments, he looked up at the small group who waited anxiously and slowly shook his head.

Lafitte died just as the clock began to strike eleven, and Carrie slipped away to sit out in back of the house on the old water bench, her arms folded around herself, rocking back and forth in the still, hot night.

They buried him the next day, near to where Adam and Molly Kingston lay. Across the road and down a little way was the spot where all the rest of the faithful family servants had been buried, but such distinctions no longer seemed valid to Carrie.

* * *

"Are the cakes all ready?" Susannah asked Chloe, and the Negress grinned and pointed to the countertop where three burnt sugar cakes stood in all their glory, creamy icing swirled into fancy peaks.

"There they are," Chloe said proudly. "Lordy, I don't know how long it's been since we used up that much sugar at one time. It's just like the old days . . . before the war come on."

"And here," Carrie said, edging through the door of the warming kitchen, "is the chicken." She could barely carry the dish heaped high with crusty pieces of fried chicken, and Susannah jumped to help her. They put it on the counter beside the cakes.

Molly Caroline sat in the high chair that Benjamin had made for her and munched contentedly on a molasses cookie, most of which seemed to have turned to a gooey mass that clung to her fingers and ringed her mouth.

"My goodness, just look at you," Susannah said, laughing. She hurried to wipe off her daughter, who squirmed and reached determinedly for the cookie once again.

"Let's see now," Carrie said, "do we have the tomatoes?"

"Sliced tomatoes in that bowl right there." Chloe indicated the big earthenware bowl on the table. "And the summer squash is all ready." She pointed to the huge oblong baking pan next to the tomatoes. "And the cornbread is in this here basket. Everything's ready. I'll go tell Benjamin to bring the wagon around and load it up."

It had been a month since Lafitte's death . . . a month of dry heat, cane that curled and spotted, and roads that had turned to dust. Spirits were sagging, and Carrie had suddenly decided to call a holiday for the whole place. They would all go on a picnic and have a party. Everyone would bring something.

As Carrie looked around the kitchen at all the food, she felt some small misgiving. She wasn't sure if they could afford to splurge this way, but she quickly shrugged that off. It would do them all good, she told herself firmly. It had been far too long since they'd just relaxed and had a little fun.

"Oh, Carrie, this is such a good idea!" Susannah said, as if she had read her sister's mind.

Carrie grinned at her. "Do you have everything for Molly Caroline?"

"Right here in this satchel. I'm taking two dresses in case she smears herself with cookies the way she was about to a minute ago. And I have her rag doll and the wooden blocks that Josephus made for her."

"Don't forget a quilt in case she gets sleepy."

"I won't."

Chloe came back into the kitchen. "Benjamin's got the wagon outside. And Justice and Tana are here."

They loaded the food into the wagon, laughing and talking, exchanging greetings with Justice and Tana. Molly Caroline's eyes sparkled, and she clapped her hands and babbled as if she knew that something special was afoot.

Chloe and Benjamin went in the wagon, and Susannah and the baby rode with Justice and Tana. Carrie rode ahead on Majestic.

Long before they reached the agreed-upon spot, which was near to the river, they could hear the high pitch of Josephus's fiddle and the deeper twang of Willie's old guitar. A half-Indian Negro named Charlie Lonestar provided the rhythm by drumming on a piece of hollow log.

Couples were already dancing, and food was piling up on the makeshift tables the men had put together. There were platters of fried fish and shrimp and succulent crayfish. Sweet potatoes roasting in a fire pit sent a delicious aroma through the air. Pans of peach cobbler and shortcakes waited. Everything was covered over to keep the flies away.

Justice observed it all from the sidelines, grinning. "Reminds me of the times when your daddy used to give parties," he said to Carrie who stood beside him. "We always had one after the sugar makin'. Everybody for miles around would come."

"I can remember some of them," Carrie said. "Suzy and I used to beg Mama to let us sit up late so that we could watch all the dancing."

She walked around and talked. "How are you feeling, Bessie?" Carrie asked Willie's woman, who was pregnant again.

She already had three, and the youngest was busy scaling his mother's rounded abdomen. She pulled him up into her arms. "Fine, Miss Carrie, fine."

Old Toby, who was the only one of the old slaves from the quarters left alive now—his wife Nadine had died last winter—sat in a chair and jiggled a lumpy old foot in time to the music. Though he was stone deaf now, he seemed to feel the vibrations. Josephus's woman Sara stood behind him. She had made the old man her special charge. Carrie patted him on the shoulder and smiled at him. He was stone deaf now. There was no use trying to talk to him, but his eyes lit as he recognized her.

"He looks good, Sara," Carrie told her. "Let me know if he needs anything."

"I will, Miss Carrie," the woman said, and Carrie passed on.

One of the younger women, Effie, brought her special pickles for Carrie to taste, and Carrie told her how good they were. Thanking the girl, she saw Susannah coming toward her with Molly Caroline and went to meet her.

"Can you believe I came off without her diapers?" Susannah said. "She's sure to be wet before long. If you'll take her, I'll drive the wagon back to the house and get them."

"I'll go," Carrie told her sister. "I can take Majestic and be there and back in a few minutes. Where did you leave them?"

"They must be in the back hall," Susannah said. "I had them all folded. Honestly, Carrie, I don't see how I could have come off without them."

Molly Caroline babbled her little unintelligible sounds and smiled at Carrie, reaching out to her aunt with her fat little hands.

"Let her come with me," Carrie said, reaching for the child. She often rode her niece in front of the saddle, as her father had once ridden her.

They found Majestic grazing contentedly beneath the trees where Carrie had left him and Molly Caroline giggled as Carrie swung her up then mounted herself, taking the little girl into the protective circle of her arms.

Carrie kept to the grass, it was easier riding now that the roads were so dusty, and a few minutes later she circled the barns and the stables.

Disengaging her niece's chubby fingers from Majestic's mane, Carrie swung Molly Caroline down and they went in through the back door, the house quiet and cool in the late afternoon. In the

372

hall, she checked the bench and searched through the linen press but the diapers were nowhere to be seen.

"Now where do you suppose your mommy could have left them?" she said to the baby. Molly Caroline babbled "Ma-ma," and patted at Carrie's face.

Carrie looked in the warming kitchen. They weren't there. Finally, she decided that they must be up in Suzy's room beside the crib. The child was growing heavy on her arm so Carrie settled her in the highchair and handed her a wooden spoon. "You wait here. I'll be right back." Molly Caroline began at once to bang happily.

Carrie went through the house to the front hall, aware of the tall case clock, the waxed floor, and the polished walnut table with its bowl of brightly colored zinnias. She paused for a moment, filled with love for it all. Perhaps a great deal had changed, she thought, but Kingston's Landing was the same . . . this house was the same, and she was going to do her best to keep it that way always.

She found the diapers upstairs as she had expected, right beside Molly Caroline's crib on the small table. She gathered them up and went back out into the hall, stopping for a moment in her own room to see that the draperies were drawn against the late afternoon sun.

She continued down the stairs and back through the house, aware that Molly Caroline's banging had ceased for the moment. She heard the child laughing and smiled herself. But as she came to the kitchen doorway the smile froze. Beau Canfield stood there, Molly Caroline in his arms.

Carrie gasped, the diapers falling to the floor. She darted into the room to snatch the baby away from him. Molly Caroline, who'd been gurgling happily, looked startled, her lower lip puckered.

Beau regarded Carrie with a look of annoyance, one perfect eyebrow slanted upward. "Good God, Carrie, you don't think I mean her any harm, do you?"

Carrie eyed him warily. "The way you didn't mean any harm to Suzy? Or to me, Beau?"

He shrugged, elegant as usual, ruffles perfect.

"What are you doing here?" Carrie demanded, patting Molly Caroline to head off the threatened tears.

"I should think that would be self-evident. I wanted to see the child."

"I don't know if I believe that," Carrie snapped.

"It seems, my dear Carrie," he frowned, "that your temper hasn't improved a bit. But despite what you may think, I do have feelings. She *is* my daughter."

"Not legally, she isn't."

"Legally? What does legality have to do with it! She's my child, Carrie! My only child, so far as I know," he added. "Is it so hard to understand that I might just want to see her . . . see what she looks like?"

Carrie was taken aback by his outburst. His voice, usually so smooth, had been ragged, underlined with a truth she had never heard there before. Molly Caroline had decided to ignore the adults' conversation and was all smiles again, tugging at the buttons of Carrie's blouse.

Beau looked at his daughter for a long moment. "She is beautiful. Isn't she?"

"Yes," Carrie said.

"Do you think she looks like me?"

Carrie nodded truthfully. "A little like you. A little like Suzy."

"Do you need money?" he said. "I could provide her with whatever—"

"No," Carrie cut him off. "She's fine. We just want you to leave us alone, Beau."

He walked over to the window and stood looking out for a moment then turned back, a jaunty set to his shoulders. "I'm sure you won't believe this," he smiled his old smile, his eyes moving up and down the length of her suggestively, "but I am truly sorry that things worked out so badly between us, Carrie."

Carrie regarded him coldly. "Tell me, Beau . . . Were you ever anything that you claimed to be? Did you ever *really* run the blockade into Charleston?"

His eyebrows raised. "Of course I did. Many times. At the risk of my life and," he grinned, "the fattening of my pocketbook. But if it will make you feel any better about it, my dear, I did

374

not play favorites. I took my money from the North as well as the South.''

"You were never anything but a profiteer," Carrie said scornfully.

"Call it what you will." He came back to stand near to her and the baby. "The war made me a rich man. It gave me everything I wanted . . . except you, Carrie." His eyes narrowed slightly as he gazed at her.

"Stop it, Beau," she said.

He laughed. "I admit that you've taken on a certain aura for me . . . probably because you're the only woman I ever set out to get and didn't. But," his shoulders lifted beneath the well-cut jacket, "even I know when to quit."

He picked up his hat from the table where he'd left it. "You needn't worry about my bothering you again. I'm going to Europe soon. I've decided to live there. The atmosphere is much more agreeable to a man of my tastes."

He held out a hand to Molly Caroline who seized it at once and started to tug at the gold ring on his finger. He looked at the child a long time, his face betraying nothing, and then nodded to Carrie.

"Thank you for letting me see her."

He was into the hallway when he turned back for a moment, grinning. "There is one other thing you might like to know, Carrie. I was the one who told the Yankees about your brother being here. It evened the score for that lump on the head you gave me."

He was still standing, half turned toward her, laughing, one eyebrow mockingly aslant, when the sound of a gunshot crashed against Carrie's ears. She would remember it forever afterward, remember the way his eyes opened wide and his hand went to his chest.

He made a long, drawn-out sound, as if he were saying "Ah . . ." and then tried to look down the hallway, but his head was jerking, beyond control. He slumped slowly to the floor, stiffened, then lay still.

Molly Caroline had started to shriek at the loud noise. Carrie stood there staring at Beau, at the sudden, bright red stain that was spreading along the ruffles of his white shirtfront. She held back the scream that rose in her own throat and, after a moment of paralysis, forced herself to move out into the hallway. A thin, pale figure stood there, Adam Kingston's old dueling pistol in her hand.

"Oh, my God . . . Suzy!" Carrie whispered. "Suzy . . . what have you done!"

The pistol dropped to the floor with a clatter as Susannah's lips drew back. She began a high-pitched keening which joined crazily with Molly Caroline's squalling. As Carrie drew near, her sister grabbed the red-faced baby, clutching it to her so tightly that the child cried all the louder.

"Stop it, Suzy. Stop, you're scaring her."

"I couldn't let him hurt her . . . He would have taken us away! I couldn't let him!" Susannah babbled.

"Oh, dear Lord," Carrie groaned, "you're wrong. He wasn't—" She broke off. Her sister wasn't really hearing her.

"I . . . I came back to tell you where I left the diapers. I heard him. I heard Beau. I knew he'd come for us . . ." Her voice was stretched and thin, with an hysterical edge.

"Listen to me, Suzy," Carrie said sharply. "I want you to take Molly Caroline, go upstairs to your room, and wait for me. Do you hear me? Will you do that?"

Susannah nodded and Carrie gave her a little push toward the stairs. "Go ahead now . . . I'll come up," she said, and as her sister took a hesitant step or two, Carrie turned back to Beau.

It took only a glance to confirm her worst fears. There was no sign of breathing. His lips were parted slightly, the eyes that had always seemed so dark for his fair skin, stared glassily at the wall. She choked back the hot rising in her throat. It was clear there was nothing she could do for him.

She realized that Susannah was still standing where she had left her. Molly Caroline's cries had subsided to whimpers, her face turned into her mother's neck. Carrie went slowly back to them, her own legs trembling. She could feel the film of perspiration on her face.

"Come on." She put her arm around her sister. "Let's go upstairs."

Once there, Susannah allowed her to take Molly Caroline and put her in her crib. The child rolled onto her stomach, drew her legs up and popped a thumb into her mouth. Susannah sat on the side of the bed, her face colorless.

"He would have made us go away with him, Carrie. I couldn't let him have Molly Caroline," she whispered.

"Don't think about it, honey," Carrie said. "Just stretch out here on the bed. Lie back." She did as Carrie told her. "Just close your eyes and don't think of anything right now."

Carrie's brain was racing. She would not let Suzy be hurt anymore than she had been already. She knew what had to be done. She fought back the urge to cry. She could cry later.

"Suzy . . ." she smoothed back a strand of hair from her sister's damp forehead, "honey, I'm going to go back to the picnic and get Justice and Benjamin. I'll tell everyone you have a headache. I want you to stay right here in your room while I'm gone."

Susannah nodded.

"Do you promise? You'll wait right here until I come back for you?"

"Yes," Susannah said and closed her eyes.

Back at the picnic, Carrie managed to smile while slowly working her way toward Justice.

"Meet me at the house as soon as you can," she whispered to him just as he was ending a dance with Tana. "Don't let anyone know," she added.

She said the same thing to Benjamin as he mopped up the juices on his plate with a huge piece of cornbread. He stood up slowly and stretched, exclaiming loudly how full he was, and a moment later slipped away through the trees. If anyone saw him, they would have sworn that he was just going off to relieve himself.

Once they were back at the house, the two men took charge. They wrapped Beau's body in an old quilt and hefted it between them.

"Clean that up good," Justice jerked his head toward the bloodstains on the floor, and then he and Benjamin carried their unwieldy burden out to a rickety old wagon they'd brought from the barn.

Carrie did as he said, scrubbing the wide floorboards with a brush and soapy water, then rubbing until the floor was dry and waxing the wood to a soft sheen. Her father's old pistol was put back in its case.

Afterward she didn't ask them what they had done with Beau's body. She only knew that they were gone for about two hours, long enough to go far back into the bayous where the vegetation grew rampantly and decayed just as quickly, more springing up to take its place . . . where wild creatures fed, and where quicksand pits could swallow an animal—or a man—and leave no trace.

A few days later, the overseer at the old Gayerre place rode by Justice's cabin and asked if he might have seen Beau Canfield. When Justice replied that he hadn't, the pudgy overseer wiped a red handkerchief across his multiple chins and spat a stream of tobacco juice out of the corner of his mouth, swearing disgustedly.

"He's a queer one, that one is. You never know when he's comin' or leavin'. Shit, I ain't even got my pay for this month!"

27

CARRIE SAT BEHIND HER FATHER'S OLD DESK IN THE STUDY, going over the books and the bills one last time. There it was, all clearly penned out, the figures precise and undeniable. Her creditors were demanding payment and there was nothing to pay them with. It was as simple as that.

She'd known it for weeks, but still had clung to the hope that something, *anything*, would happen to get her through. Finally, ten days ago, she'd faced up to the heartbreaking truth. She'd gone down to New Orleans and asked Leroy Tate to make arrangements to sell Kingston's Landing.

In the days since she'd tried her best to keep the others from knowing how much it hurt her. With a feigned enthusiasm she'd painted a bright picture of the new life that awaited them in California. George Pierre had written that he'd obtained a teaching position there, and she, Susannah and Molly Caroline, Chloe and Benjamin would be going out to join him once the place was sold. And maybe, Carrie thought, it would be a good thing for Susannah. Her sister had drawn even farther into herself since the day of the picnic, never truly at ease unless she was with Molly Caroline. Perhaps California would let her forget, or at least come to terms with the memories of Beau Canfield.

Carrie got up now and paced the room restlessly. She had to keep telling herself that it would all work out for the best, or it would kill her. She had fought so long and hard to keep the place. And she could have, too, but for the bad-luck weather and never being able to borrow enough money to put in the really big crops that would have paid off with handsome profits. She might have anyway if the summer hadn't been so hot and dry. The cane in the fields now would never pay even half her debts when it was turned into sugar.

She pulled back the thin white curtain and looked out the window. The magnolia tree nearby looked cool and lush, as if in defiance of the dusty road that led down toward the barn and the stables, but the gardenia bushes that edged the road had turned dry and brown-spotted with hardly a bloom to see.

The place looked deserted. It was, almost. She had had to let most of the hands go because she didn't have the money to pay them. The quarters were all but empty. All the families had left. Old Toby had died two weeks after the picnic.

Carrie let the curtain fall and hurried from the room, struggling to keep back the tears. There was something she had to do, and she might as well do it now.

She walked down to the barn and saddled up Majestic, who had come trotting in from the lot the moment he saw her—she always had a little piece of sugar or a bit of corn to give him. The worn cypress posts, the stalls, the smells of leather and feed and horses assailed her with memories that would always be a part of her.

Still fighting the tears, she tightened the cinch, and leading the animal outside, she swung up onto the sidesaddle, bringing her heel down lightly against the sleek side of the gelding and giving him his head.

They went along the road by the river, and she watched the gulls dip and circle above the mighty current. Pale, cream caps topped the waves. Far back in the bright afternoon sky, a line of clouds lay swollen and purple, as if they might hold rain. "Too late now," she muttered.

She turned back toward the place where Maisonfleur had once been, skirted around it, then headed for the burial plot.

It was pleasant there. Lafitte's grave had grown over now. Mosses shone faintly green on the stones for Uncle Etienne and her grandfather, old Monsieur Moreau. Birds chattered and scolded in the nearby branches of the live oak trees. A slight breeze had sprung up.

Carrie left Majestic standing and went to the pair of graves where her parents were buried, studying the carved marble tombstones, the grape clusters and flowers and curlicues. . . The grass stirred gently.

It occurred to her that to have to sell the land where her ancestors and all the people she had loved rested was perhaps the worst part of it. She stood rigidly, as if for their judgment.

"I tried, Papa," she said, dry-eyed now. "I tried so hard. But I can't make it. I'm having to sell the place, Papa. I'm sorry . . ." She turned to all of them. "I'm sorry . . ."

The hot swelling in her throat was choking her. She ran back to the horse and swung up to send him galloping wildly, it didn't matter which way. But after a while at such a killing pace, she realized that the gelding's sides were pumping and he was dark with sweat.

She pulled him up and got down from the saddle to fling herself prone in the tall grass, burying her face in the fragrance of it, breathing in the deep and fecund smell of the land itself . . . and she let all the tears come that she had held back for so long, sobbing her heart out into the rich Louisiana soil.

She finally rolled over and lay on her back, quietly watching the clouds move slowly in a turquoise sky. Majestic had cooled down, but she felt guilty about him now and went to him and rubbed the velvety nose. "I'm sorry, boy," she said softly. "I didn't mean for us to run so hard . . . so far."

They were near the river, and she heard the deep blast of the steamboat whistle. That would be the newspapers, and maybe some mail, she thought. She smoothed her tousled hair back and mounted Majestic once again.

As she emerged from the trees, the steamboat was in full view. Carrie put Majestic into an easy trot along the river road.

She was a sidewheeler, three-tiered and loaded with passengers who waved from the rails and called out to the pretty girl atop the chestnut gelding. The great paddles beat rhythmically, churning the muddy water to send a fine froth of bubbles in its wake, and the deep whistle sounded again.

Carrie pulled Majestic up to the landing just as the pilot skillfully brought the big boat in to the dock. A steward called a greeting and tossed the packet of newspapers down onto the cypress planking. A gentleman with a thin mustache leaned forward over the rail and gravely tipped his hat to Carrie. And a little girl in pink ribbons clutched her mother's skirt with one hand and waved with the other as the whistle sounded its warning once again and the boat edged back and moved out into midstream.

There was a letter from Leroy Tate, and Carrie didn't wait to get back up to the house, but opened it and read it right there.

> I didn't expect to settle the matter so soon, but I have found an out-of-state buyer for Kingston's Landing. If you can be in my office on Friday morning at nine o'clock, we can sign the papers.

"Not this time, you ain't! You ain't goin' down to New Orleans lookin' like a field hand!" Chloe scolded as she dragged Carrie's crinoline out of the armoire and looked over the line of dresses that hadn't been worn in many months.

The other times Carrie had made the trip down to the city on business, she had gone and returned in one day and had worn her velvet riding habit, which was in better condition than any of her other riding outfits. She hardly knew what it felt like to have hoops on anymore.

"If you got to sell this place, then whoever buys it is goin' to know that he's buyin' it from a lady!" Chloe went on, leaving no room at all for argument. "Let's see now, You goin' down on Thursday, and this is Tuesday . . ."

She made Carrie soak her roughened hands in cream, covering them over with old white gloves while she slept. Buttermilk was applied lavishly to her face. Her nails were trimmed, and her hair was washed and rinsed until it gleamed with chestnut highlights.

Susannah even got into the spirit of it and dug out some unpatched underwear and a nightgown from her trunk for Carrie to take along, loaning her sister her string of coral beads besides.

Carrie was touched by their concern for her, and she tried not to let them see how heavy her heart really was.

On Thursday, she took the afternoon packet down and, once in the city, went directly to see Mattie, who was clearly busy and happy. Carrie promised that Chloe and Benjamin would have time to visit before they all left for California.

After that, she went to Prosper's and had tea with him.

"I am sorry, *ma chère*," he consoled her. "But who knows. Something quite wonderful may happen when you least expect it." His dark eyes gleamed, the waxed points of his mustache quivered.

"Perhaps," Carrie said. "At least—" she forced herself to assume a gay manner—"I'm going to enjoy myself while I'm in town. In fact, if you would excuse me now, I think I'm going to take myself off and do all the things I haven't done for a long time."

"Such as . . ." he prompted.

"Oh . . ." She thought for a moment. "I'm going to the confectioner's to buy something sinfully sweet. And I may even go by the dressmaker's. After all, tomorrow I'll be coming into some money," she said ruefully. "Of course," she added hastily, "I won't be spending too much on clothes and such. I hope to start a business of some kind when we get to California."

Prosper nodded. "Shall I drive you?"

"No, thank you. I'd like to walk. I want to remember everything."

Prosper's hand came out to rest lightly on her arm, and his black eyes grew soft. He understood.

She did go to Madame Louisa's and looked at all the beautiful materials and the latest fashions in the stacks of magazines. She inspected laces and buttons and frog closings and beribboned bonnets.

They would all come to the shop, she vowed, just as soon as the deal was closed and she had the money. She did not intend to allow herself to sink into a trough of despair. Susannah and Molly Caroline both needed clothes. And she'd seen a rose watered silk that would be perfect for Chloe. It wouldn't cost that much. And she mustn't forget Benjamin. They'd go to the tailor and have him fitted with a new suit and hat. When they sailed for California, they would not look like beggars.

She bade Madame Louisa good day and walked along the banquette, looking in the shop windows and enjoying the bustle of the streets. A parrot squawked from his cage in an open doorway. Potted vines trailed from second-story balconies that were railed with delicate ironwork.

She caught sight of her reflection in the window of a small coffee shop and stopped for a moment to gaze at the young woman she saw there. She was wearing her blue challis dress, cut wide at the neckline to show an expanse of neck and bosom that was no longer creamy but golden with the constant exposure to sun. Beneath her wide leghorn straw hat, her hair hung in shiny chestnut tendrils, but Chloe's buttermilk treatment for her face had been a failure. The sprinkling of freckles across her nose was as pronounced as before.

Sighing, she raised the white ruffled parasol that she'd been carrying closed and continued on along the banquette. Perhaps now that she would no longer be working on the plantation, she would gradually get to look and act like a lady again. The thought was not much comfort.

She walked to Jackson Square and strolled around the bronze statue of the "savior of New Orleans," Old Hickory himself, Andrew Jackson, the seventh president of the United States, looking suitably impressive on his rearing horse. The words, THE UNION MUST AND SHALL BE PRESERVED, were cut deeply into the base, the sun glinting off them. They had been put there by order of General Benjamin Butler during his tenure as commanding general of New Orleans. Had it really only been three years ago, she mused, that "Beast" Butler had earned the enmity not only of New Orleanians but of Southerners in general? It seemed longer . . . a lifetime away, so much had happened since then.

People came and went through the square. A young mother herded her two small sons ahead of her, while not far away a pair of nuns walked with suitably downcast eyes. An elderly Creole gentleman swung his walking stick and smiled.

In a moment, Carrie's attention was drawn to an old Negro woman, small and birdlike in her dark green skirt and kerchief. She was carrying a tray of pralines and stopped to hawk them in her singsong gombo, tilting her head this way and that, smiling as she extolled the virtues of her creamy, rich pecan candies.

Carrie was considering whether to buy one when a deep and familiar voice came from behind her. "We'll take two, please."

She whirled to see a gold watchchain stretching across a royal blue silk waistcoat, her eyes traveling upward to a strong cleft chin beneath a dark full mustache, and finally to clear gray eyes. Everything in the world stood perfectly still for a moment. Rance stood there smiling at her, incredibly handsome in a well-cut fawn-colored suit, his hat in his hand.

"Two, Michie . . . two . . . ." The old Negress wrapped a pair of the candies in paper, and Rance handed her a coin.

Rance stood holding the pralines, still smiling at Carrie. "I didn't get these for myself, you know," he said, handing them to her.

Able to move at last, she took the candies with fingers that still felt numb. "Rance . . ." she said, smiling back at him. That was all she seemed able to say.

"Hello, Carrie."

"I . . . I . . ." She tried to get herself together. "I didn't expect to see you here in New Orleans."

"I had a thing or two that I needed to see about."

"Yes, of course. Well . . . you're looking . . . well," she finished lamely, acutely conscious of her freckled nose and her tanned skin.

"So are you," he said, and his eyes moved over her in a way that made shivers run along her back. "Why don't we sit down over here." He indicated a stone bench nearby.

384

As they made their way to it, Carrie warned herself silently. Rance's presence in New Orleans didn't mean anything. He certainly hadn't come to see her. And she was no longer a silly, young girl. She mustn't act like one.

Since the bench was shaded, she lowered her parasol and put it beside her, turning to face him calmly. "It's really a coincidence to run into you," she said. "I'm only down to the city for a few days myself. I was just walking about town. Enjoying it."

"Oh? You're at Kingston's Landing then?"

"Yes," she said.

"And how is Suzy?"

Carrie's attempt at light conversation faltered. "Suzy is . . . very changed," she said honestly. "Sometimes it's hard to remember that she's only nineteen. It's as if she got old too soon." She hesitated, then told him. "She has a child, Rance. A little girl."

His brows knitted. "Canfield?"

She nodded.

"I ought to kill him!" he said his face hardening. "I always heard stories about him, but—"

She drew a deep breath, stopped him. "Actually, he . . . disappeared some time back. No one seems to know what happened. But—" She steered the subject away from Beau— "Molly Caroline, the baby, is the sweetest, prettiest little thing. You must—" She stopped herself. She had almost said, you must come and see her.

They were silent for a moment.

"Tell me," she said lightly, "how is Nora?"

He had seemed lost in his own thoughts, but now his head came up, and he regarded her with a puzzled expression in the gray eyes. "I haven't the faintest idea."

Carrie stared at him. "I don't understand," she said. "Your wife . . ."

"*Wife?*" The surprise on his face suddenly gave way to understanding. "You thought that I . . . that Nora and I . . ." He let his breath out in a rush and leaned forward, hunching his shoulders slightly. "Good Lord, Carrie, Nora and I were never married!"

Carrie could feel her lower jaw drop, but she closed her mouth promptly. She felt slightly dizzy. All this time she had supposed that the wedding had taken place as scheduled. "Oh . . ." She searched for something to say. "I . . . I'm sorry."

He laughed. "I'm not," he said gently. "Thank heaven, we both found out in time how wrong it was." The breeze ruffled his dark hair, and he grinned at her. "You haven't eaten your candy," he said.

She looked down at the wrapped candies that lay untouched in her lap. "No," she said. "I don't feel very hungry right now."

His hand sought hers, those strong fingers closing gently. "Perhaps you will be later," he said. "Would you allow me to take you to dinner this evening?"

It was as if a bird fluttered in her chest, but her voice was very steady as she answered. "I'd like that very much, Rance."

Prosper was letting Carrie use the house on Dumaine Street as usual, and he'd insisted on sending over his servant girl, Delphine. Carrie had protested that she didn't need anyone to look after her, but now she was delighted to have the girl.

Together they had heated the water on the big iron stove in the kitchen and dragged the copper tub in there so they wouldn't have to carry the buckets so far. Carrie stripped down and got into the lavender-scented water, and Delphine scrubbed her back and helped her wash her hair.

"It seems to me, Mademoiselle Carrie," the girl said as she rinsed Carrie's hair with rain water taken from the barrel in the courtyard, "that a very special gentleman must be calling this evening." She turned her head to one side and gave Carrie a knowing smile, then giggled. Carrie found herself joining in.

"Well, I suppose you could say that. Major—" She caught herself. "I mean, *Mr.* Stewart is taking me to dinner."

Delphine's shapely mouth formed an O. "The handsome Yankee officer?" Her eyes rolled. "Who could forget?"

"Yes . . . who *could* forget?" Carrie found herself being honest and then blushed with mortification.

Delphine pursed her mouth, her eyes twinkling. "We shall be ready for him," she declared, and hoisted another bucket of rainwater.

Once the bath was complete, she toweled Carrie's skin until it was glowing and splashed her with lavender cologne, which she took out of her own case. "My Emile loves it," she assured Carrie. She buffed Carrie's nails and, once her hair was dry, brushed it to a shimmering mass of chestnut curls.

Susannah's unpatched underwear was brought out and donned, along with a ruffled petticoat and the wide crinoline.

"Oh, if only I had a new gown . . ." Carrie agonized.

But Delphine quickly went through the armoire and selected the ivory-colored silk with the big puffed sleeves and the cascade of lace at the elbow.

"But he's *seen* that," Carrie said. "He's seen them all."

Delphine tapped her white teeth with a slender fingertip, her brows drawn together for a moment. She brightened. "Leave it to me, Mademoiselle. I shall be back shortly.

She was gone from the house for about twenty minutes and then returned with a bag on her arm and a triumphant look on her face. "I have just the thing," she said, as she withdrew a half-dozen tiny silk roses and a needle and thread from the bag. She fastened the roses with quick, invisible stitches at intervals across the top of the low-cut ivory silk bodice. And when Carrie was buttoned into it, she dug into the bag once more to produce a wide pink silk sash, which she tied in a large bow in back.

"Nearly perfect . . ." She stood back and surveyed her handiwork. "You need some jewelry . . . a locket . . . something . . ."

"I know what." Carrie's eyes sparkled as she dug into her case and came up with Susannah's pink coral beads. Then she stood back and looked at herself in the mirror, almost astonished at the radiant reflection she saw there. She had gotten so used to seeing herself in the rough work clothes she'd found serviceable around the plantation, it was hard to believe that the enchanting woman she saw in the glass was her.

She turned to Delphine and hugged her, the two of them giggling again like girls just as the bell sounded.

"Oh, my goodness!" Carrie gasped, suddenly nervous.

"Monsieur Stewart will be quite dazzled," Delphine purred. "And remember, Mademoiselle . . . I shall be far in back in my quarters when you and Monsieur return, and," she added archly, "I am a *very* sound sleeper."

"Delphine!" Carrie said, blushing to the roots of her hair. But the girl was already away to answer the door and show Rance in, after which she tactfully withdrew.

When she saw him, Carrie wondered if it weren't *she* who should be dazzled by Rance. He was splendid in a black broadcloth suit with a white brocaded silk waistcoat and white ruffled shirt. But then his gray eyes moved slowly up and down the length of her.

"My God . . . you look beautiful!" he said, smiling, and then sobered to offer his arm gravely. "I have a hackney waiting. Shall we go?"

He took her to a place on St. Louis Street called Antoine's. It was not fancy. The tables, china, and cutlery were serviceable and plain, but the food and the service were acknowledged to be the best in the city.

Rance ordered for them, and they started with oysters on the halfshell, followed by pompano in white wine sauce with crabmeat and diced shrimp, asparagus with lemon crumbs, and artichoke hearts marinated in oil and vinegar. It was all mouthwateringly delicious, but the truth was, Carrie could barely swallow she was so excited and nervous at seeing Rance again.

They spoke of the war and its aftermath. He told her of his return home to find that his father was dead.

"Oh, Rance," she said, "I'm so sorry." Instinctively she put her hand out to his.

He nodded, his eyes darkening with memories. "They said he called for me . . . at the last. I like to believe that that meant he had forgiven me for choosing to fight with the Union."

"I'm sure it did." She pressed his fingers and then drew her hand back shyly.

"Sherman's men spared the house," Rance went on, "but destroyed the dikes. No way to raise rice there now. The system of dikes kept the sea water out," he explained. "Rice has to have fresh water to grow; sea water kills it. And the whole system was terribly expensive to build in the first place. Most of the other plantations had the same kind of damage. I doubt if there's anyone left in that part of the country with that kind of money now."

"But the land is still there," Carrie said.

"Yes. Perhaps on some of it I could grow cotton. Or sugar."
He laughed.

"Perhaps," she said. She didn't tell him that she was being
forced to sell Kingston's Landing. She didn't want him to feel in
any way sorry for her. If she had understood him, he was only
going to be in New Orleans for a few days, and there was no
reason why he should ever know.

They finished their food, and the proprietor, Monsieur Antoine
Alciatore himself, a handsome man with a full dark beard and
mustache, came by the table to ask if everything had been
satisfactory and to supervise the making and serving of the
wickedly strong Café Brulôt. The coffee, laced with brandy,
curaçao, sugar, and spices, made Carrie feel quite light-headed,
and as she caught a glimpse of herself in a mirror, she saw that
her cheeks were softly rosy, her eyes golden in the gaslight.

Back at the house on Dumaine Street, Carrie found that Delphine
was as good as her word. She was nowhere to be seen, but the
wall sconces were lit, and two white candles flickered atop a tea
table. A decanter of brandy and two glasses were on a tray
nearby.

"Well . . ." Carrie said, taking Rance's hat and putting it
aside along with her shawl. "Delphine seems to have put out
some of Prosper's brandy. Would you like some?"

"No," he said.

She turned to look at him standing there before the French
doors. The candlelight played along that hard cheek, caught the
gray eyes, highlighted the dark thick hair. He seemed very tall
standing there, one hand resting lightly at his belt, the other at
his side.

"No?" she said softly.

"No," he repeated. He held out his hand, and she met his
eyes with hers.

"Rance . . ." she said, and his name was like music on her
tongue. It was true her hand was trembling as she extended it to
him, but it was only with anticipation. She was a woman. She
knew that there might only be this last night . . . but she wanted
it with all her heart.

The moment their palms met, he pulled her to him. "Carrie
. . . oh, Carrie . . ." he said, and his hard-muscled body scorched

the length of her. His mouth came down to drown out the gasp that escaped her lips. He kissed her slowly, as if in wonder, growling deep in his throat, and then drew back to look at her face, tracing her brows, her nose, her lips with his fingertip. "Oh, God, Carrie . . ."

His mouth was on hers again, this time searching, his tongue parting her lips, thrusting, his hands moving along her back until her whole body was tingling, crying for more . . . more . . . She could smell the mingled scents of her lavender cologne, brandy, his cigar.

He ran his hand lightly over the tops of her breasts, and the already swollen nipples grew harder, pushed against the ruffled camisole and the bodice of her dress. She moaned softly, and his gray eyes smoldered with the unasked question.

"Carrie . . . I've wanted you for so long," he said hoarsely.

Her chin came up, and she faced him squarely. "And I have wanted you," she whispered, as honest as she'd ever been in her life.

The dark fires deep within those gray eyes flamed, and before she realized his intention, he had swept her up into powerful arms and was striding toward the stairs. Carrie turned her face into his chest and could feel the banded muscles, could hear the strong and steady beat of his heart, which seemed in tune with her own, and she abandoned herself totally.

At the top of the stairs, Rance turned toward the bedroom where the door was ajar, the lamps lit. Delphine had turned down the bed cover invitingly; two huge pillows covered with white ruffled shams resting against the tall rosewood headboard.

The door kicked shut behind him, Rance put Carrie down beside the high bed and slowly began to undress her, his big hands caressing her skin as he bared it, making her moan and sway, scarcely able to stand the desire that burned through her flesh. He moved his fingertips along the line where the tanned skin gave way to milky white breasts, nipples swollen and dark as plums.

"Dear God . . . you're so beautiful!" he whispered, pulling her against his hard manhood. And as if in a fever, the rest of their clothing was stripped off, their need for one another urgent, immediate.

They sank into the soft feather mattress, bodies molding, lips and tongues meeting. Rance's long, sinewy legs parted hers, and as he thrust into the soft wetness, she gasped. The pleasure was so sharp, so intense . . . yet that pleasure rose and soared as he moved, first slowly and then faster, carrying her to peaks of ecstasy she had not reached even on that long ago morning in the thicket. She cried out and whimpered with each new sensation, and she moved against him, letting him guide her, her body arching upward to meet his.

She could see the fine sheen of perspiration that glistened over his body, see the ripple of tendon and muscle beneath the skin, and she gloried in the hard maleness of him, gloried in this man who possessed her completely, who claimed her as his own . . . if only for this night. And then she heard herself wail, and it was as if she had exploded into a thousand lovely colors just an instant before he did.

After a long moment of lying spent, Rance slid off of her and drew her into the curve of his arm. Her head was against his shoulder, his hand gently stroking her hair, and they lay there, silent in their contentment, bodies resonating with the exquisite thing that had just happened between them.

They kissed, still wordless, as if each of them were afraid to break that blissful enchantment, and Carrie, who had never been so happy, drifted to sleep in the safety of his arms.

She awoke sometime later to find Rance sleeping soundly, one arm flung above his head, the other still around her. She lay there totally contented for a moment and then slid carefully out from his encircling arm and out of the bed.

Her clothing lay in a heap on the rug. She grinned, felt herself blush at her nakedness, but made no move to go to the chest and get herself a nightgown. Instead she turned out the lamps and went to the windows to draw back the heavy draperies and let the cool night air in, welcoming it against her bare body, lifting up her hair to let it fan her neck.

The room was silvered with moonlight, and she went back to lie down beside Rance once again, studying his face, the well-shaped brows, the straight nose, the deep-clefted chin. She had carried it, she realized, in her heart all this time.

She closed her eyes to see it still there behind her eyelids, and when she opened them again, he was looking at her, sleepy-lidded, a half-smile on his lips.

"Hello . . ." he whispered huskily.

"Hello." She was suddenly shy at having been caught staring at him while he slept, especially since both of them were lying there naked "I . . . I didn't mean to wake you," she stammered.

"Why not?" he teased.

She didn't know how to answer that, and she merely shivered as he ran his forefinger gently down her bare stomach. And she gasped when he followed the course of his finger with his lips, kissing down the length of her to the soft triangle of hair. "Rance!" she got out, her breath coming fast.

He laughed at her and brought his face up to bury it between her breasts and then sought her lips, kissing her long and tenderly. She could feel the rising manhood of him and was surprised to find her own need so sharp, so urgent once again.

She murmured her encouragement, and this time slowly and most thoroughly, Rance made love to her, left her replete, filled with a kind of contentment she had never known existed.

When she awakened next, it was to sense the bright shaft of sunlight piercing through the open window. She lay still, eyes closed yet, to revel in the moment. Birds chirped in the tree branches just outside the house, and the breeze was pleasant with the morning's freshness. She knew that she only had to reach her hand out to touch Rance's shoulder, run her fingers along the dark, curled hair that furred that broad chest. She stretched and turned, only to look over at an empty pillow and a rumpled sheet, and the smile faded from her lips.

"Rance," she called softly, and sat up to find the room empty, his clothes gone. Perhaps he had gotten hungry and gone downstairs, she told herself.

Hurriedly she flung off the linen sheet that covered her and searched out her wrapper, buttoning it to the throat as she went out into the hallway and down the stairs.

"Rance . . ." she called again, but the foyer was empty, as was the sitting room and the library. She heard a noise in the kitchen and went back along the hallway to find Delphine turning out a pan of hot corn muffins.

"Good morning," Carrie said. She could see by the knowing

look in the girl's eyes that she knew full well Rance had spent the night, so she took a deep breath and came directly to the question.

"Have you . . . seen Mr. Stewart, Delphine?" she asked.

Delphine straightened and put aside the thick pot holder. "No, I didn't, Miss Carrie," she said. "But I heard him go out about a half-hour ago. I guess it was him. I heard the front door open and close."

"Yes . . . well, thank you, Delphine."

"Breakfast be ready in a few minutes. Should I set two plates or one?" Delphine called after her, but Carrie's mind was not on food at the moment. He might have left a note for her . . . in the foyer or the sitting room.

She hurried to look, but there was nothing. And finally she went to stand and look out into the courtyard. The camelias were heavy with buds.

Questions clamored within her. Had she been too forward, too open in her desire for him? Would it have been better if she'd pretended to be shy and unwilling, so that he could persuade her? Oh, God, it had been so perfect. Why had he left without a word?

She folded her arms around her middle. He had not said that he loved her last night. And she blamed him for nothing. She had asked for no promises. Yet the thought that she might never see him again was almost more than she could bear.

There *was* her blood, her heritage. Was that why he had chosen to go . . . quickly and quietly before she woke up?

Tears scalded her eyes, gathered in her throat to choke her, but she held them back sternly. She was due at Leroy Tate's office in an hour to sign the papers on Kingston's Landing.

She would be there.

The old clerk, Simpson, announced her, and Leroy Tate came out as he always did so that he might escort her personally into his office. "You're looking lovely, as usual, Carrie," he said. He had long ago started to use her given name, and now he straightened his spectacles, and his eyes warmed to the lavender dress with its high lace collar and purple velvet neckband, and the straw bonnet with white ruching that framed her face prettily.

"Thank you, Leroy," she said, trying her best to smile.

Besides the approval in the banker's eyes, she thought she detected something else there . . . apprehension, which was unlike him. She put it down to his knowing that this would be a very difficult day for her.

Simpson beamed at her, bobbing his head the way he always did, his thin white hair escaping in all directions from the band of his green eyeshade. The ancient clerk handed his boss a folder of papers, and Tate nodded his thanks.

"Has the buyer arrived?" Carrie asked, scarcely able to get the words out.

"Yes. He's waiting in my office." After a quick glance toward the teller's cages to make sure that the two young men were properly busy, Tate swung open the railing gate and held it for Carrie. "Shall we go in?" he asked, a faintly uneasy smile on his heavy-jawed face.

"Yes, please," Carrie said. She wanted to get it over with now . . . wanted to make the cut as quickly and cleanly as possible. Maybe that's what Rance had done, too. She didn't know, would probably never know. But she would be all business in there, she told herself briskly. No one would be able to see that she had lost what mattered to her most . . . both on the same day. She'd lost Rance again, she told herself miserably, she was all but convinced of it now. And she was signing away Kingston's Landing . . . probably to someone who could never love it as she did.

She made a conscious effort to sweep her face of all emotion and walked purposefully into the room, her skirts rustling, her white kid slippers tapping against the wide wooden floorboards. But just inside the doorway, she stopped dead still, her cheeks draining of color.

"Good morning, Carrie," Rance drawled. He rose from one of the leather chairs in front of Leroy Tate's desk.

She could only stare and look from one man to the other as Tate fidgeted with his watchchain. "I believe the two of you know each other," he said.

"Yes, we do," Rance said pleasantly. He was handsome in a fine gray broadcloth suit, the white ruffled shirtfront gleaming, set off by a black stock and waistcoat. "Won't you sit here, Carrie."

He stood waiting, his eyes on her, and though Carrie didn't know if she could breathe, much less move, she managed somehow to walk to the chair and sit down. The two men followed suit.

"Well . . ." Tate said nervously, tapping his fingertips together and clearing his throat. "I suppose, Carrie, that since you've decided that you want to sell the plantation, it's a little better to have a friend buy it. Wouldn't you say?" He gave a hesitant little laugh.

She didn't answer him but turned to search Rance's face. "You . . .?" The word came out in a whisper.

He nodded, his expression unreadable.

"But why?" she burst out. "I don't understand."

He shrugged. "I heard it was for sale. I decided to buy it."

"But . . ." She began to stammer.

"You do want to sell it, don't you?" his eyes locked with hers.

"No. I . . . I mean, yes," she said finally.

He nodded and turned toward the desk. "You have the papers ready?" he asked Tate.

"Right here. Mr. Stewart has met your price to the dollar, Carrie." The banker took the papers from the folder that Simpson had given him earlier and placed them on the desk facing Rance and Carrie. "I'll just have to get your signatures." He dipped his pen into the inkwell and handed it to Carrie. "Right here, Carrie . . . and here."

Carrie's hand shook noticeably, and she turned and looked at Rance for a long moment, pen poised.

"Well?" he said.

She turned and signed quickly in the places that Leroy had indicated and then passed the pen over to him, looking away as he put his name there, listening to the scratch of the pen, the dip in the inkwell, scratching again.

"Well, then . . . that does it," Tate said, his voice falsely hearty.

"It does," Rance agreed. "Tell me, Mr. Tate, did you take care of that other matter for me?"

"I certainly did. You have only to sign right here, Mr. Stewart."

Carrie could hardly contain herself. What in the world was Rance up to? Why was he doing this . . . and why hadn't he told her last night that he was the buyer she'd be meeting?

He had signed the second paper and now stood up. "If you would allow us a moment in private, Mr. Tate," he said.

"Of course . . . of course." Tate suddenly got very busy gathering up the folder and retrieving his spectacles, which he'd left on the desktop. "Just take your time. I'll be outside," he said, avoiding Carrie's eyes.

Rance escorted the banker to the door and shut it firmly behind him, then turned back and stood there tall and broad-shouldered. He seemed to fill the room.

"Rance." Carrie came to her feet to confront him with more assurance than she actually felt, "I would like you to tell me what on earth you think you're doing?"

"I've just bought Kingston's Landing," he said coolly.

"I know that," she said. "What I don't understand is why?" The serious set to his face and his silence now frightened her. She was flooded with memories of last night . . . of his arms around her, of that hard, beautiful body against hers. God, what was happening?

"I don't understand," she repeated, "but maybe that doesn't matter." She twisted the strings of her reticule, fingers interlocking. "I guess what Leroy said was right. I *would* rather you had it than . . . than anyone else. And . . . and you don't have to worry about last night." She was determined that he not feel any guilt or responsibility for her. "I mean—"

"Carrie, would you just be quiet for once and listen to me!" he interrupted her, his jaw set to a hard, straight line.

She nodded meekly.

"Good!" He thrust the paper he was holding at her. "I want you to have this," he growled.

She scanned it quickly and then reread it to make sure she had seen it correctly. The paper she held in her hand gave Kingston's Landing back to her.

She jerked her head up and stared at him. "Oh, no . . ." she said. "I can't let you do this!"

"You can't stop me," he answered calmly.

"Oh, yes, I can! Leroy!" she called, and started toward the door, but Rance put out a hand to grab her, clasping her wrist firmly.

"Damn it, Carrie, you're supposed to be listening to me! Now will you just sit down and shut up until you've heard what I have to say!"

Their eyes locked and struggled for a moment, but his iron stare won, and Carrie reluctantly did as she was told.

Rance nodded, rolling his lips together in a tight line. He walked about the room as if he were inspecting the files and the leather books and the umbrella stand.

Suddenly he turned. "I love you, Carrie," he said intently, the hard lines of his face now softened. "It's why I came back. I think that I loved you from that first day . . . from the moment I came around the corner of the house and saw you giving Corporal Hagerty the very devil."

Carrie had grown weak, a fierce, hot joy bubbling through her.

He had paused only briefly, now rushed on. "I want you to marry me."

"Oh, Rance . . ." she breathed. And then it was like a slashing knife as reality cut through her. "But, you know . . ." Her voice trembled. "You know we couldn't. The law . . ."

"I don't give a damn about the law! And I don't give a good damn in hell who your grandmother was!" he exploded. "Except," he added gently, "she must have been a hell of a woman if she was anything at all like you."

"But—"

"Will you be quiet and listen to me!" he growled. "I know the law of Louisiana says we can't marry. But there are places in the world where no such idiotic laws exist! I love you. I want you to marry me. I want you for my wife."

Carrie was trembling, head spinning. She could hardly believe that she was hearing Rance say things that she hadn't even dared to dream. But she could sense something else in him, something that was holding her at arm's length still, no matter what he'd said.

"There's more," he confirmed her feeling. "And only you,

my darling, can make this decision. And I want you to think about it very carefully before you do.''

"I don't understand," she said, softly. "What decision, Rance?"

"When I arrived back in New Orleans," he said, "I went straight to Prosper, and he told me that you were going to have to sell Kingston's Landing."

"He never told me—" Carrie began.

"No," Rance cut her off. "I made him promise he wouldn't. And poor Mr. Tate out there as well." He grinned wryly. "You see, I always knew how much you loved Kingston's Landing, but it was only after I spoke with Prosper that I realized how much it might hurt you if you had to leave it. I decided that you must have the choice.

"As you know, my father was a staunch supporter of the South. But, ironically, all his money was in Northern banks at the start of the war and stayed there quite safely. With his death, I became fairly well-off. I am well able to give you Kingston's Landing, Carrie. It's yours forever.''

She still didn't quite know what he was getting at. "Rance . . ." she began, but he shook his head.

"Don't. I've only a little more to say now," he said firmly. "With the money from the transaction here today, you can go back to the plantation and do with it what you wish. Make it as successful as it used to be. Or . . . you can come away with me. And I'll make you my wife, my darling . . . my cherished wife.''

"Oh . . .'' The sound, small and quivering, escaped her trembling lips, but he held up his hand once again to forestall any reply from her.

"I know that you have others to think of. I assure you that they will be taken care of. Kingston's Landing can be their home with an overseer to run the place. Or, when we get settled, you could send for whomever you wish . . . Suzy and the baby . . . Chloe, Benjamin. However you'd want it. But the thing you must understand is that we would probably only be able to come back here to visit occasionally. I've consulted an attorney and, though Louisiana law is vague on the subject, he believes it unlikely that the authorities would allow us to live here permanently as husband and wife. And I will have it no other way. I couldn't do that to you."

Before she could say a word, he had taken his hat from the hall tree in the corner. "I don't want you to feel that you're pressured. It's your choice, and I want you to make it freely." His eyes softened, grew dark and tender. "I'll always love you, Carrie . . . no matter what you decide."

He turned away to the door. "I'll be at the St. Charles until three o'clock tomorrow afternoon. If I don't hear from you before then, I'll know what your answer is."

He didn't look back, and Carrie sat there, paralyzed for a moment, unable to absorb quite all he had said. If she wished it, he had made it possible for her to have Kingston's Landing . . . the thing she had thought she wanted most in the world.

But through the open doorway she could see him walking away, walking away from her forever, and she started up from her chair. Dear God, there was not the slightest doubt in her mind about what she wanted. Kingston's Landing would always be close to her heart . . . but Rance *was* her heart.

"Rance . . . Rance!" she called, rushing after him, past the startled clerks and Leroy Tate, past the gaping tellers and the dour-faced, fat lady in line. And as she threw herself into Rance's arms, old Simpson stood to watch, his eyeshade askew, pen in hand.

"Come, come, Simpson," a beaming Leroy Tate said with mock sternness, "don't be gawking at our customers now!" And Simpson sank back down to his desk, ducking his head but peeking all the same through the green shade.

The tellers leaned out of their cages, grinning, and even the fat lady smiled faintly as that lovely young woman whispered something into the ear of the tall and handsome man, whereupon he caught her to him, throwing back his head and laughing, swinging her off her feet and around in a whirl of petticoats and white kid slippers . . . and then kissing her as if he would never let her go again.

ABOUT THE AUTHOR: A seventh-generation Kentuckian, Betty Layman Receveur still lives in Louisville, where she was born and grew up, with her husband John. She has three sons by a former marriage, the youngest of whom lives with them, and her husband has three daughters.

A professional author, Miss Receveur has two previous historical romances to her credit, including MOLLY GALLAGHER, the story of CARRIE KINGSTON's mother. About wanting to write, she says: "When I was a child, I read every book I could get my hands on. At one point I remember being afraid that I would finish all the books in the library and there would be nothing left for me to read. Perhaps that's why I started to write my own books once I'd grown up." Her husband is also a writer, and they have four typewriters at home—just to be safe. It's a rare time that the sound of clicking keys doesn't echo through their house.

Miss Receveur's passions are old houses, antique furniture, and Silky Terriers—and her beautiful Kentucky.

Ballantine's World of Historical Romance...